ACCLAIM FOR JEFF SMITH'S

Named an all-time top ten graphic novel by **Time** magazine.

"As sweeping as the 'Lord of the Rings' cycle, but much funnier." —Andrew Arnold, **Time.com**

★"This is first-class kid lit: exciting, funny, scary, and resonant enough that it will stick with readers for a long time." —Publishers Weekly, *starred review*

"One of the best kids' comics ever." —Vibe *magazine*

"**BONE** *is storytelling at its best, full of endearing, flawed characters whose adventures run the gamut from hilarious whimsy . . . to thrilling drama.*" —Entertainment Weekly

"[This] sprawling, mythic comic is spectacular." —SPIN *magazine*

"*Jeff Smith's cartoons are irresistible. Every gorgeous sweep of his brush speaks volumes.*" —Frank Miller, creator of Sin City

OTHER *BONE* BOOKS

Out from Boneville

The Great Cow Race

Eyes of the Storm

The Dragonslayer

Rock Jaw: Master of the Eastern Border

Old Man's Cave

Ghost Circles

Treasure Hunters

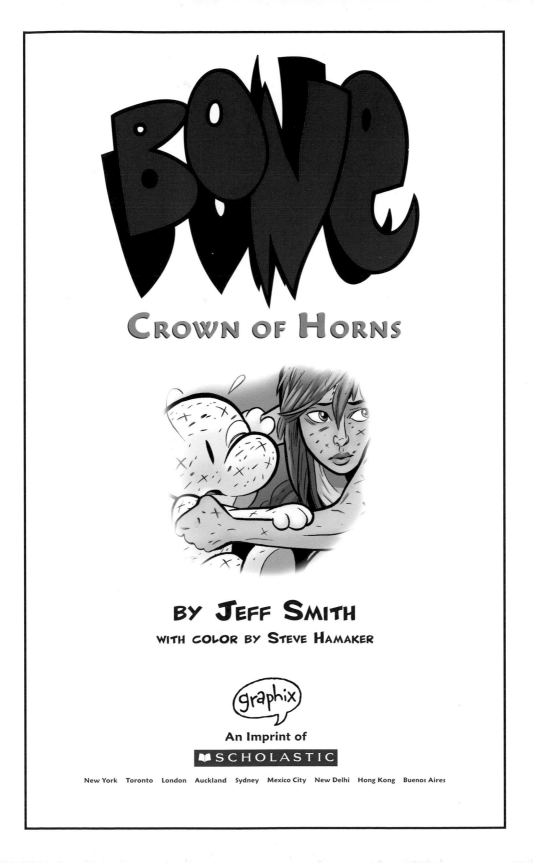

BONE

CROWN OF HORNS

BY JEFF SMITH

WITH COLOR BY STEVE HAMAKER

graphix

An Imprint of

📖**SCHOLASTIC**

New York   Toronto   London   Auckland   Sydney   Mexico City   New Delhi   Hong Kong   Buenos Aires

This book is for Paul Pope and Terry Moore

Copyright © 2009 by Jeff Smith.

The chapters in this book were originally published in the comic book *BONE* and are copyright © 2003 and 2004 by Jeff Smith. *BONE*® is © 2009 by Jeff Smith.

All rights reserved. Published by Graphix, an imprint of Scholastic Inc., *Publishers since 1920.* SCHOLASTIC, GRAPHIX, and associated logos are trademarks and/or registered trademarks of Scholastic Inc.

Library of Congress Catalog Card Number 9568403.

ISBN-13 978-0-439-70631-5 — ISBN-10 0-439-70631-9

ISBN 0-439-70632-7 (paperback)

ACKNOWLEDGMENTS

Harvestar Family Crest designed by Charles Vess

Map of *The Valley* by Mark Crilley

Color by Steve Hamaker

10 9 8 7 6 5   11 12 13

First Scholastic edition, February 2009

Book design by David Saylor

Printed in Singapore 46

CONTENTS

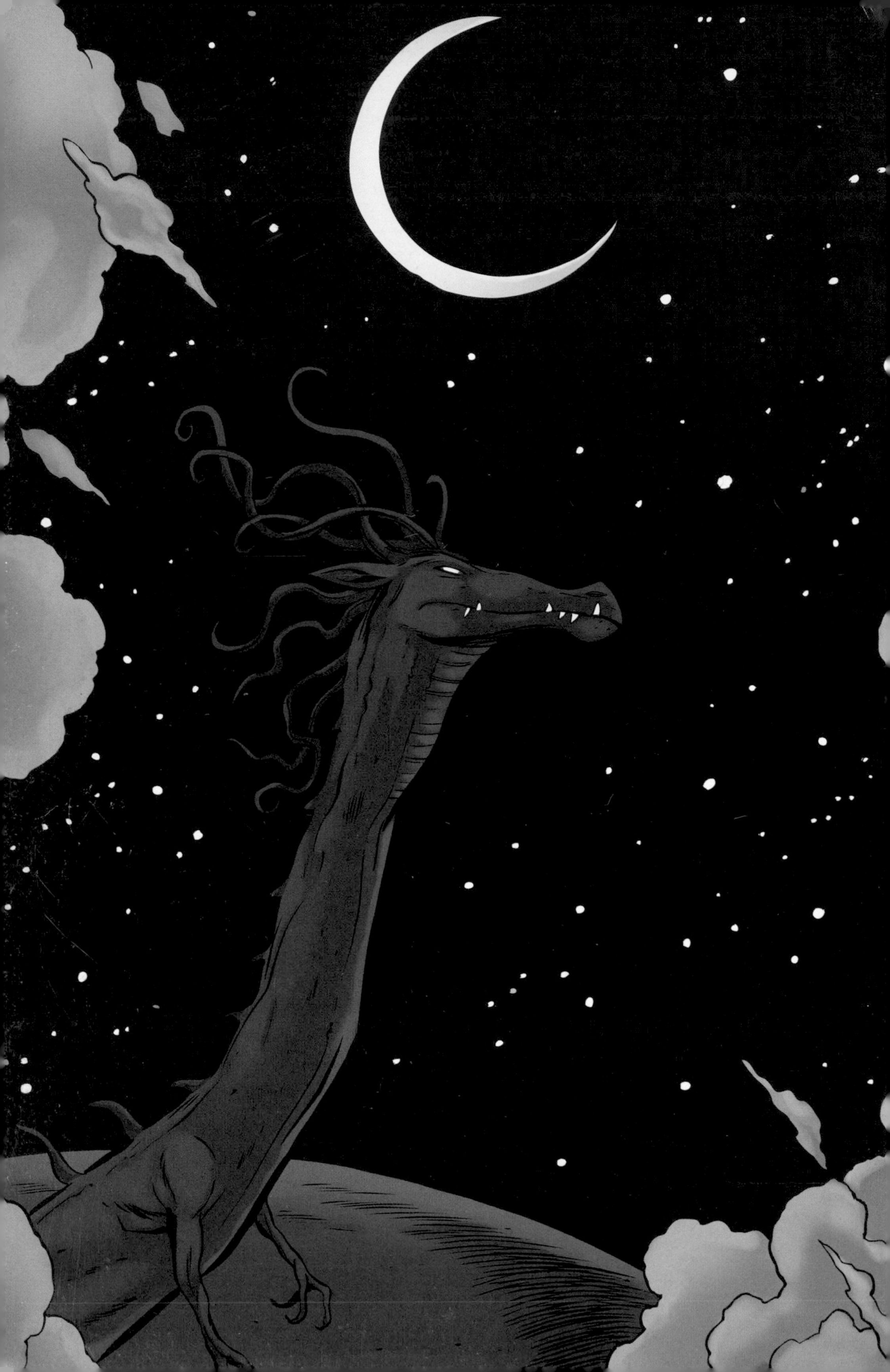

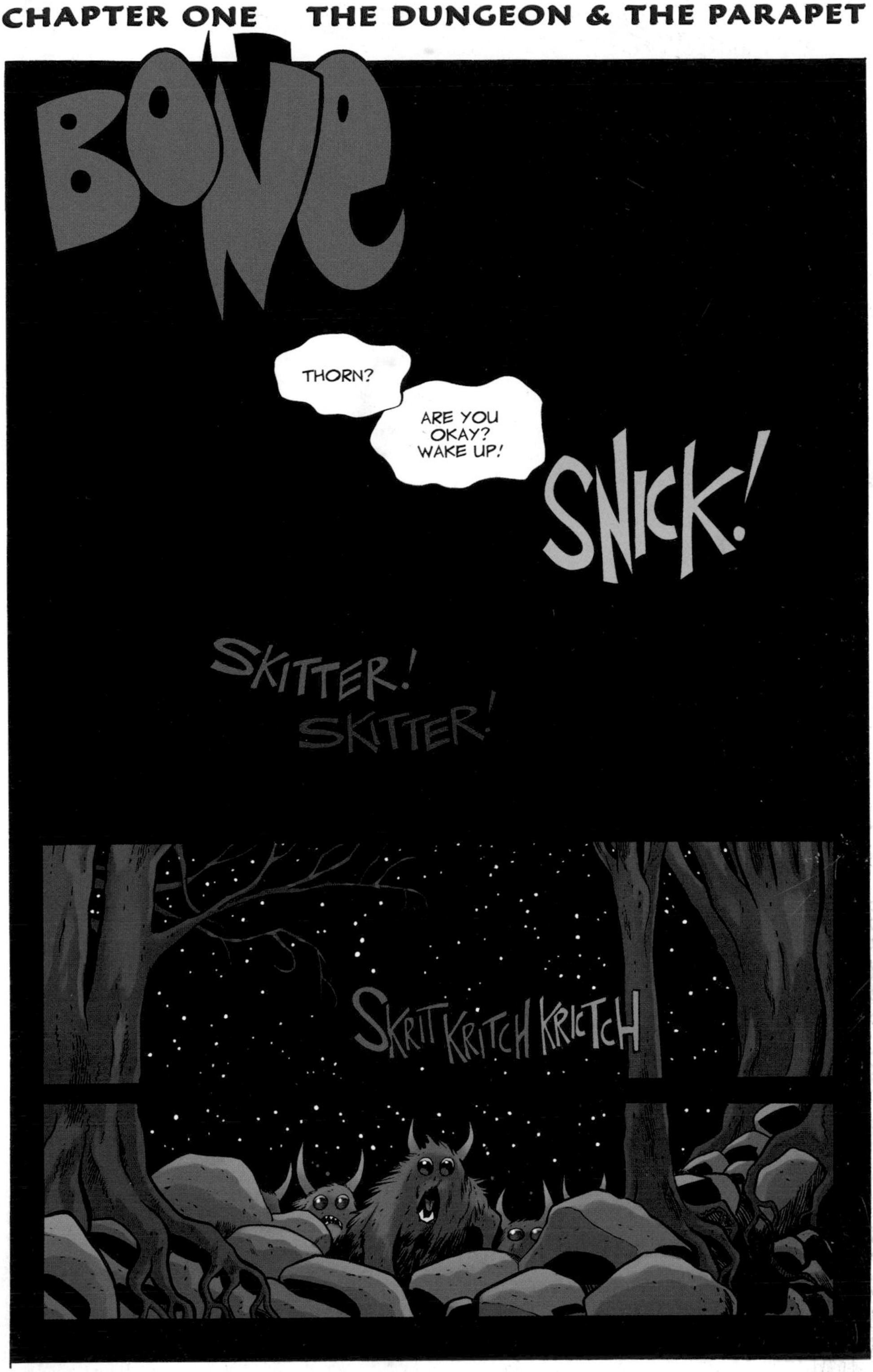
BONE
THORN?
ARE YOU OKAY? WAKE UP!
SNICK!
SKITTER! SKITTER!
SKRIT KRITCH KRICTCH

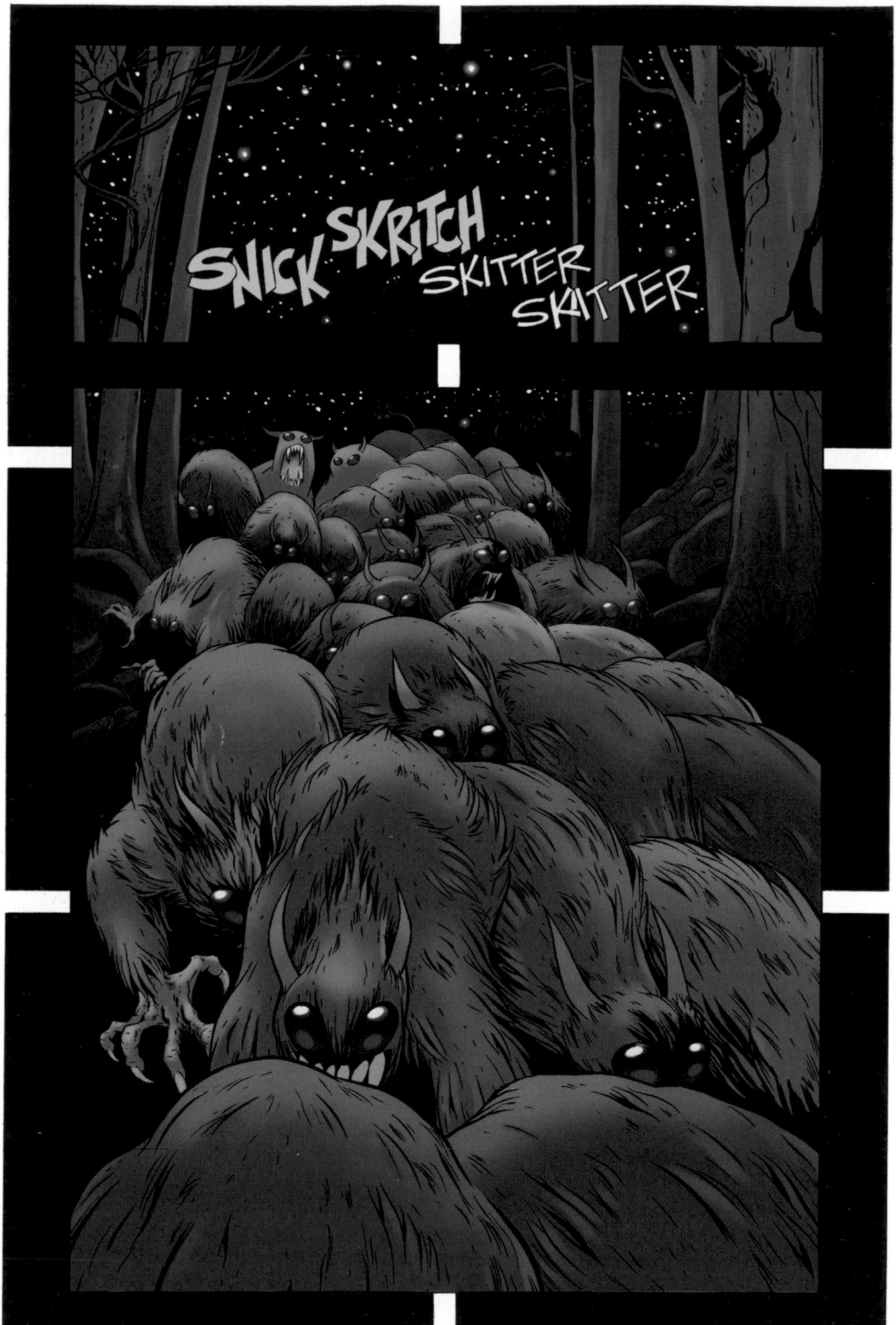
SNICK SKRITCH
SKITTER
SKITTER

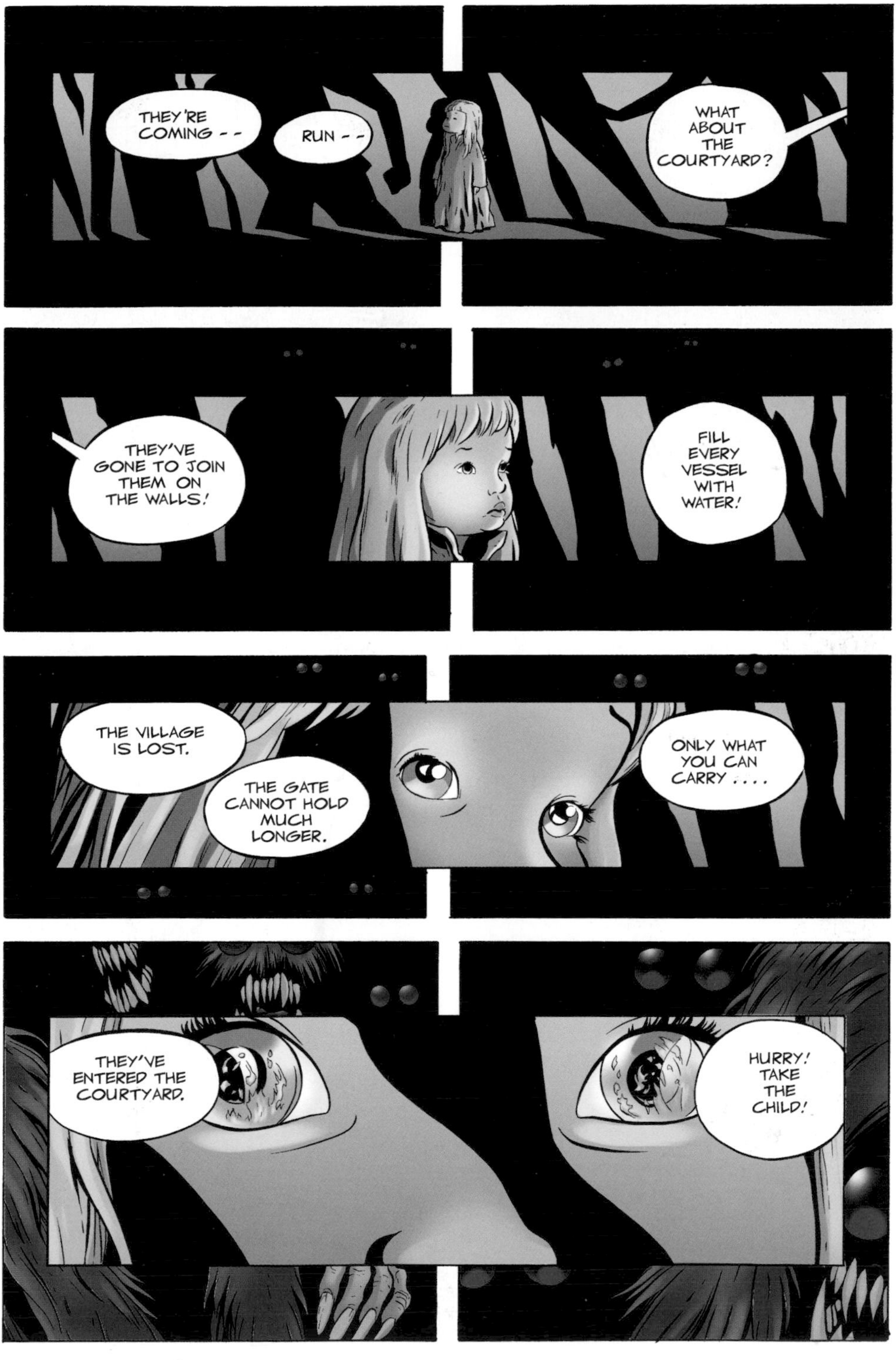
THEY'RE COMING - -
RUN - -
WHAT ABOUT THE COURTYARD?
THEY'VE GONE TO JOIN THEM ON THE WALLS!
FILL EVERY VESSEL WITH WATER!
THE VILLAGE IS LOST.
THE GATE CANNOT HOLD MUCH LONGER.
ONLY WHAT YOU CAN CARRY . . . .
THEY'VE ENTERED THE COURTYARD.
HURRY! TAKE THE CHILD!

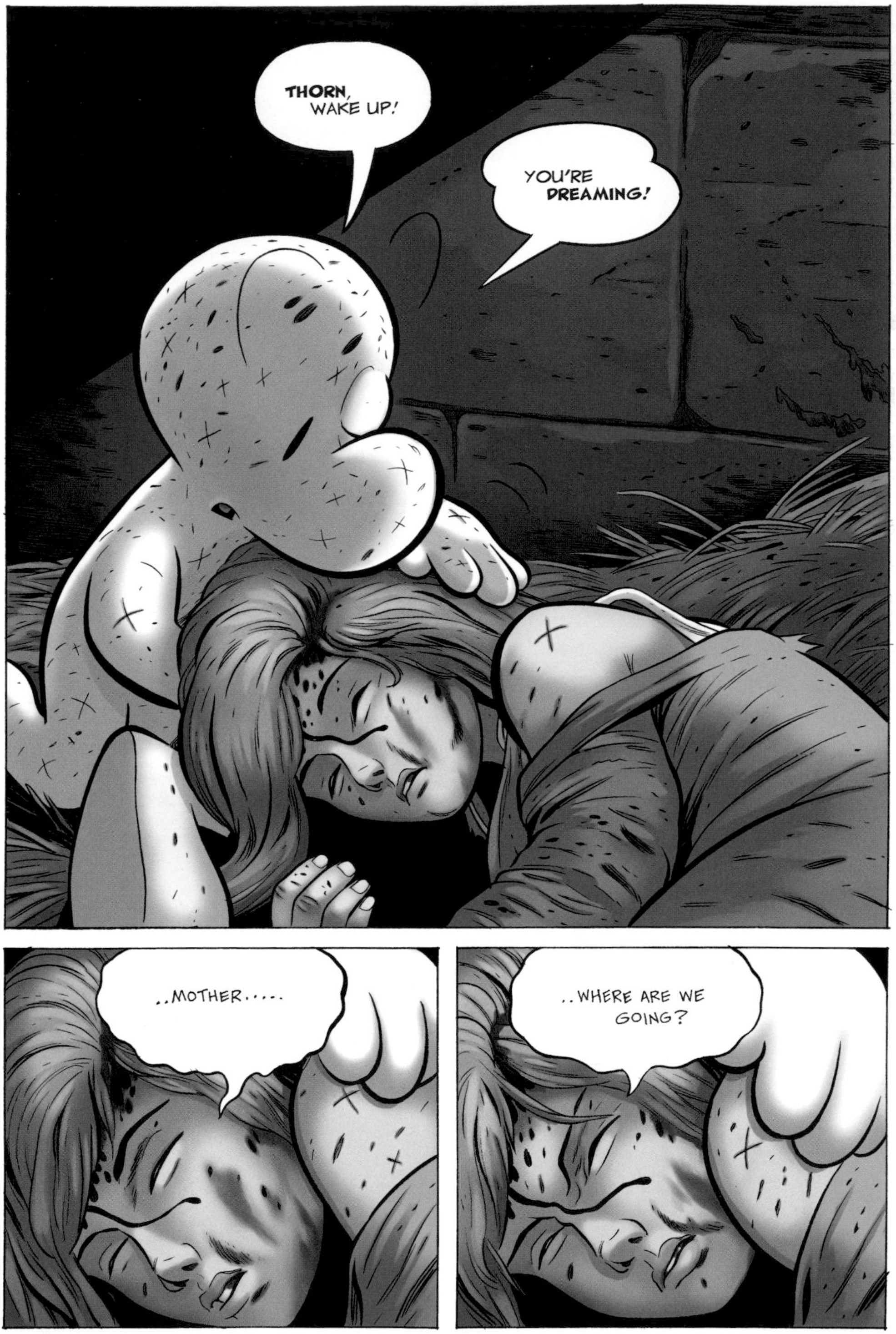
THORN, WAKE UP!
YOU'RE DREAMING!
..MOTHER.....
..WHERE ARE WE GOING?

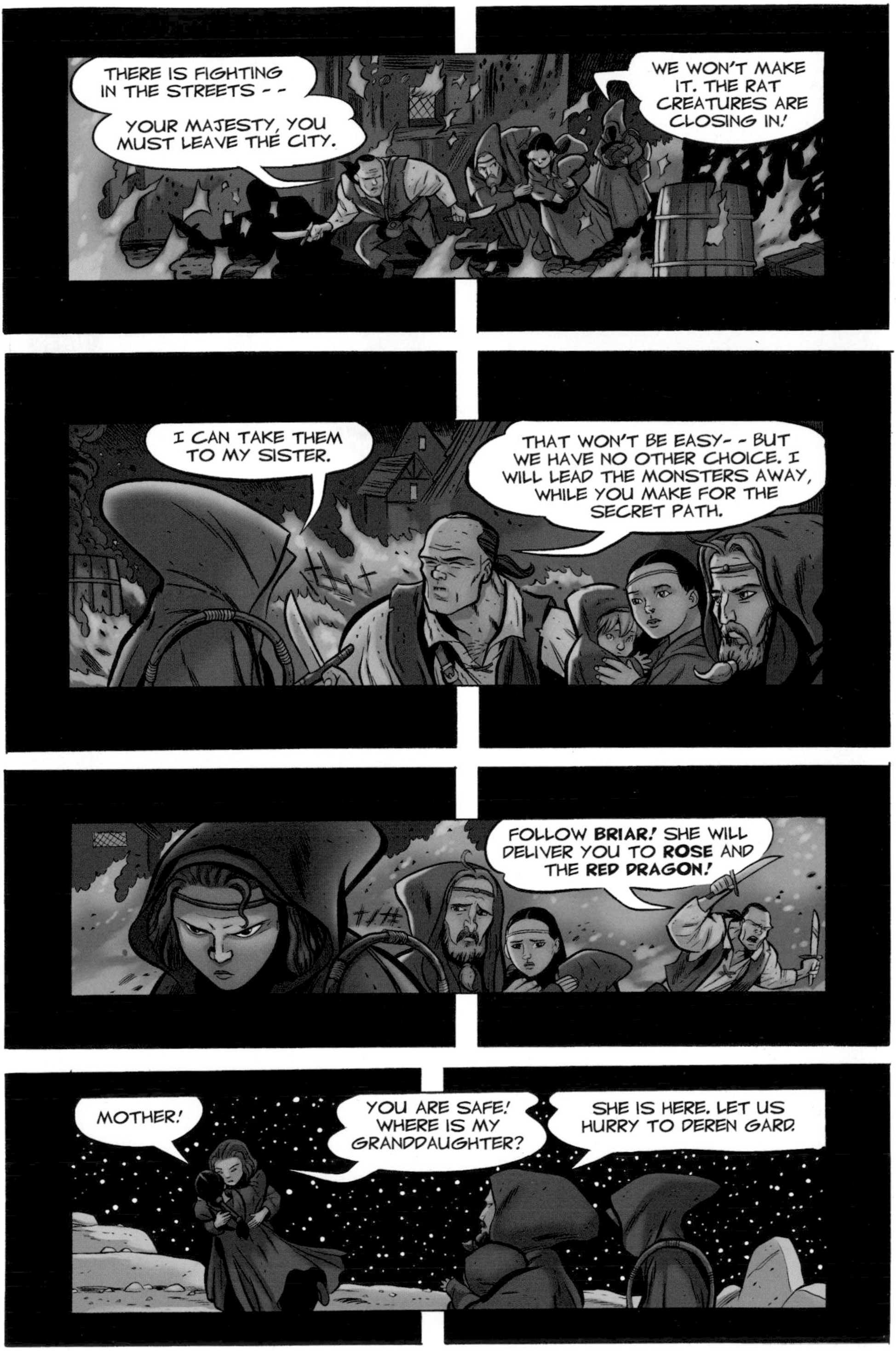
THERE IS FIGHTING IN THE STREETS - -
YOUR MAJESTY, YOU MUST LEAVE THE CITY.
WE WON'T MAKE IT. THE RAT CREATURES ARE CLOSING IN!
I CAN TAKE THEM TO MY SISTER.
THAT WON'T BE EASY- - BUT WE HAVE NO OTHER CHOICE. I WILL LEAD THE MONSTERS AWAY, WHILE YOU MAKE FOR THE SECRET PATH.
FOLLOW BRIAR! SHE WILL DELIVER YOU TO ROSE AND THE RED DRAGON!
MOTHER!
YOU ARE SAFE! WHERE IS MY GRANDDAUGHTER?
SHE IS HERE. LET US HURRY TO DEREN GARD.

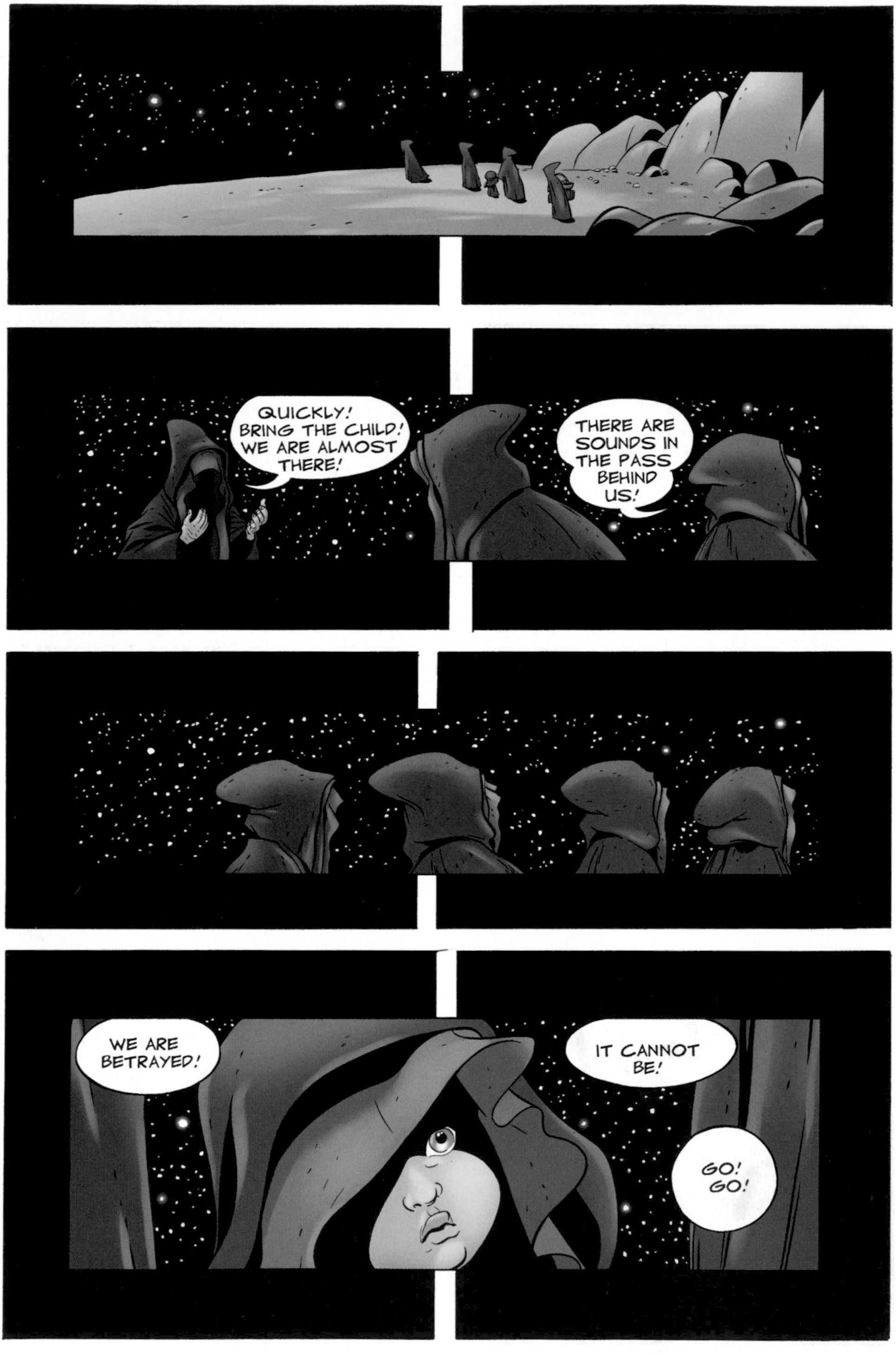
QUICKLY! BRING THE CHILD! WE ARE ALMOST THERE!
THERE ARE SOUNDS IN THE PASS BEHIND US!
WE ARE BETRAYED!
IT CANNOT BE!
GO! GO!

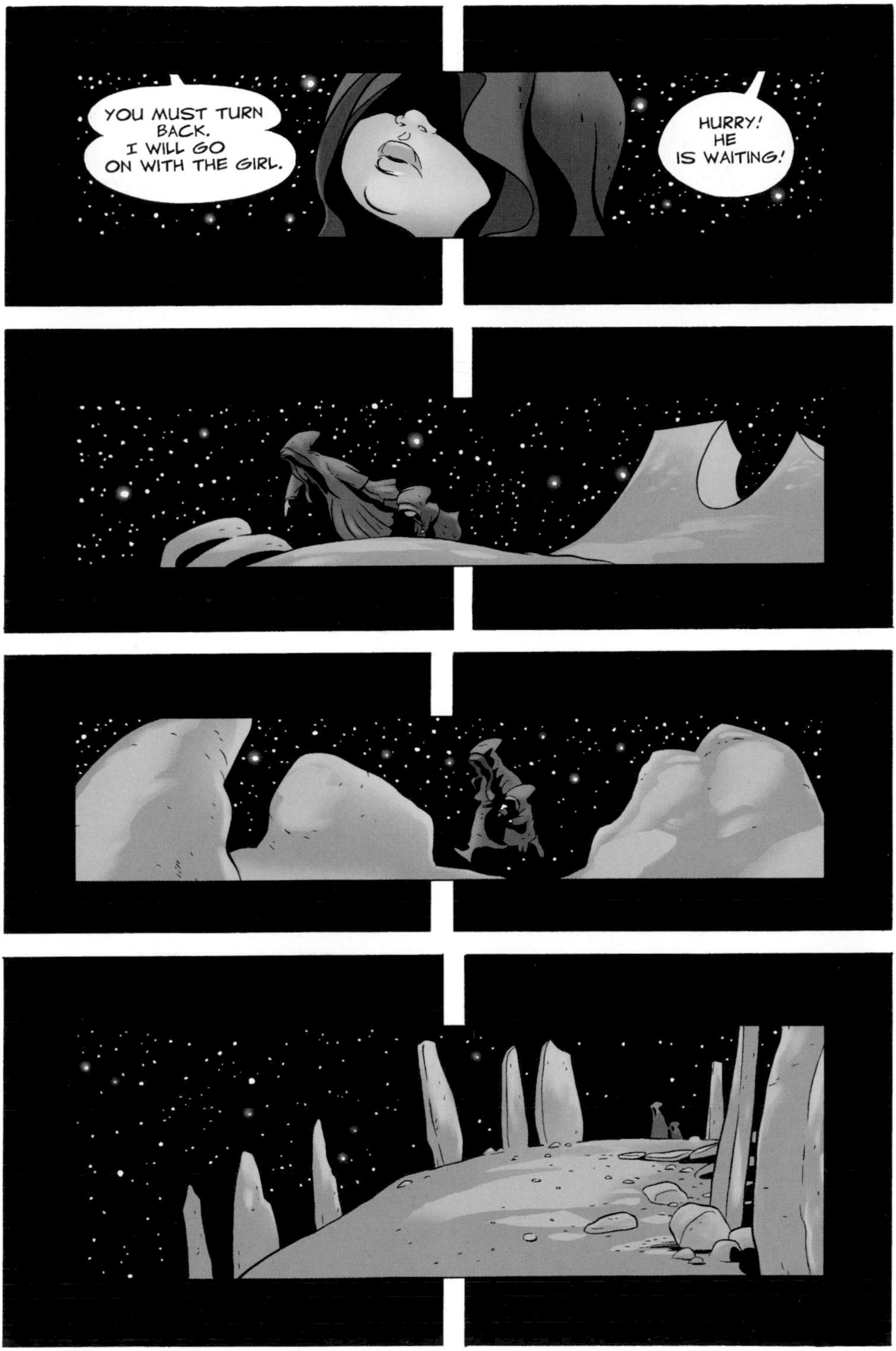
YOU MUST TURN BACK. I WILL GO ON WITH THE GIRL.
HURRY! HE IS WAITING!

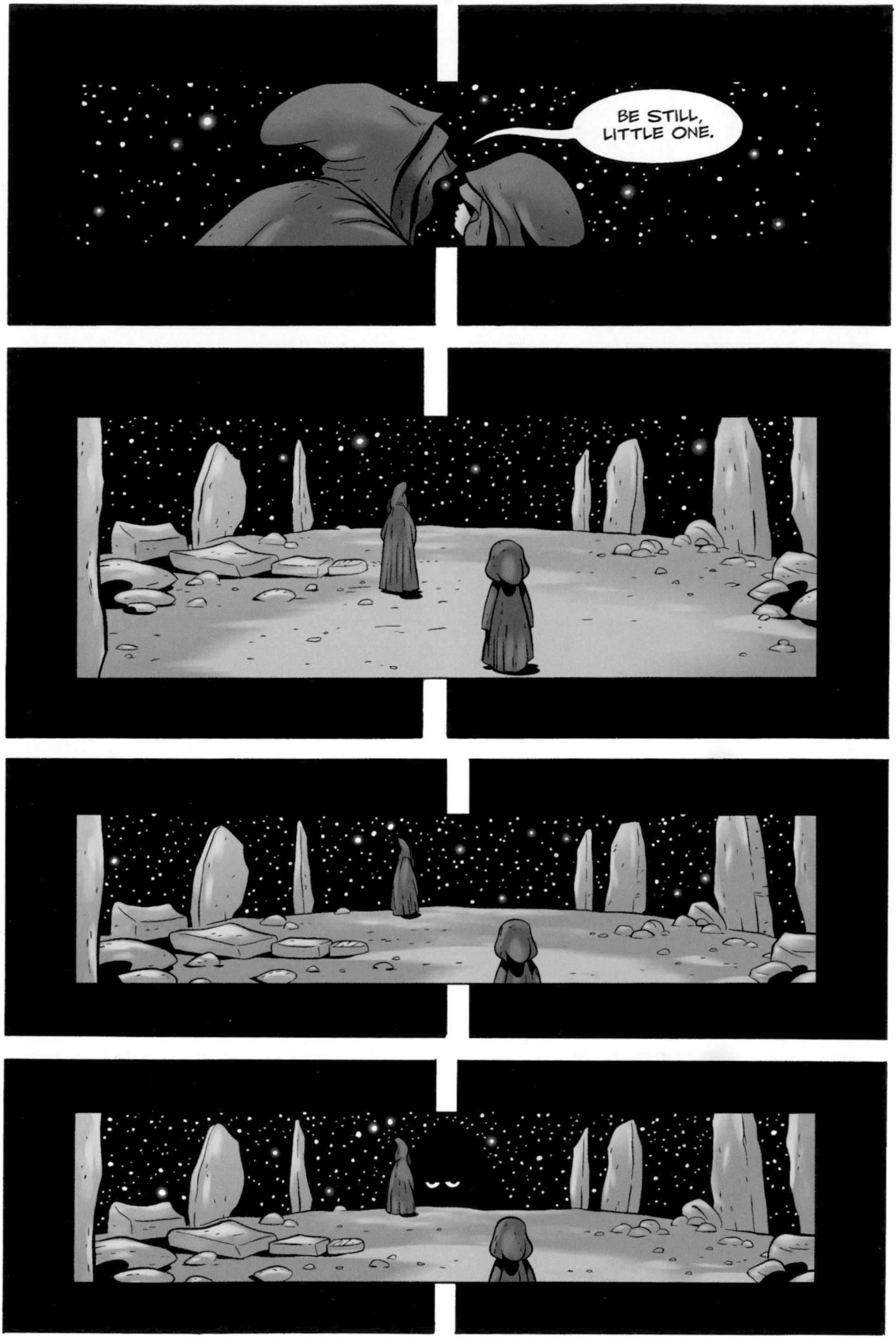
BE STILL, LITTLE ONE.

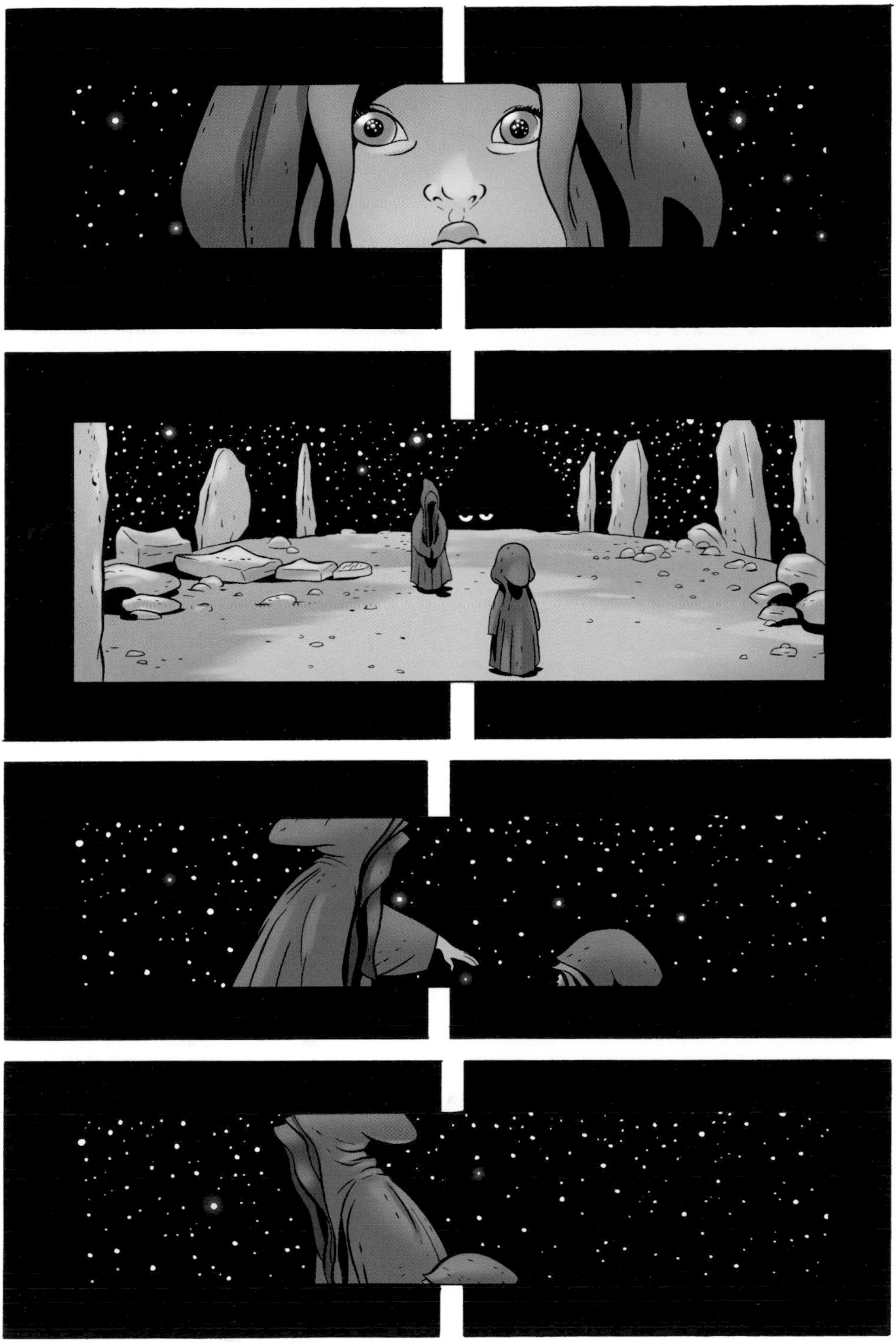

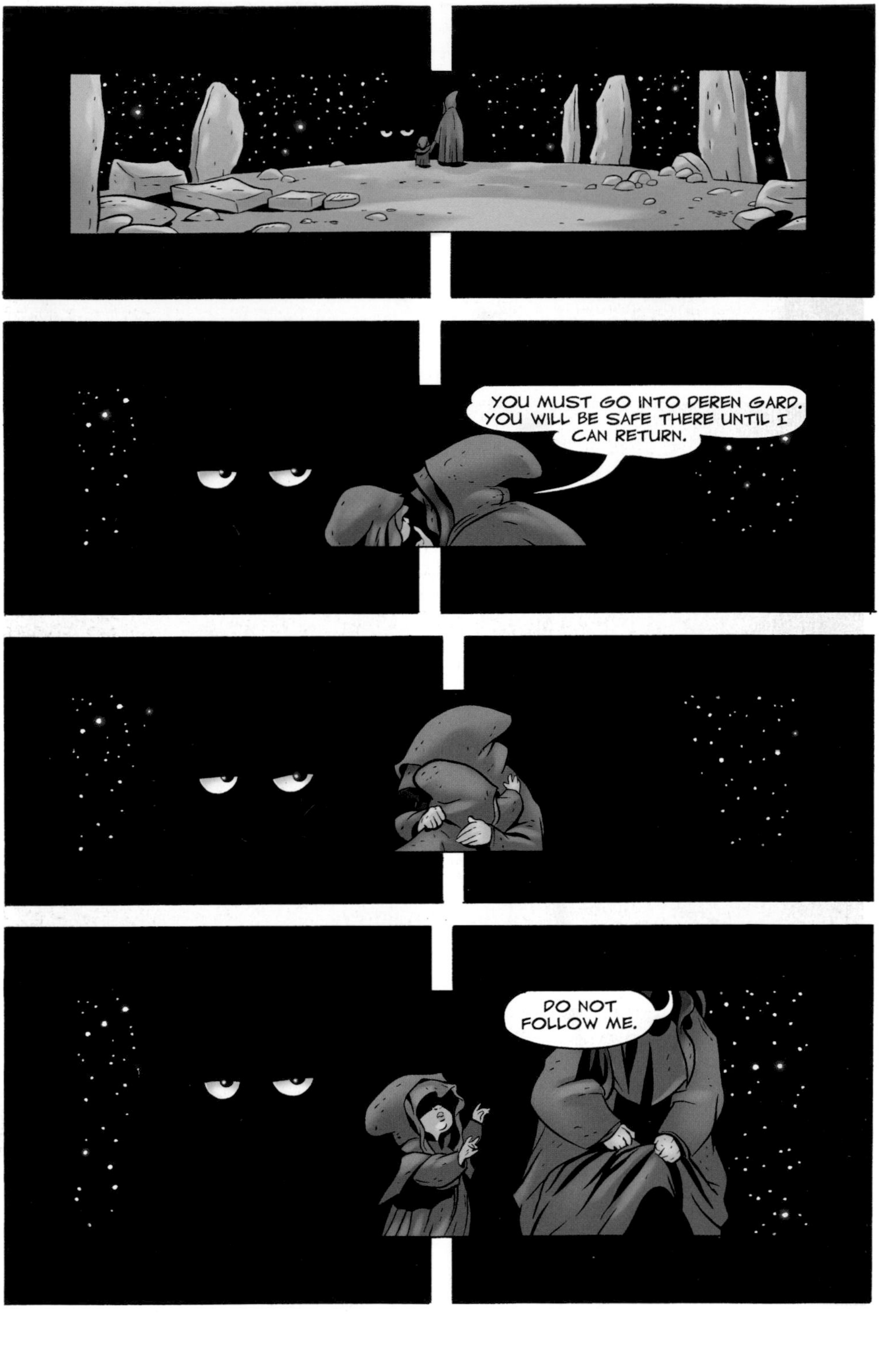
YOU MUST GO INTO DEREN GARD. YOU WILL BE SAFE THERE UNTIL I CAN RETURN.
DO NOT FOLLOW ME.

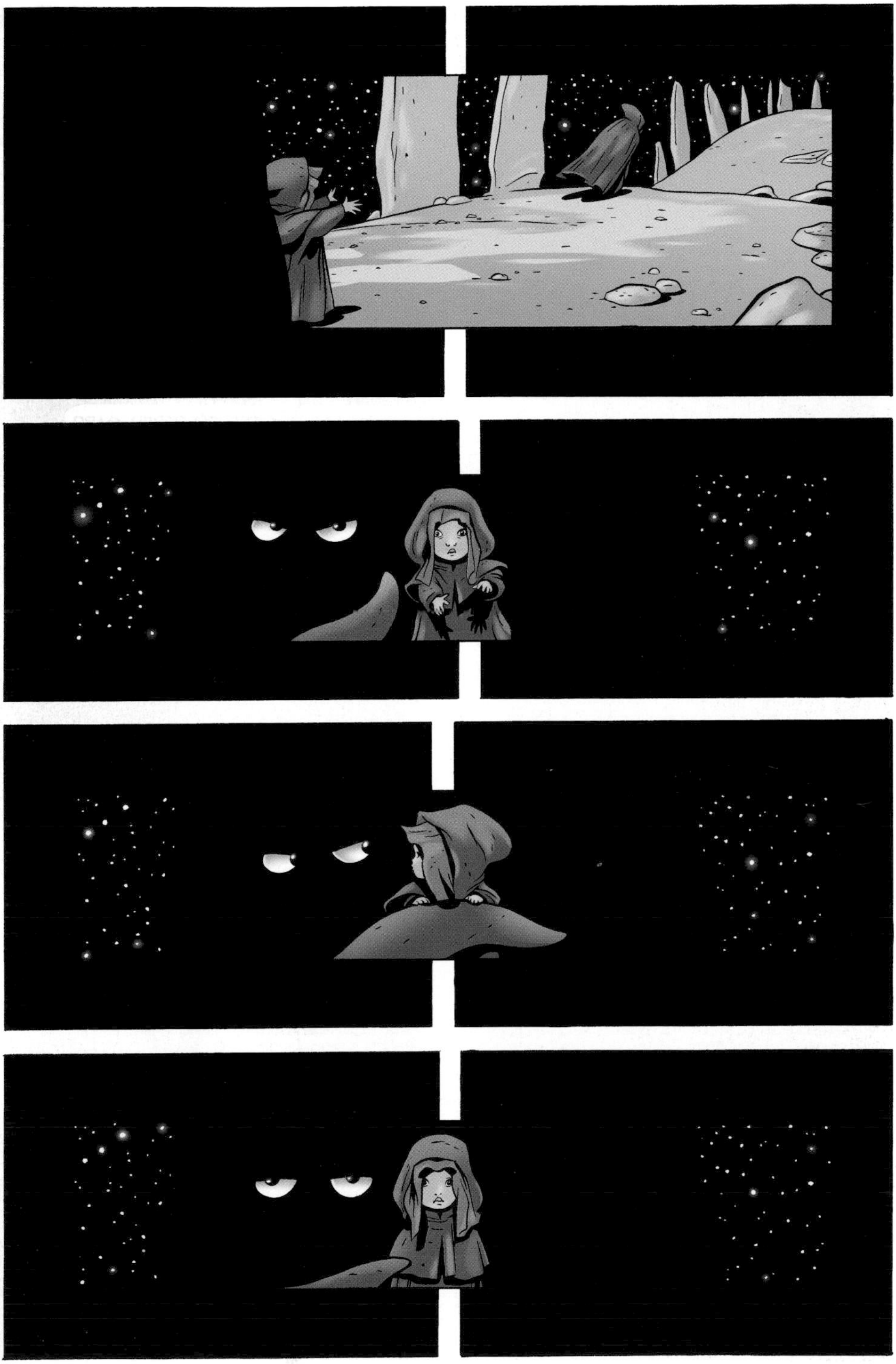

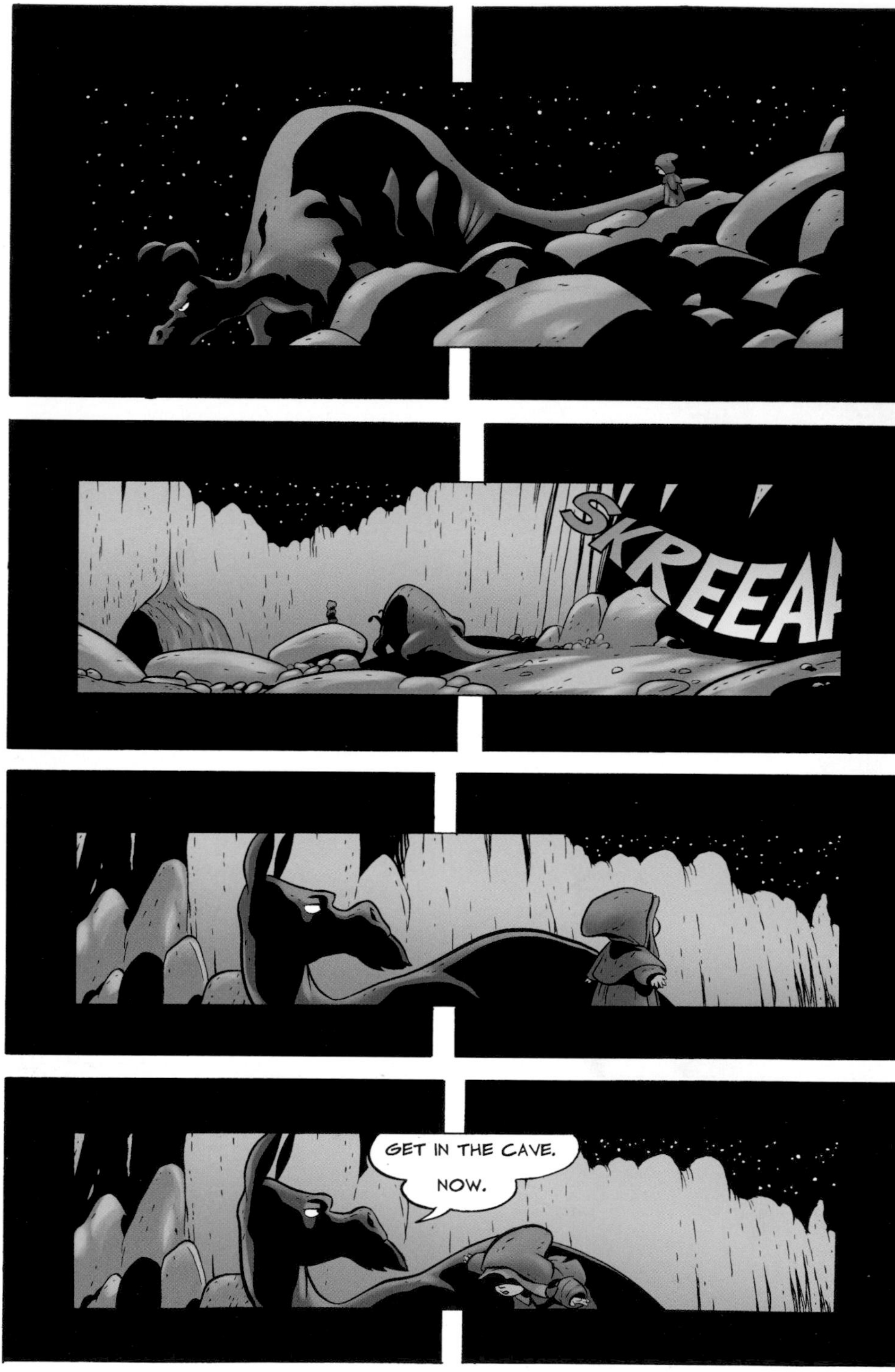
SKREEAP
GET IN THE CAVE.
NOW.

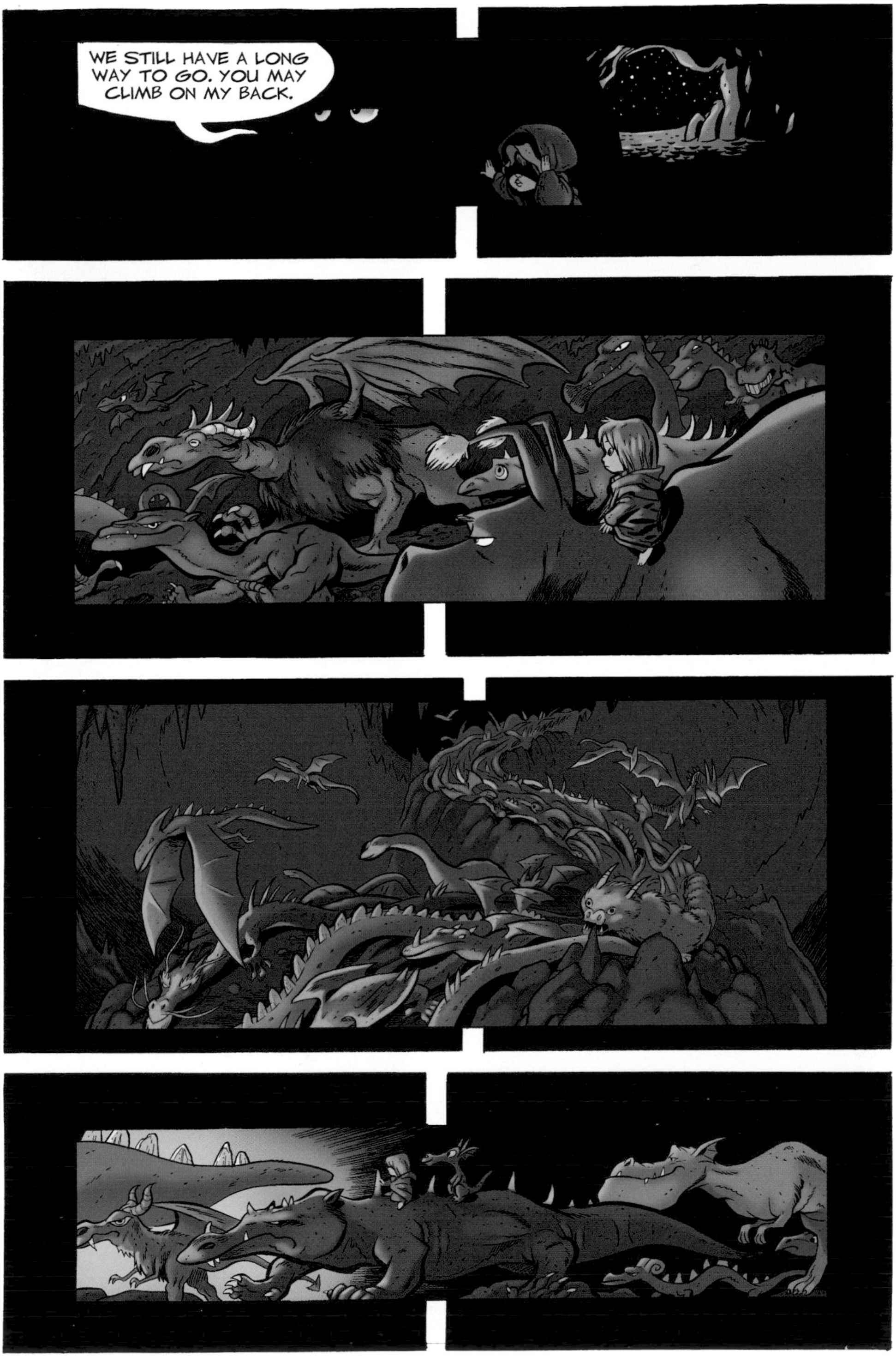
WE STILL HAVE A LONG WAY TO GO. YOU MAY CLIMB ON MY BACK.

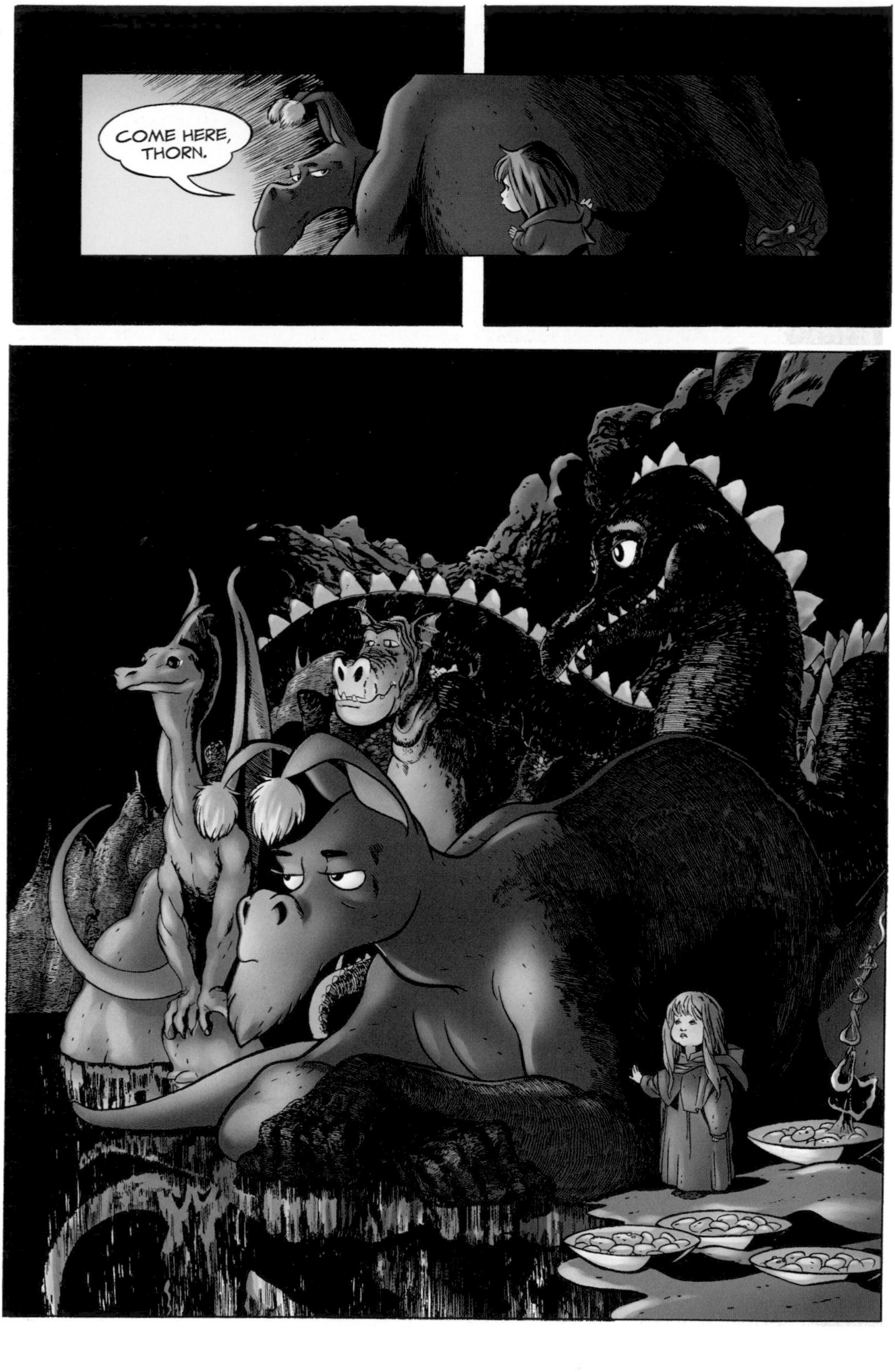
COME HERE, THORN.

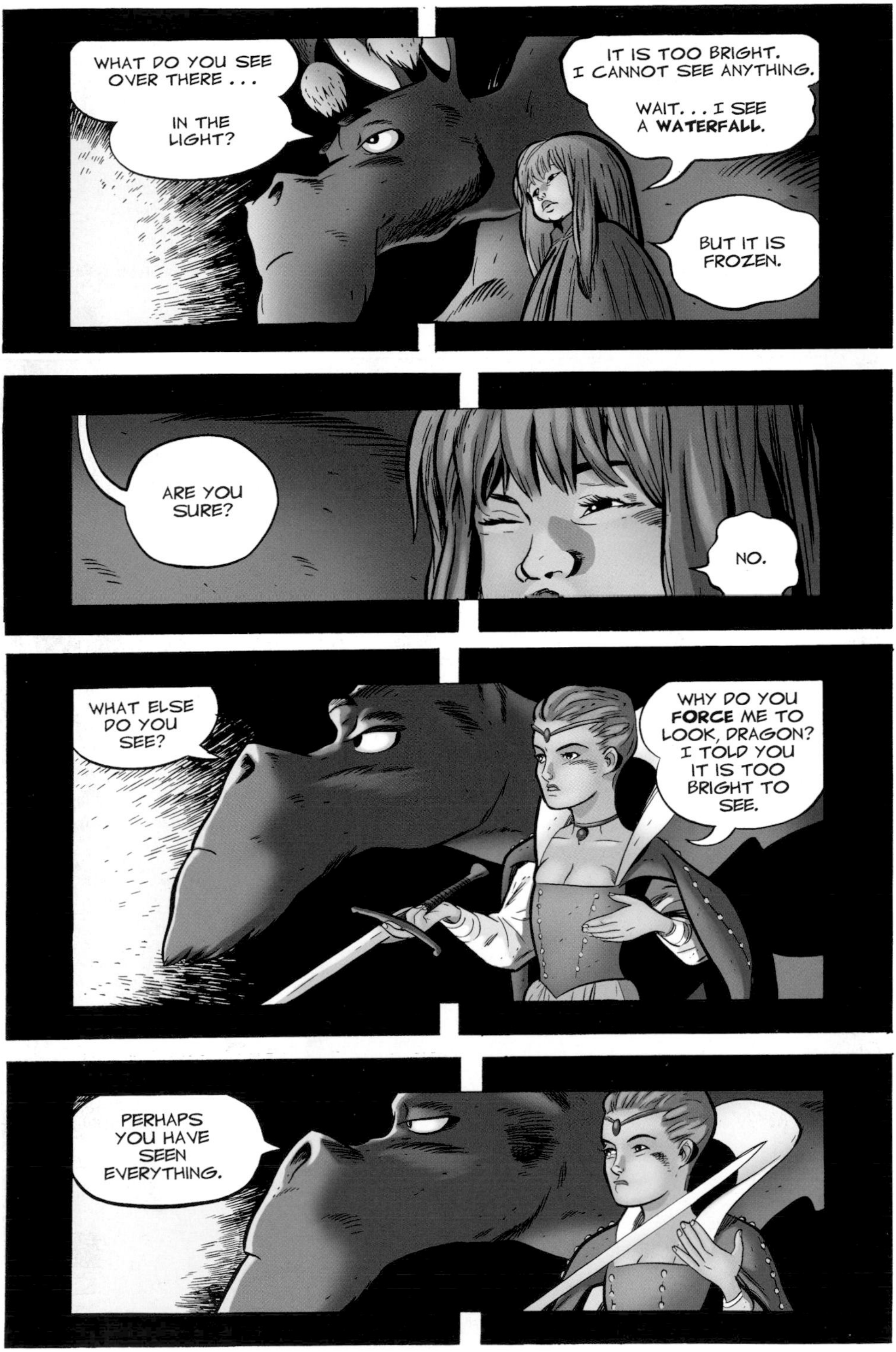
WHAT DO YOU SEE OVER THERE . . .
IN THE LIGHT?
IT IS TOO BRIGHT. I CANNOT SEE ANYTHING.
WAIT. . . I SEE A **WATERFALL.**
BUT IT IS FROZEN.
ARE YOU SURE?
NO.
WHAT ELSE DO YOU SEE?
WHY DO YOU **FORCE** ME TO LOOK, DRAGON? I TOLD YOU IT IS TOO BRIGHT TO SEE.
PERHAPS YOU HAVE SEEN EVERYTHING.

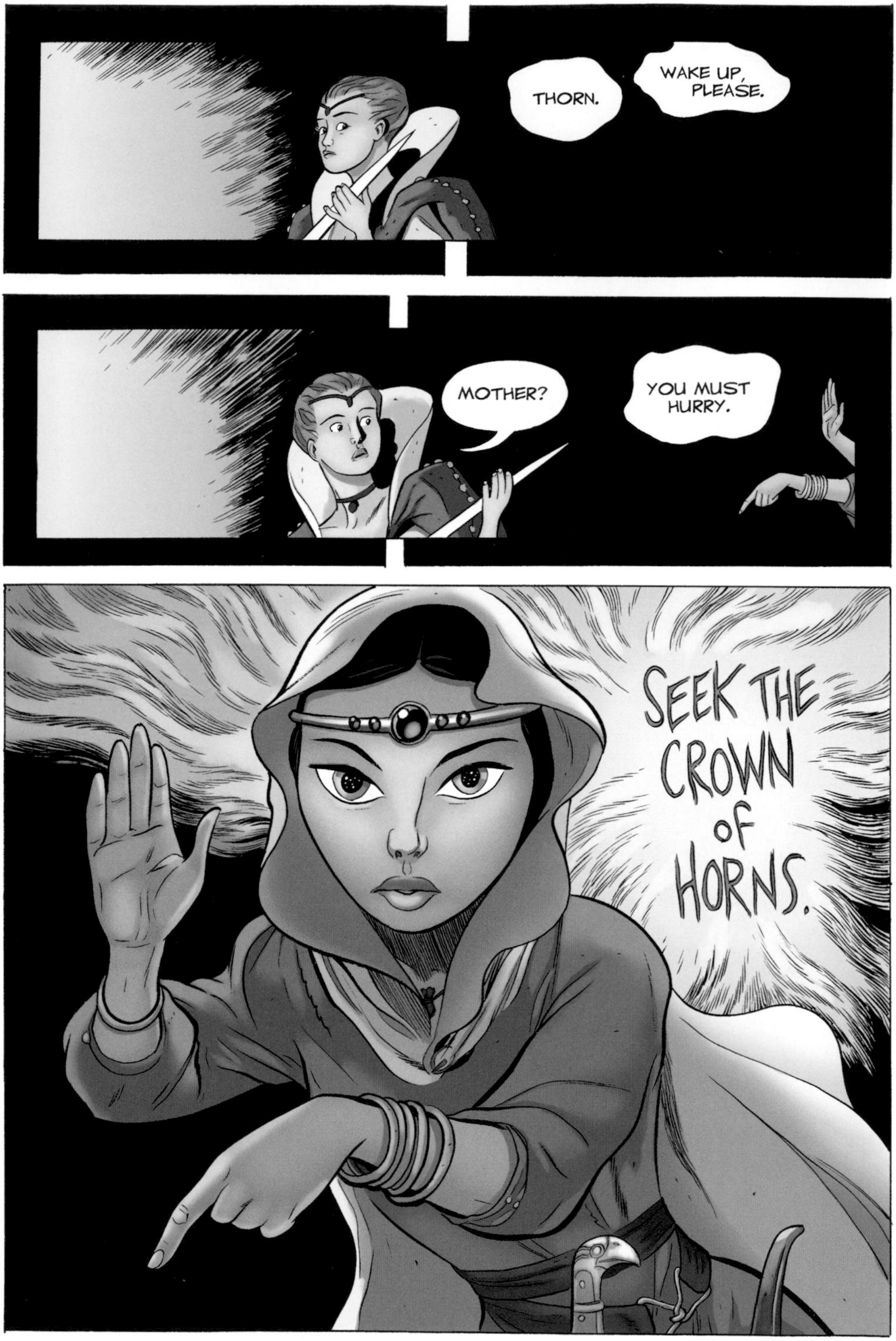
THORN.
WAKE UP, PLEASE.
MOTHER?
YOU MUST HURRY.
SEEK THE CROWN of HORNS.

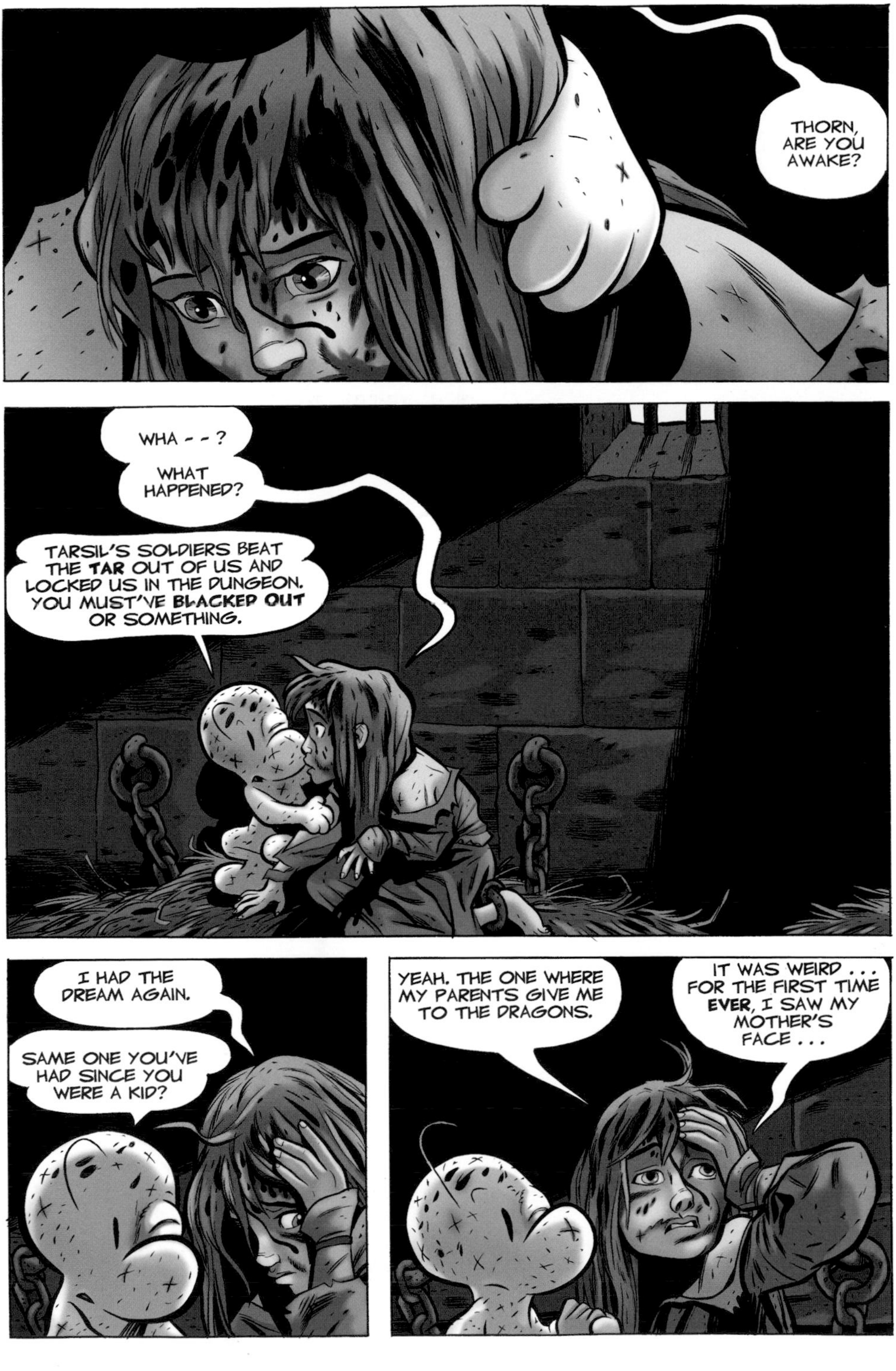
THORN, ARE YOU AWAKE?
WHA - - ?
WHAT HAPPENED?
TARSIL'S SOLDIERS BEAT THE TAR OUT OF US AND LOCKED US IN THE DUNGEON. YOU MUST'VE BLACKED OUT OR SOMETHING.
I HAD THE DREAM AGAIN.
SAME ONE YOU'VE HAD SINCE YOU WERE A KID?
YEAH. THE ONE WHERE MY PARENTS GIVE ME TO THE DRAGONS.
IT WAS WEIRD . . . FOR THE FIRST TIME EVER, I SAW MY MOTHER'S FACE . . .

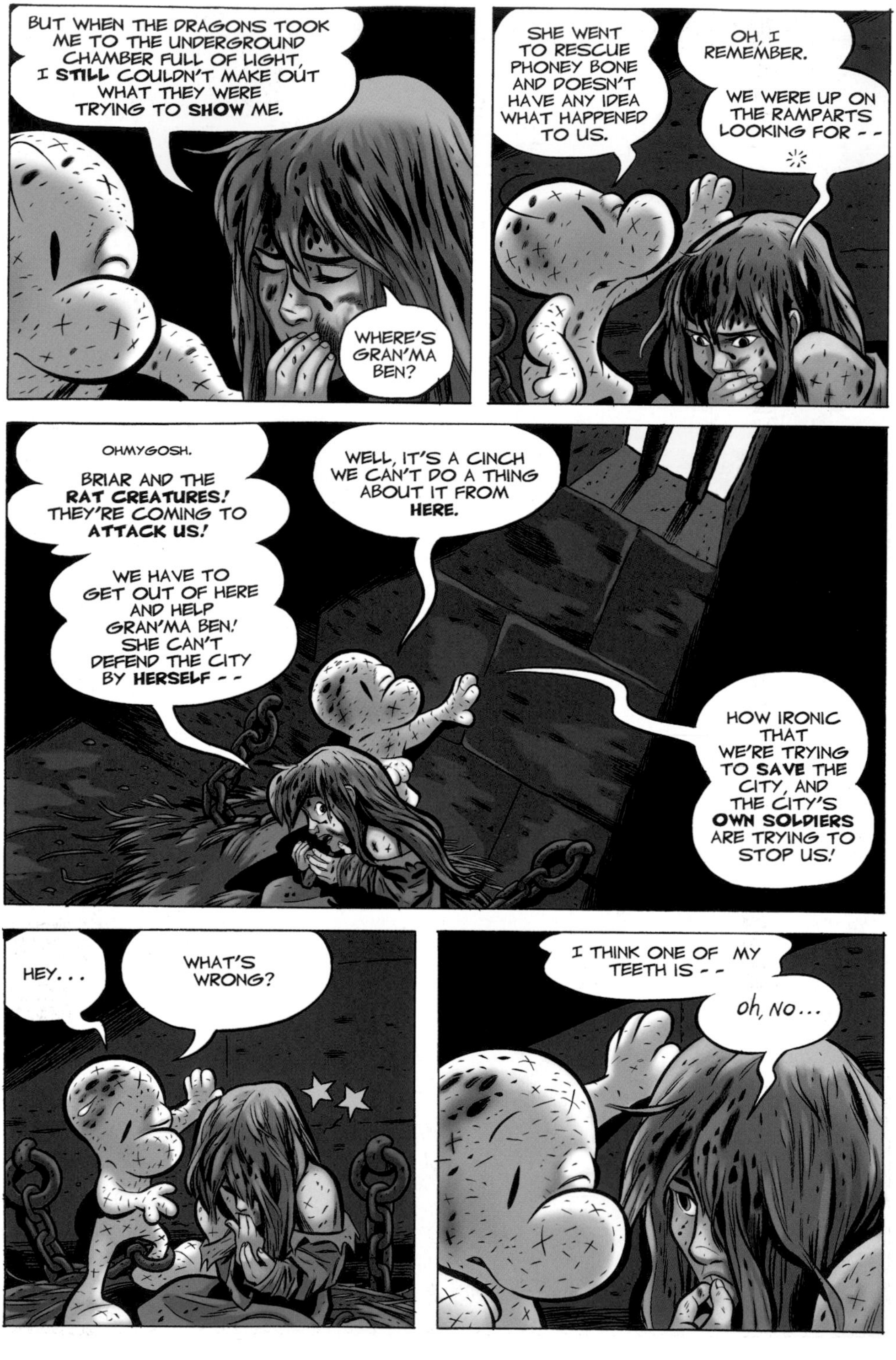
BUT WHEN THE DRAGONS TOOK ME TO THE UNDERGROUND CHAMBER FULL OF LIGHT, I STILL COULDN'T MAKE OUT WHAT THEY WERE TRYING TO SHOW ME.
WHERE'S GRAN'MA BEN?
SHE WENT TO RESCUE PHONEY BONE AND DOESN'T HAVE ANY IDEA WHAT HAPPENED TO US.
OH, I REMEMBER.
WE WERE UP ON THE RAMPARTS LOOKING FOR - -
OHMYGOSH.
BRIAR AND THE RAT CREATURES! THEY'RE COMING TO ATTACK US!
WE HAVE TO GET OUT OF HERE AND HELP GRAN'MA BEN! SHE CAN'T DEFEND THE CITY BY HERSELF - -
WELL, IT'S A CINCH WE CAN'T DO A THING ABOUT IT FROM HERE.
HOW IRONIC THAT WE'RE TRYING TO SAVE THE CITY, AND THE CITY'S OWN SOLDIERS ARE TRYING TO STOP US!
HEY. . .
WHAT'S WRONG?
I THINK ONE OF MY TEETH IS - -
oh, No . . .

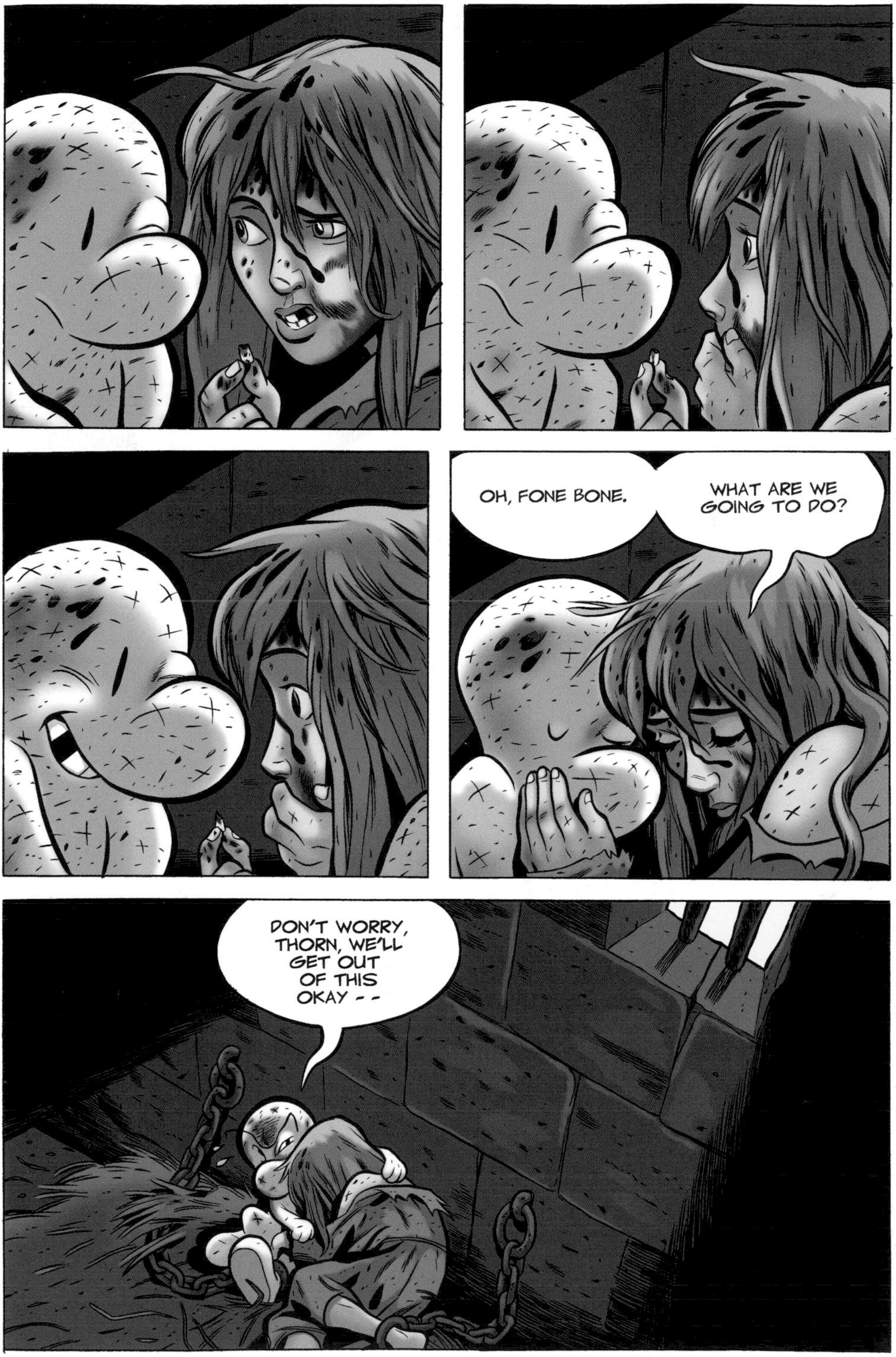
OH, FONE BONE.
WHAT ARE WE GOING TO DO?
DON'T WORRY, THORN, WE'LL GET OUT OF THIS OKAY - -

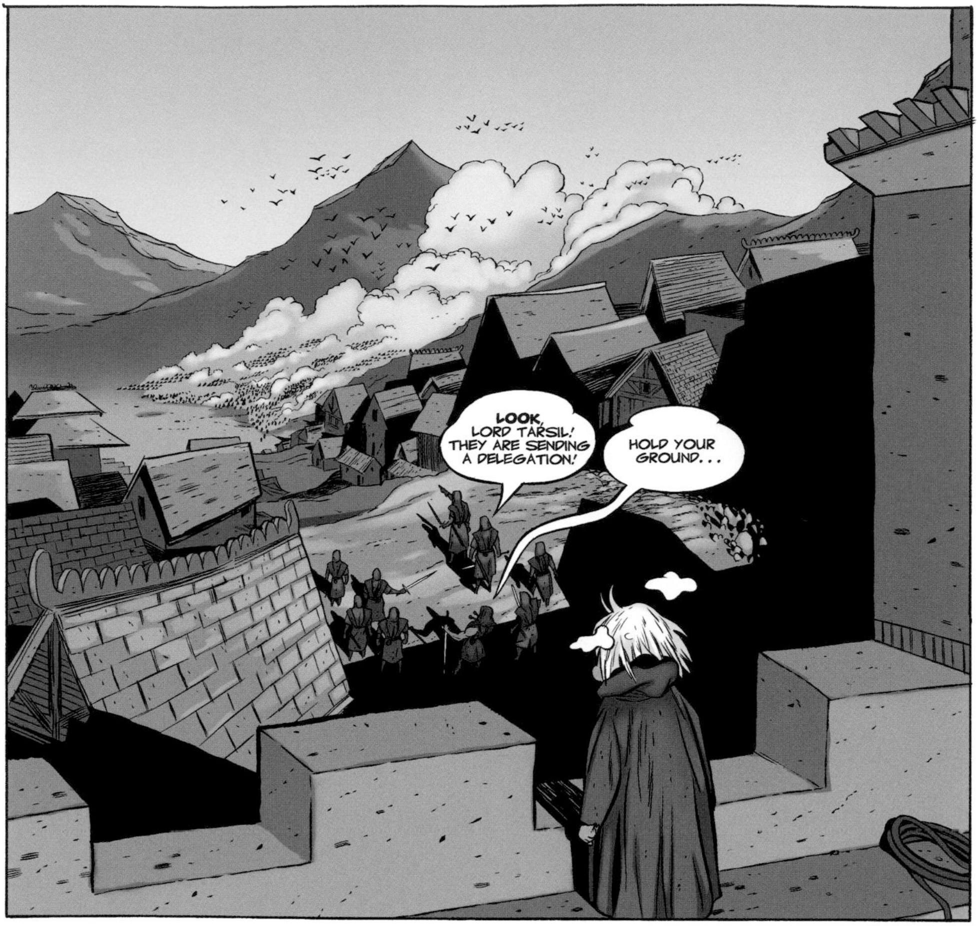
LOOK, LORD TARSIL! THEY ARE SENDING A DELEGATION!
HOLD YOUR GROUND...

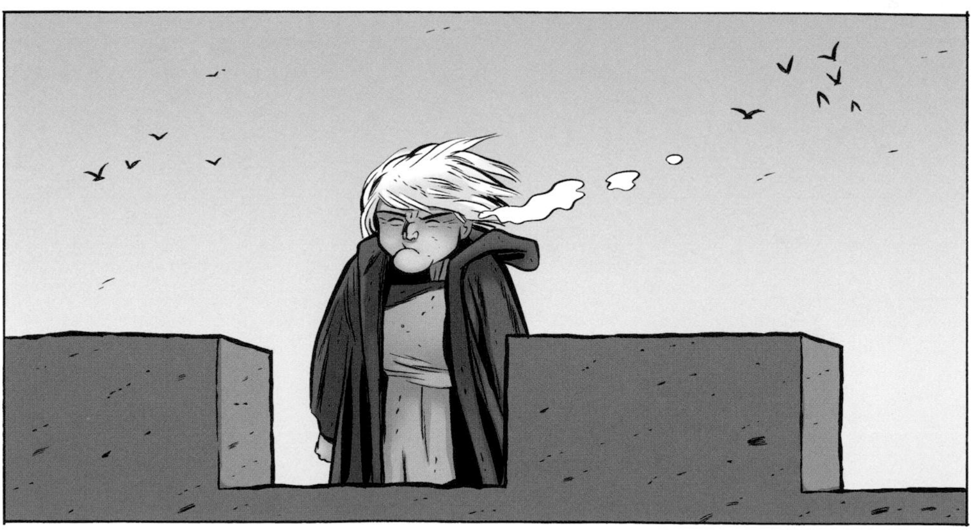

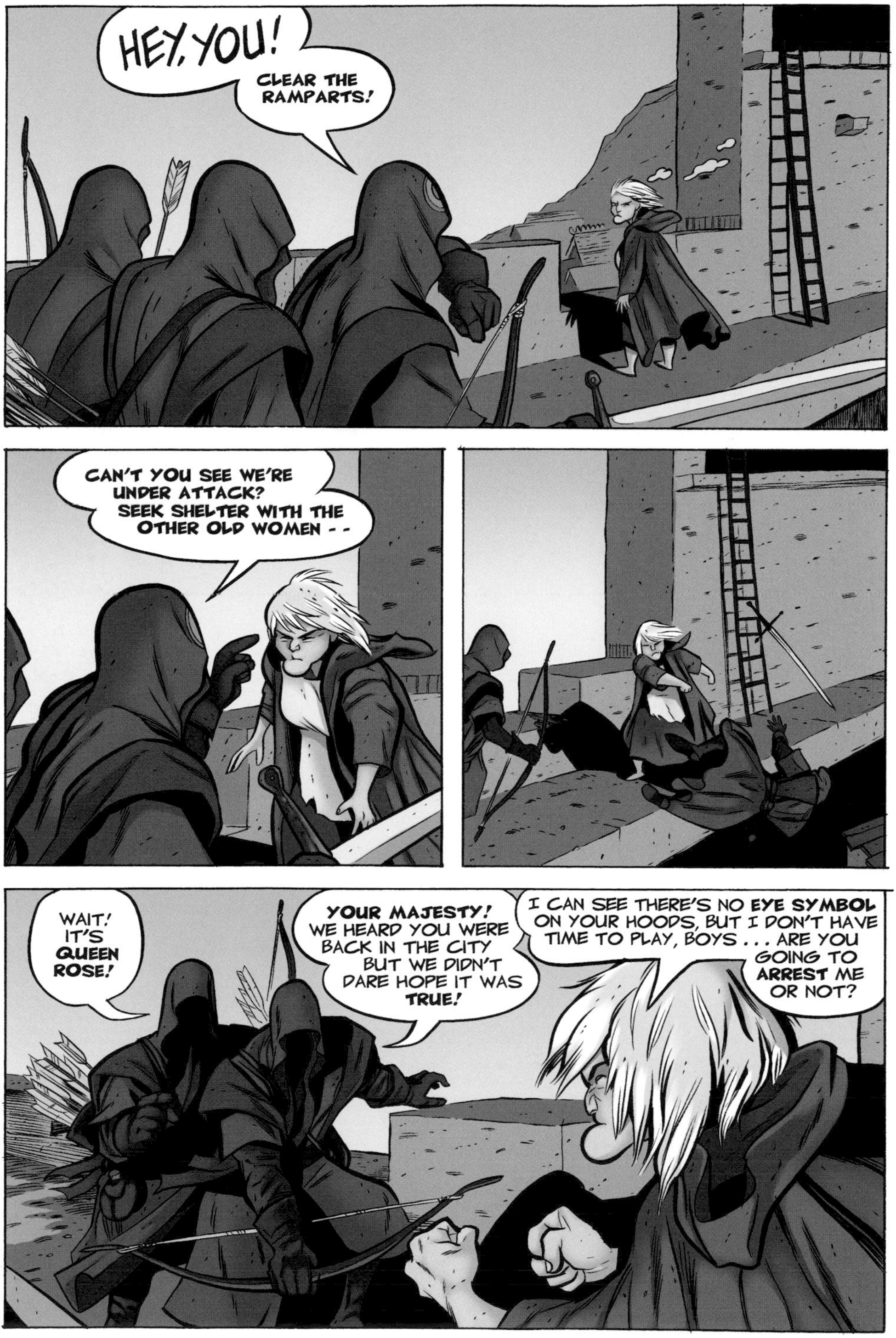
HEY, YOU!
CLEAR THE RAMPARTS!
CAN'T YOU SEE WE'RE UNDER ATTACK? SEEK SHELTER WITH THE OTHER OLD WOMEN - -
WAIT! IT'S QUEEN ROSE!
YOUR MAJESTY! WE HEARD YOU WERE BACK IN THE CITY BUT WE DIDN'T DARE HOPE IT WAS TRUE!
I CAN SEE THERE'S NO EYE SYMBOL ON YOUR HOODS, BUT I DON'T HAVE TIME TO PLAY, BOYS . . . ARE YOU GOING TO ARREST ME OR NOT?

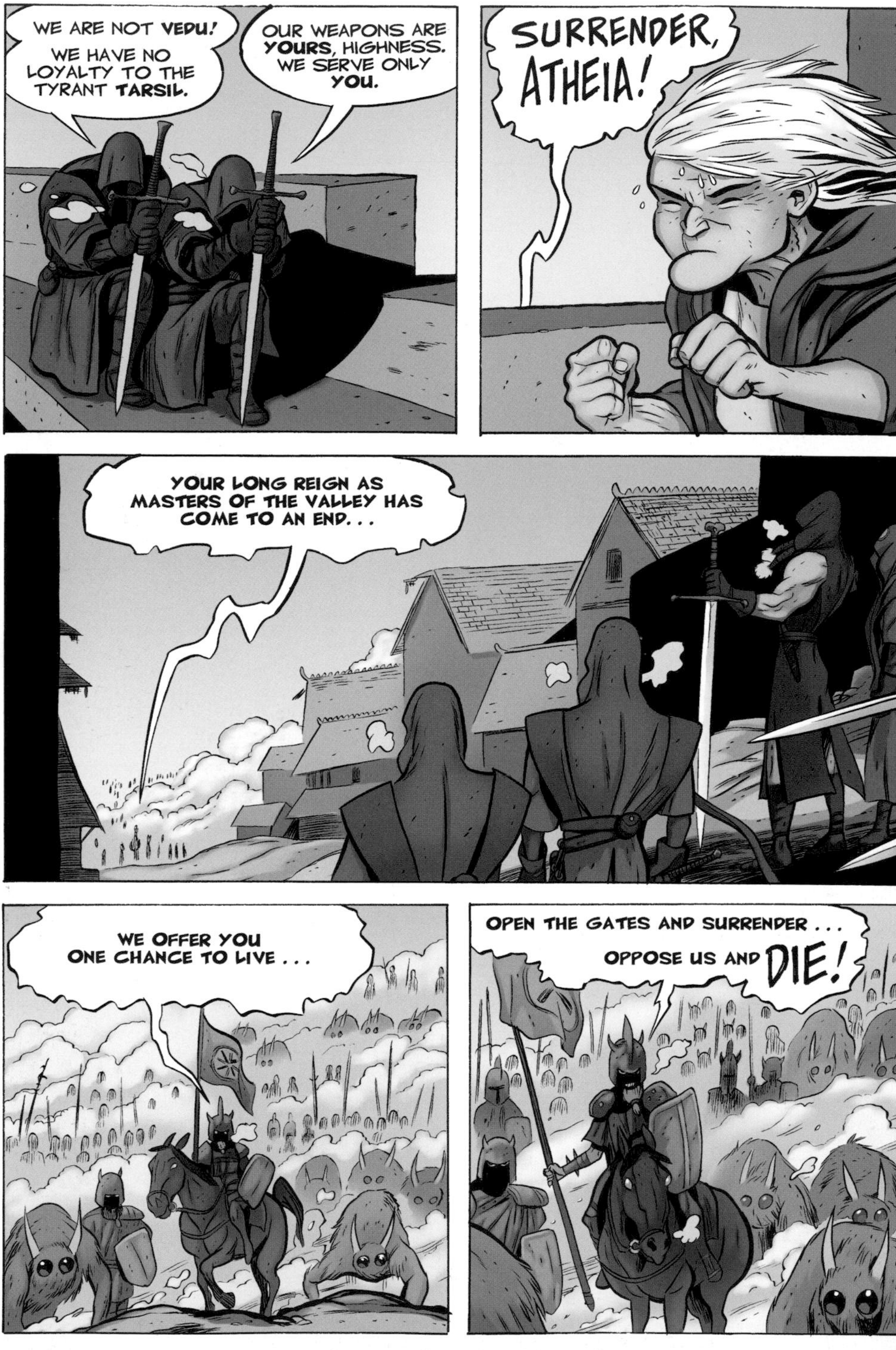
WE ARE NOT VEDU! WE HAVE NO LOYALTY TO THE TYRANT TARSIL.
OUR WEAPONS ARE YOURS, HIGHNESS. WE SERVE ONLY YOU.
SURRENDER, ATHEIA!
YOUR LONG REIGN AS MASTERS OF THE VALLEY HAS COME TO AN END . . .
WE OFFER YOU ONE CHANCE TO LIVE . . .
OPEN THE GATES AND SURRENDER . . .
OPPOSE US AND DIE!

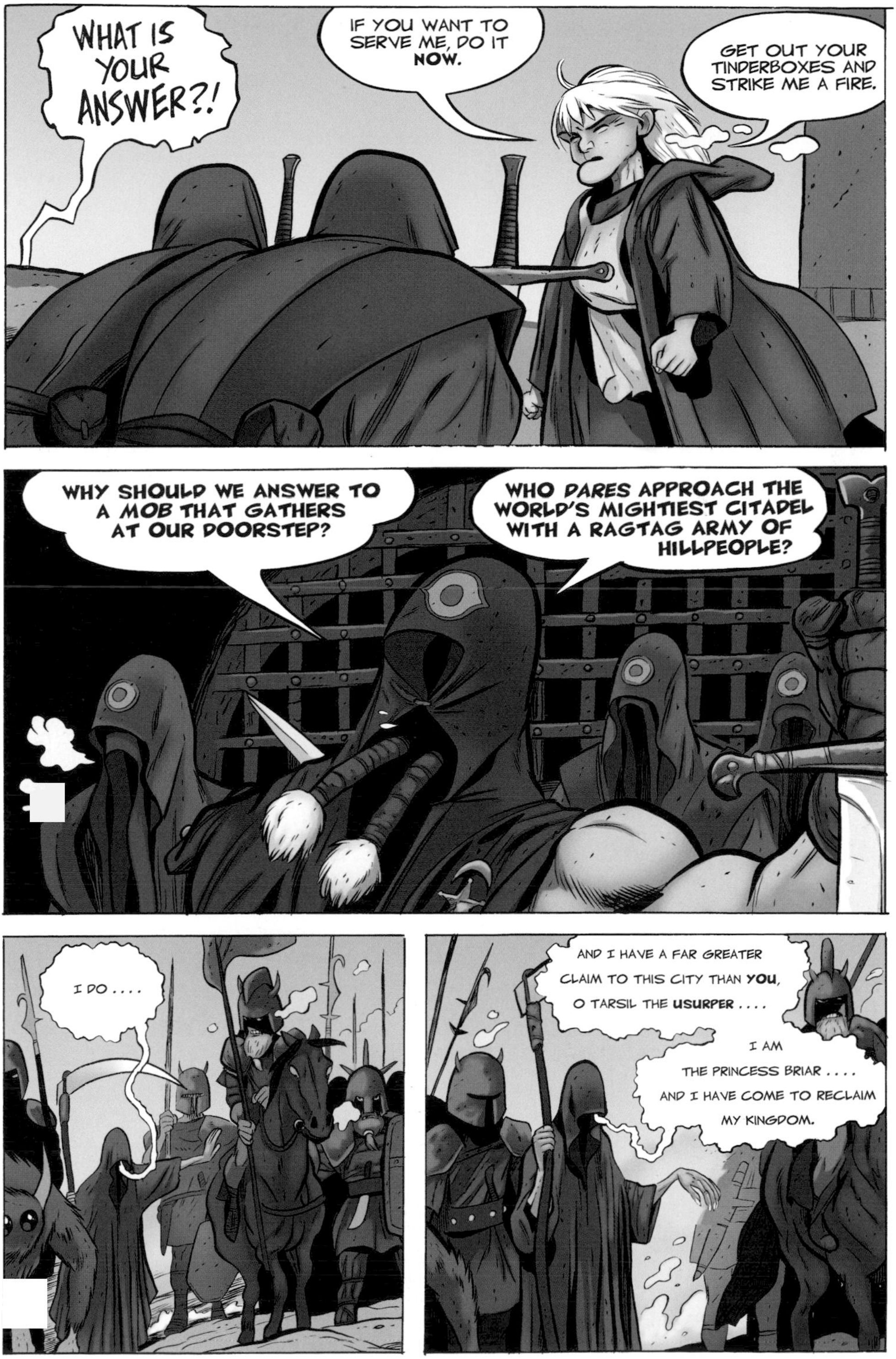
WHAT IS YOUR ANSWER?!
IF YOU WANT TO SERVE ME, DO IT NOW.
GET OUT YOUR TINDERBOXES AND STRIKE ME A FIRE.
WHY SHOULD WE ANSWER TO A MOB THAT GATHERS AT OUR DOORSTEP?
WHO DARES APPROACH THE WORLD'S MIGHTIEST CITADEL WITH A RAGTAG ARMY OF HILLPEOPLE?
I DO ....
AND I HAVE A FAR GREATER CLAIM TO THIS CITY THAN YOU, O TARSIL THE USURPER ....
I AM THE PRINCESS BRIAR .... AND I HAVE COME TO RECLAIM MY KINGDOM.

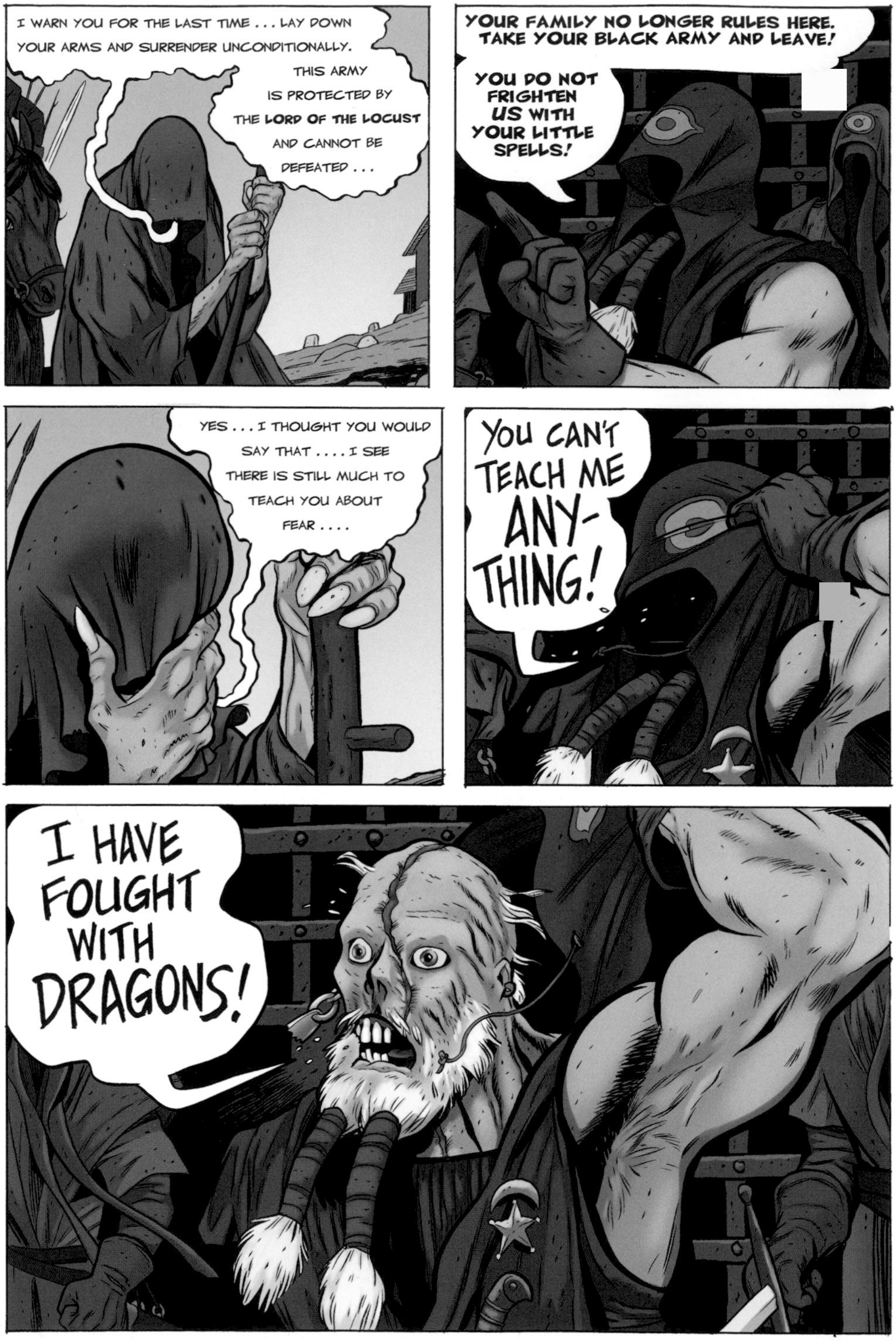
I WARN YOU FOR THE LAST TIME . . . LAY DOWN YOUR ARMS AND SURRENDER UNCONDITIONALLY.
THIS ARMY IS PROTECTED BY THE LORD OF THE LOCUST AND CANNOT BE DEFEATED . . .
YOUR FAMILY NO LONGER RULES HERE. TAKE YOUR BLACK ARMY AND LEAVE!
YOU DO NOT FRIGHTEN US WITH YOUR LITTLE SPELLS!
YES . . . I THOUGHT YOU WOULD SAY THAT . . . . I SEE THERE IS STILL MUCH TO TEACH YOU ABOUT FEAR . . . .
YOU CAN'T TEACH ME ANY-THING!
I HAVE FOUGHT WITH DRAGONS!

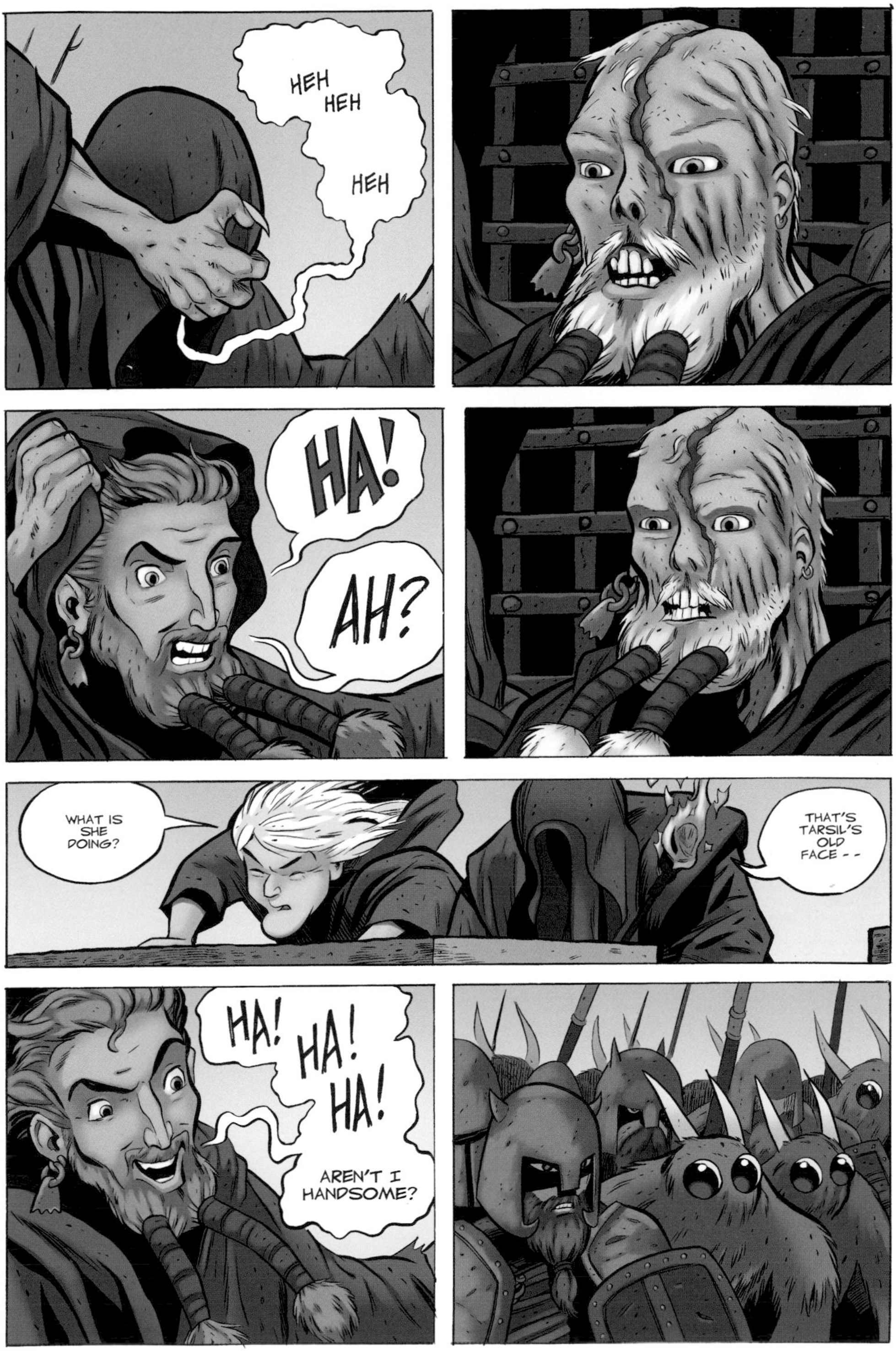
HEH
HEH
HEH
HA!
AH?
WHAT IS SHE DOING?
THAT'S TARSIL'S OLD FACE --
HA! HA! HA!
AREN'T I HANDSOME?

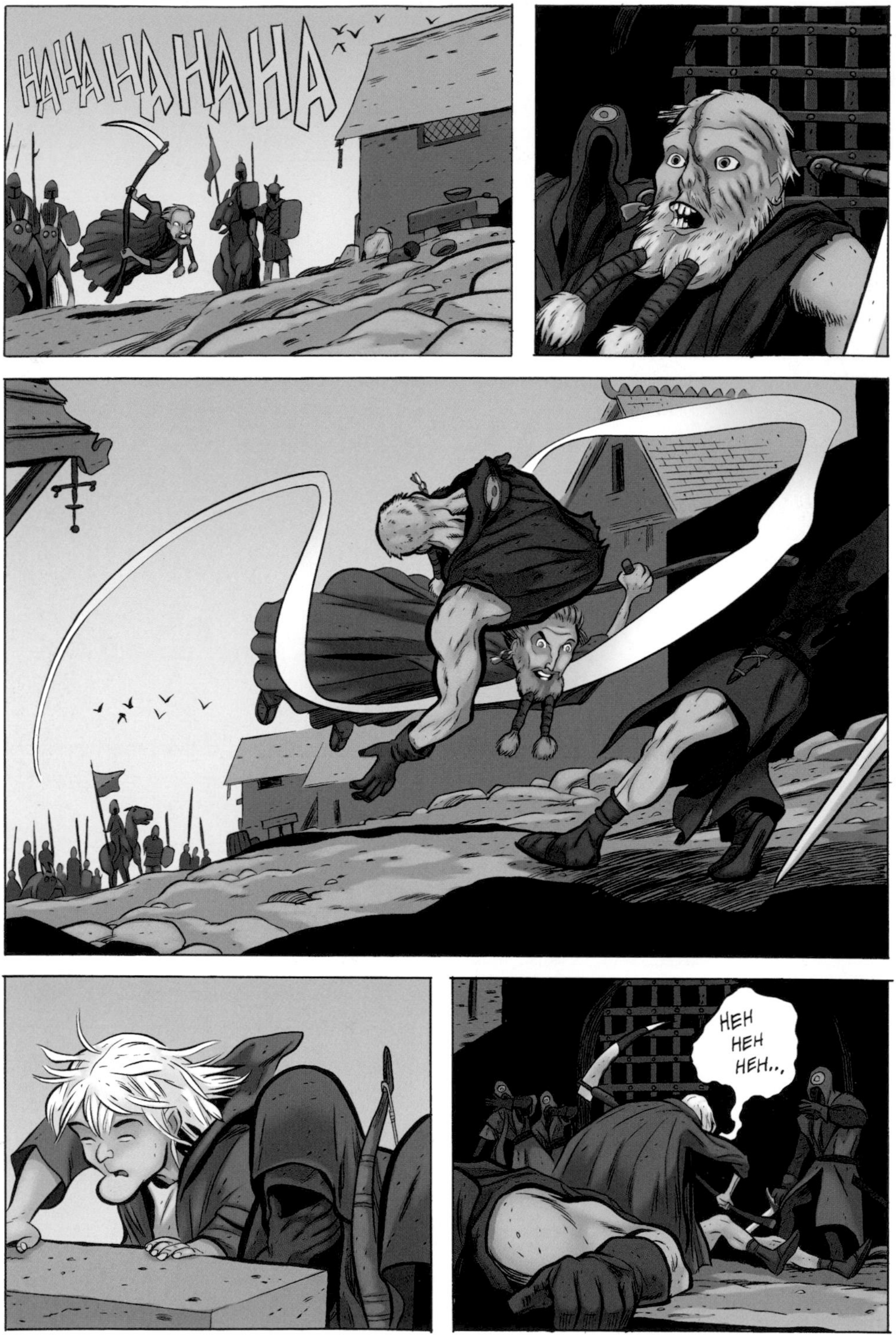
HAHAHAHAHAHA
HEH HEH HEH...

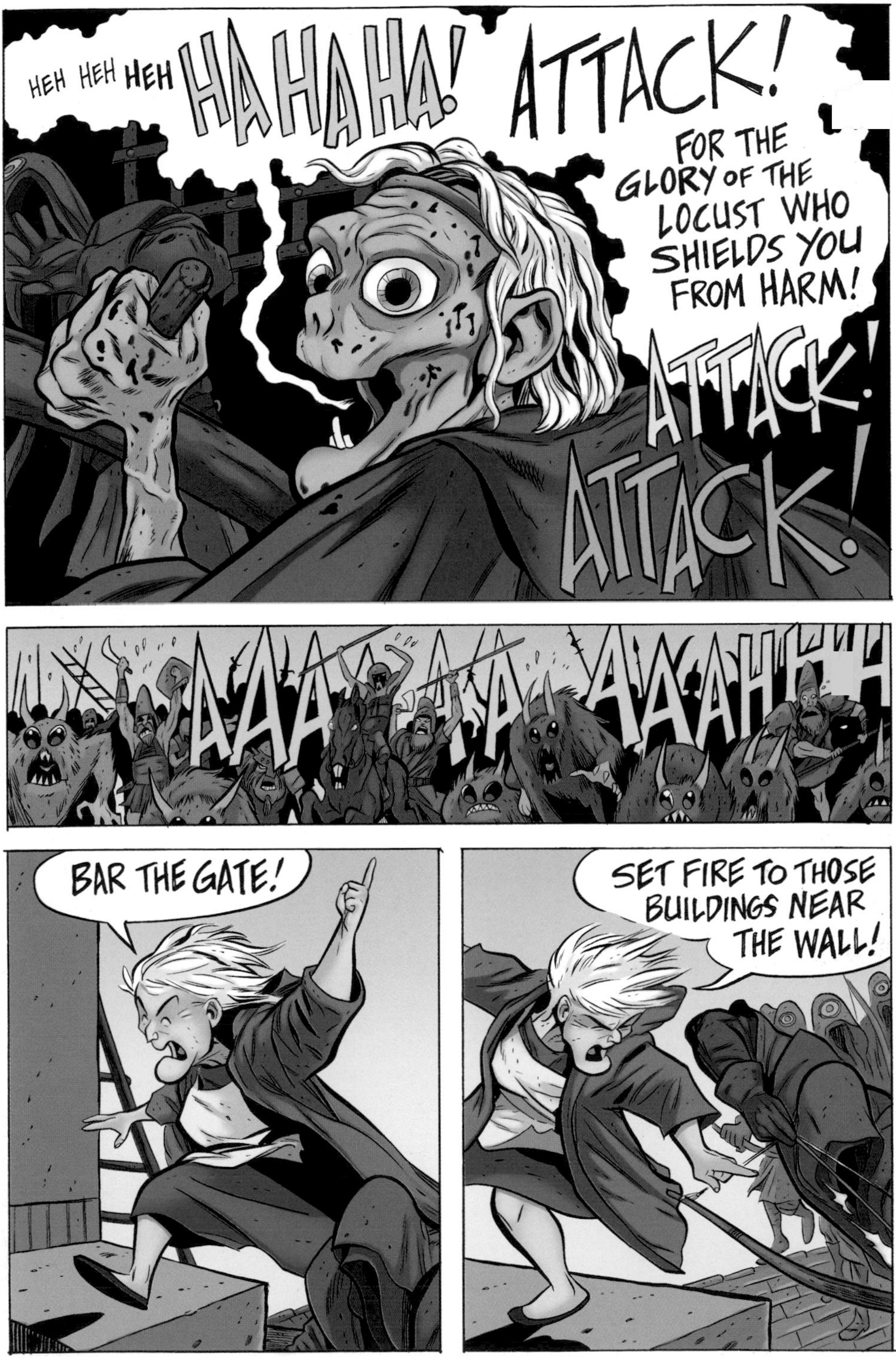
HEH HEH HEH HAHAHA! ATTACK!
FOR THE GLORY OF THE LOCUST WHO SHIELDS YOU FROM HARM!
ATTACK! ATTACK!
AAAAAAAAAHHH
BAR THE GATE!
SET FIRE TO THOSE BUILDINGS NEAR THE WALL!

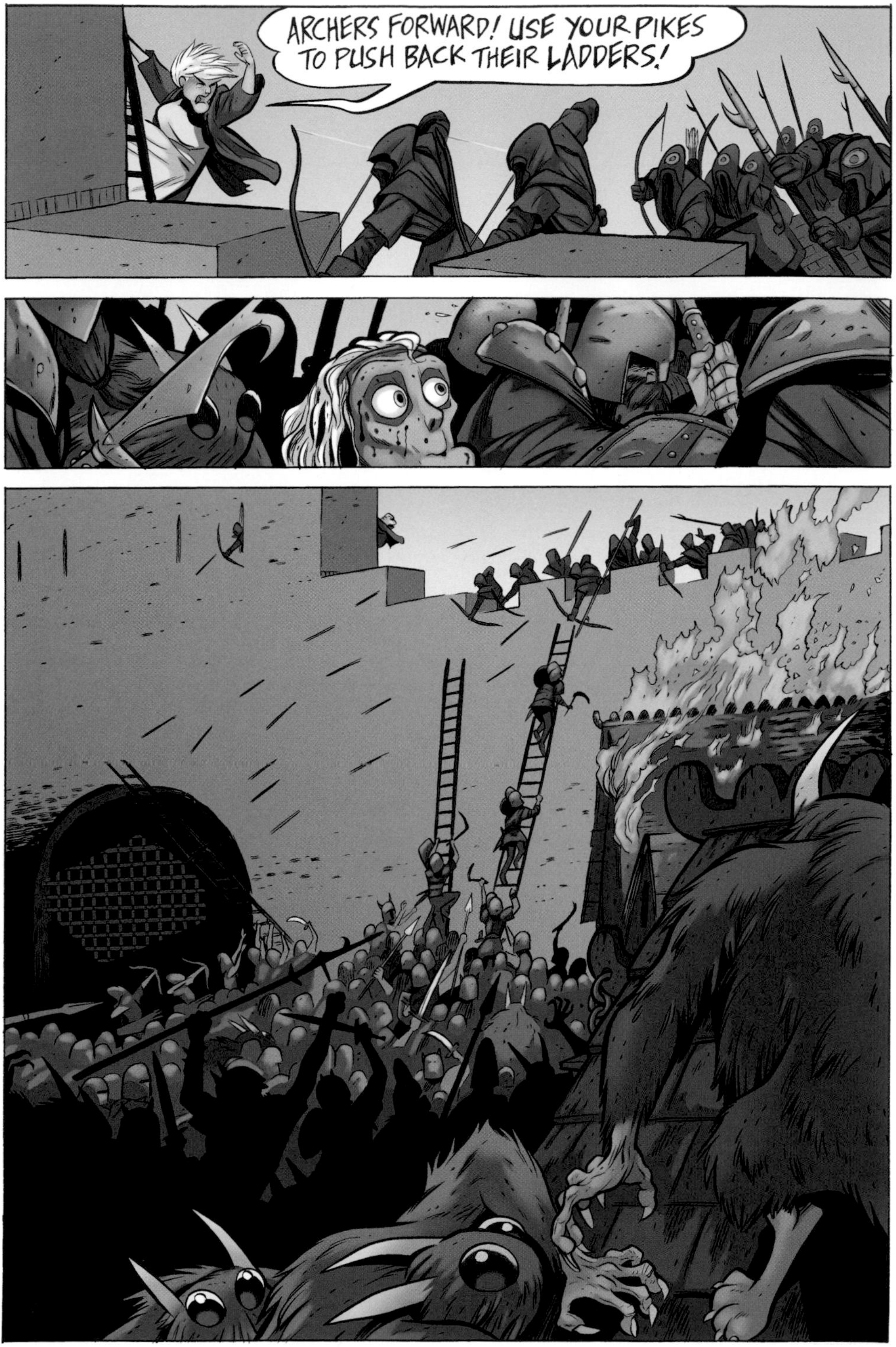
ARCHERS FORWARD! USE YOUR PIKES TO PUSH BACK THEIR LADDERS!

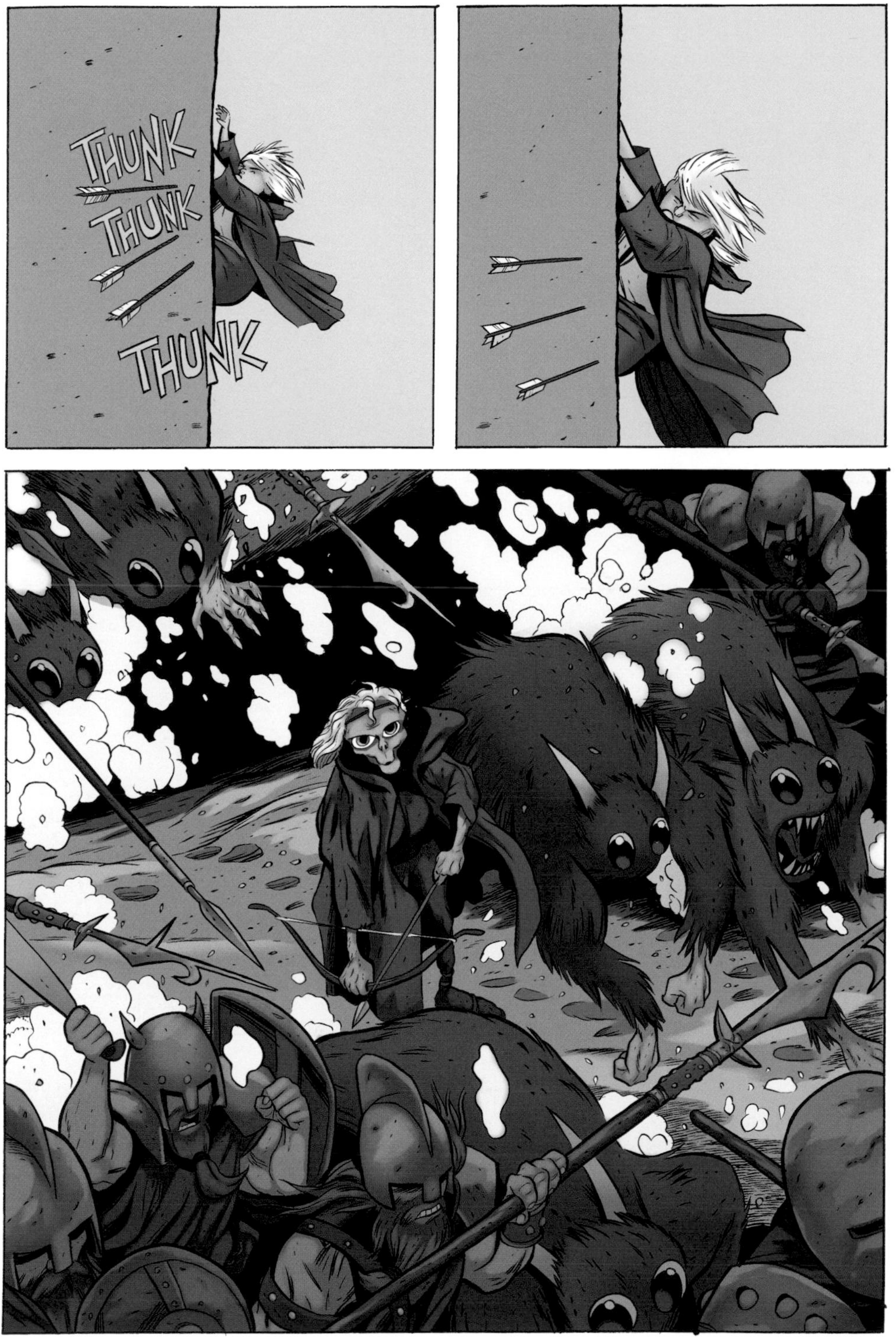
THUNK
THUNK
THUNK

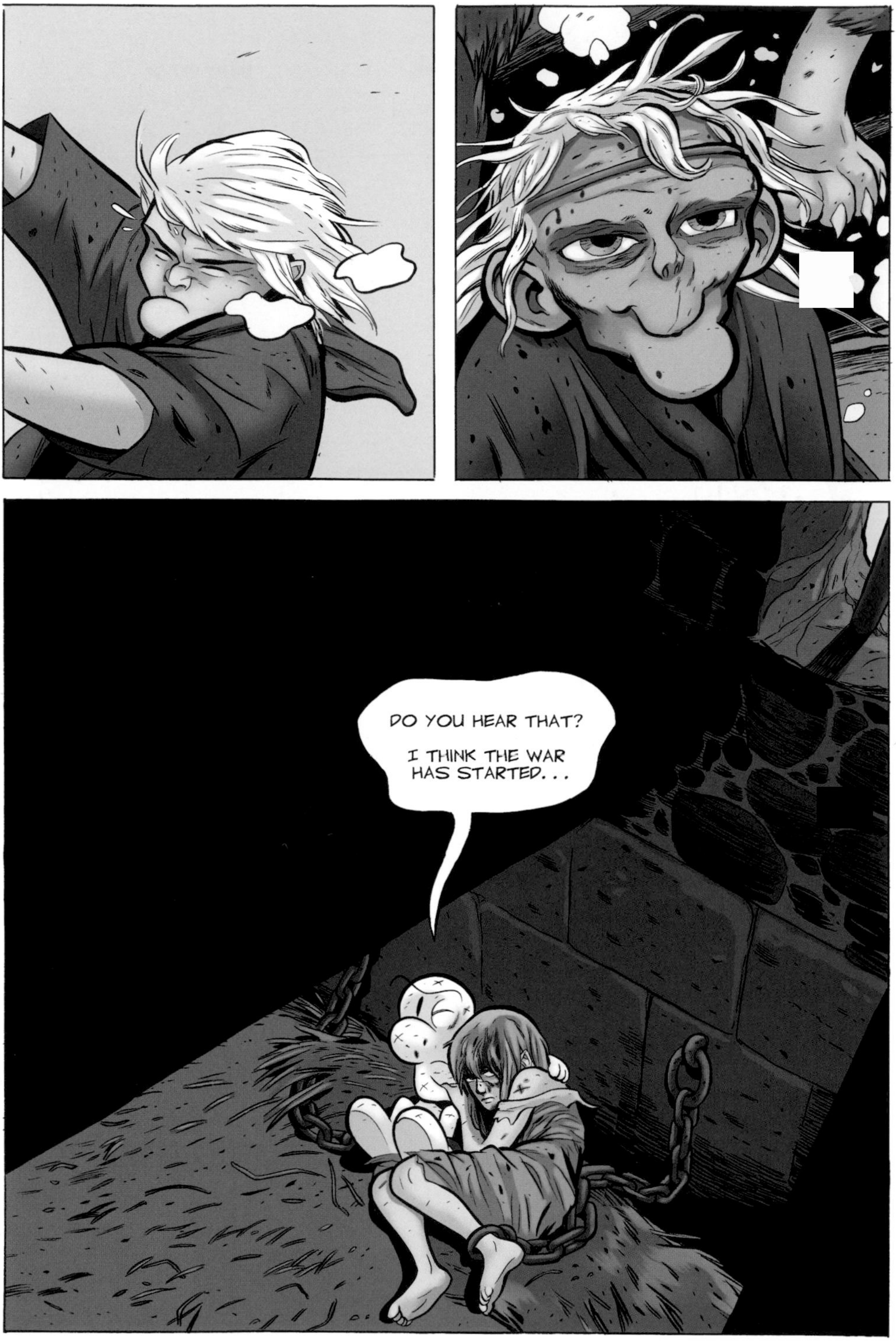
DO YOU HEAR THAT?
I THINK THE WAR HAS STARTED. . .

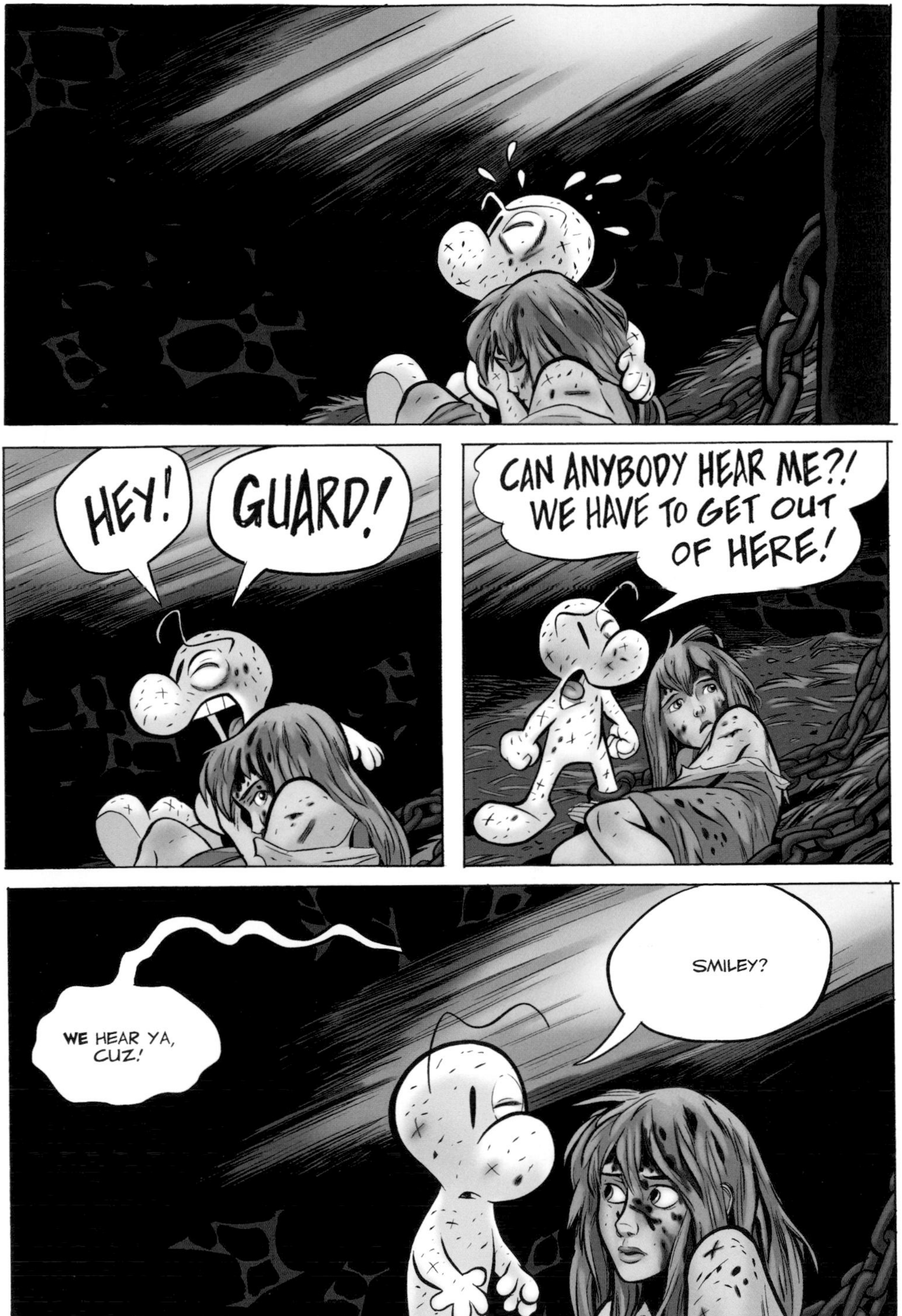
HEY!
GUARD!
CAN ANYBODY HEAR ME?! WE HAVE TO GET OUT OF HERE!
WE HEAR YA, CUZ!
SMILEY?

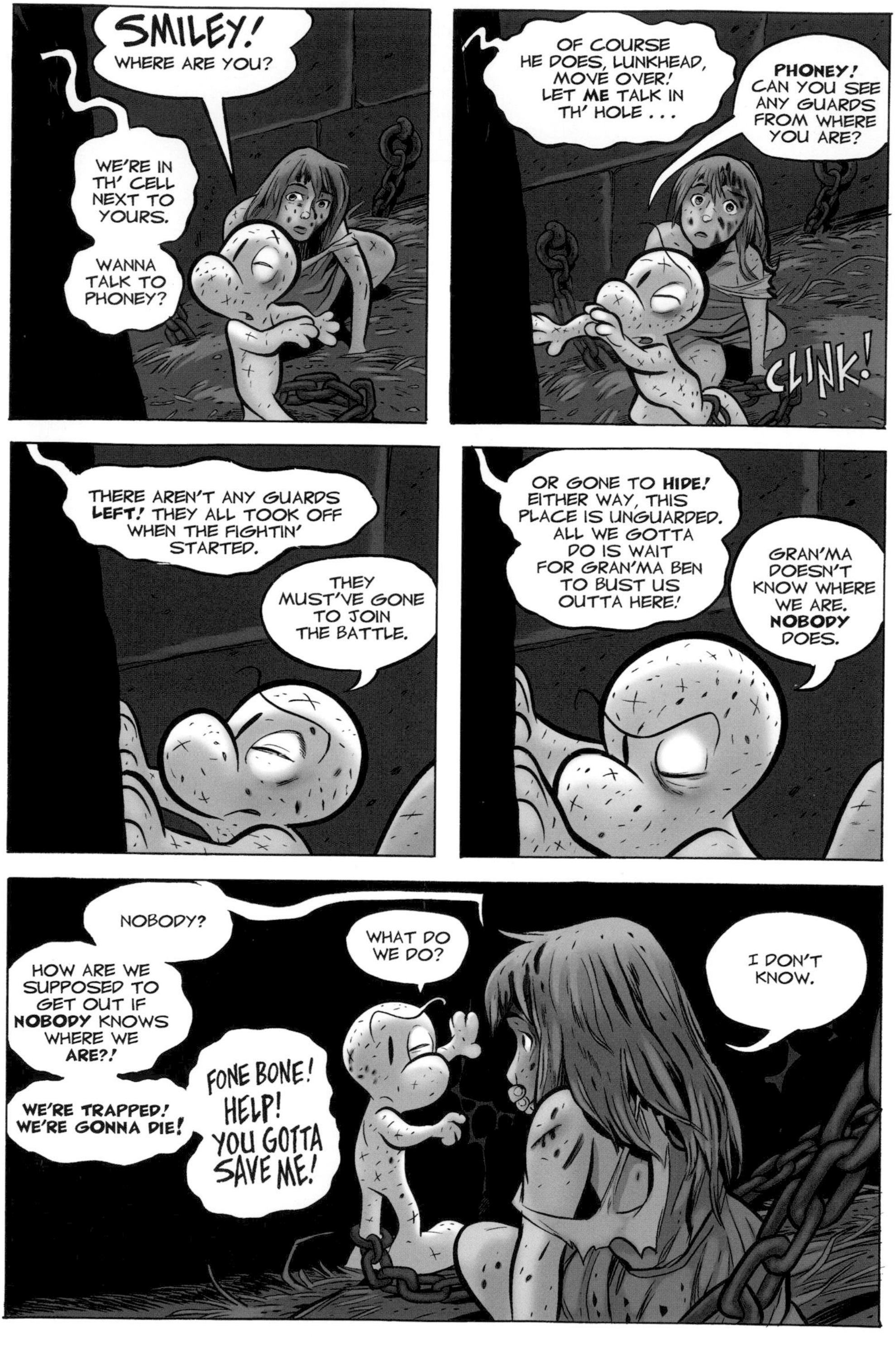
SMILEY! WHERE ARE YOU?
WE'RE IN TH' CELL NEXT TO YOURS.
WANNA TALK TO PHONEY?
OF COURSE HE DOES, LUNKHEAD, MOVE OVER! LET ME TALK IN TH' HOLE . . .
PHONEY! CAN YOU SEE ANY GUARDS FROM WHERE YOU ARE?
CLINK!
THERE AREN'T ANY GUARDS LEFT! THEY ALL TOOK OFF WHEN THE FIGHTIN' STARTED.
THEY MUST'VE GONE TO JOIN THE BATTLE.
OR GONE TO HIDE! EITHER WAY, THIS PLACE IS UNGUARDED. ALL WE GOTTA DO IS WAIT FOR GRAN'MA BEN TO BUST US OUTTA HERE!
GRAN'MA DOESN'T KNOW WHERE WE ARE. NOBODY DOES.
NOBODY?
HOW ARE WE SUPPOSED TO GET OUT IF NOBODY KNOWS WHERE WE ARE?!
WE'RE TRAPPED! WE'RE GONNA DIE!
FONE BONE! HELP! YOU GOTTA SAVE ME!
WHAT DO WE DO?
I DON'T KNOW.

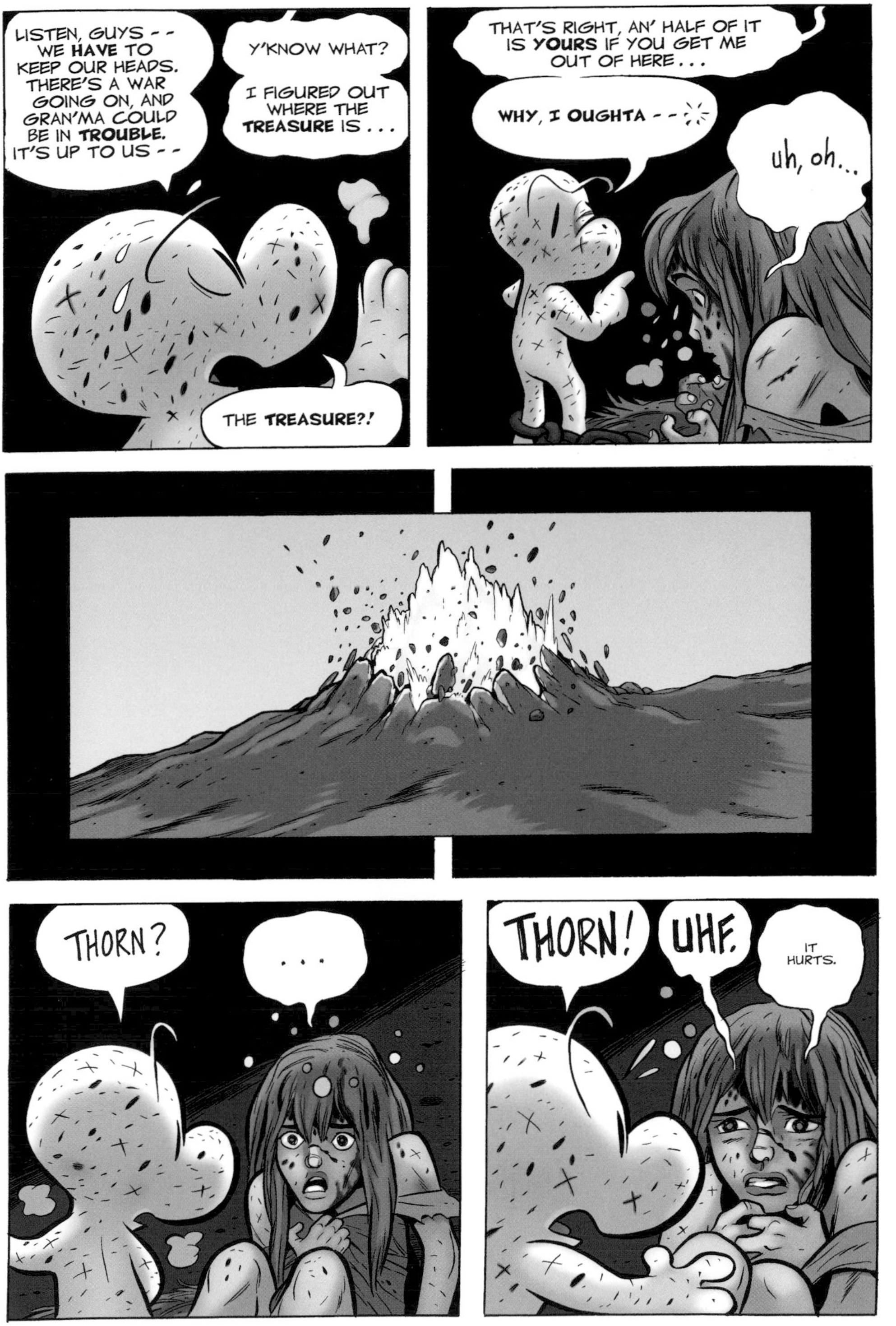
LISTEN, GUYS - - WE HAVE TO KEEP OUR HEADS. THERE'S A WAR GOING ON, AND GRAN'MA COULD BE IN TROUBLE. IT'S UP TO US - -
Y'KNOW WHAT?
I FIGURED OUT WHERE THE TREASURE IS . . .
THE TREASURE?!
THAT'S RIGHT, AN' HALF OF IT IS YOURS IF YOU GET ME OUT OF HERE . . .
WHY, I OUGHTA - -
uh, oh...
THORN?
. . .
THORN!
UHF.
IT HURTS.

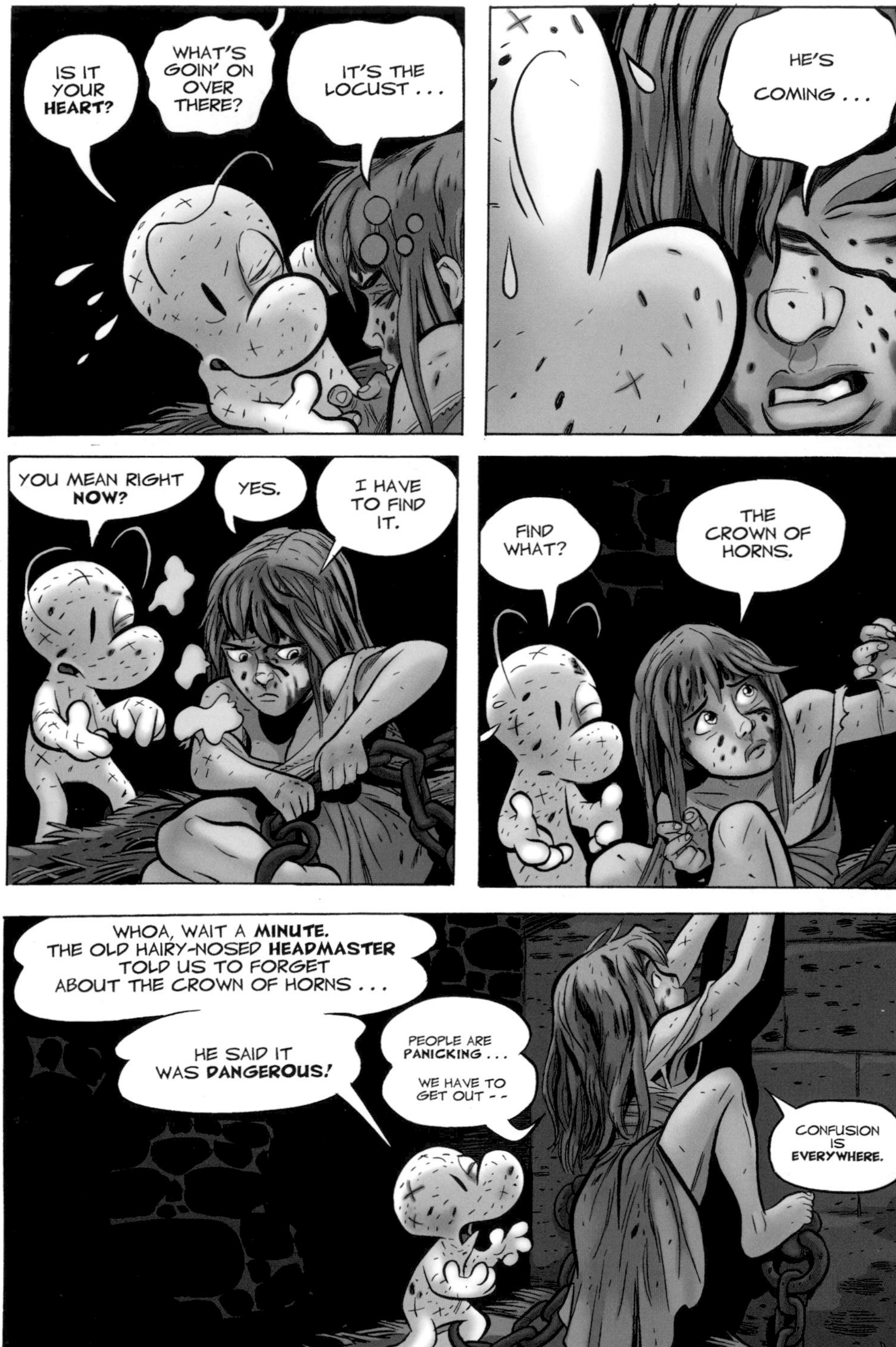
IS IT YOUR HEART?
WHAT'S GOIN' ON OVER THERE?
IT'S THE LOCUST . . .
HE'S COMING . . .
YOU MEAN RIGHT NOW?
YES.
I HAVE TO FIND IT.
FIND WHAT?
THE CROWN OF HORNS.
WHOA, WAIT A MINUTE. THE OLD HAIRY-NOSED HEADMASTER TOLD US TO FORGET ABOUT THE CROWN OF HORNS . . .
HE SAID IT WAS DANGEROUS!
PEOPLE ARE PANICKING . . .
WE HAVE TO GET OUT - -
CONFUSION IS EVERYWHERE.

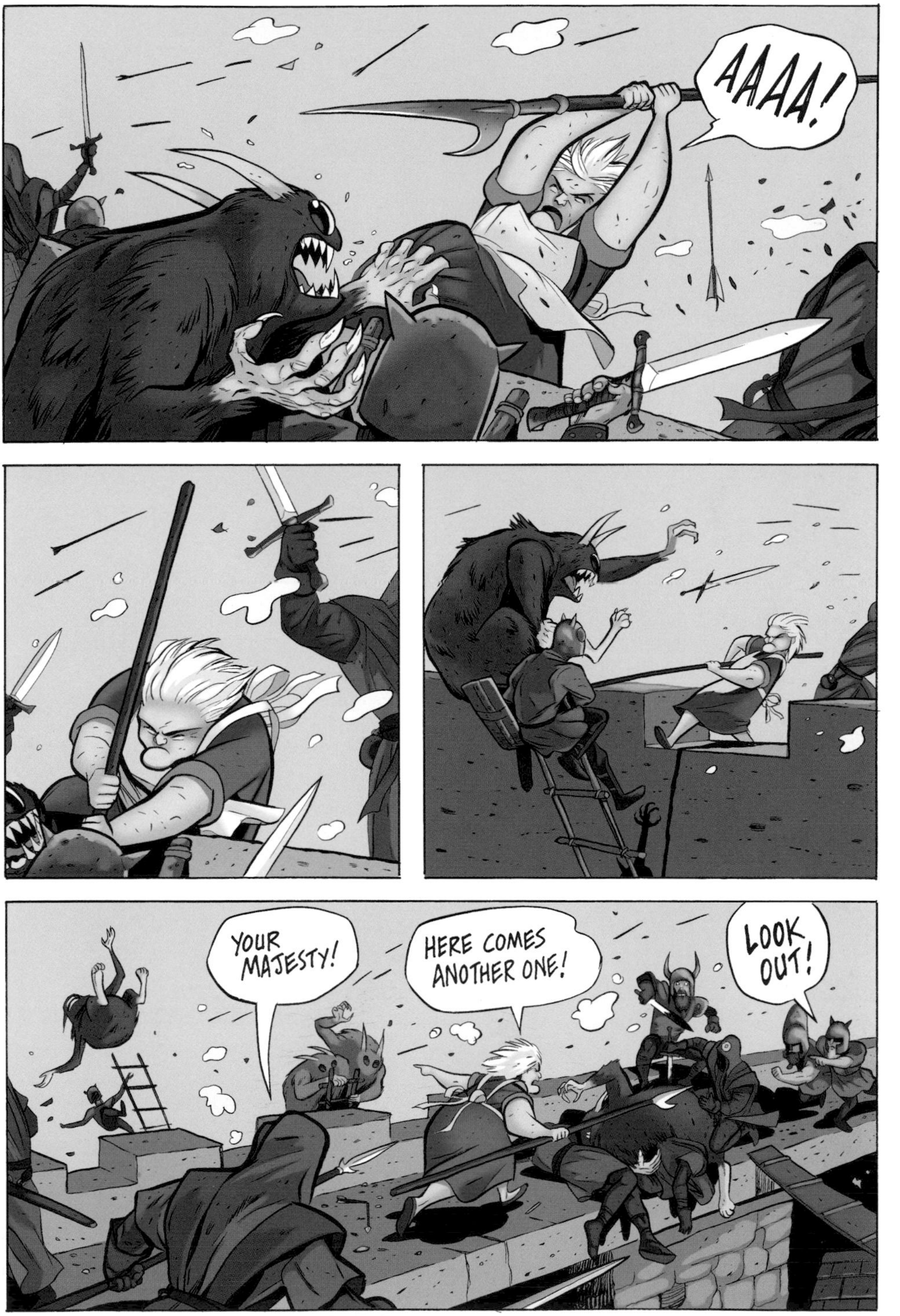
AAAA!
YOUR MAJESTY!
HERE COMES ANOTHER ONE!
LOOK OUT!

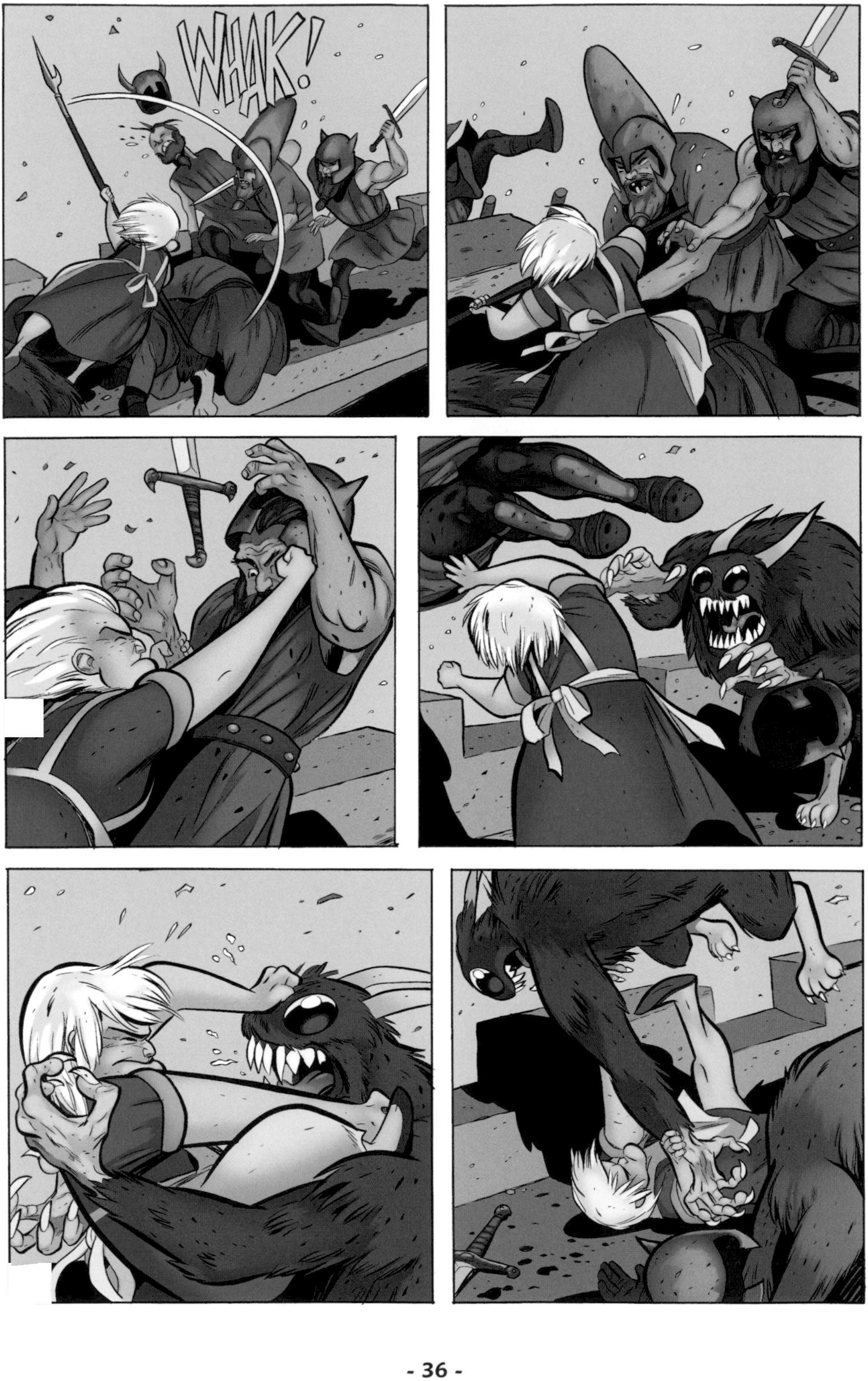
WHAK!

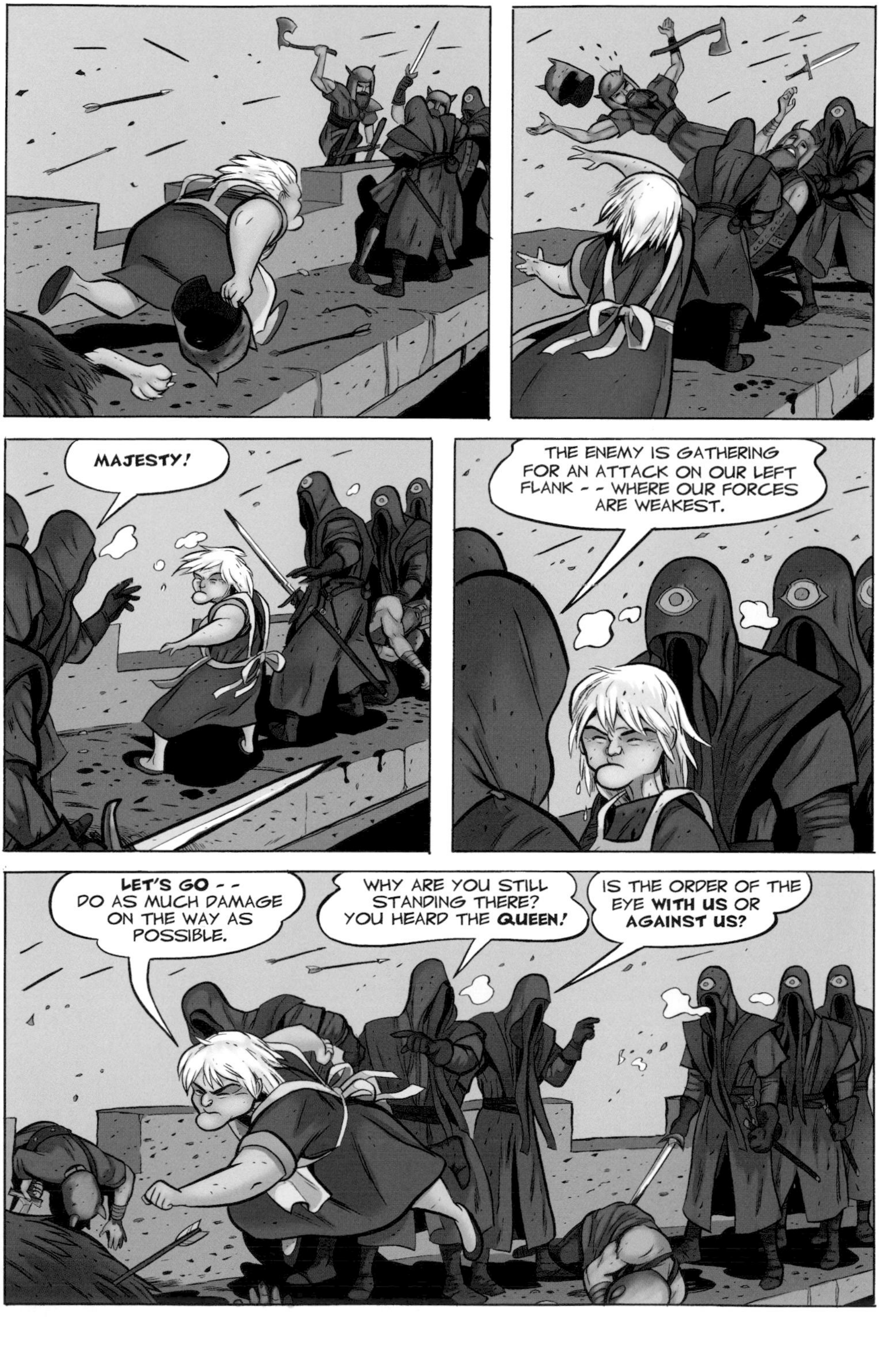
MAJESTY!
THE ENEMY IS GATHERING FOR AN ATTACK ON OUR LEFT FLANK -- WHERE OUR FORCES ARE WEAKEST.
LET'S GO -- DO AS MUCH DAMAGE ON THE WAY AS POSSIBLE.
WHY ARE YOU STILL STANDING THERE? YOU HEARD THE QUEEN!
IS THE ORDER OF THE EYE WITH US OR AGAINST US?

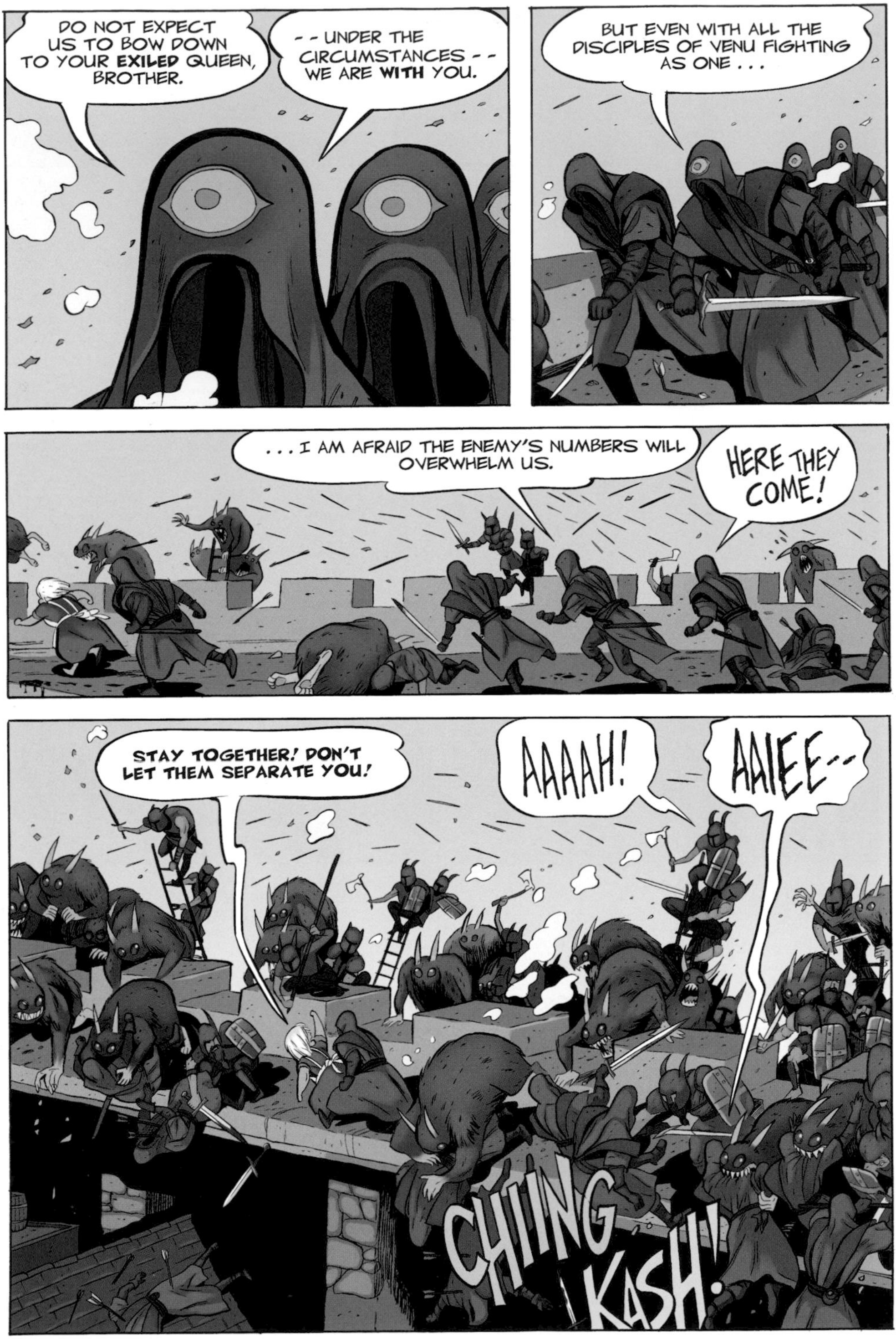
DO NOT EXPECT US TO BOW DOWN TO YOUR EXILED QUEEN, BROTHER.
- - UNDER THE CIRCUMSTANCES - - WE ARE WITH YOU.
BUT EVEN WITH ALL THE DISCIPLES OF VENU FIGHTING AS ONE . . .
. . . I AM AFRAID THE ENEMY'S NUMBERS WILL OVERWHELM US.
HERE THEY COME!
STAY TOGETHER! DON'T LET THEM SEPARATE YOU!
AAAAH!
AAIEE- -
CHING KASH!

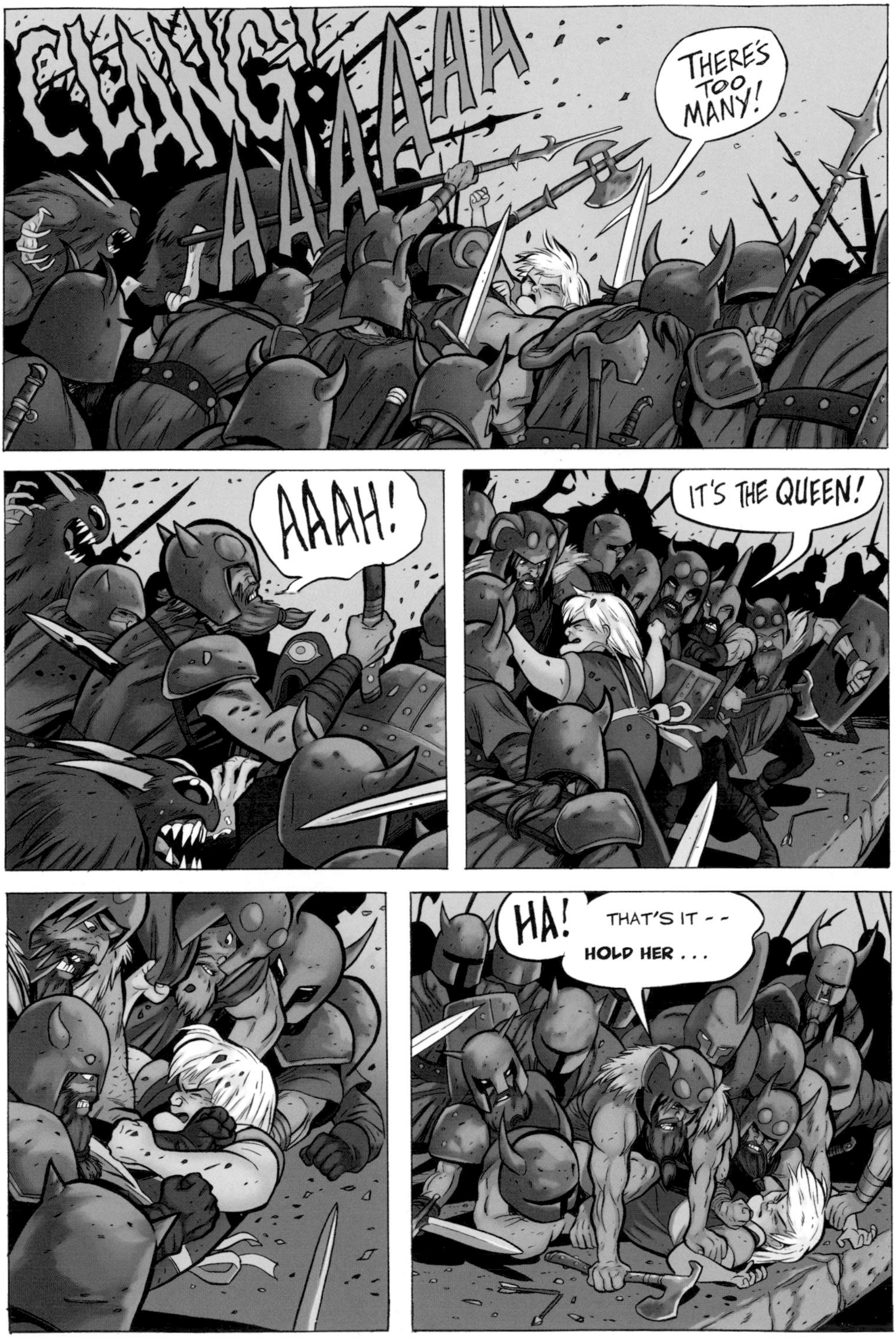
CLANG!
AAAAAAAA
THERE'S TOO MANY!
AAAH!
IT'S THE QUEEN!
HA!
THAT'S IT - -
HOLD HER . . .

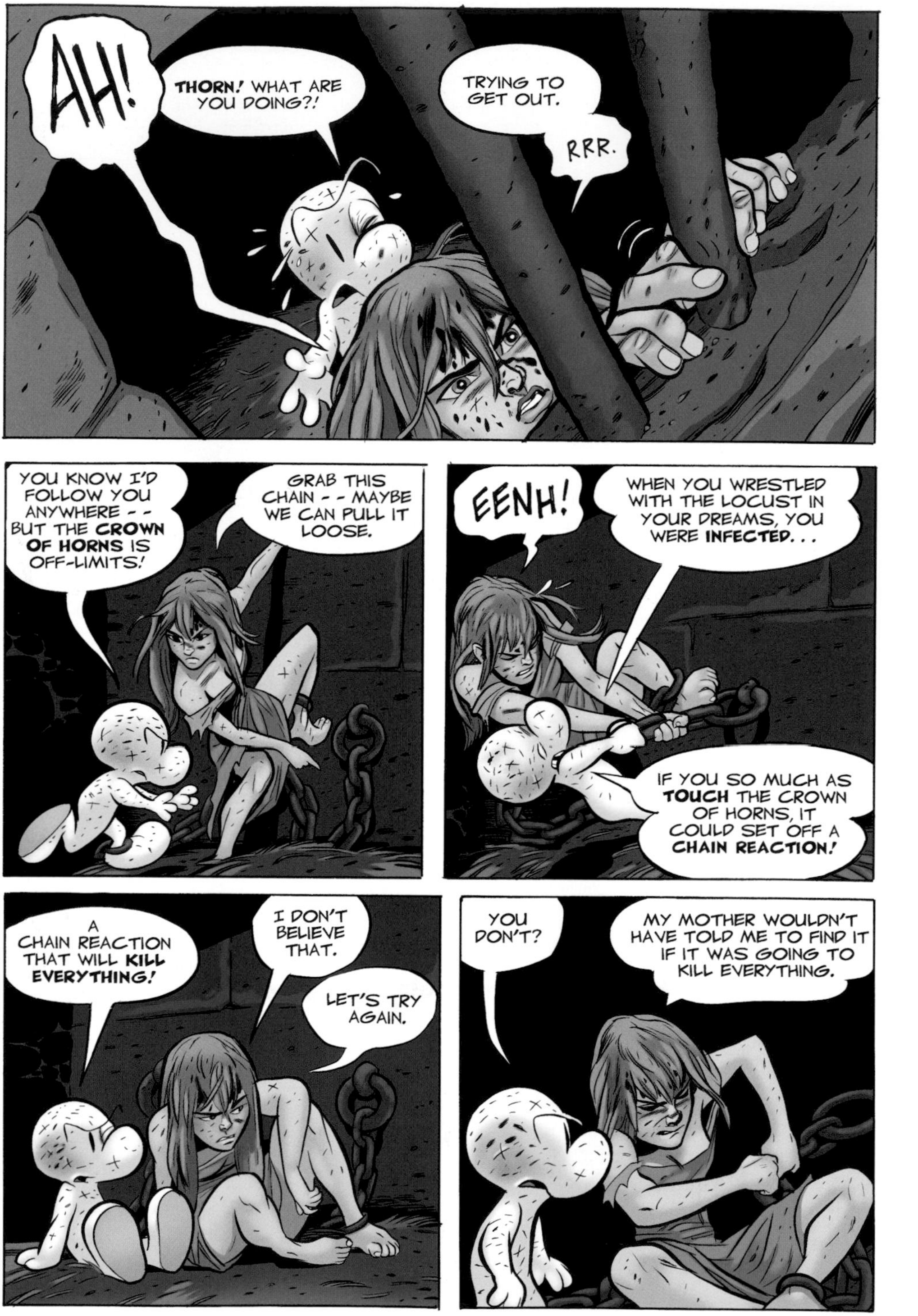
AH!
THORN! WHAT ARE YOU DOING?!
TRYING TO GET OUT.
RRR.
YOU KNOW I'D FOLLOW YOU ANYWHERE -- BUT THE CROWN OF HORNS IS OFF-LIMITS!
GRAB THIS CHAIN -- MAYBE WE CAN PULL IT LOOSE.
EENH!
WHEN YOU WRESTLED WITH THE LOCUST IN YOUR DREAMS, YOU WERE INFECTED...
IF YOU SO MUCH AS TOUCH THE CROWN OF HORNS, IT COULD SET OFF A CHAIN REACTION!
A CHAIN REACTION THAT WILL KILL EVERYTHING!
I DON'T BELIEVE THAT.
LET'S TRY AGAIN.
YOU DON'T?
MY MOTHER WOULDN'T HAVE TOLD ME TO FIND IT IF IT WAS GOING TO KILL EVERYTHING.

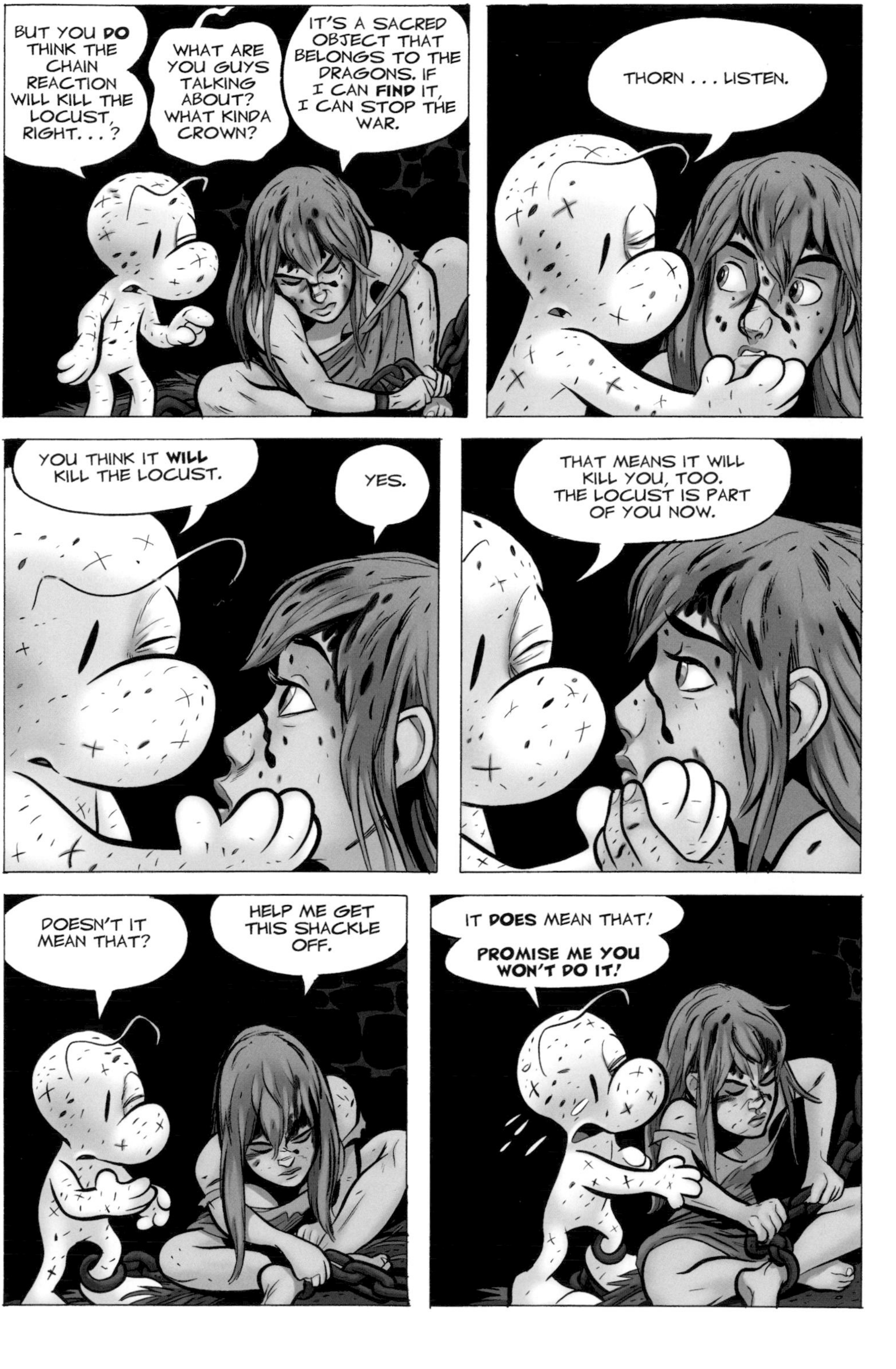
BUT YOU **DO** THINK THE CHAIN REACTION WILL KILL THE LOCUST, RIGHT. . . ?
WHAT ARE YOU GUYS TALKING ABOUT? WHAT KINDA CROWN?
IT'S A SACRED OBJECT THAT BELONGS TO THE DRAGONS. IF I CAN **FIND** IT, I CAN STOP THE WAR.
THORN . . . LISTEN.
YOU THINK IT **WILL** KILL THE LOCUST.
YES.
THAT MEANS IT WILL KILL YOU, TOO. THE LOCUST IS PART OF YOU NOW.
DOESN'T IT MEAN THAT?
HELP ME GET THIS SHACKLE OFF.
IT **DOES** MEAN THAT!
PROMISE ME YOU WON'T DO IT!

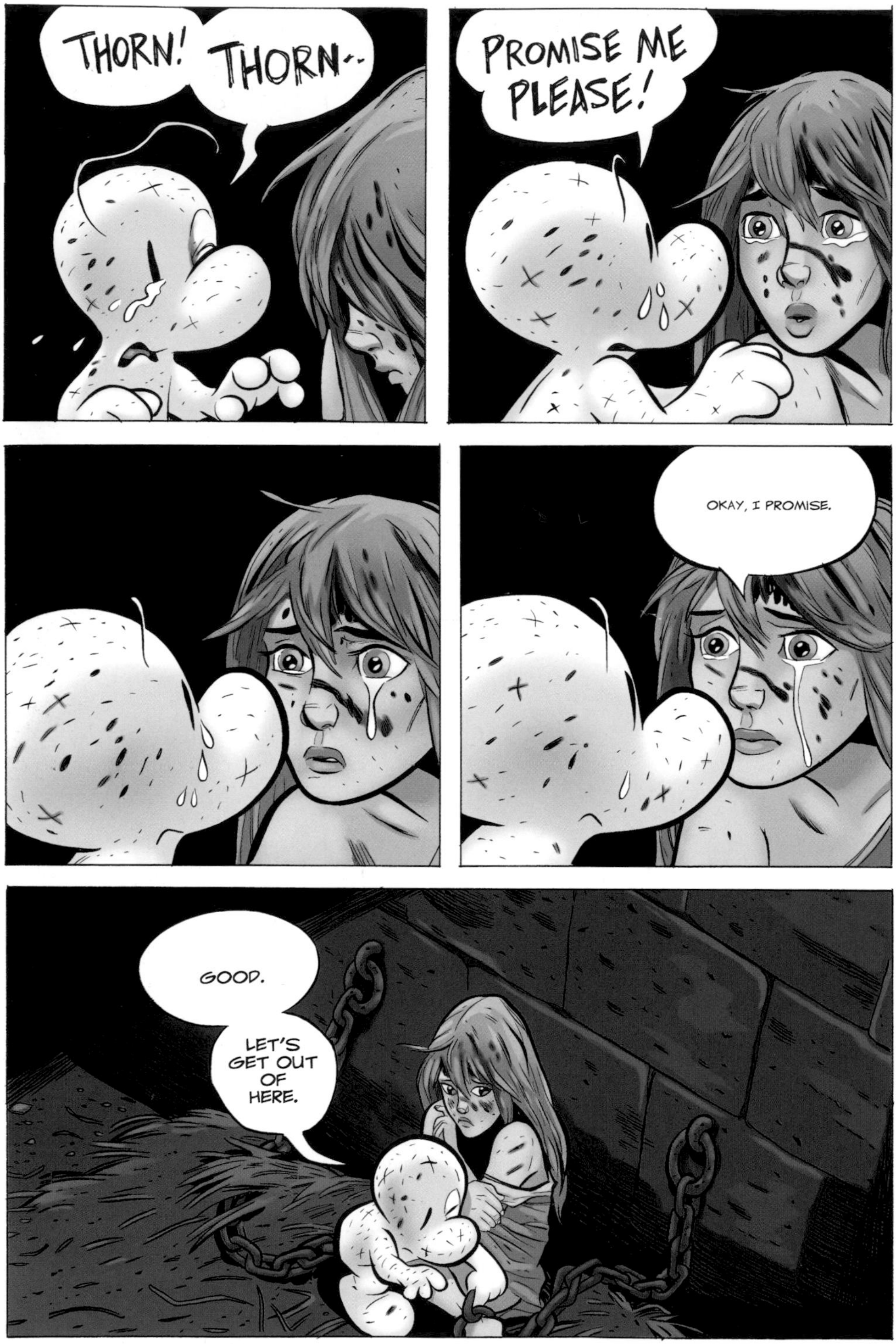
THORN!
THORN--
PROMISE ME PLEASE!
OKAY, I PROMISE.
GOOD.
LET'S GET OUT OF HERE.

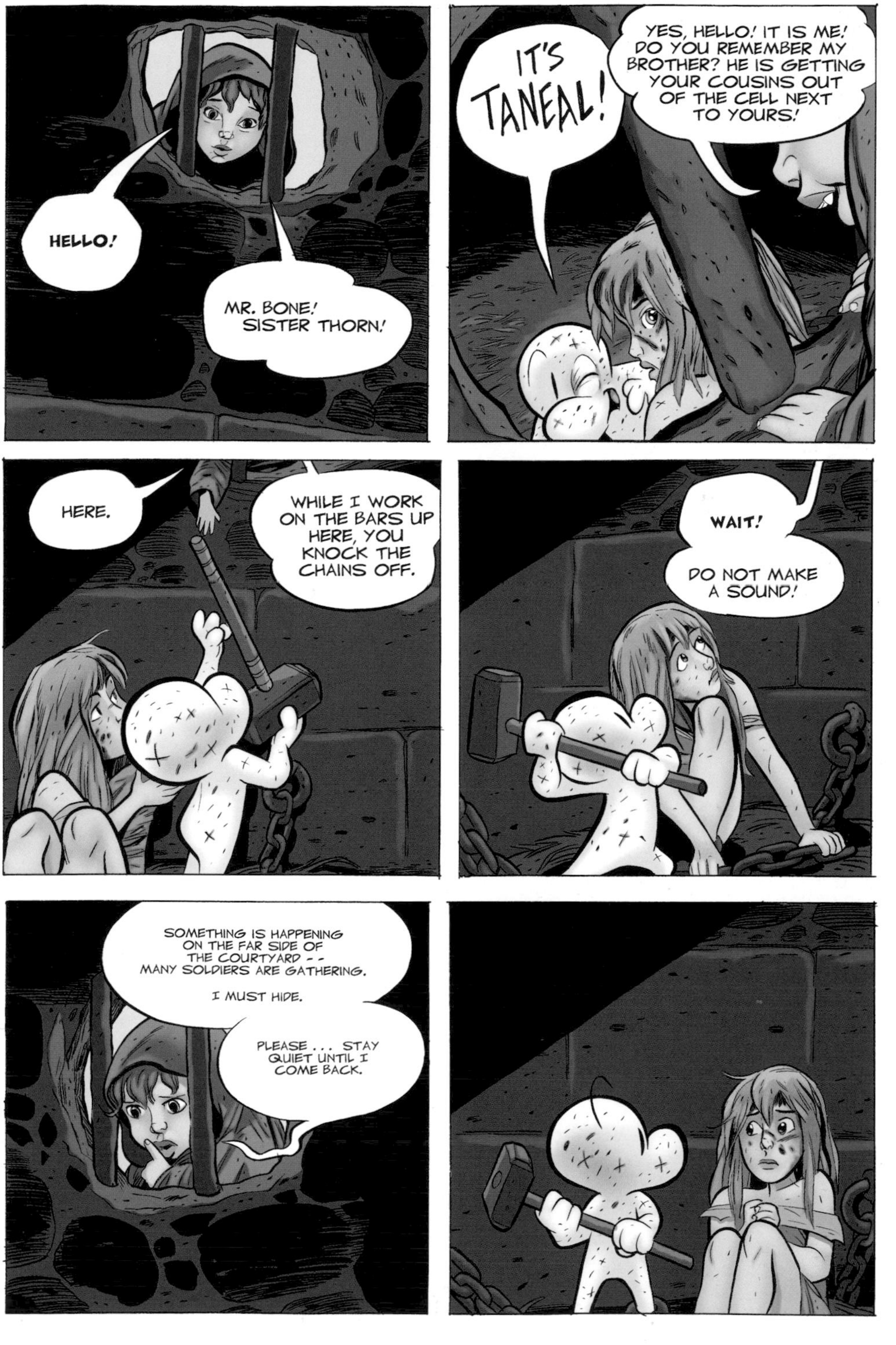
HELLO!
MR. BONE! SISTER THORN!
IT'S TANEAL!
YES, HELLO! IT IS ME! DO YOU REMEMBER MY BROTHER? HE IS GETTING YOUR COUSINS OUT OF THE CELL NEXT TO YOURS!
HERE.
WHILE I WORK ON THE BARS UP HERE, YOU KNOCK THE CHAINS OFF.
WAIT!
DO NOT MAKE A SOUND!
SOMETHING IS HAPPENING ON THE FAR SIDE OF THE COURTYARD - - MANY SOLDIERS ARE GATHERING.
I MUST HIDE.
PLEASE . . . STAY QUIET UNTIL I COME BACK.

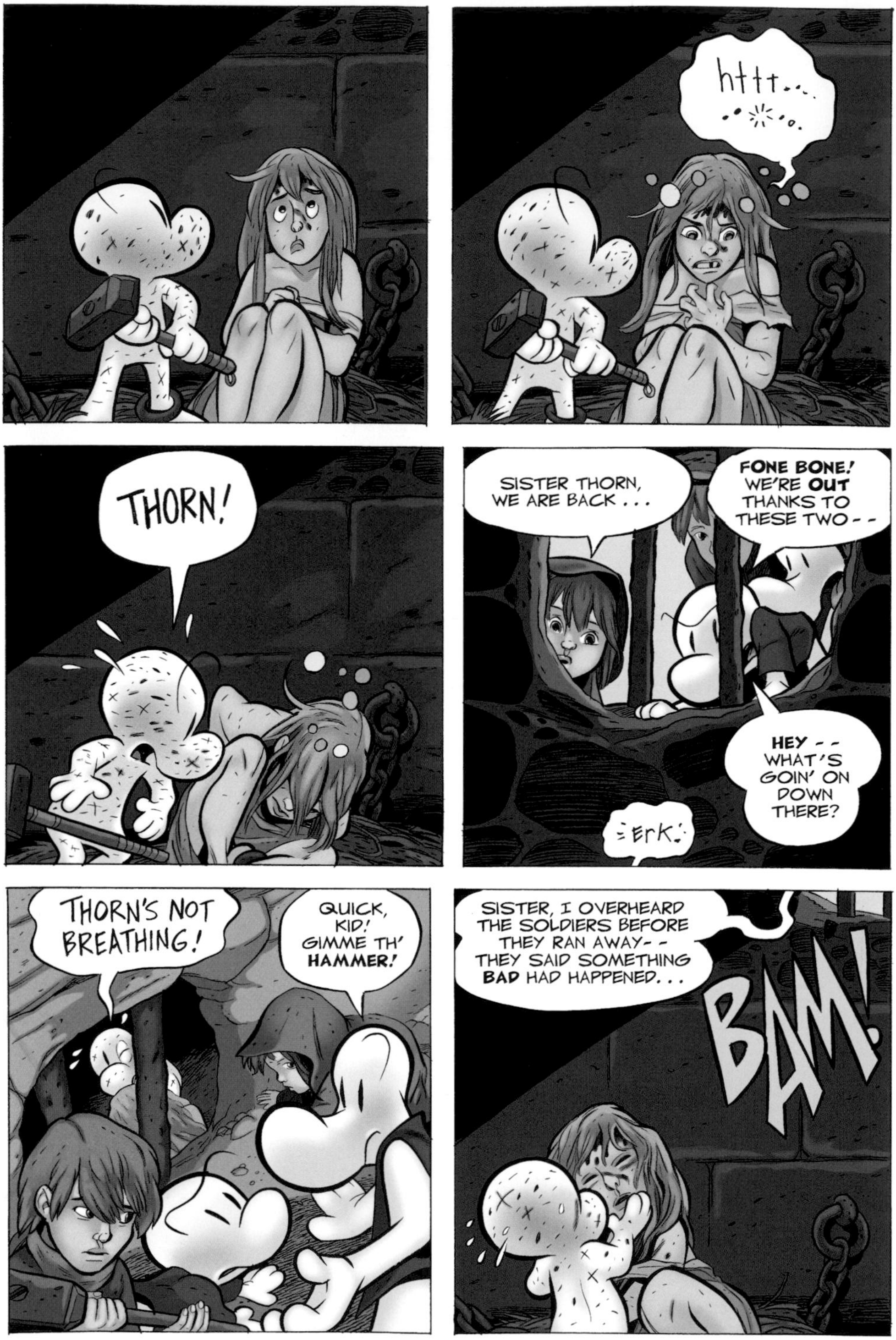
httt...
THORN!
SISTER THORN, WE ARE BACK . . .
FONE BONE! WE'RE OUT THANKS TO THESE TWO- -
HEY - - WHAT'S GOIN' ON DOWN THERE?
ERK
THORN'S NOT BREATHING!
QUICK, KID! GIMME TH' HAMMER!
SISTER, I OVERHEARD THE SOLDIERS BEFORE THEY RAN AWAY- - THEY SAID SOMETHING BAD HAD HAPPENED. . .
BAM!

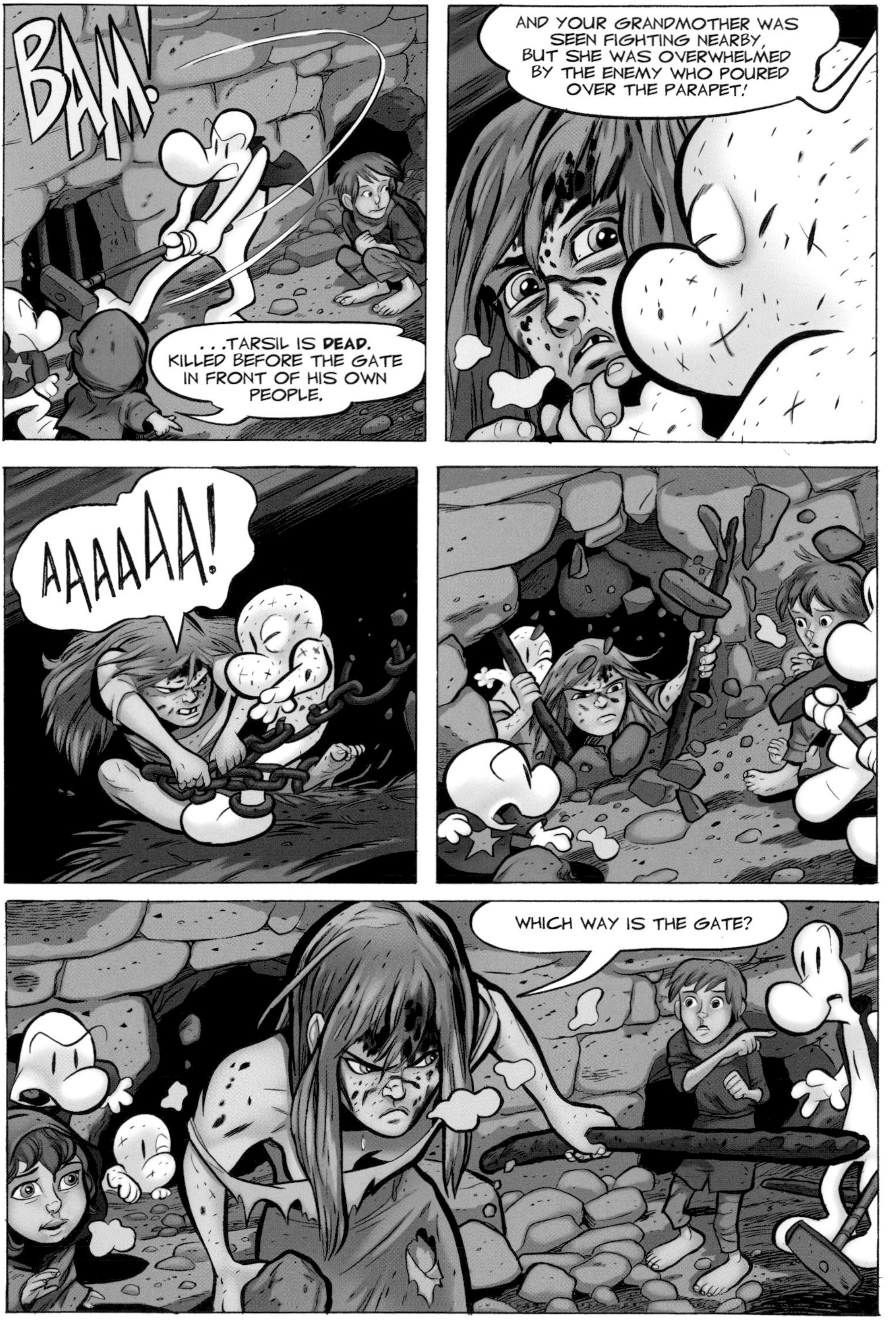
BAM!
. . .TARSIL IS DEAD. KILLED BEFORE THE GATE IN FRONT OF HIS OWN PEOPLE.
AND YOUR GRANDMOTHER WAS SEEN FIGHTING NEARBY, BUT SHE WAS OVERWHELMED BY THE ENEMY WHO POURED OVER THE PARAPET!
AAAAAA!
WHICH WAY IS THE GATE?

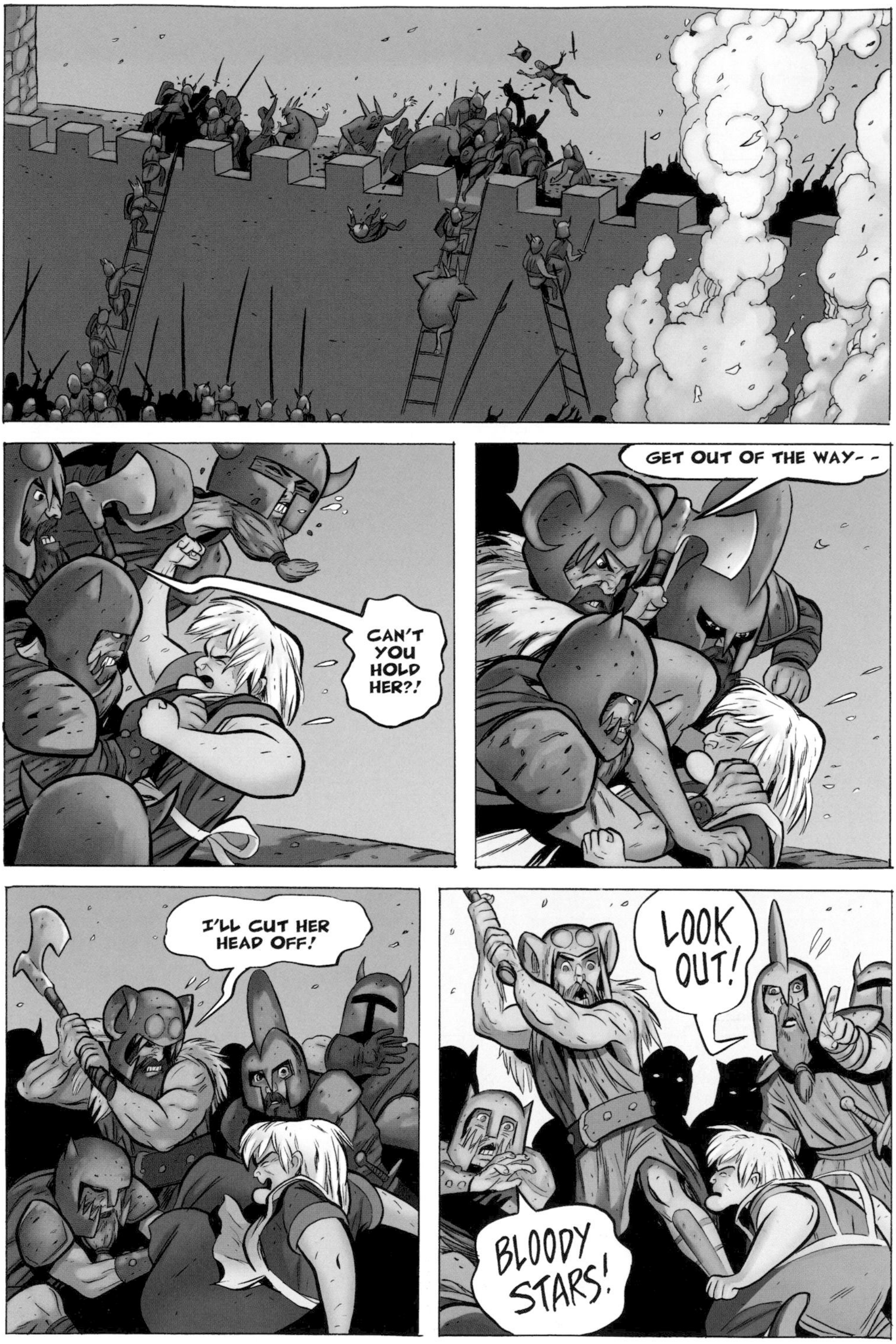
CAN'T YOU HOLD HER?!
GET OUT OF THE WAY- -
I'LL CUT HER HEAD OFF!
LOOK OUT!
BLOODY STARS!

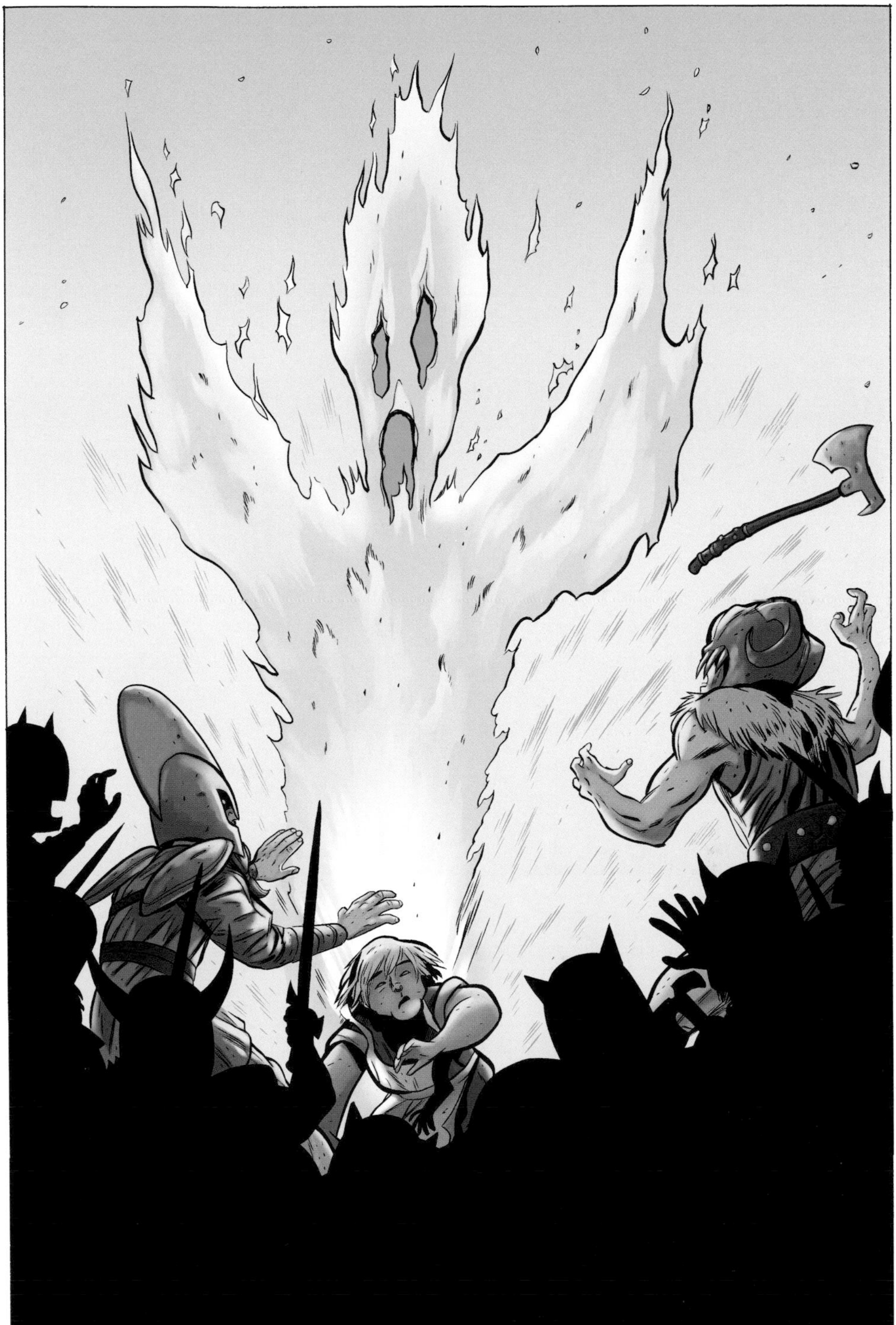

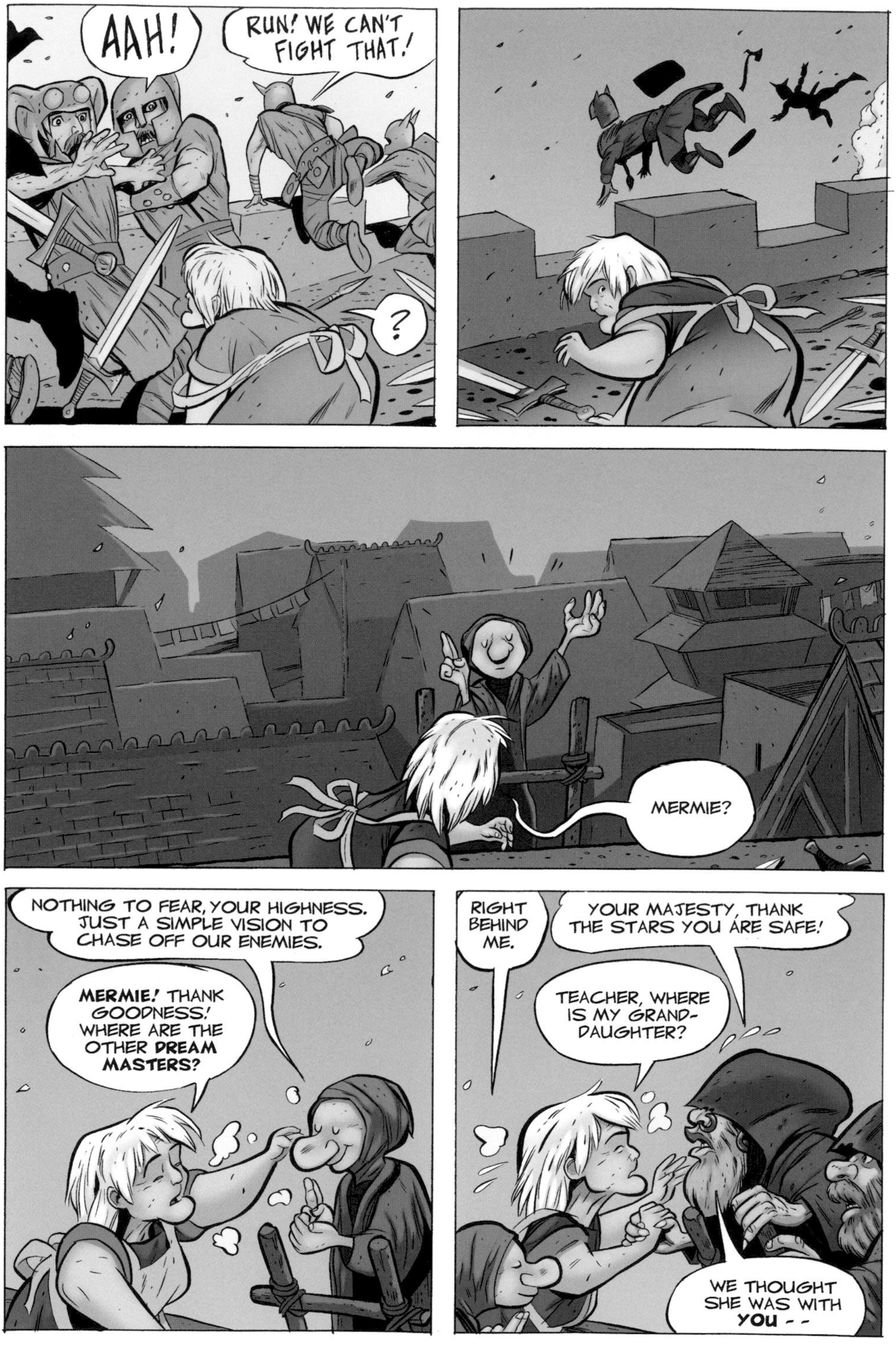
AAH!
RUN! WE CAN'T FIGHT THAT!
?
MERMIE?
NOTHING TO FEAR, YOUR HIGHNESS. JUST A SIMPLE VISION TO CHASE OFF OUR ENEMIES.
MERMIE! THANK GOODNESS! WHERE ARE THE OTHER DREAM MASTERS?
RIGHT BEHIND ME.
YOUR MAJESTY, THANK THE STARS YOU ARE SAFE!
TEACHER, WHERE IS MY GRAND-DAUGHTER?
WE THOUGHT SHE WAS WITH YOU - -

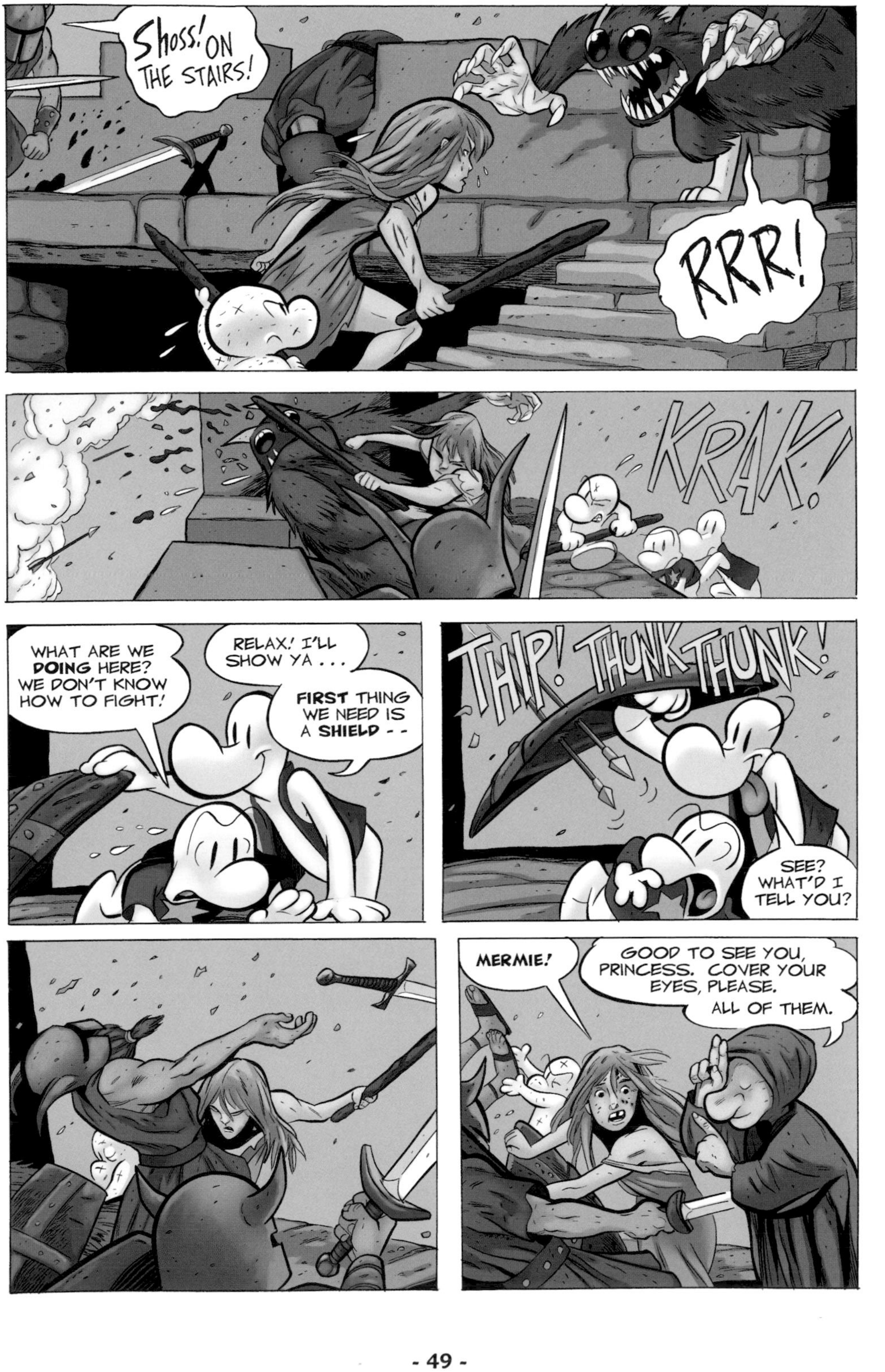
Shoss! ON THE STAIRS!
RRR!
KRAK!
WHAT ARE WE DOING HERE? WE DON'T KNOW HOW TO FIGHT!
RELAX! I'LL SHOW YA . . .
FIRST THING WE NEED IS A SHIELD - -
THIP! THUNK THUNK!
SEE? WHAT'D I TELL YOU?
MERMIE!
GOOD TO SEE YOU, PRINCESS. COVER YOUR EYES, PLEASE.
ALL OF THEM.

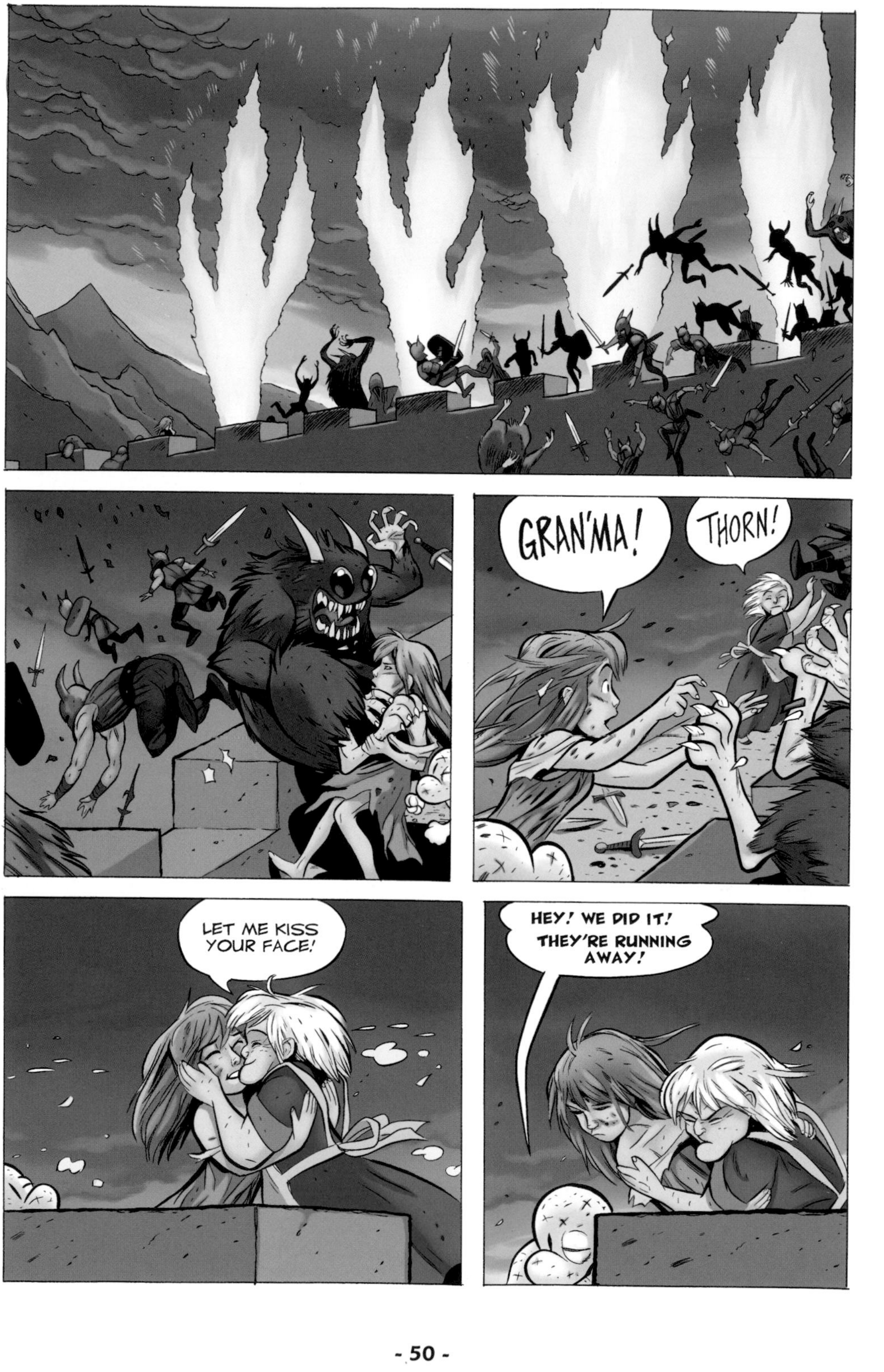
GRAN'MA!
THORN!
LET ME KISS YOUR FACE!
HEY! WE DID IT! THEY'RE RUNNING AWAY!

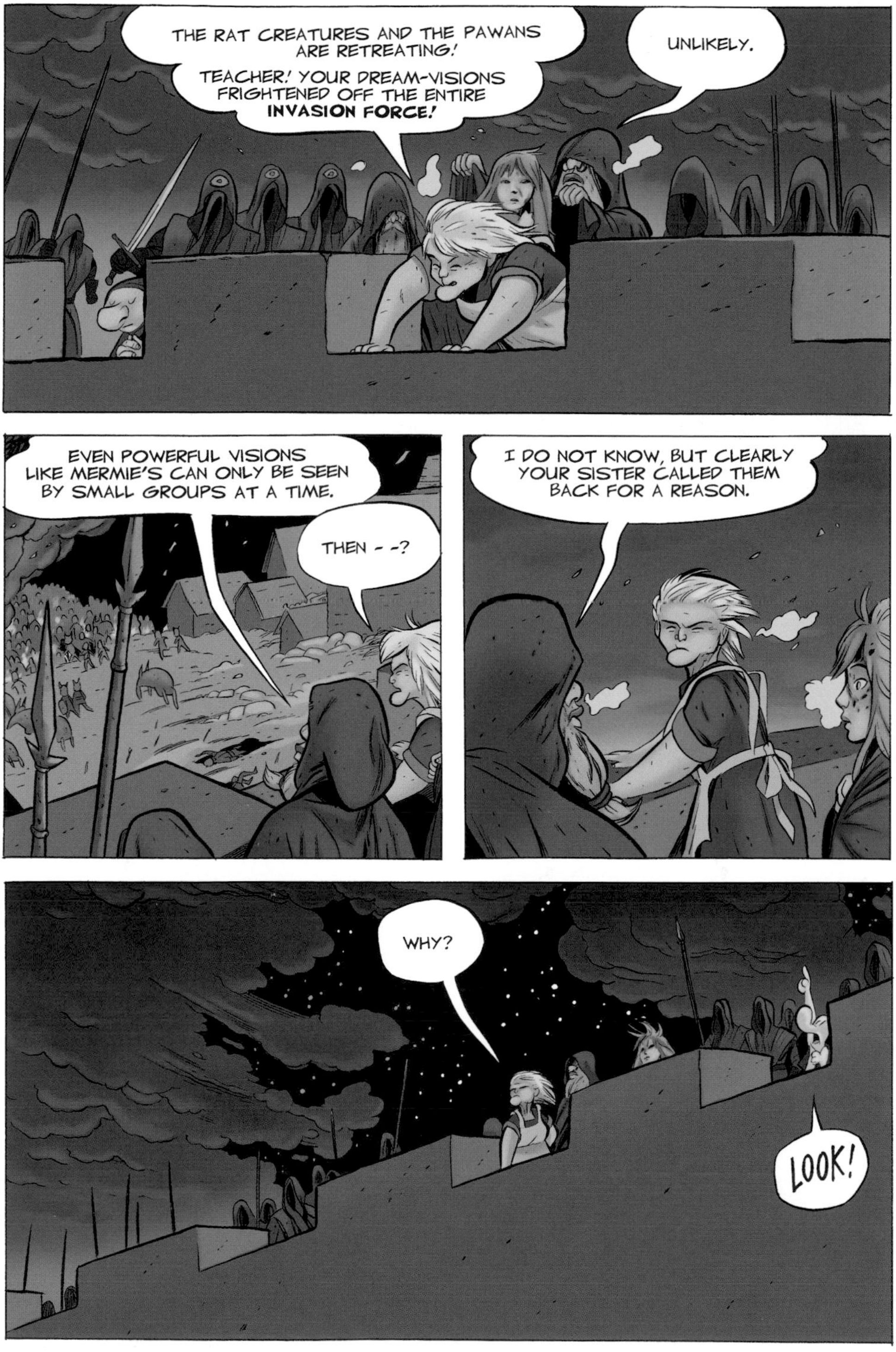
THE RAT CREATURES AND THE PAWANS ARE RETREATING!
TEACHER! YOUR DREAM-VISIONS FRIGHTENED OFF THE ENTIRE **INVASION FORCE!**
UNLIKELY.
EVEN POWERFUL VISIONS LIKE MERMIE'S CAN ONLY BE SEEN BY SMALL GROUPS AT A TIME.
THEN - -?
I DO NOT KNOW, BUT CLEARLY YOUR SISTER CALLED THEM BACK FOR A REASON.
WHY?
LOOK!

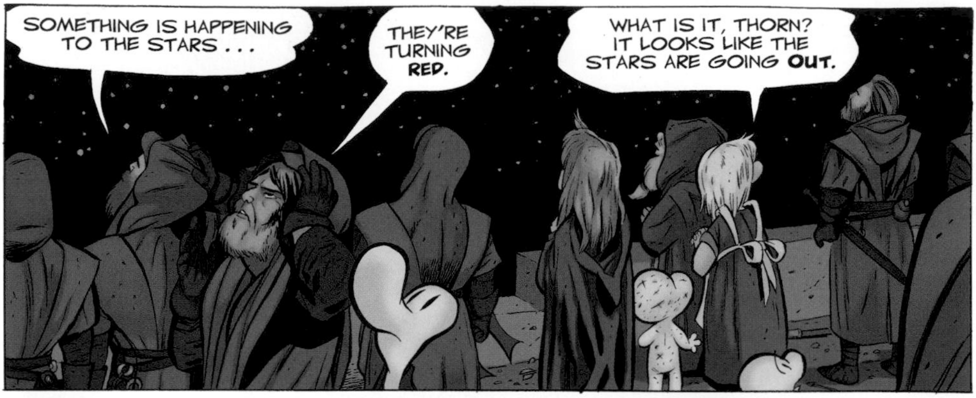
SOMETHING IS HAPPENING TO THE STARS . . .
THEY'RE TURNING RED.
WHAT IS IT, THORN? IT LOOKS LIKE THE STARS ARE GOING OUT.

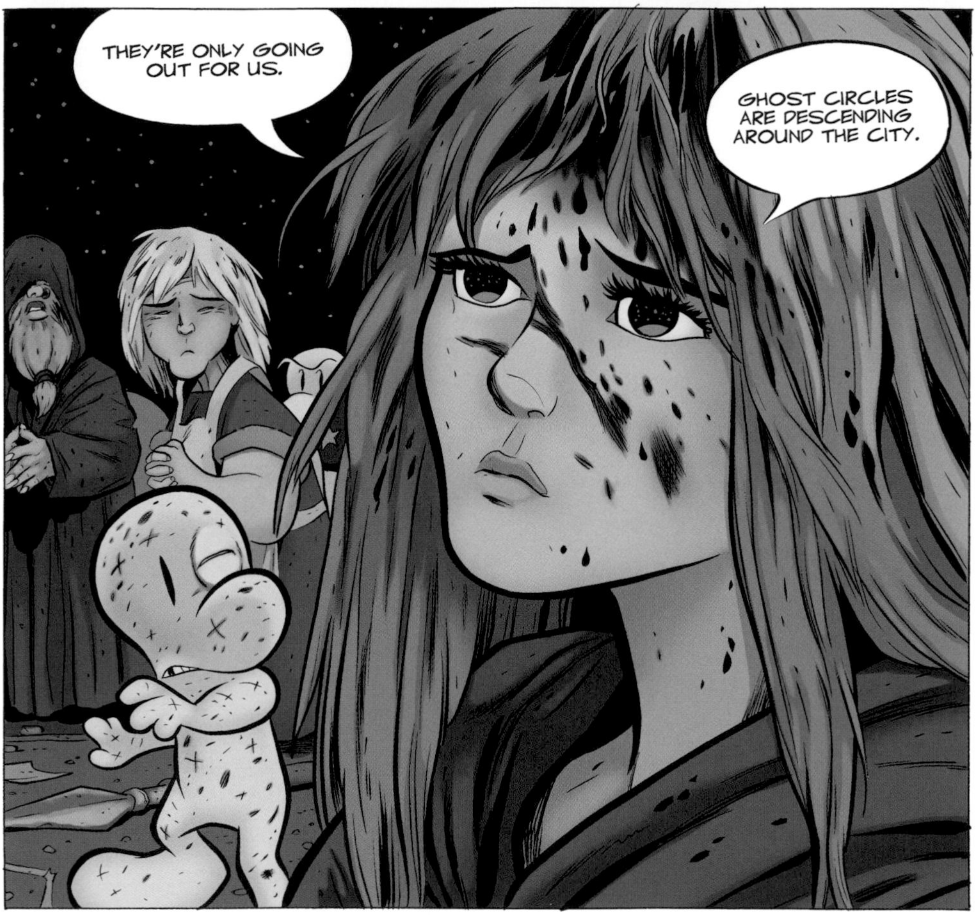
THEY'RE ONLY GOING OUT FOR US.
GHOST CIRCLES ARE DESCENDING AROUND THE CITY.

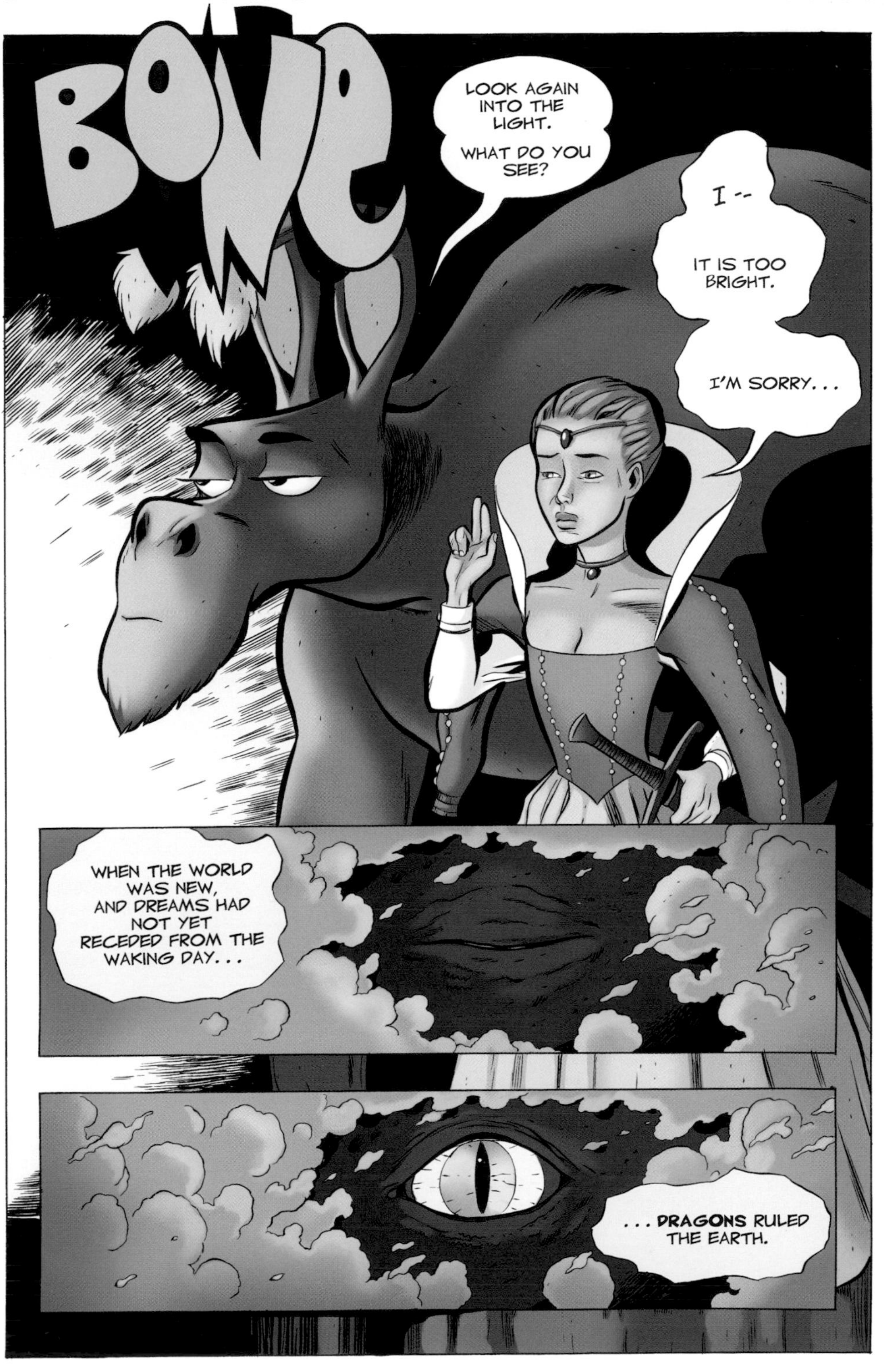
BONE
LOOK AGAIN INTO THE LIGHT.
WHAT DO YOU SEE?
I --
IT IS TOO BRIGHT.
I'M SORRY...
WHEN THE WORLD WAS NEW, AND DREAMS HAD NOT YET RECEDED FROM THE WAKING DAY...
...DRAGONS RULED THE EARTH.

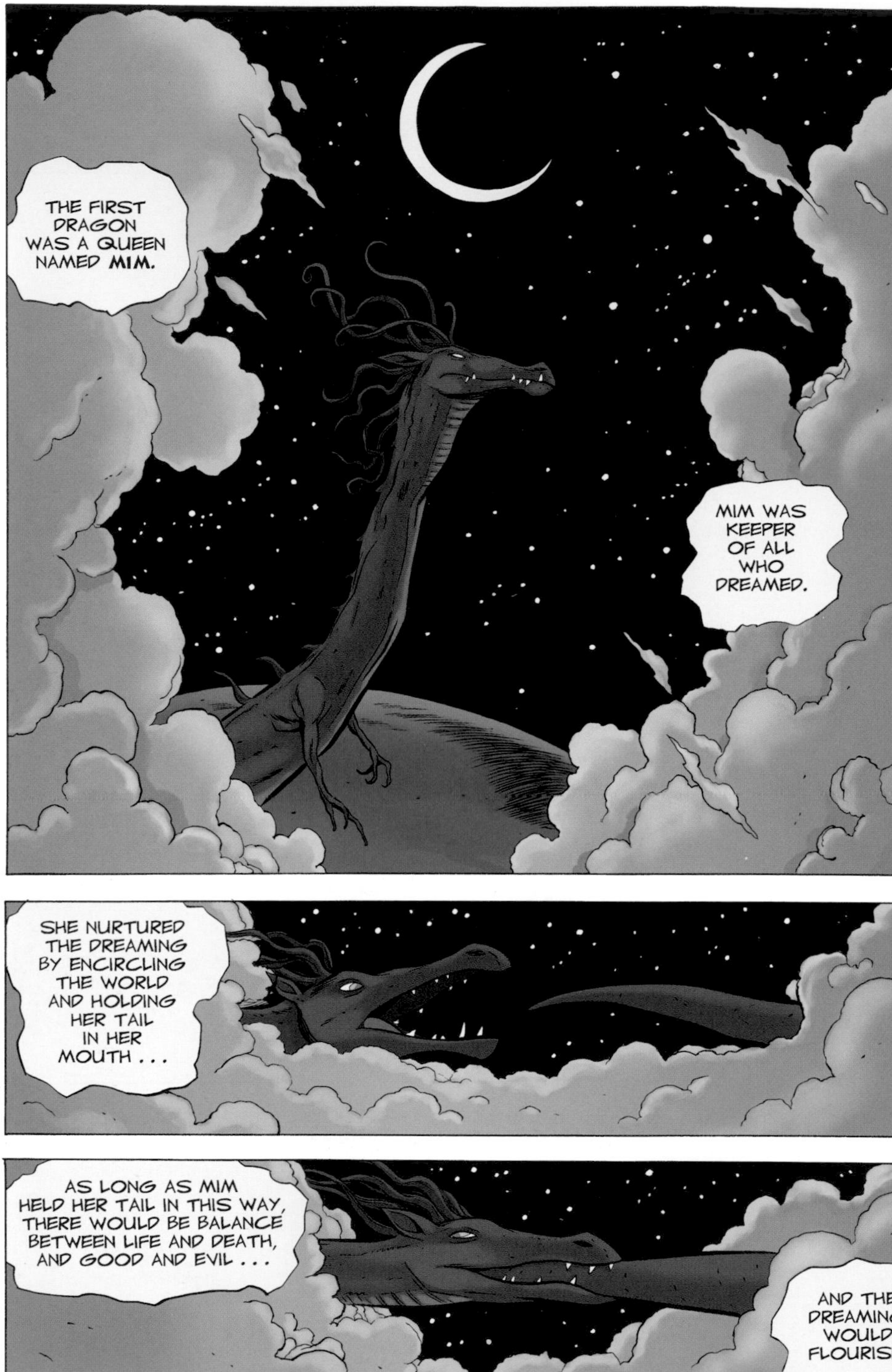
THE FIRST DRAGON WAS A QUEEN NAMED **MIM.**
MIM WAS KEEPER OF ALL WHO DREAMED.
SHE NURTURED THE DREAMING BY ENCIRCLING THE WORLD AND HOLDING HER TAIL IN HER MOUTH . . .
AS LONG AS MIM HELD HER TAIL IN THIS WAY, THERE WOULD BE BALANCE BETWEEN LIFE AND DEATH, AND GOOD AND EVIL . . .
AND THE DREAMING WOULD FLOURISH.

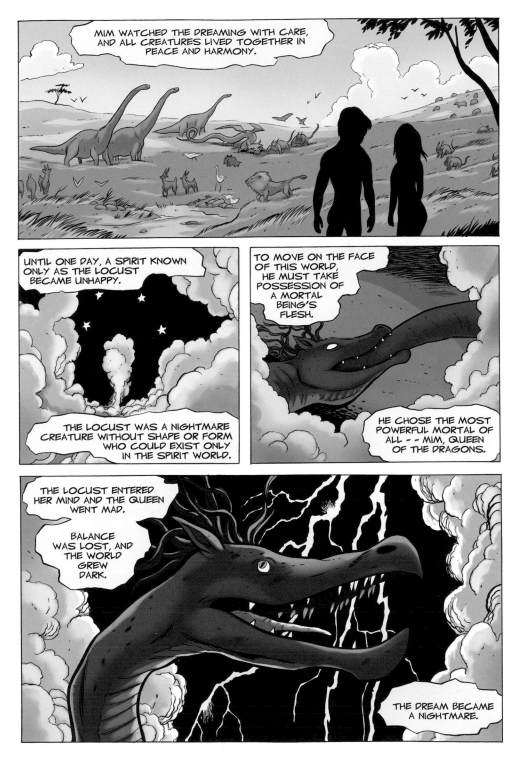

MIM WATCHED THE DREAMING WITH CARE, AND ALL CREATURES LIVED TOGETHER IN PEACE AND HARMONY.

UNTIL ONE DAY, A SPIRIT KNOWN ONLY AS THE LOCUST BECAME UNHAPPY.

THE LOCUST WAS A NIGHTMARE CREATURE WITHOUT SHAPE OR FORM WHO COULD EXIST ONLY IN THE SPIRIT WORLD.

TO MOVE ON THE FACE OF THIS WORLD, HE MUST TAKE POSSESSION OF A MORTAL BEING'S FLESH.

HE CHOSE THE MOST POWERFUL MORTAL OF ALL -- MIM, QUEEN OF THE DRAGONS.

THE LOCUST ENTERED HER MIND AND THE QUEEN WENT MAD.

BALANCE WAS LOST, AND THE WORLD GREW DARK.

THE DREAM BECAME A NIGHTMARE.

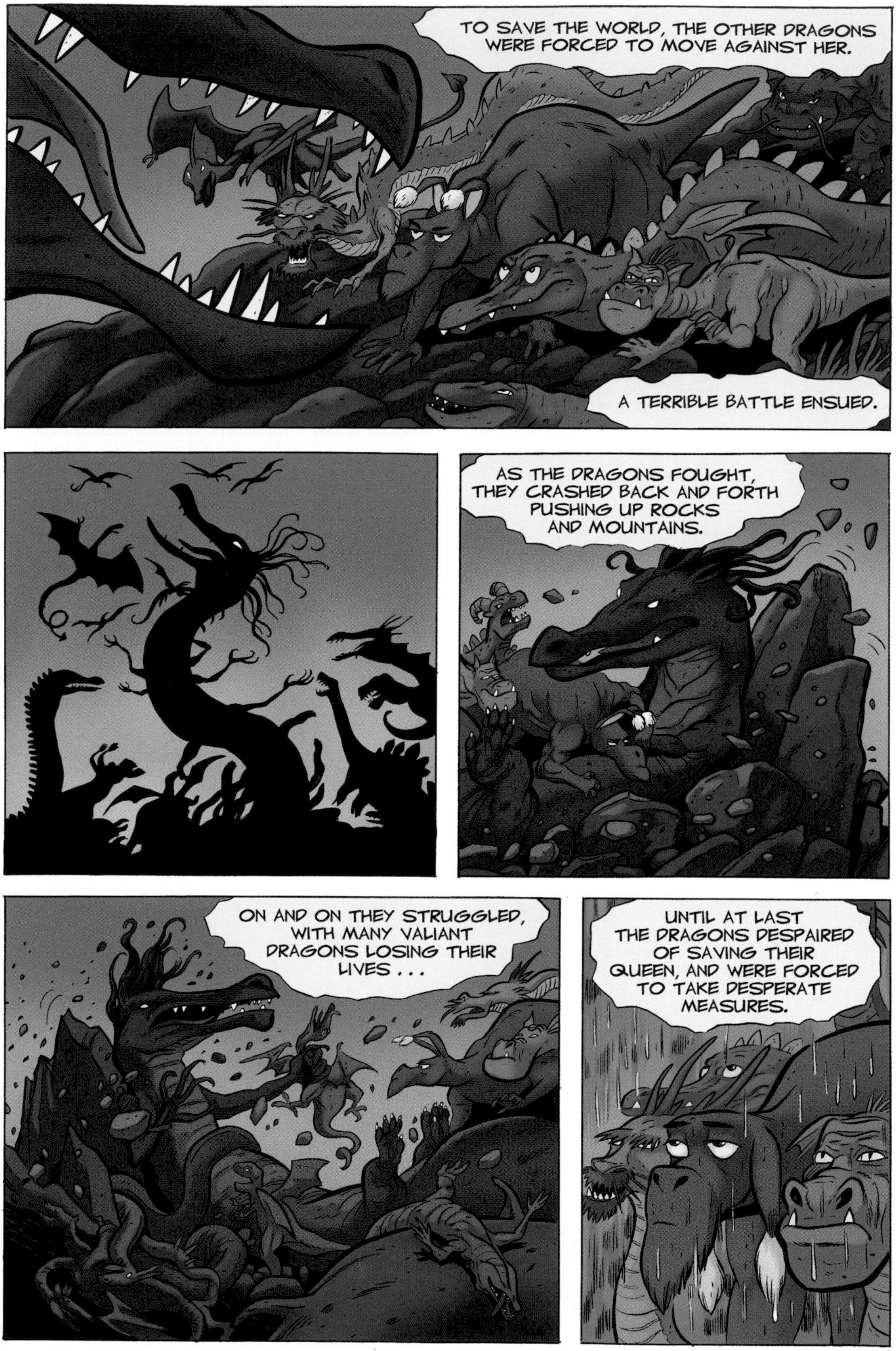
TO SAVE THE WORLD, THE OTHER DRAGONS WERE FORCED TO MOVE AGAINST HER.
A TERRIBLE BATTLE ENSUED.
AS THE DRAGONS FOUGHT, THEY CRASHED BACK AND FORTH PUSHING UP ROCKS AND MOUNTAINS.
ON AND ON THEY STRUGGLED, WITH MANY VALIANT DRAGONS LOSING THEIR LIVES . . .
UNTIL AT LAST THE DRAGONS DESPAIRED OF SAVING THEIR QUEEN, AND WERE FORCED TO TAKE DESPERATE MEASURES.

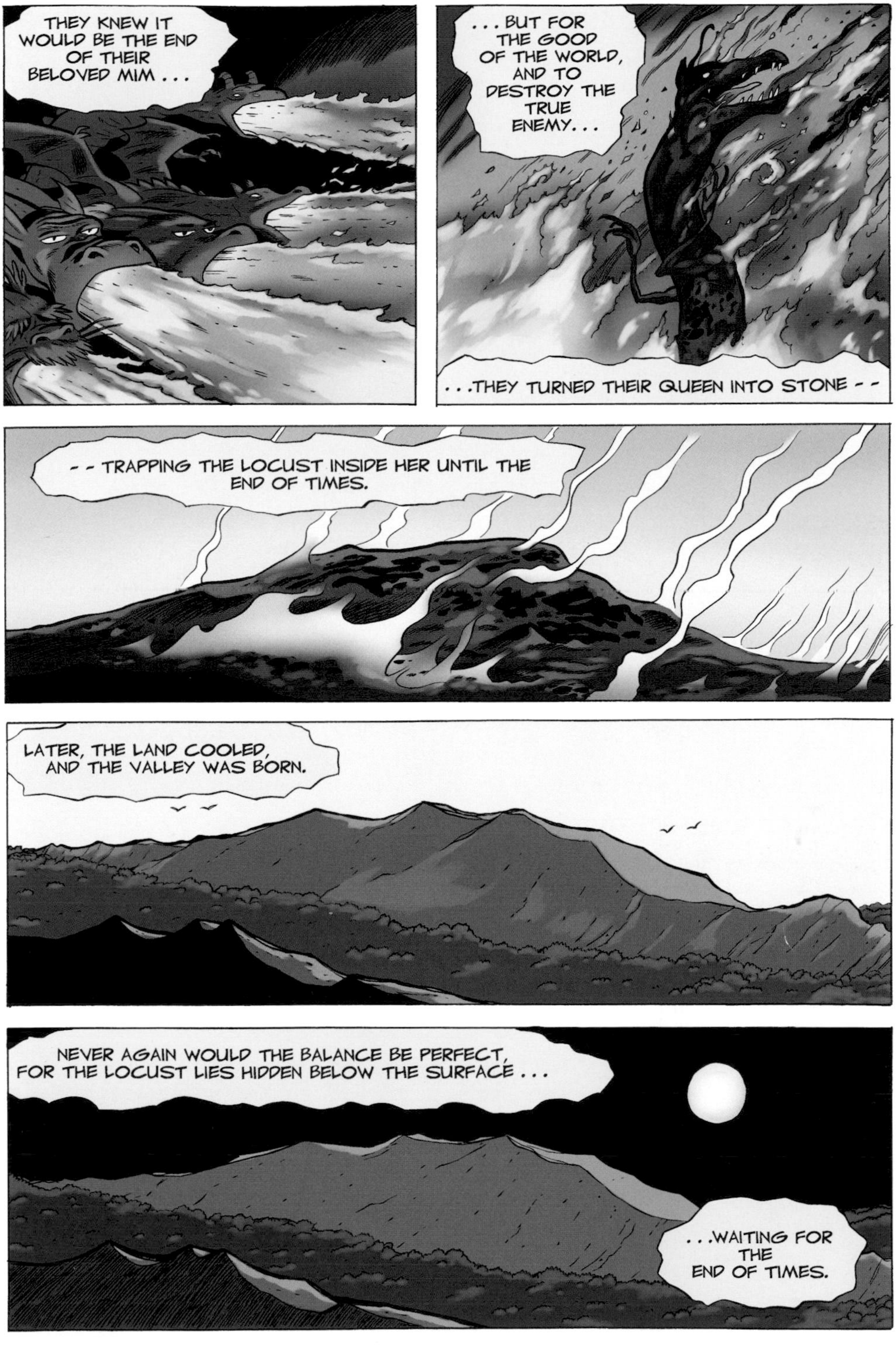
THEY KNEW IT WOULD BE THE END OF THEIR BELOVED MIM . . .
. . . BUT FOR THE GOOD OF THE WORLD, AND TO DESTROY THE TRUE ENEMY. . .
. . .THEY TURNED THEIR QUEEN INTO STONE - -
- - TRAPPING THE LOCUST INSIDE HER UNTIL THE END OF TIMES.
LATER, THE LAND COOLED, AND THE VALLEY WAS BORN.
NEVER AGAIN WOULD THE BALANCE BE PERFECT, FOR THE LOCUST LIES HIDDEN BELOW THE SURFACE . . .
. . .WAITING FOR THE END OF TIMES.

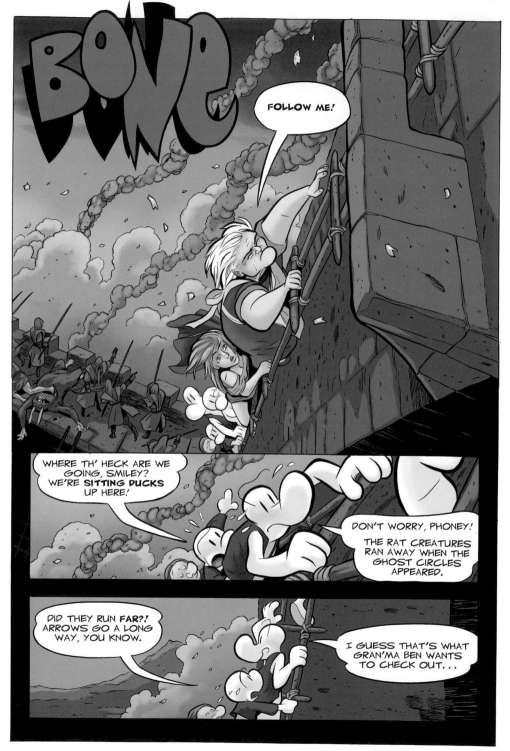

FOLLOW ME!

WHERE TH' HECK ARE WE GOING, SMILEY? WE'RE **SITTING DUCKS** UP HERE!

DON'T WORRY, PHONEY!

THE RAT CREATURES RAN AWAY WHEN THE GHOST CIRCLES APPEARED.

DID THEY RUN **FAR?!** ARROWS GO A LONG WAY, YOU KNOW.

I GUESS THAT'S WHAT GRAN'MA BEN WANTS TO CHECK OUT. . .

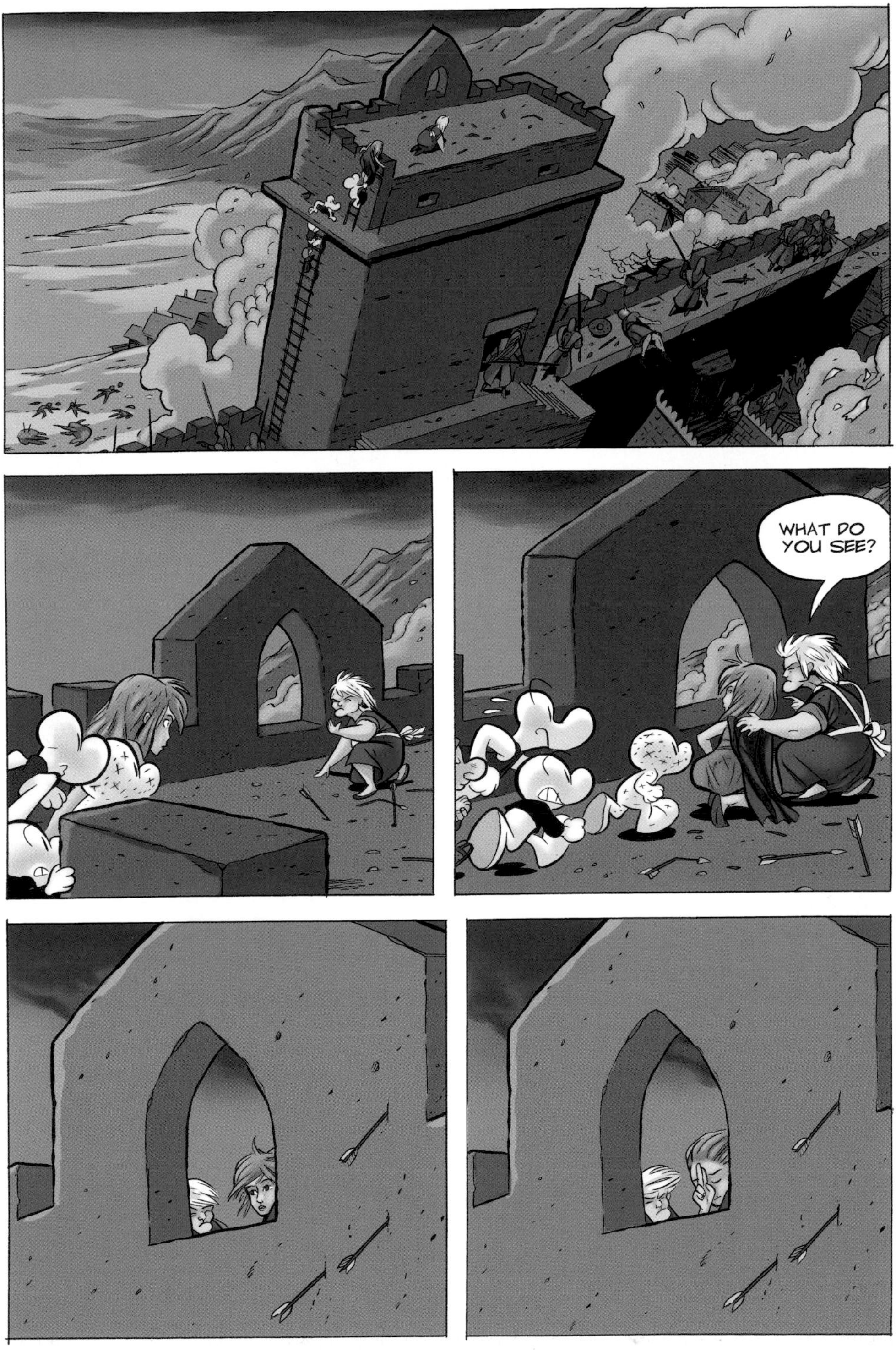
WHAT DO YOU SEE?

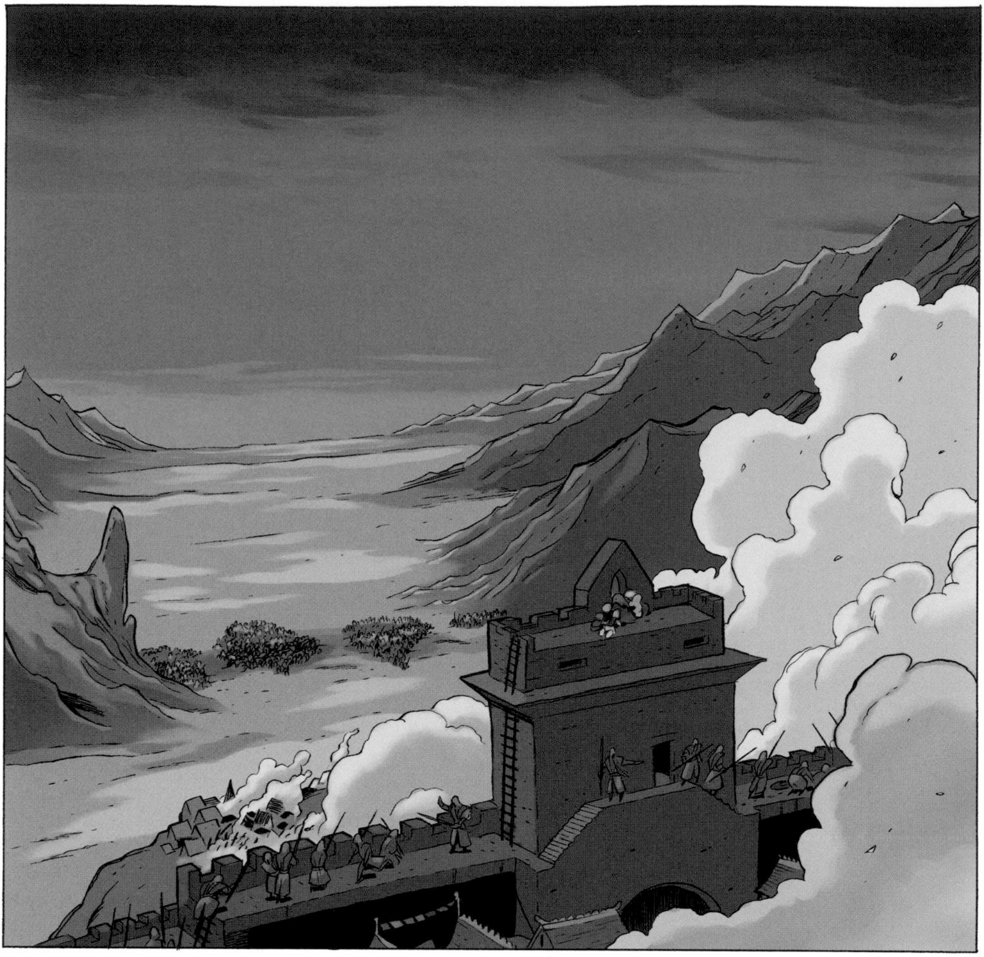

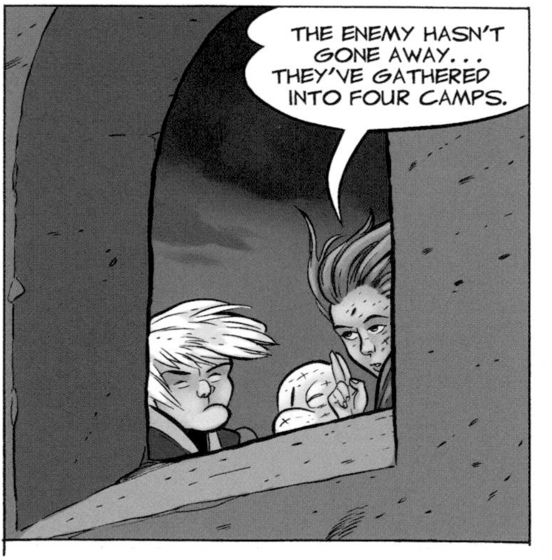
THE ENEMY HASN'T GONE AWAY. . . THEY'VE GATHERED INTO FOUR CAMPS.

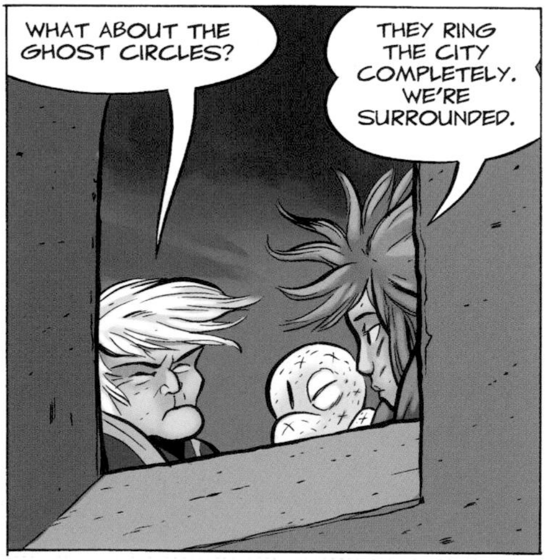
WHAT ABOUT THE GHOST CIRCLES?
THEY RING THE CITY COMPLETELY. WE'RE SURROUNDED.

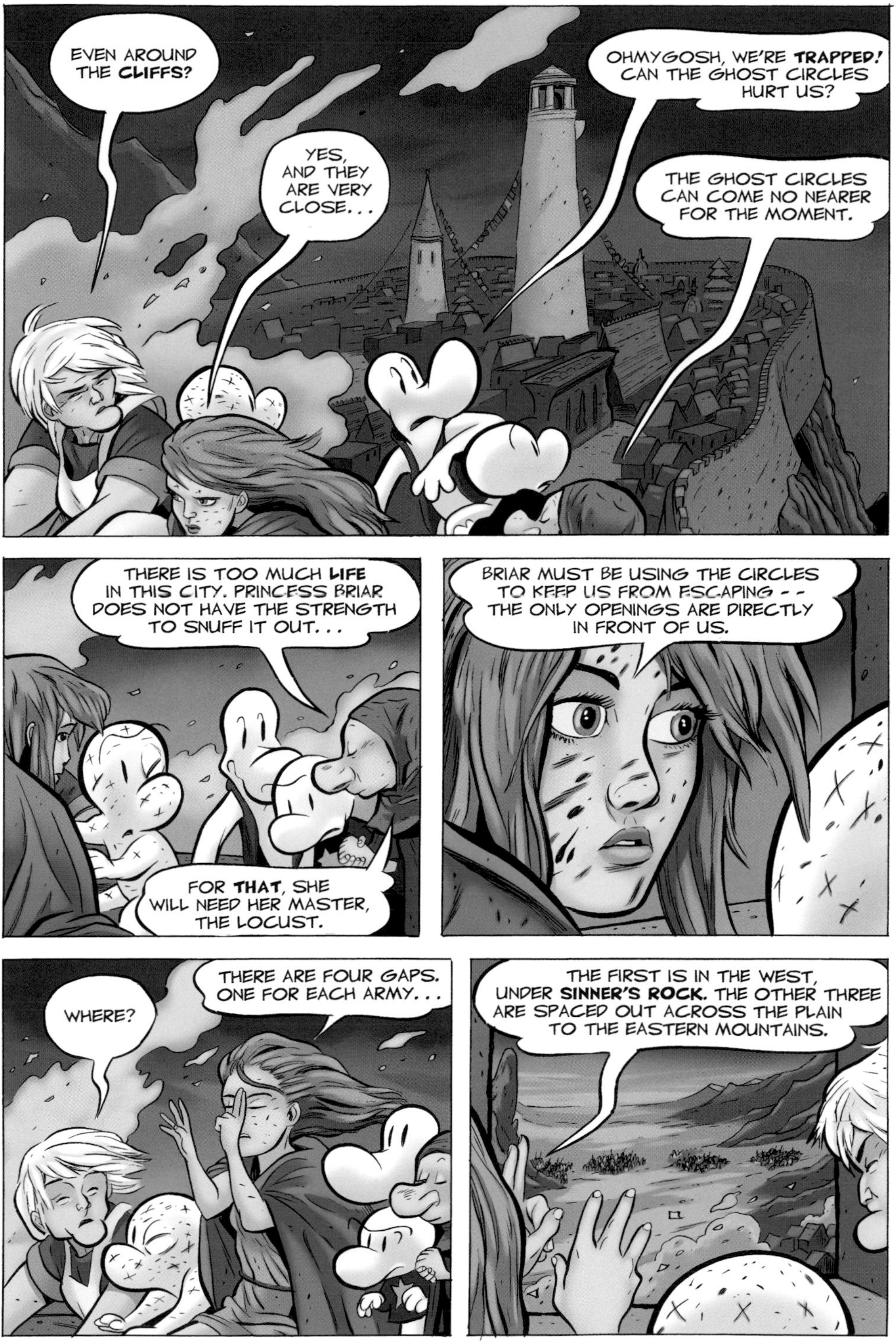
EVEN AROUND THE CLIFFS?
YES, AND THEY ARE VERY CLOSE...
OHMYGOSH, WE'RE TRAPPED! CAN THE GHOST CIRCLES HURT US?
THE GHOST CIRCLES CAN COME NO NEARER FOR THE MOMENT.
THERE IS TOO MUCH LIFE IN THIS CITY. PRINCESS BRIAR DOES NOT HAVE THE STRENGTH TO SNUFF IT OUT...
FOR THAT, SHE WILL NEED HER MASTER, THE LOCUST.
BRIAR MUST BE USING THE CIRCLES TO KEEP US FROM ESCAPING -- THE ONLY OPENINGS ARE DIRECTLY IN FRONT OF US.
WHERE?
THERE ARE FOUR GAPS. ONE FOR EACH ARMY...
THE FIRST IS IN THE WEST, UNDER SINNER'S ROCK. THE OTHER THREE ARE SPACED OUT ACROSS THE PLAIN TO THE EASTERN MOUNTAINS.

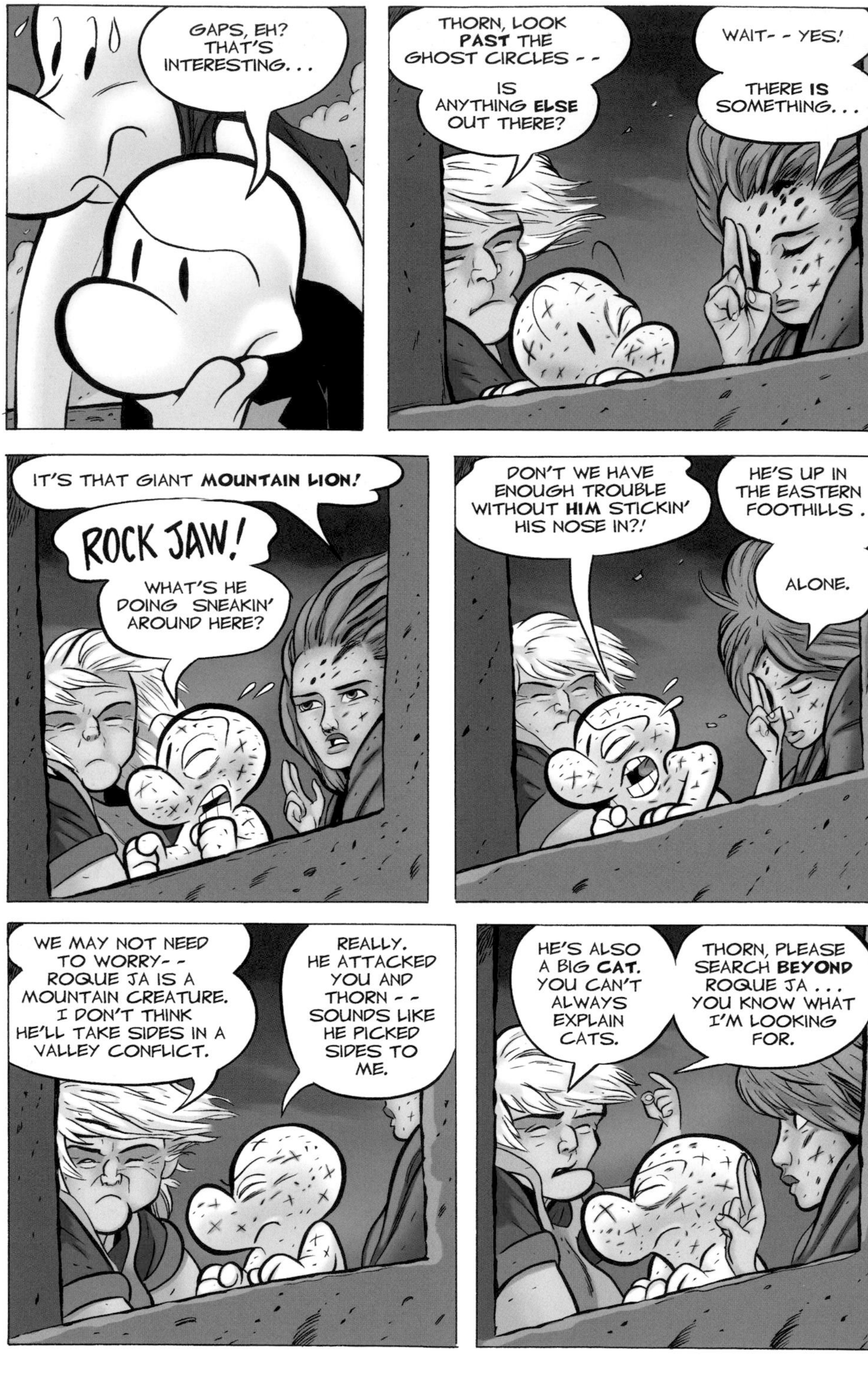
GAPS, EH? THAT'S INTERESTING...
THORN, LOOK **PAST** THE GHOST CIRCLES - -
IS ANYTHING **ELSE** OUT THERE?
WAIT- - YES!
THERE **IS** SOMETHING...
IT'S THAT GIANT **MOUNTAIN LION!**
ROCK JAW!
WHAT'S HE DOING SNEAKIN' AROUND HERE?
DON'T WE HAVE ENOUGH TROUBLE WITHOUT **HIM** STICKIN' HIS NOSE IN?!
HE'S UP IN THE EASTERN FOOTHILLS...
ALONE.
WE MAY NOT NEED TO WORRY- - ROQUE JA IS A MOUNTAIN CREATURE. I DON'T THINK HE'LL TAKE SIDES IN A VALLEY CONFLICT.
REALLY. HE ATTACKED YOU AND THORN - - SOUNDS LIKE HE PICKED SIDES TO ME.
HE'S ALSO A BIG **CAT.** YOU CAN'T ALWAYS EXPLAIN CATS.
THORN, PLEASE SEARCH **BEYOND** ROQUE JA... YOU KNOW WHAT I'M LOOKING FOR.

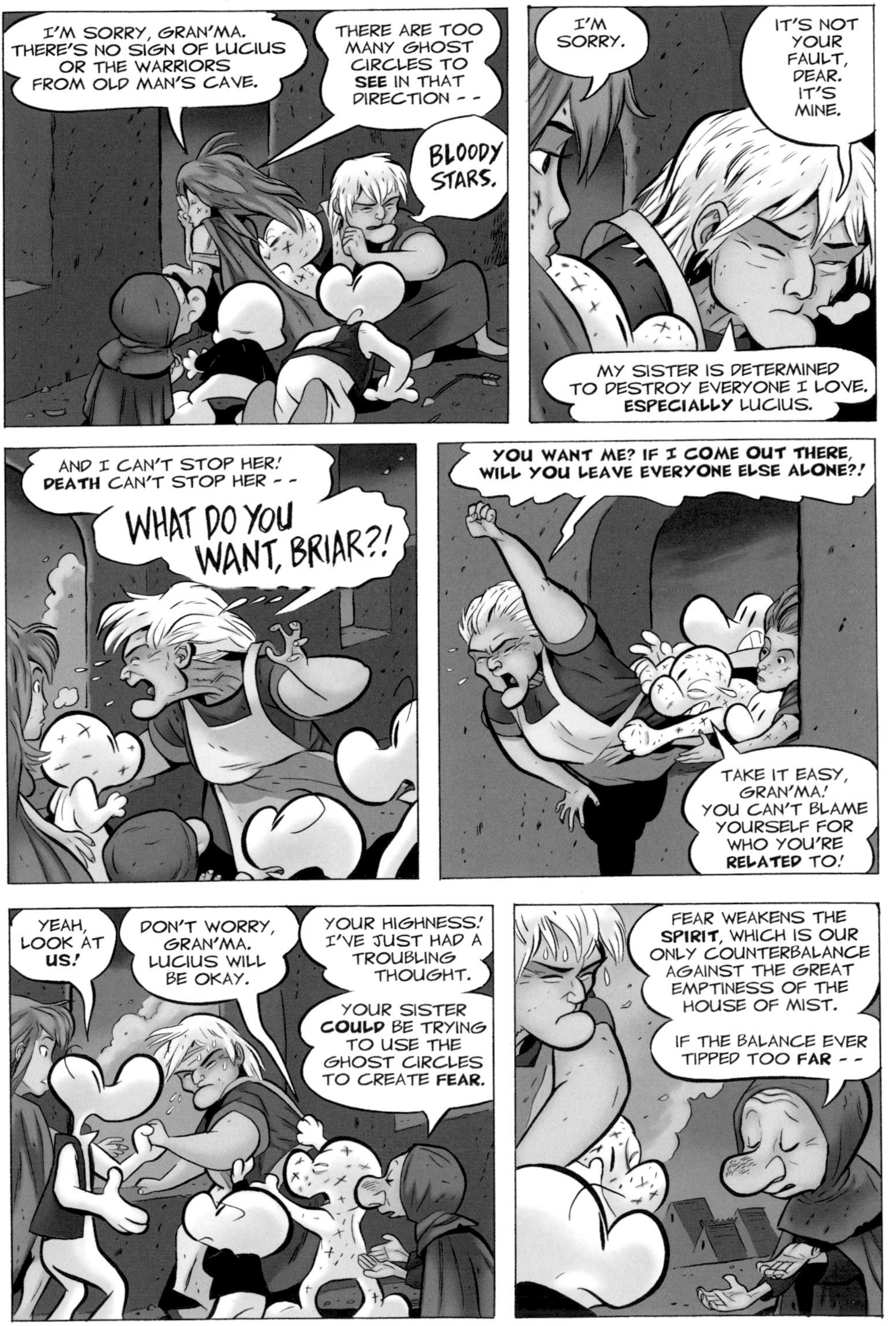
I'M SORRY, GRAN'MA. THERE'S NO SIGN OF LUCIUS OR THE WARRIORS FROM OLD MAN'S CAVE.
THERE ARE TOO MANY GHOST CIRCLES TO SEE IN THAT DIRECTION - -
BLOODY STARS.
I'M SORRY.
IT'S NOT YOUR FAULT, DEAR. IT'S MINE.
MY SISTER IS DETERMINED TO DESTROY EVERYONE I LOVE. ESPECIALLY LUCIUS.
AND I CAN'T STOP HER! DEATH CAN'T STOP HER - -
WHAT DO YOU WANT, BRIAR?!
YOU WANT ME? IF I COME OUT THERE, WILL YOU LEAVE EVERYONE ELSE ALONE?!
TAKE IT EASY, GRAN'MA! YOU CAN'T BLAME YOURSELF FOR WHO YOU'RE RELATED TO!
YEAH, LOOK AT US!
DON'T WORRY, GRAN'MA. LUCIUS WILL BE OKAY.
YOUR HIGHNESS! I'VE JUST HAD A TROUBLING THOUGHT.
YOUR SISTER COULD BE TRYING TO USE THE GHOST CIRCLES TO CREATE FEAR.
FEAR WEAKENS THE SPIRIT, WHICH IS OUR ONLY COUNTERBALANCE AGAINST THE GREAT EMPTINESS OF THE HOUSE OF MIST.
IF THE BALANCE EVER TIPPED TOO FAR - -

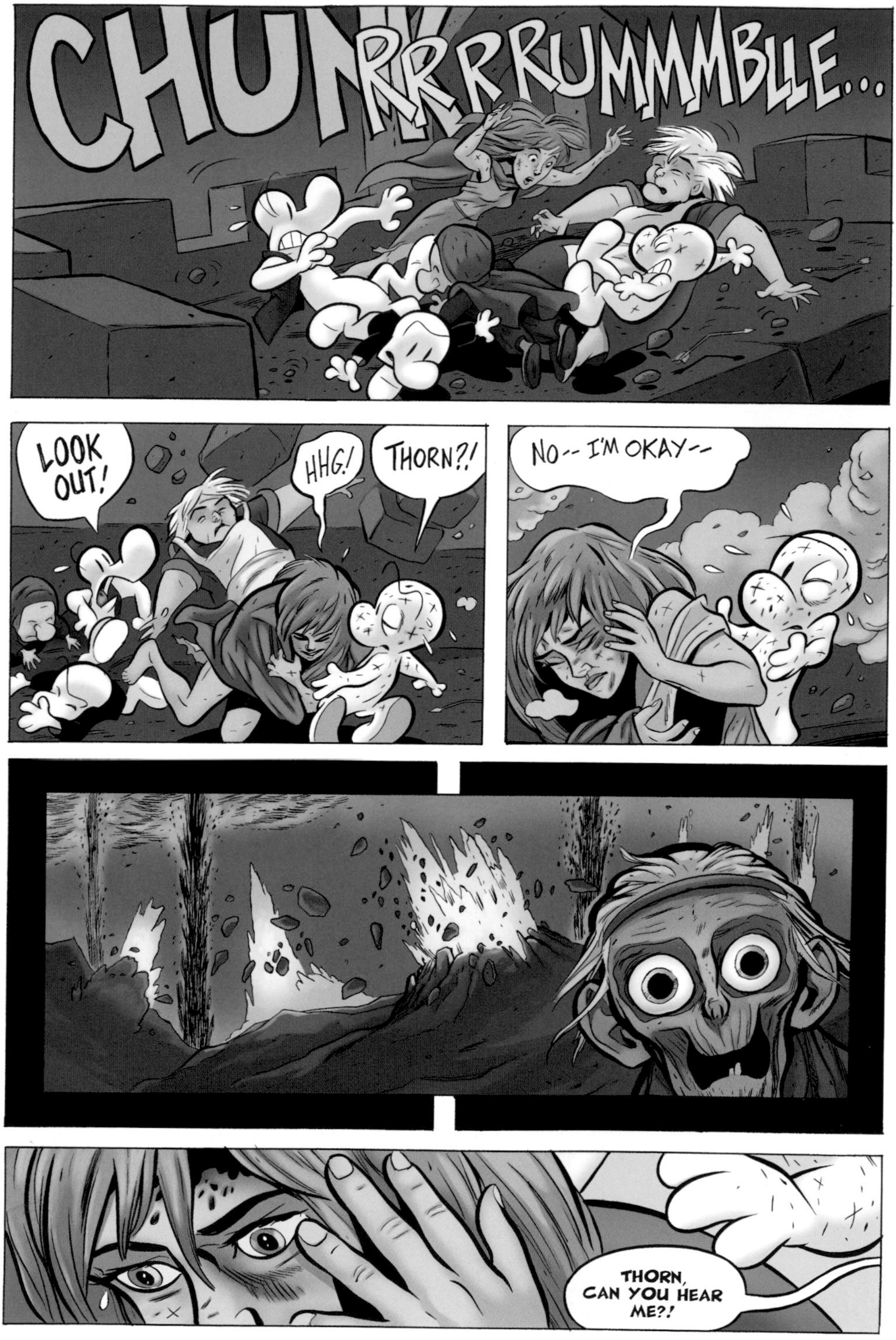
CHUNKRRRRUMMMBLLE...
LOOK OUT!
HHG!
THORN?!
NO-- I'M OKAY--
THORN, CAN YOU HEAR ME?!

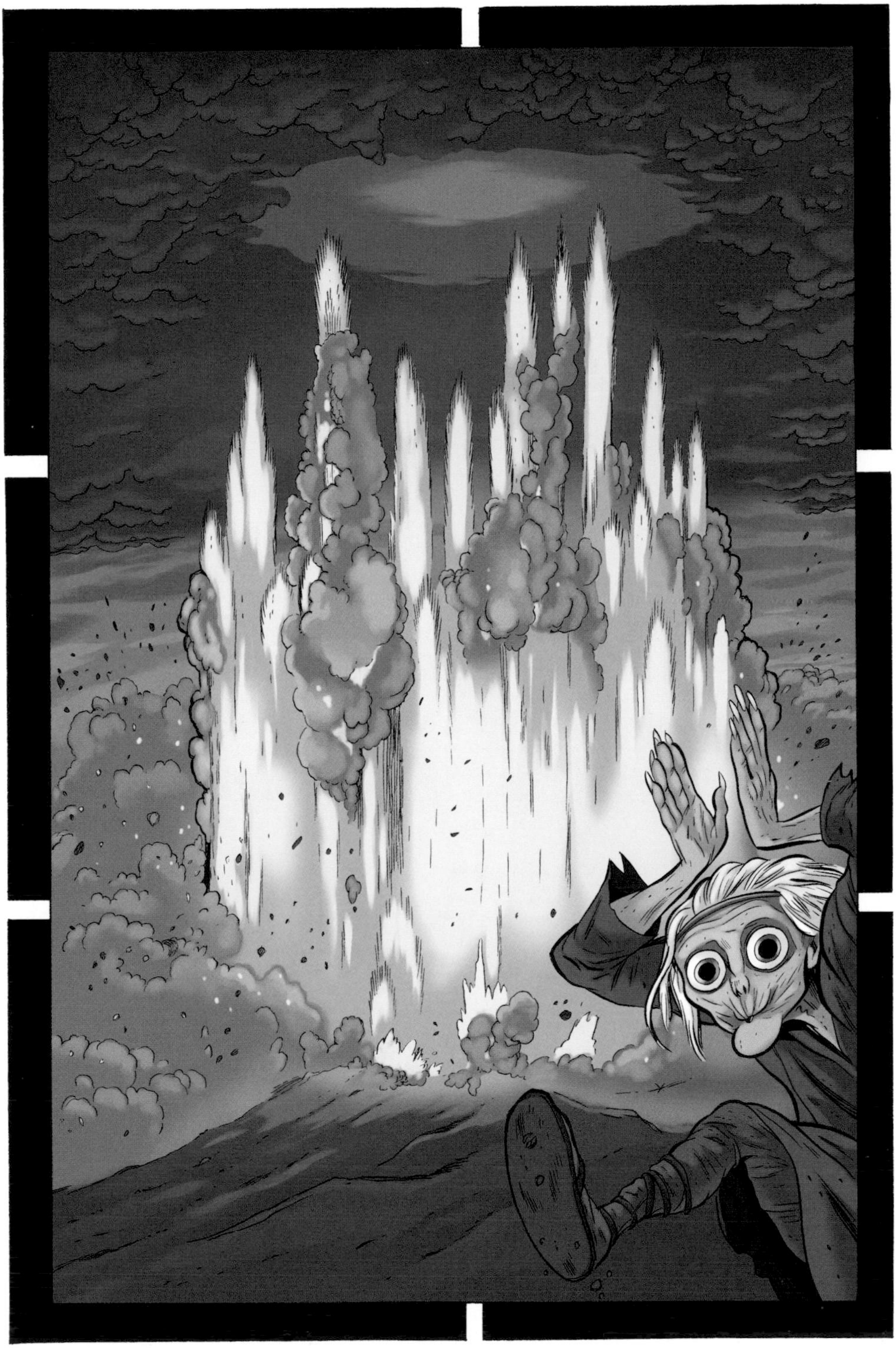

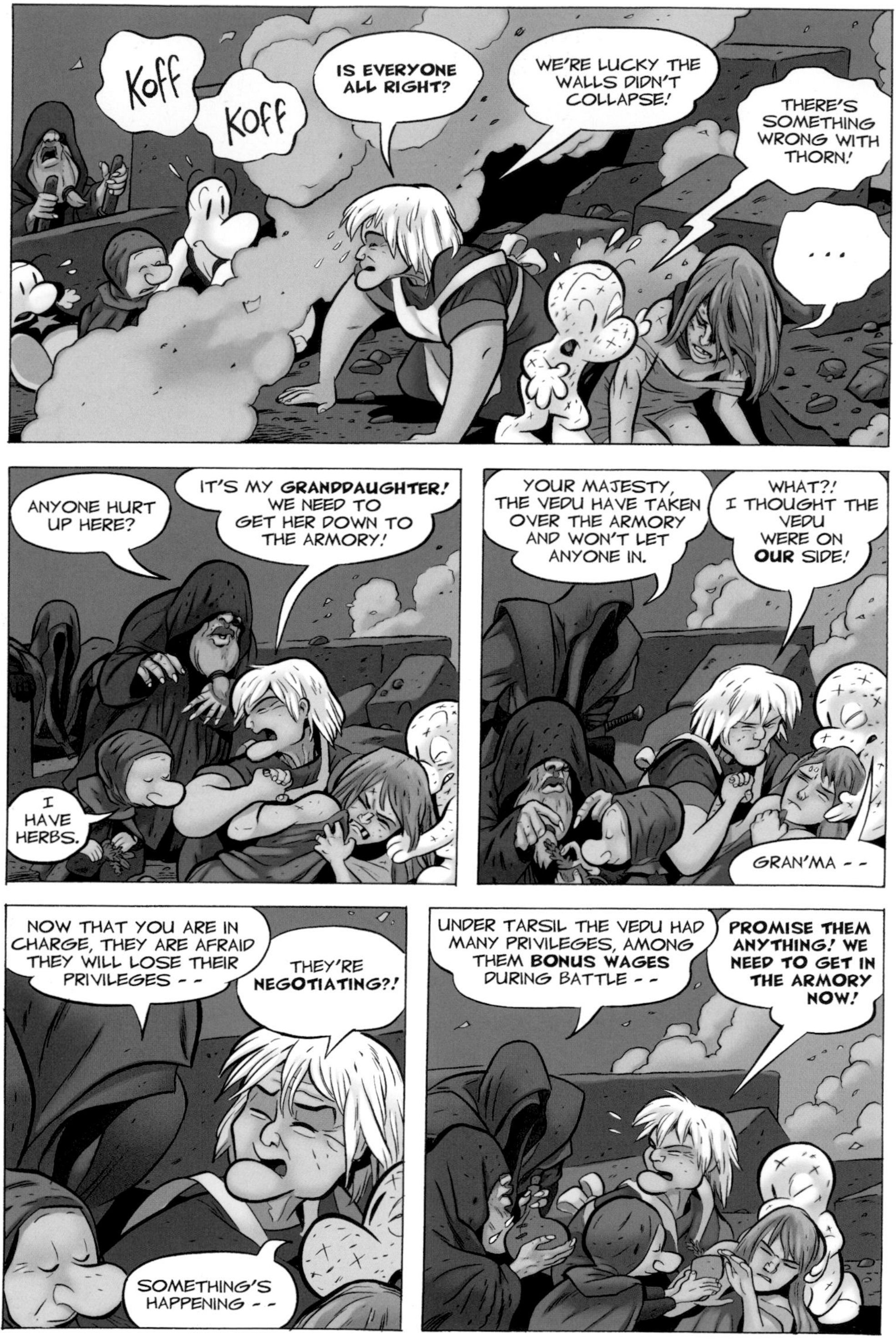
KOFF
KOFF
IS EVERYONE ALL RIGHT?
WE'RE LUCKY THE WALLS DIDN'T COLLAPSE!
THERE'S SOMETHING WRONG WITH THORN!
. . .
ANYONE HURT UP HERE?
IT'S MY GRANDDAUGHTER! WE NEED TO GET HER DOWN TO THE ARMORY!
I HAVE HERBS.
YOUR MAJESTY, THE VEDU HAVE TAKEN OVER THE ARMORY AND WON'T LET ANYONE IN.
WHAT?! I THOUGHT THE VEDU WERE ON OUR SIDE!
GRAN'MA --
NOW THAT YOU ARE IN CHARGE, THEY ARE AFRAID THEY WILL LOSE THEIR PRIVILEGES --
THEY'RE NEGOTIATING?!
SOMETHING'S HAPPENING --
UNDER TARSIL THE VEDU HAD MANY PRIVILEGES, AMONG THEM BONUS WAGES DURING BATTLE --
PROMISE THEM ANYTHING! WE NEED TO GET IN THE ARMORY NOW!

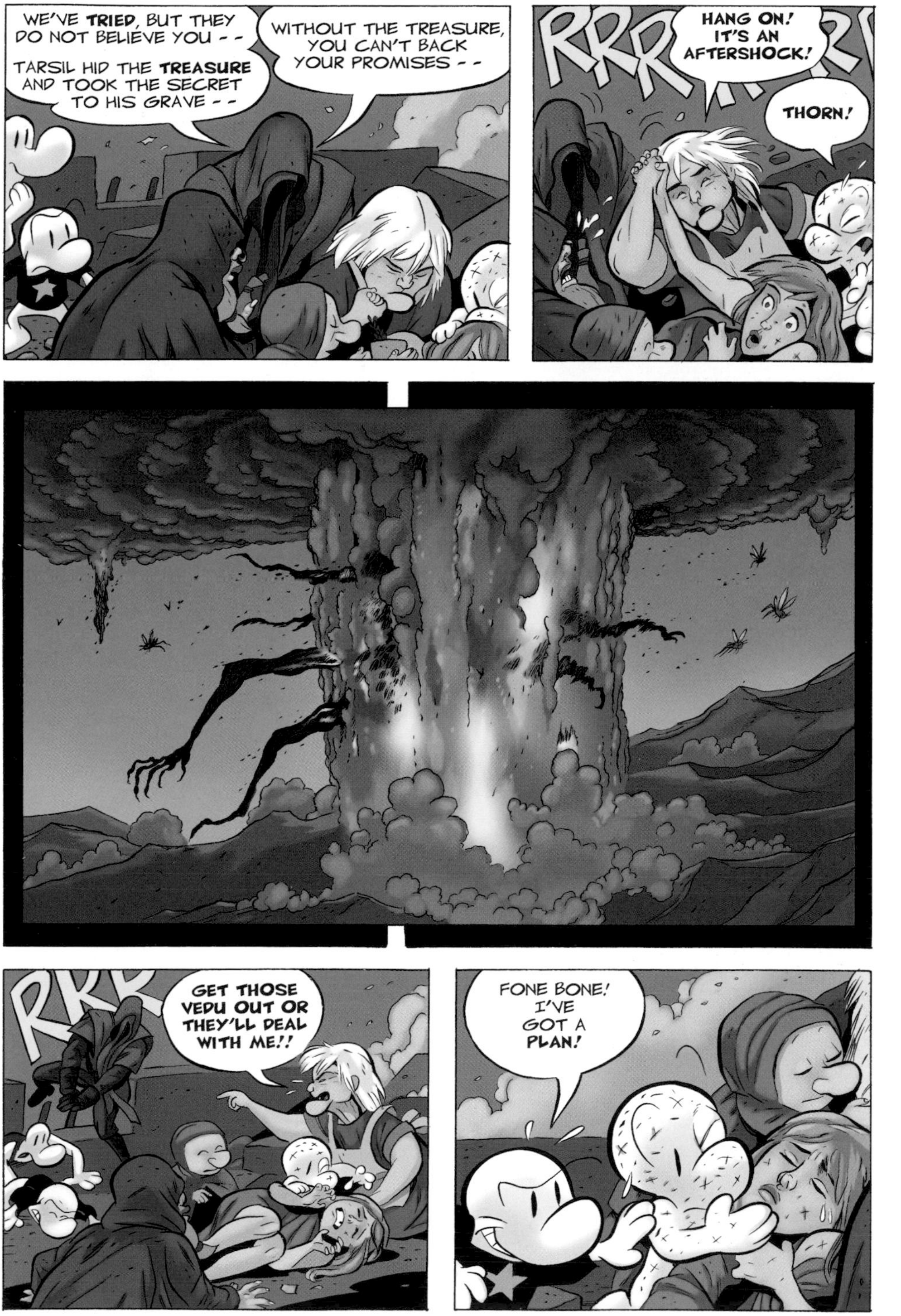
WE'VE TRIED, BUT THEY DO NOT BELIEVE YOU - -
TARSIL HID THE TREASURE AND TOOK THE SECRET TO HIS GRAVE - -
WITHOUT THE TREASURE, YOU CAN'T BACK YOUR PROMISES - -
RRRR
HANG ON! IT'S AN AFTERSHOCK!
THORN!
RRR
GET THOSE VEDU OUT OR THEY'LL DEAL WITH ME!!
FONE BONE! I'VE GOT A PLAN!

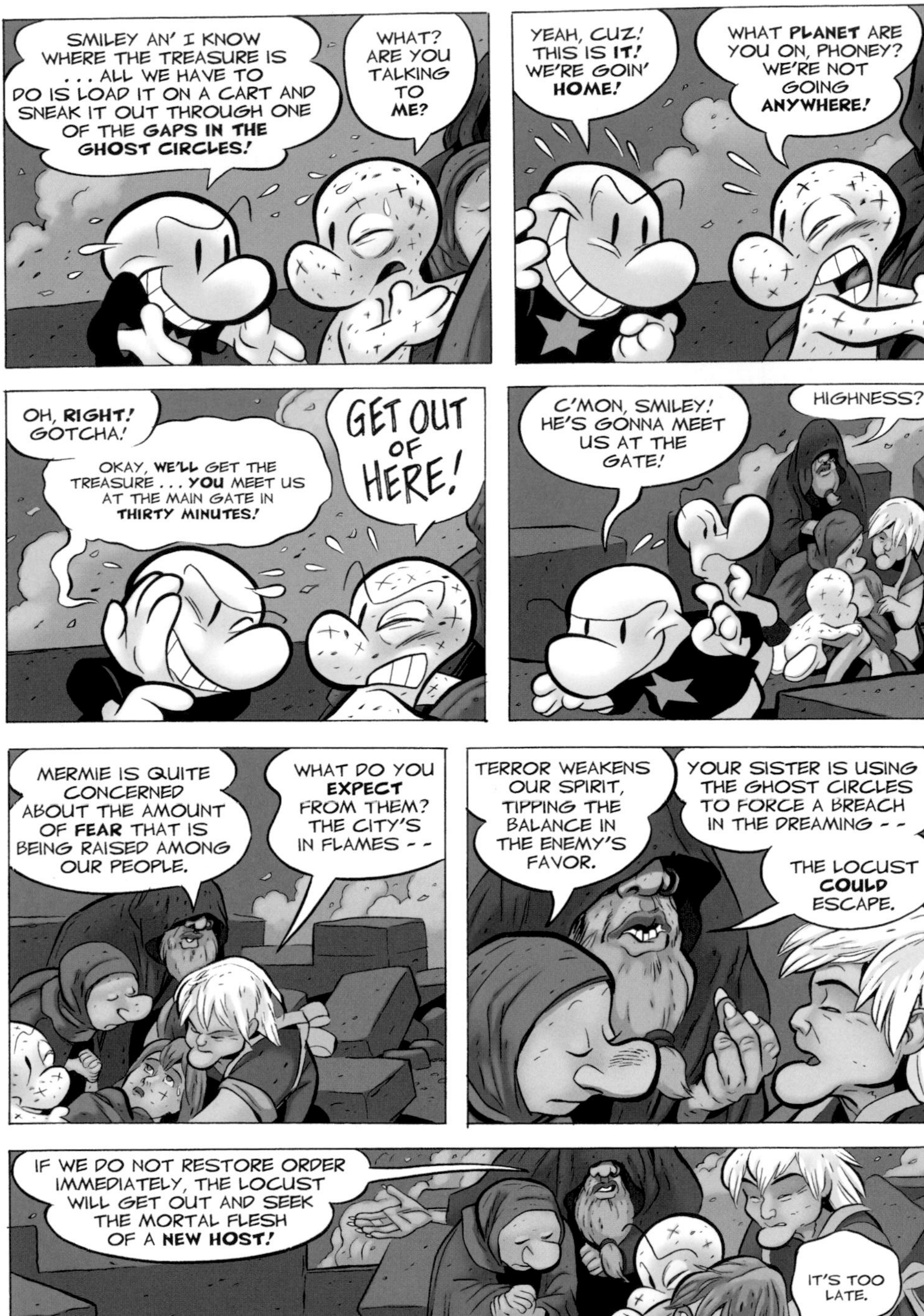
SMILEY AN' I KNOW WHERE THE TREASURE IS . . . ALL WE HAVE TO DO IS LOAD IT ON A CART AND SNEAK IT OUT THROUGH ONE OF THE GAPS IN THE GHOST CIRCLES!
WHAT? ARE YOU TALKING TO ME?
YEAH, CUZ! THIS IS IT! WE'RE GOIN' HOME!
WHAT PLANET ARE YOU ON, PHONEY? WE'RE NOT GOING ANYWHERE!
OH, RIGHT! GOTCHA!
OKAY, WE'LL GET THE TREASURE . . . YOU MEET US AT THE MAIN GATE IN THIRTY MINUTES!
GET OUT OF HERE!
C'MON, SMILEY! HE'S GONNA MEET US AT THE GATE!
HIGHNESS?
MERMIE IS QUITE CONCERNED ABOUT THE AMOUNT OF FEAR THAT IS BEING RAISED AMONG OUR PEOPLE.
WHAT DO YOU EXPECT FROM THEM? THE CITY'S IN FLAMES - -
TERROR WEAKENS OUR SPIRIT, TIPPING THE BALANCE IN THE ENEMY'S FAVOR.
YOUR SISTER IS USING THE GHOST CIRCLES TO FORCE A BREACH IN THE DREAMING - -
THE LOCUST COULD ESCAPE.
IF WE DO NOT RESTORE ORDER IMMEDIATELY, THE LOCUST WILL GET OUT AND SEEK THE MORTAL FLESH OF A NEW HOST!
IT'S TOO LATE.

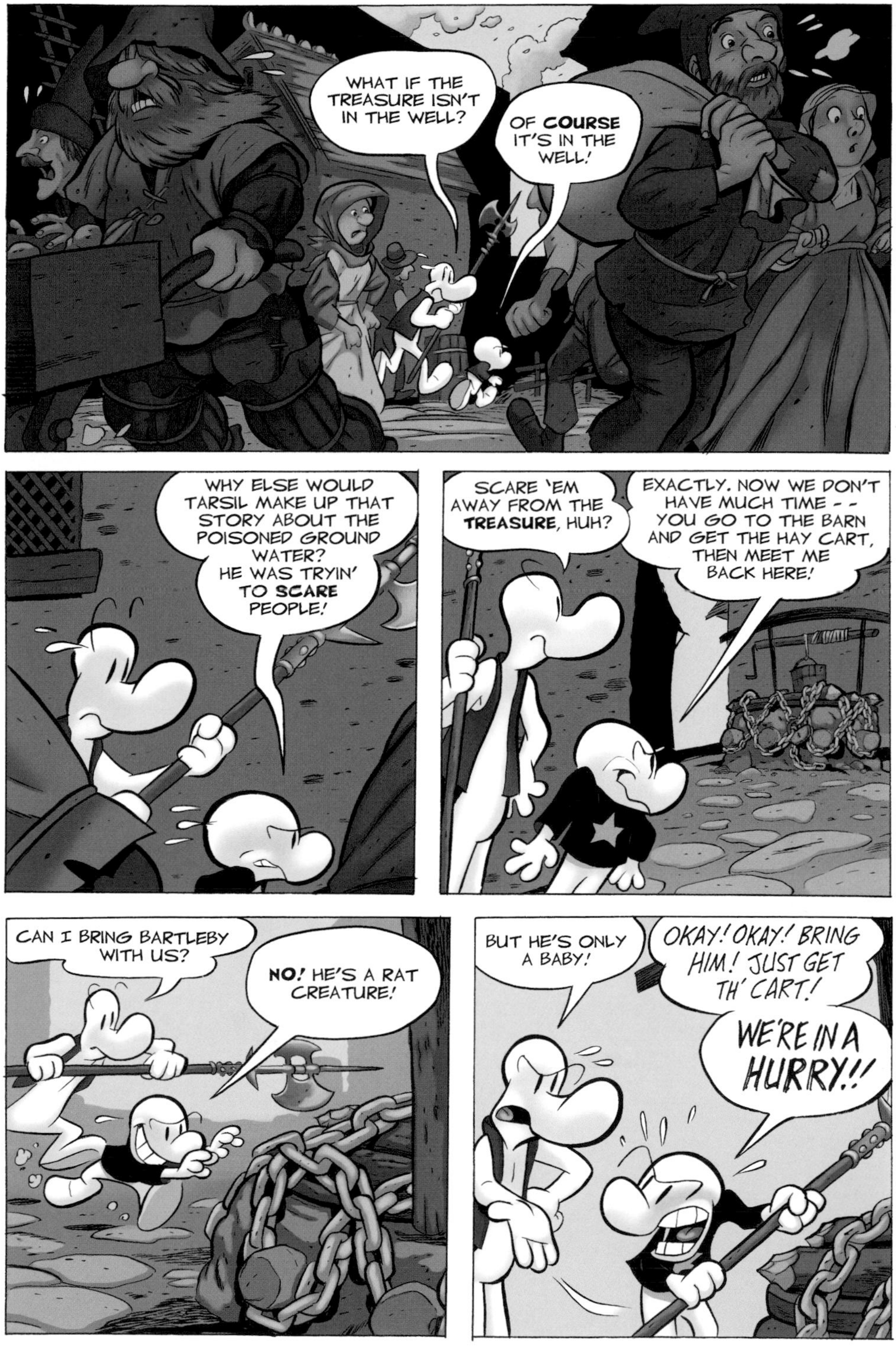
WHAT IF THE TREASURE ISN'T IN THE WELL?
OF **COURSE** IT'S IN THE WELL!
WHY ELSE WOULD TARSIL MAKE UP THAT STORY ABOUT THE POISONED GROUND WATER? HE WAS TRYIN' TO **SCARE** PEOPLE!
SCARE 'EM AWAY FROM THE **TREASURE**, HUH?
EXACTLY. NOW WE DON'T HAVE MUCH TIME -- YOU GO TO THE BARN AND GET THE HAY CART, THEN MEET ME BACK HERE!
CAN I BRING BARTLEBY WITH US?
NO! HE'S A RAT CREATURE!
BUT HE'S ONLY A BABY!
OKAY! OKAY! BRING HIM! JUST GET TH' CART!
WE'RE IN A HURRY!!

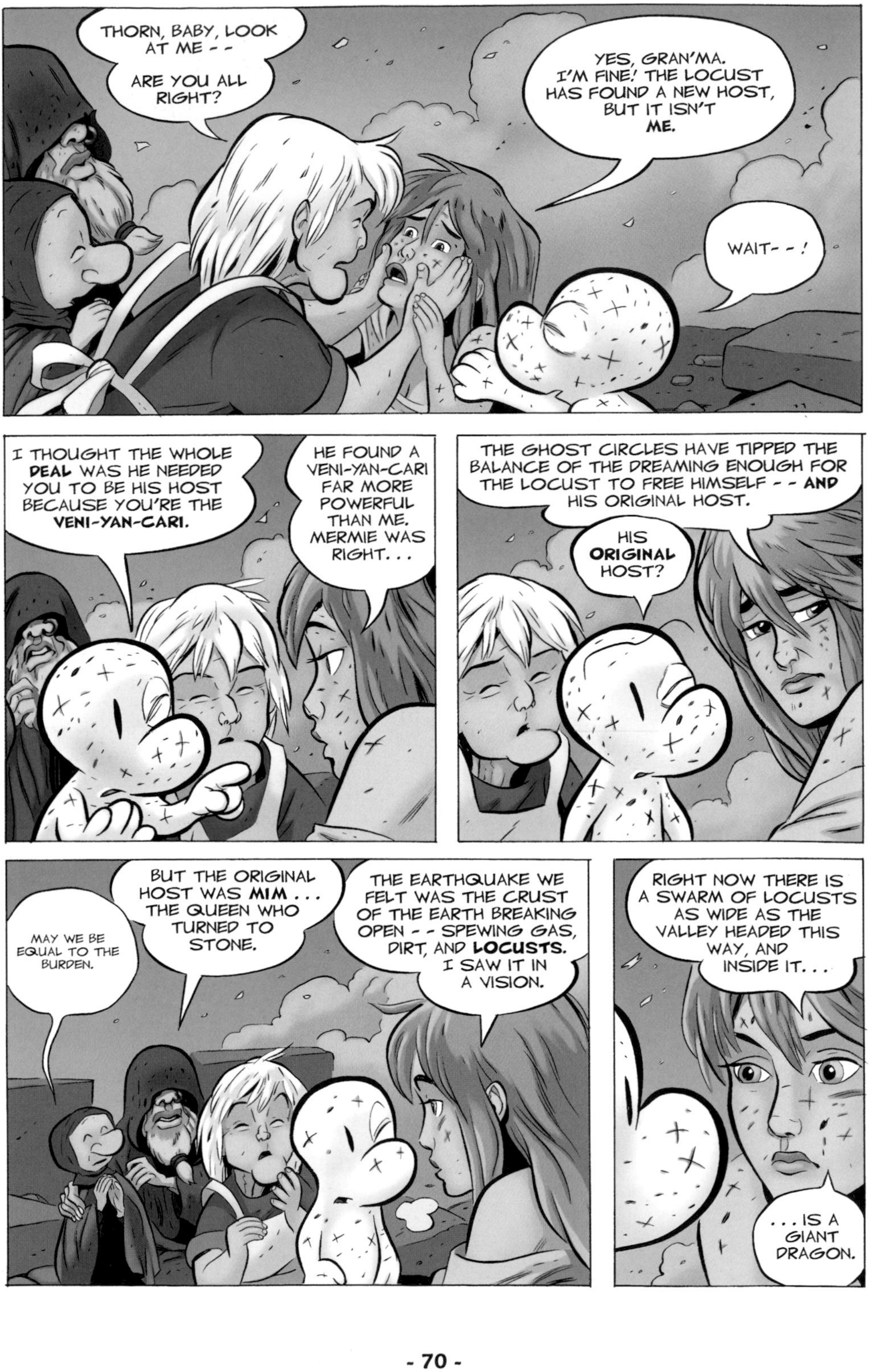
THORN, BABY, LOOK AT ME - -
ARE YOU ALL RIGHT?
YES, GRAN'MA. I'M FINE! THE LOCUST HAS FOUND A NEW HOST, BUT IT ISN'T ME.
WAIT- - !
I THOUGHT THE WHOLE DEAL WAS HE NEEDED YOU TO BE HIS HOST BECAUSE YOU'RE THE VENI-YAN-CARI.
HE FOUND A VENI-YAN-CARI FAR MORE POWERFUL THAN ME. MERMIE WAS RIGHT. . .
THE GHOST CIRCLES HAVE TIPPED THE BALANCE OF THE DREAMING ENOUGH FOR THE LOCUST TO FREE HIMSELF - - AND HIS ORIGINAL HOST.
HIS ORIGINAL HOST?
MAY WE BE EQUAL TO THE BURDEN.
BUT THE ORIGINAL HOST WAS MIM . . . THE QUEEN WHO TURNED TO STONE.
THE EARTHQUAKE WE FELT WAS THE CRUST OF THE EARTH BREAKING OPEN - - SPEWING GAS, DIRT, AND LOCUSTS. I SAW IT IN A VISION.
RIGHT NOW THERE IS A SWARM OF LOCUSTS AS WIDE AS THE VALLEY HEADED THIS WAY, AND INSIDE IT. . .
. . . IS A GIANT DRAGON.

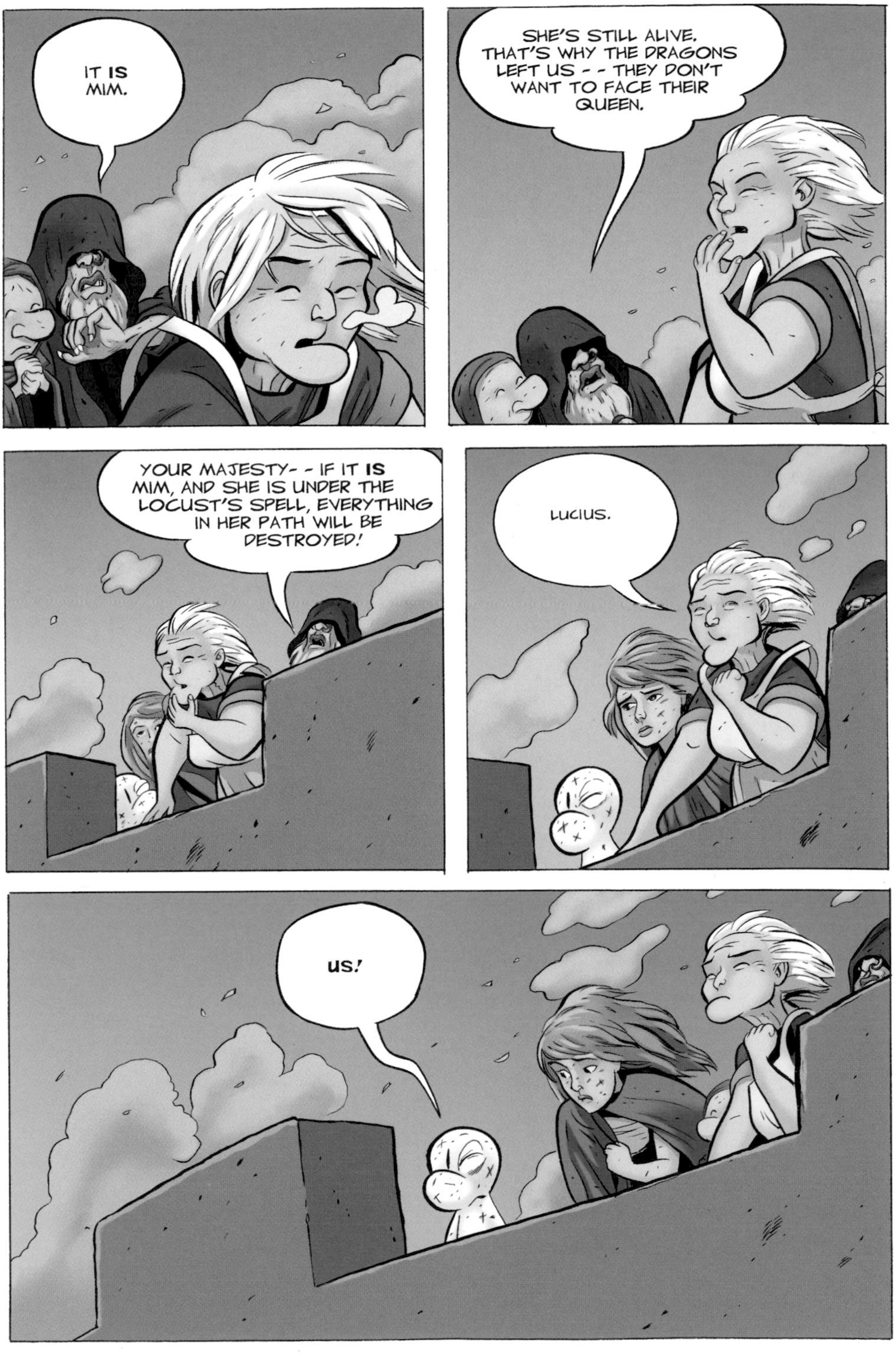
IT IS MIM.
SHE'S STILL ALIVE. THAT'S WHY THE DRAGONS LEFT US - - THEY DON'T WANT TO FACE THEIR QUEEN.
YOUR MAJESTY- - IF IT IS MIM, AND SHE IS UNDER THE LOCUST'S SPELL, EVERYTHING IN HER PATH WILL BE DESTROYED!
LUCIUS.
US!

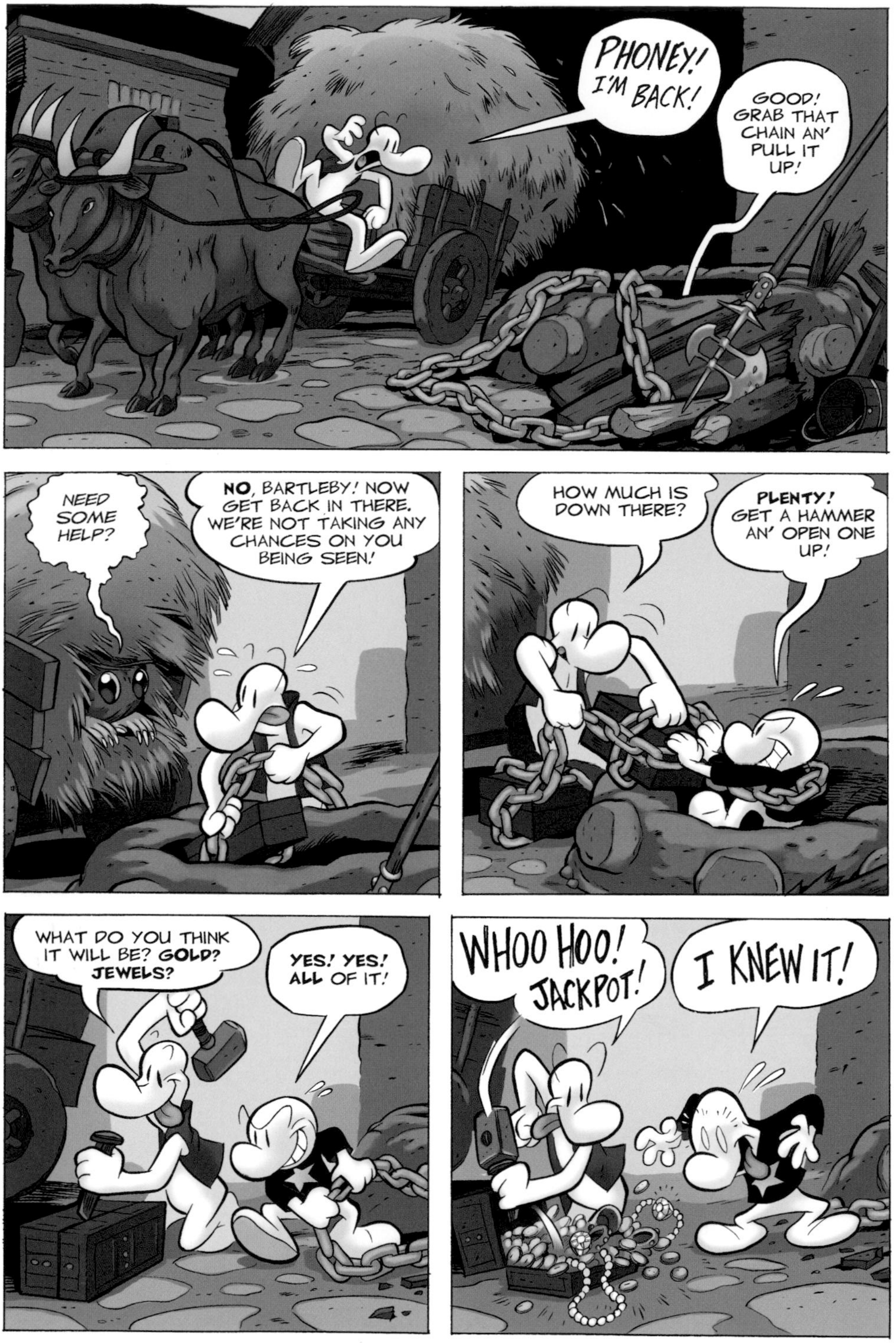
PHONEY! I'M BACK!
GOOD! GRAB THAT CHAIN AN' PULL IT UP!
NEED SOME HELP?
NO, BARTLEBY! NOW GET BACK IN THERE. WE'RE NOT TAKING ANY CHANCES ON YOU BEING SEEN!
HOW MUCH IS DOWN THERE?
PLENTY! GET A HAMMER AN' OPEN ONE UP!
WHAT DO YOU THINK IT WILL BE? GOLD? JEWELS?
YES! YES! ALL OF IT!
WHOO HOO! JACKPOT!
I KNEW IT!

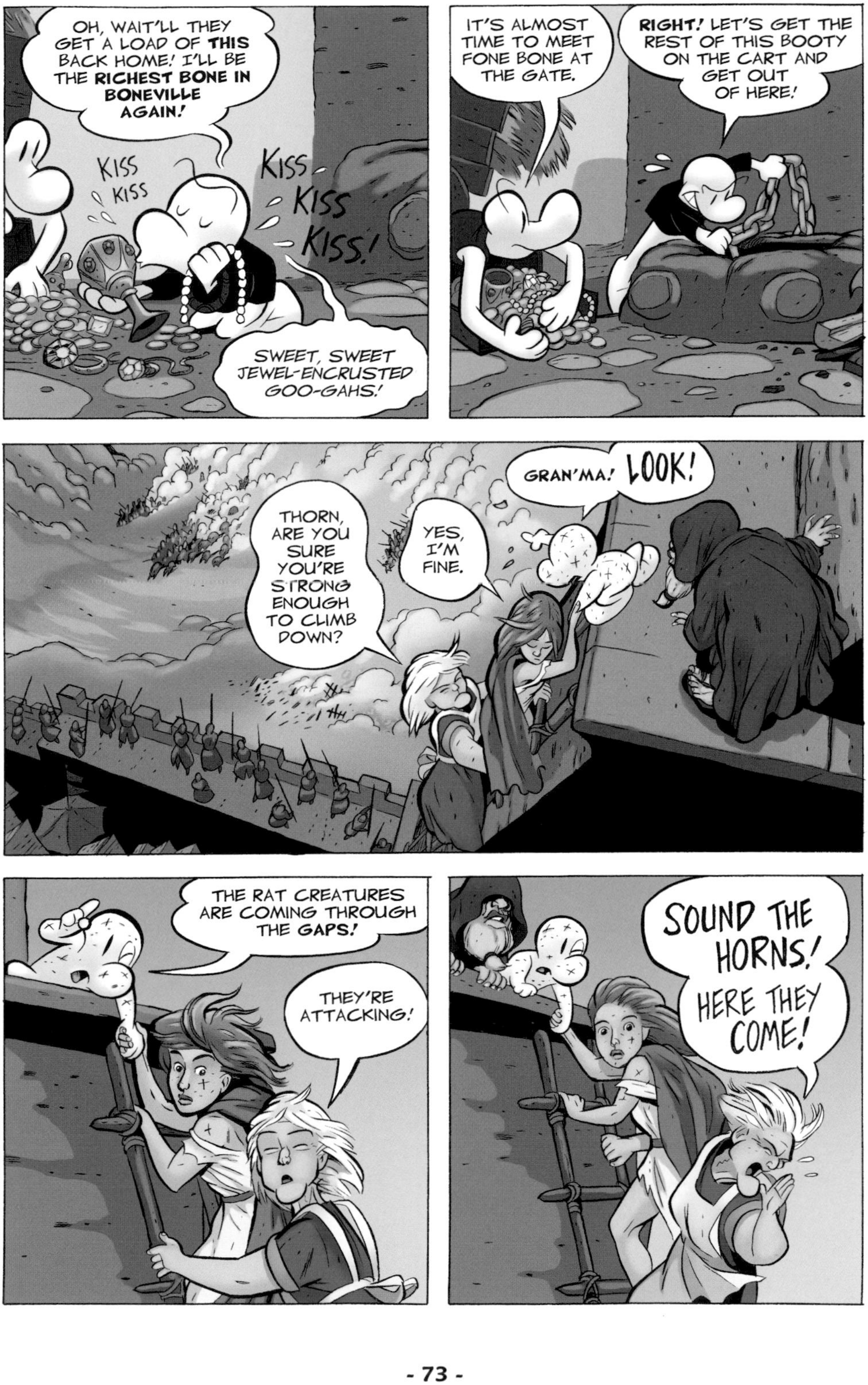
OH, WAIT'LL THEY GET A LOAD OF THIS BACK HOME! I'LL BE THE RICHEST BONE IN BONEVILLE AGAIN!
KISS KISS
KISS KISS KISS!
SWEET, SWEET JEWEL-ENCRUSTED GOO-GAHS!
IT'S ALMOST TIME TO MEET FONE BONE AT THE GATE.
RIGHT! LET'S GET THE REST OF THIS BOOTY ON THE CART AND GET OUT OF HERE!
THORN, ARE YOU SURE YOU'RE STRONG ENOUGH TO CLIMB DOWN?
YES, I'M FINE.
GRAN'MA! LOOK!
THE RAT CREATURES ARE COMING THROUGH THE GAPS!
THEY'RE ATTACKING!
SOUND THE HORNS! HERE THEY COME!

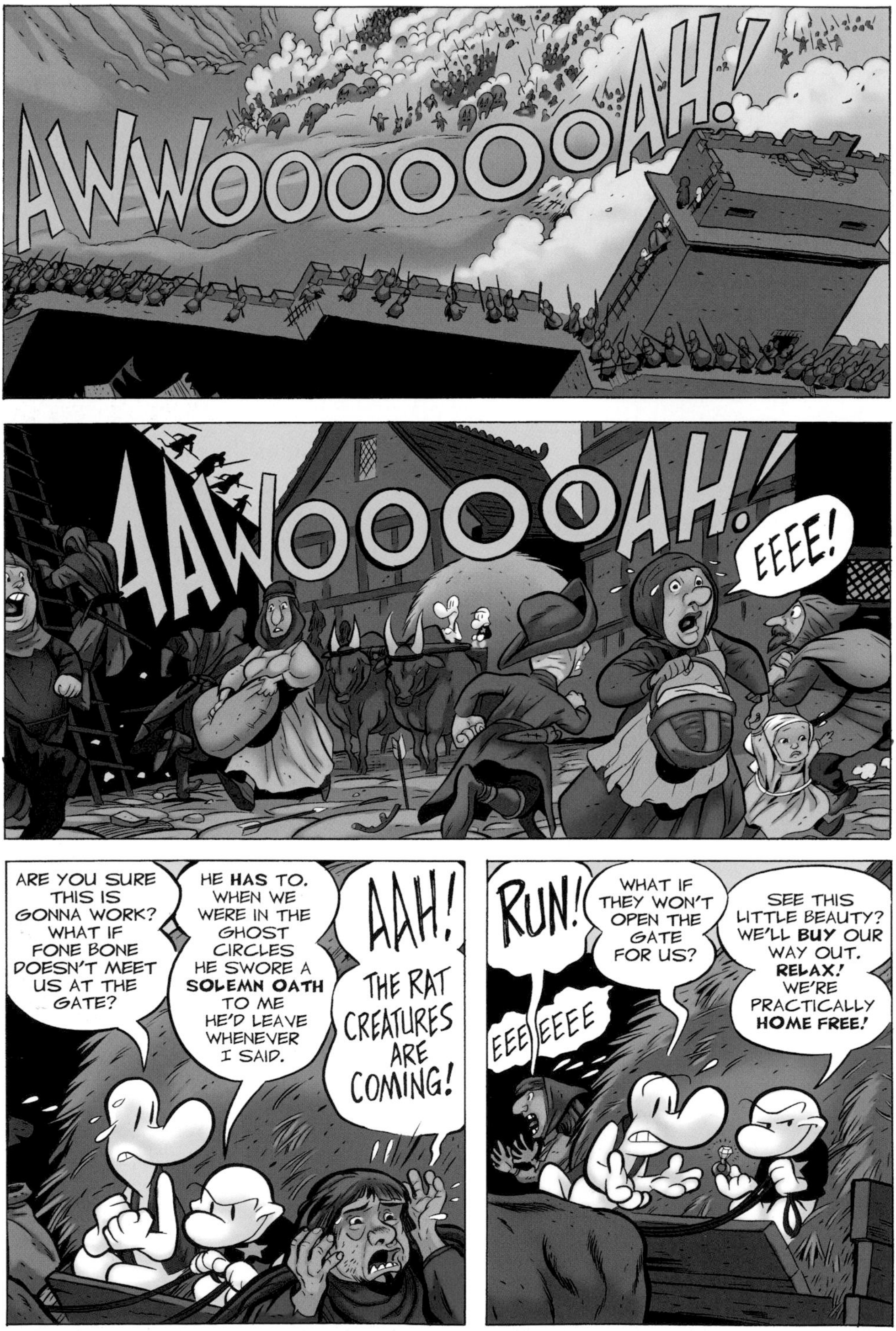
AWWOOOOOOAH!
AAWOOOOOAH!
EEEE!
ARE YOU SURE THIS IS GONNA WORK? WHAT IF FONE BONE DOESN'T MEET US AT THE GATE?
HE **HAS** TO. WHEN WE WERE IN THE GHOST CIRCLES HE SWORE A **SOLEMN OATH** TO ME HE'D LEAVE WHENEVER I SAID.
AAH!
THE RAT CREATURES ARE COMING!
RUN!
EEEEEEE
WHAT IF THEY WON'T OPEN THE GATE FOR US?
SEE THIS LITTLE BEAUTY? WE'LL **BUY** OUR WAY OUT. **RELAX!** WE'RE PRACTICALLY **HOME FREE!**

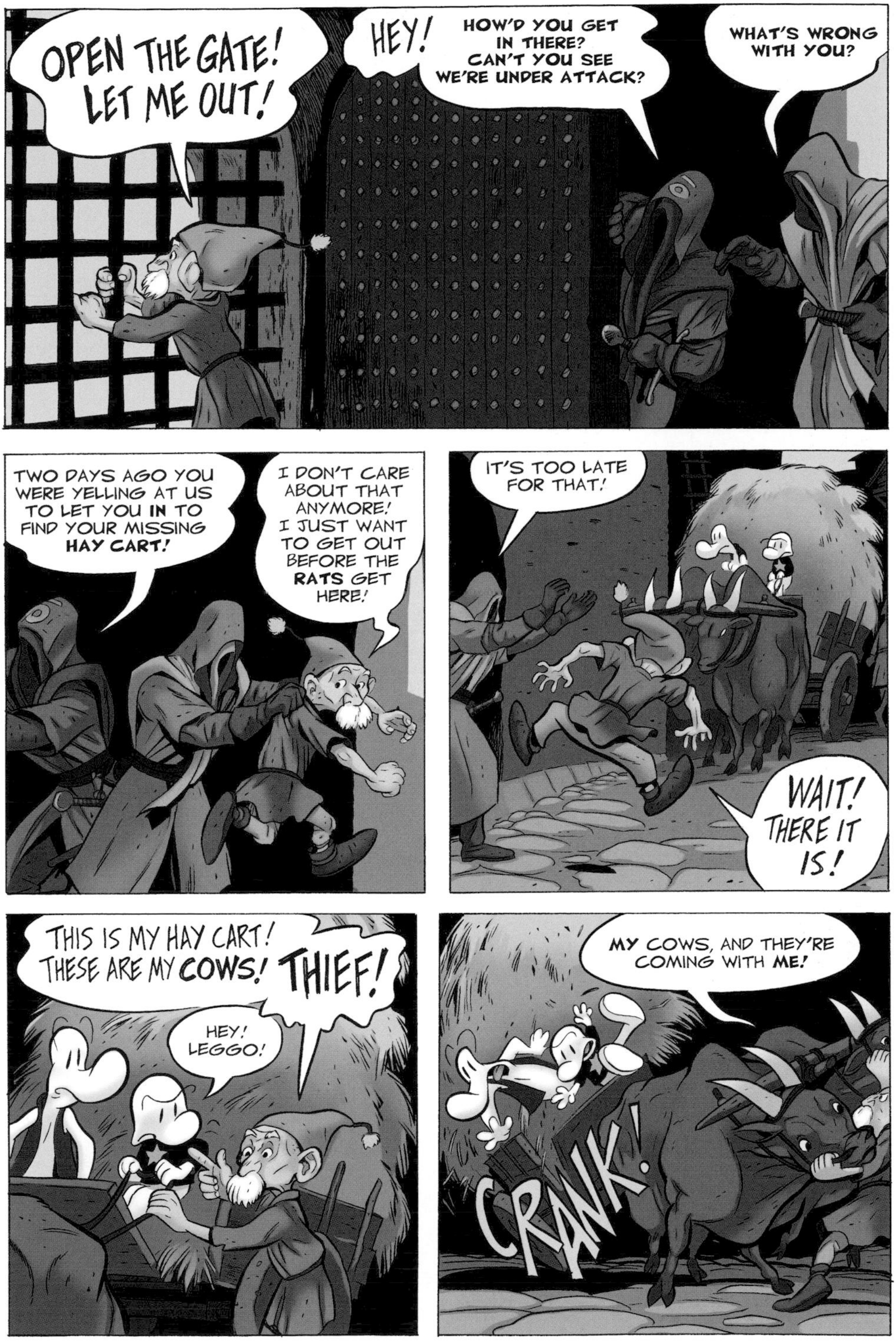
OPEN THE GATE! LET ME OUT!
HEY!
HOW'D YOU GET IN THERE? CAN'T YOU SEE WE'RE UNDER ATTACK?
WHAT'S WRONG WITH YOU?
TWO DAYS AGO YOU WERE YELLING AT US TO LET YOU IN TO FIND YOUR MISSING HAY CART!
I DON'T CARE ABOUT THAT ANYMORE! I JUST WANT TO GET OUT BEFORE THE RATS GET HERE!
IT'S TOO LATE FOR THAT!
WAIT! THERE IT IS!
THIS IS MY HAY CART! THESE ARE MY COWS!
THIEF!
HEY! LEGGO!
MY COWS, AND THEY'RE COMING WITH ME!
CRANK!

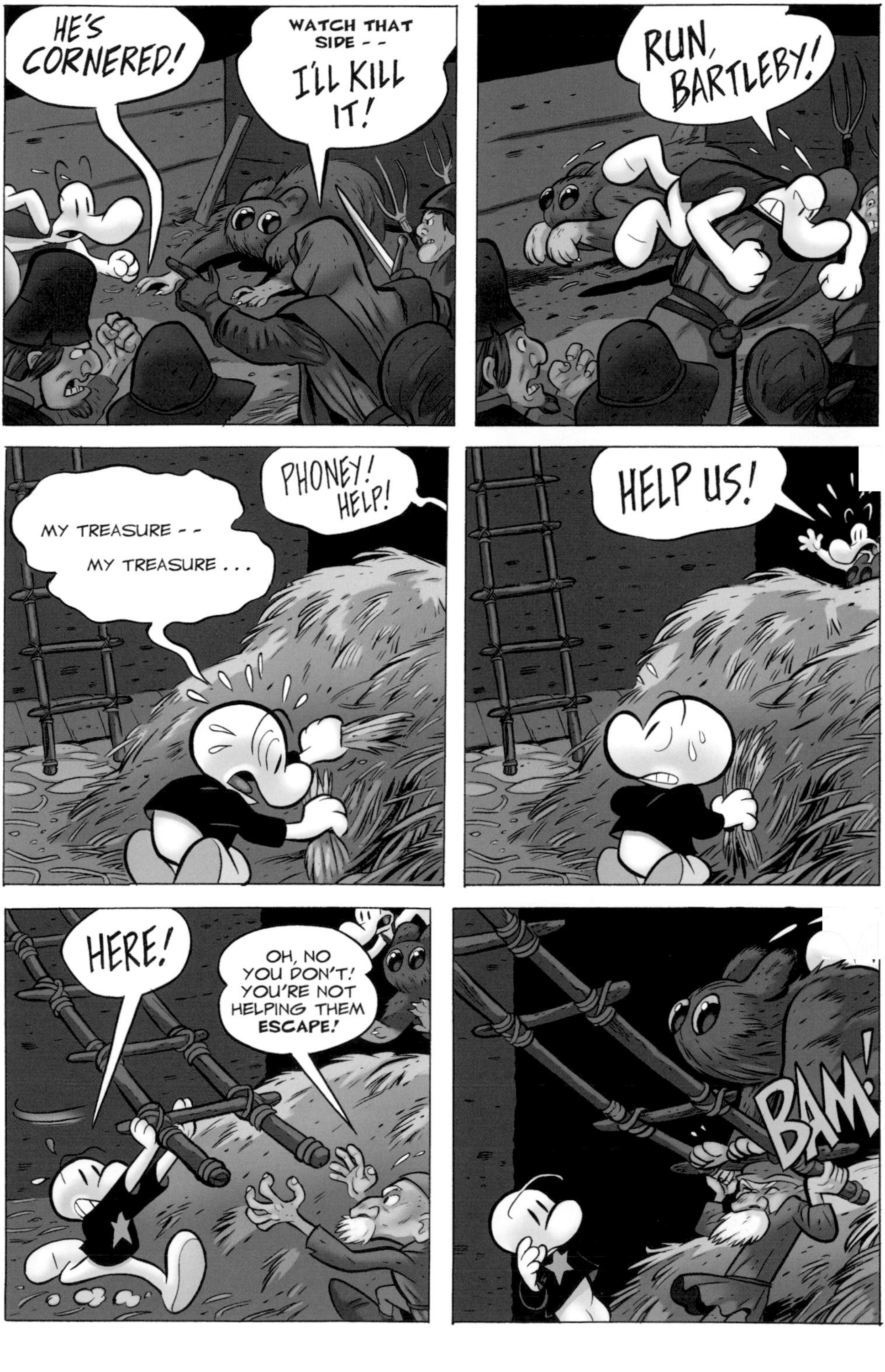
HE'S CORNERED!
WATCH THAT SIDE - -
I'LL KILL IT!
RUN, BARTLEBY!
PHONEY! HELP!
MY TREASURE - -
MY TREASURE . . .
HELP US!
HERE!
OH, NO YOU DON'T! YOU'RE NOT HELPING THEM ESCAPE!
BAM!

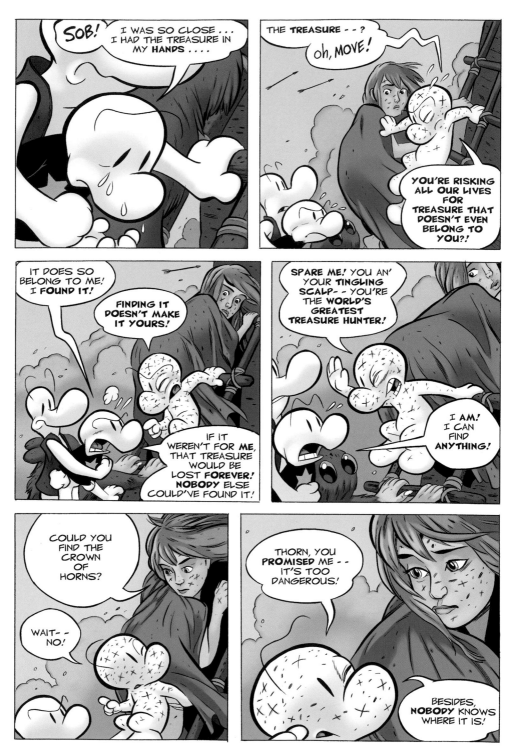

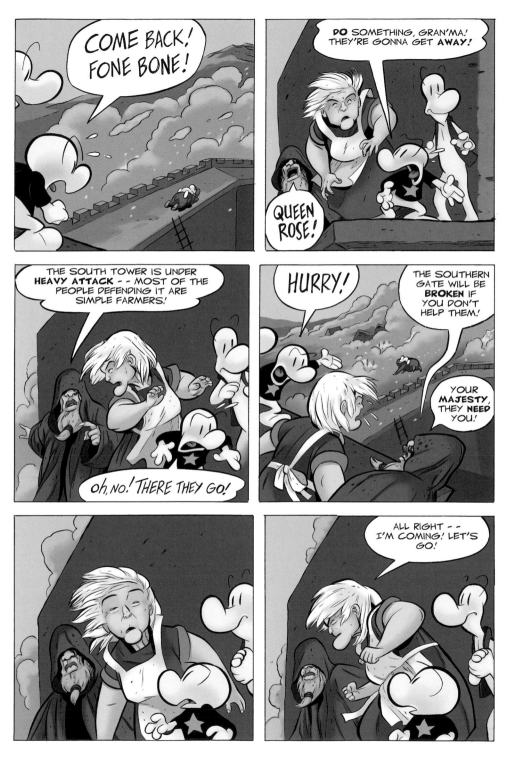

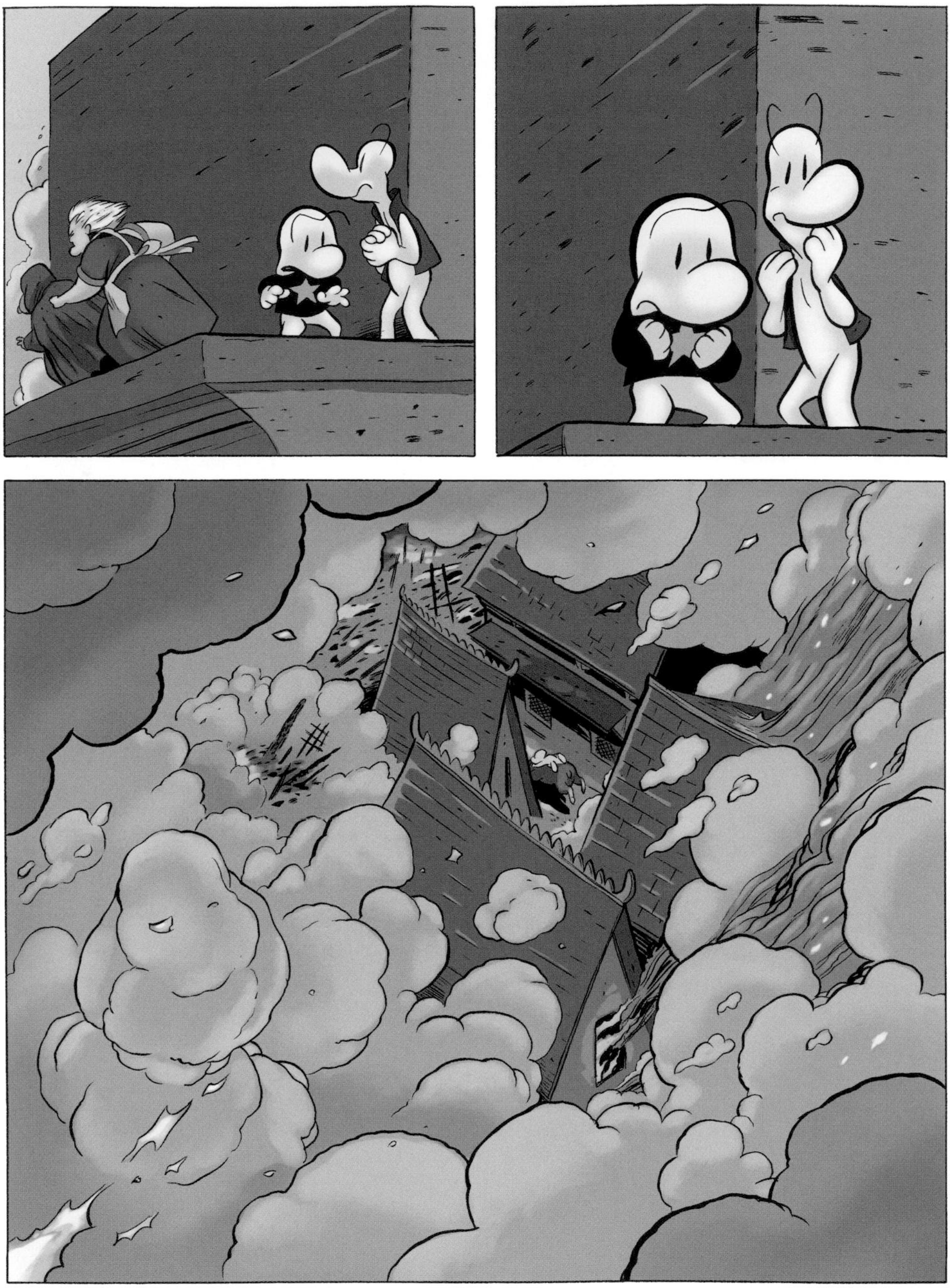

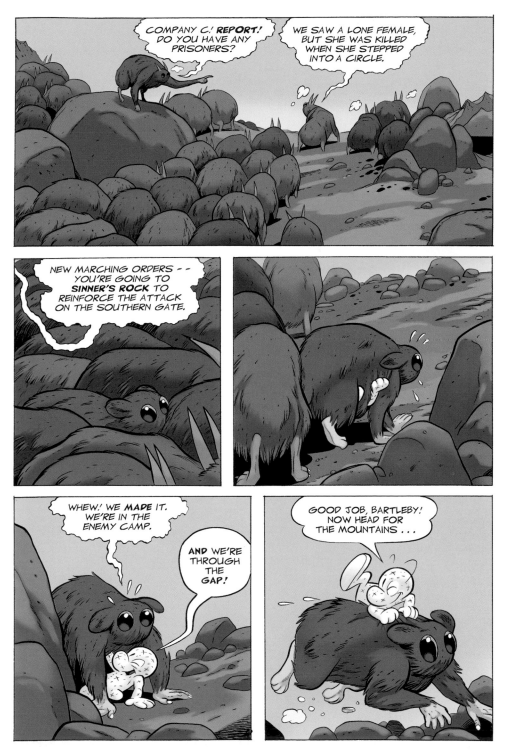

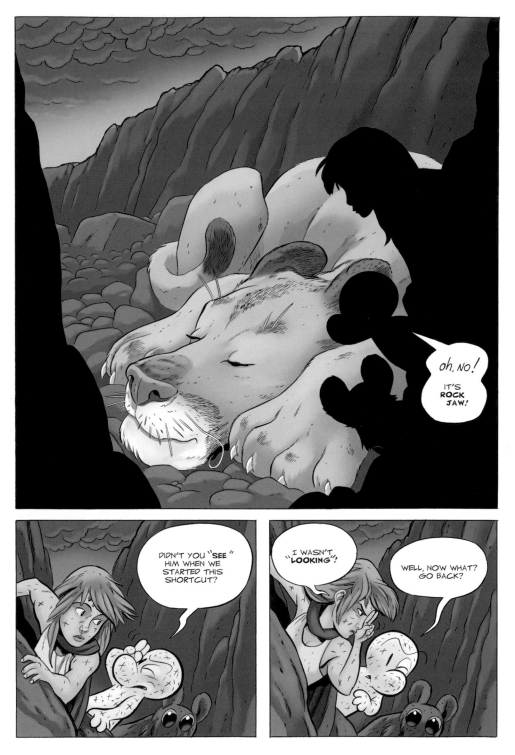

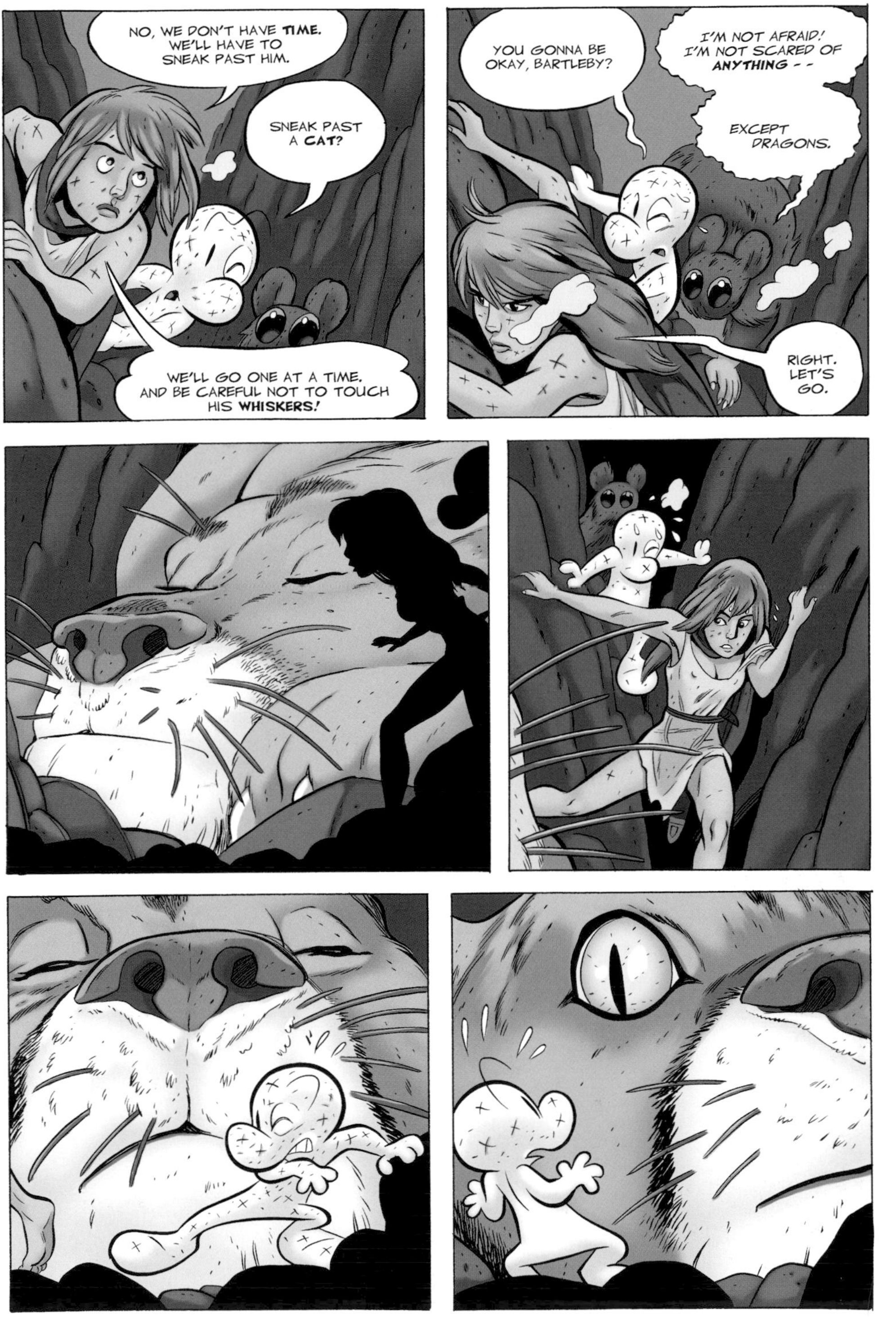
NO, WE DON'T HAVE **TIME.** WE'LL HAVE TO SNEAK PAST HIM.
SNEAK PAST A **CAT?**
WE'LL GO ONE AT A TIME. AND BE CAREFUL NOT TO TOUCH HIS **WHISKERS!**
YOU GONNA BE OKAY, BARTLEBY?
I'M NOT AFRAID! I'M NOT SCARED OF **ANYTHING** - -
EXCEPT DRAGONS.
RIGHT. LET'S GO.

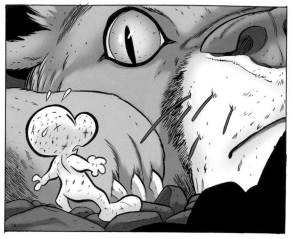

RUN, FONE BONE!

WAIT!

PUT YOUR SWORD AWAY.

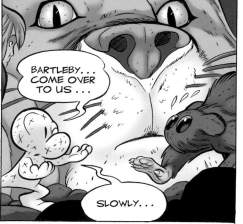

BARTLEBY... COME OVER TO US...

SLOWLY...

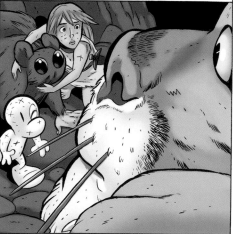

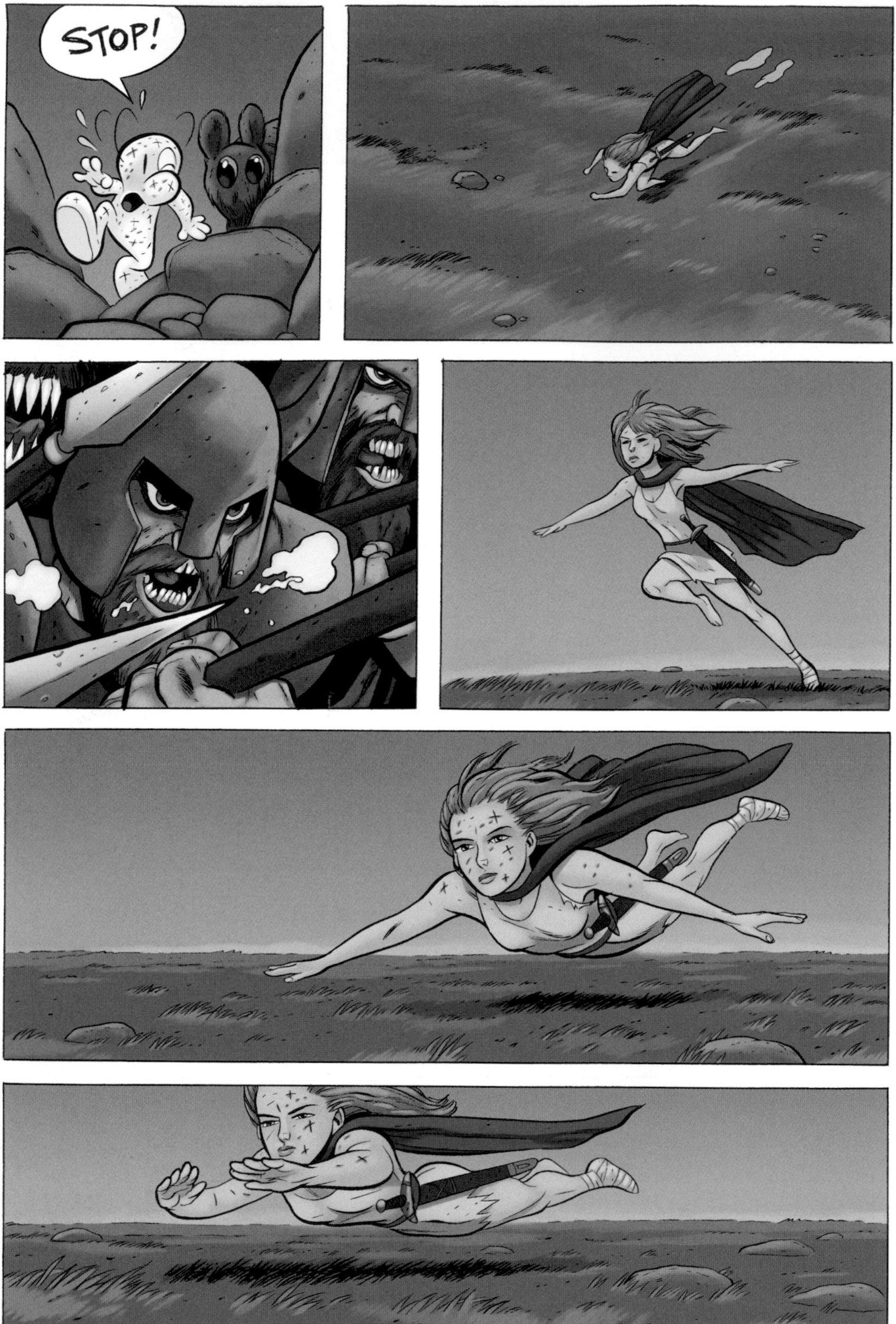
STOP!

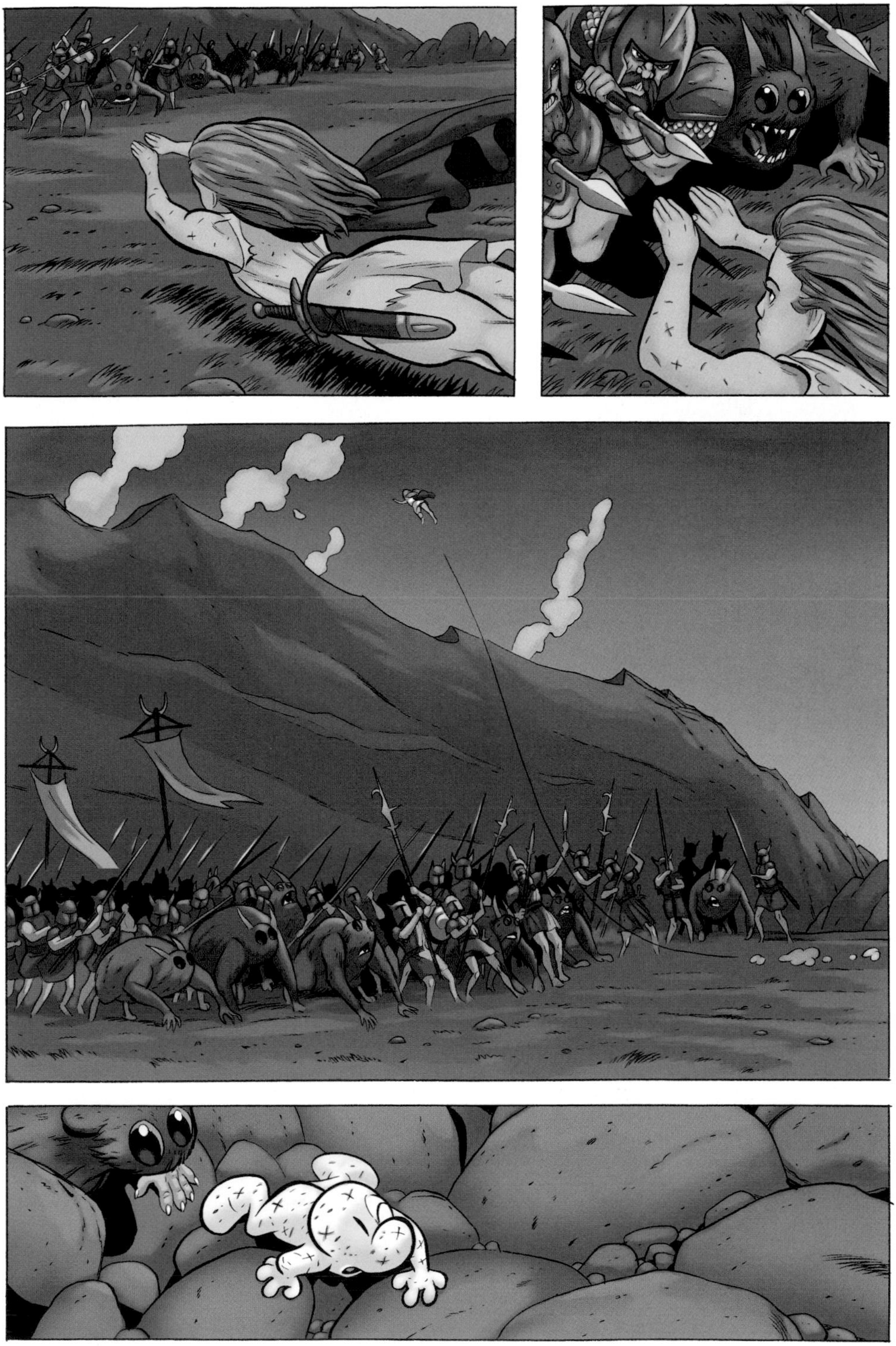

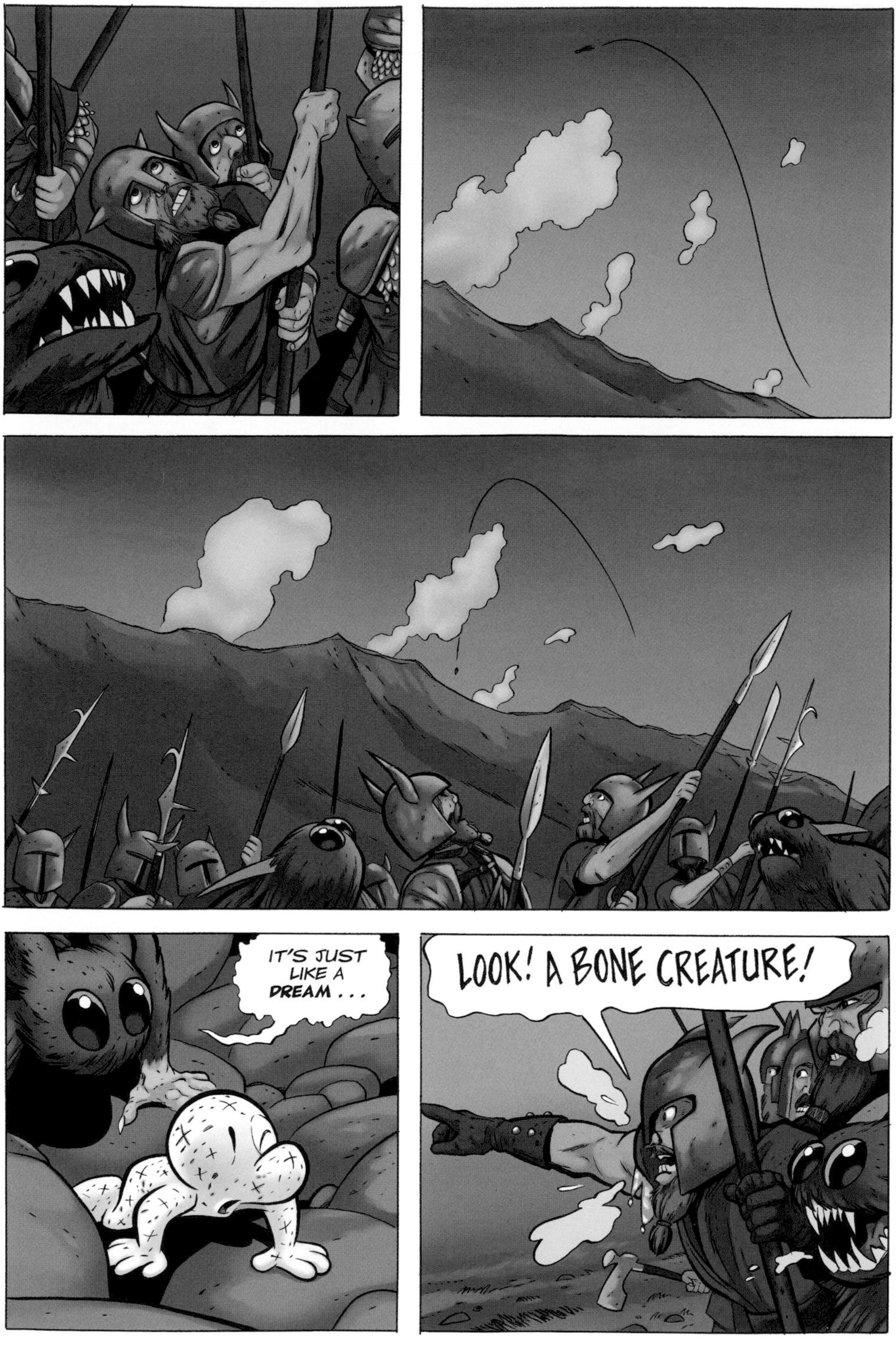
IT'S JUST LIKE A DREAM . . .
LOOK! A BONE CREATURE!

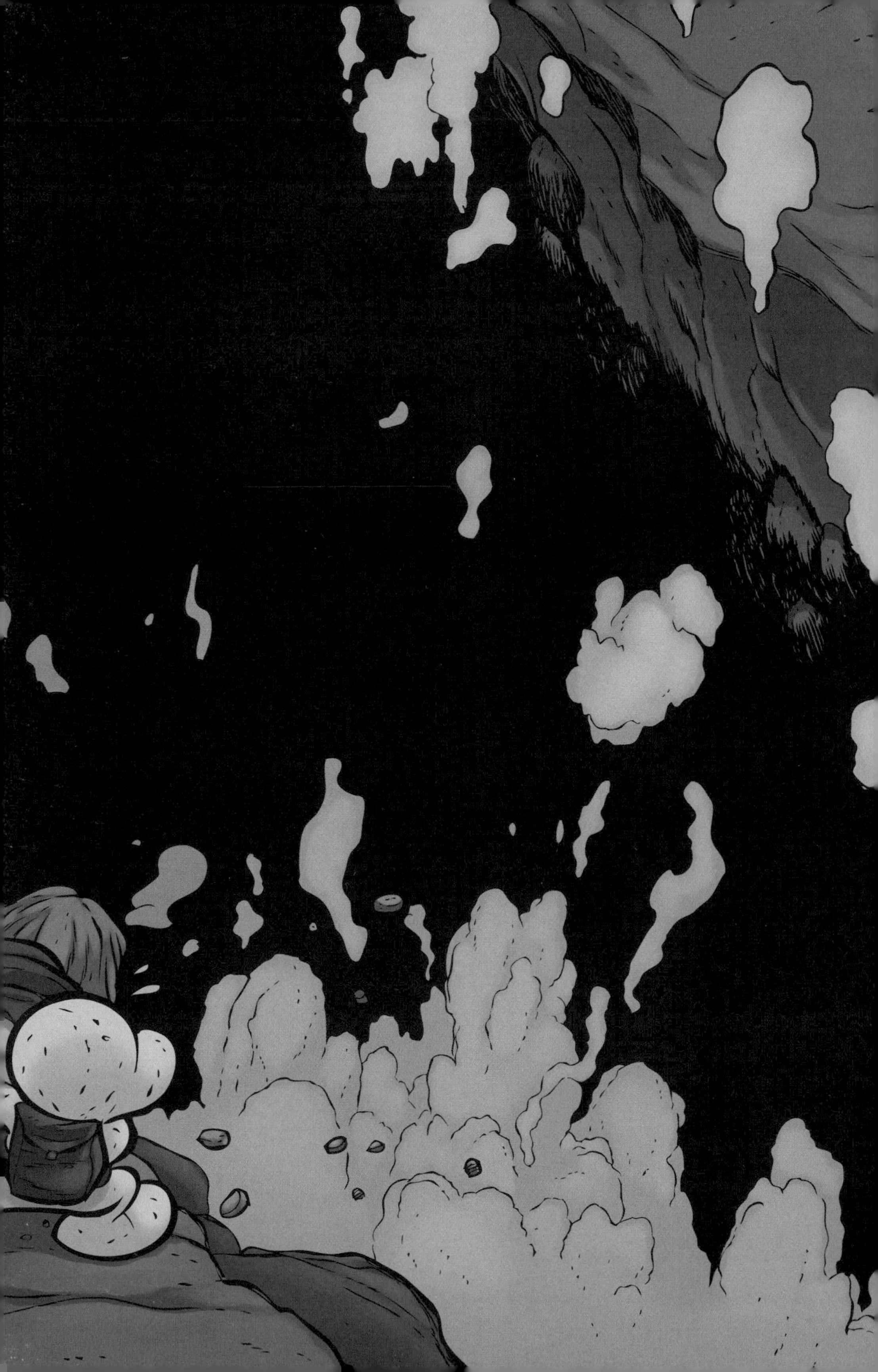

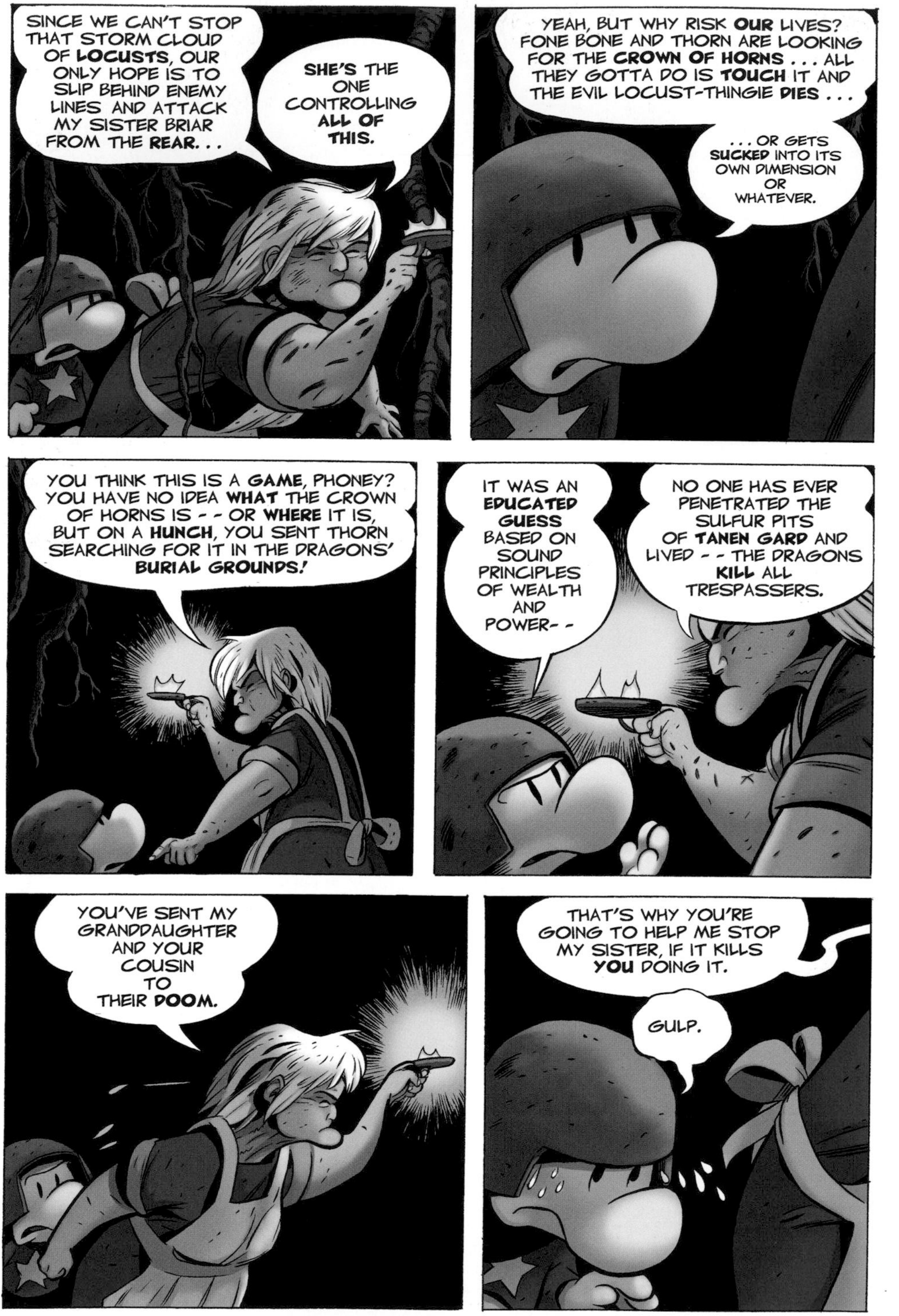
SINCE WE CAN'T STOP THAT STORM CLOUD OF LOCUSTS, OUR ONLY HOPE IS TO SLIP BEHIND ENEMY LINES AND ATTACK MY SISTER BRIAR FROM THE REAR...
SHE'S THE ONE CONTROLLING ALL OF THIS.
YEAH, BUT WHY RISK OUR LIVES? FONE BONE AND THORN ARE LOOKING FOR THE CROWN OF HORNS . . . ALL THEY GOTTA DO IS TOUCH IT AND THE EVIL LOCUST-THINGIE DIES . . .
. . . OR GETS SUCKED INTO ITS OWN DIMENSION OR WHATEVER.
YOU THINK THIS IS A GAME, PHONEY? YOU HAVE NO IDEA WHAT THE CROWN OF HORNS IS - - OR WHERE IT IS, BUT ON A HUNCH, YOU SENT THORN SEARCHING FOR IT IN THE DRAGONS' BURIAL GROUNDS!
IT WAS AN EDUCATED GUESS BASED ON SOUND PRINCIPLES OF WEALTH AND POWER- -
NO ONE HAS EVER PENETRATED THE SULFUR PITS OF TANEN GARD AND LIVED - - THE DRAGONS KILL ALL TRESPASSERS.
YOU'VE SENT MY GRANDDAUGHTER AND YOUR COUSIN TO THEIR DOOM.
THAT'S WHY YOU'RE GOING TO HELP ME STOP MY SISTER, IF IT KILLS YOU DOING IT.
GULP.

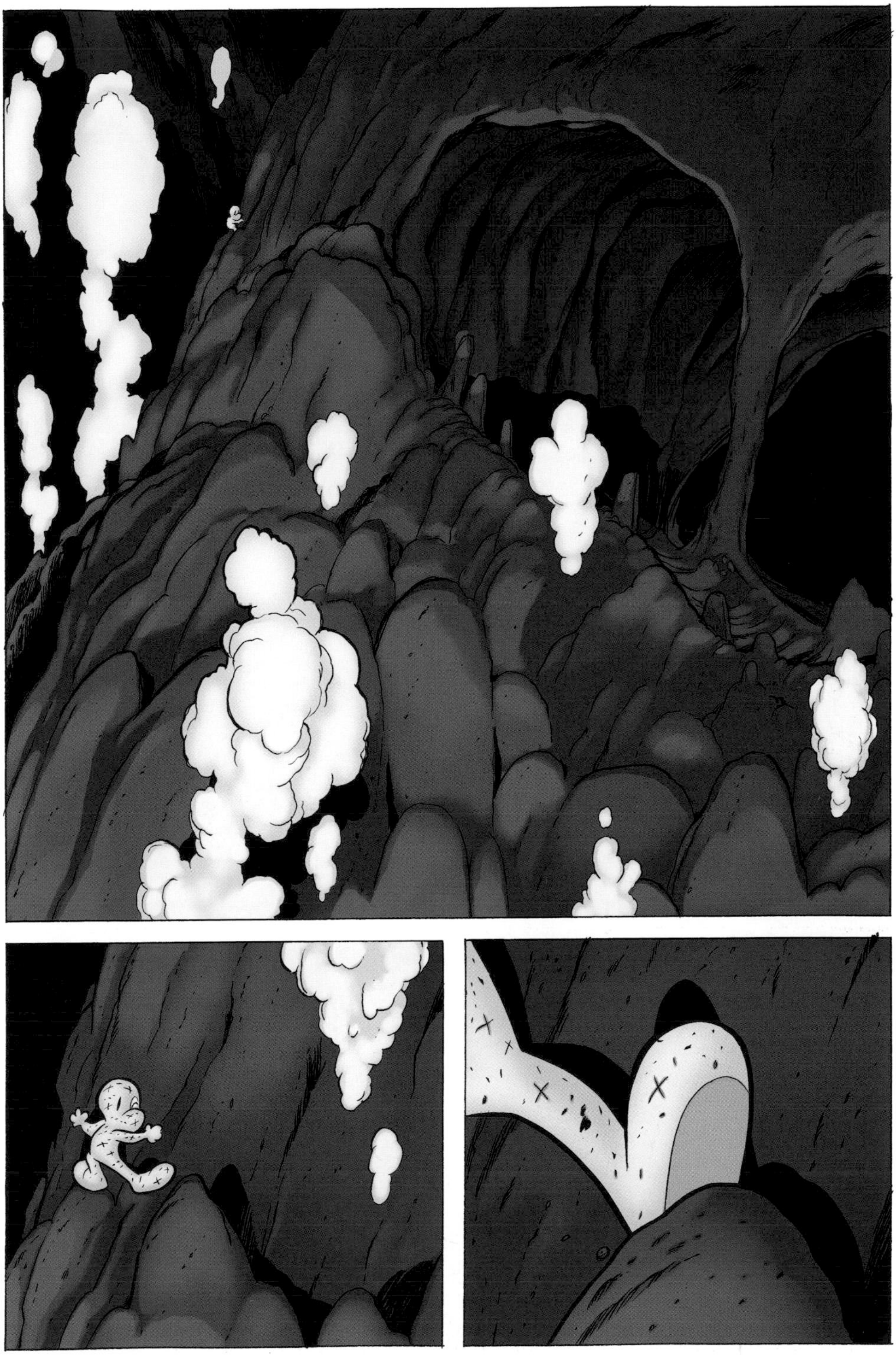

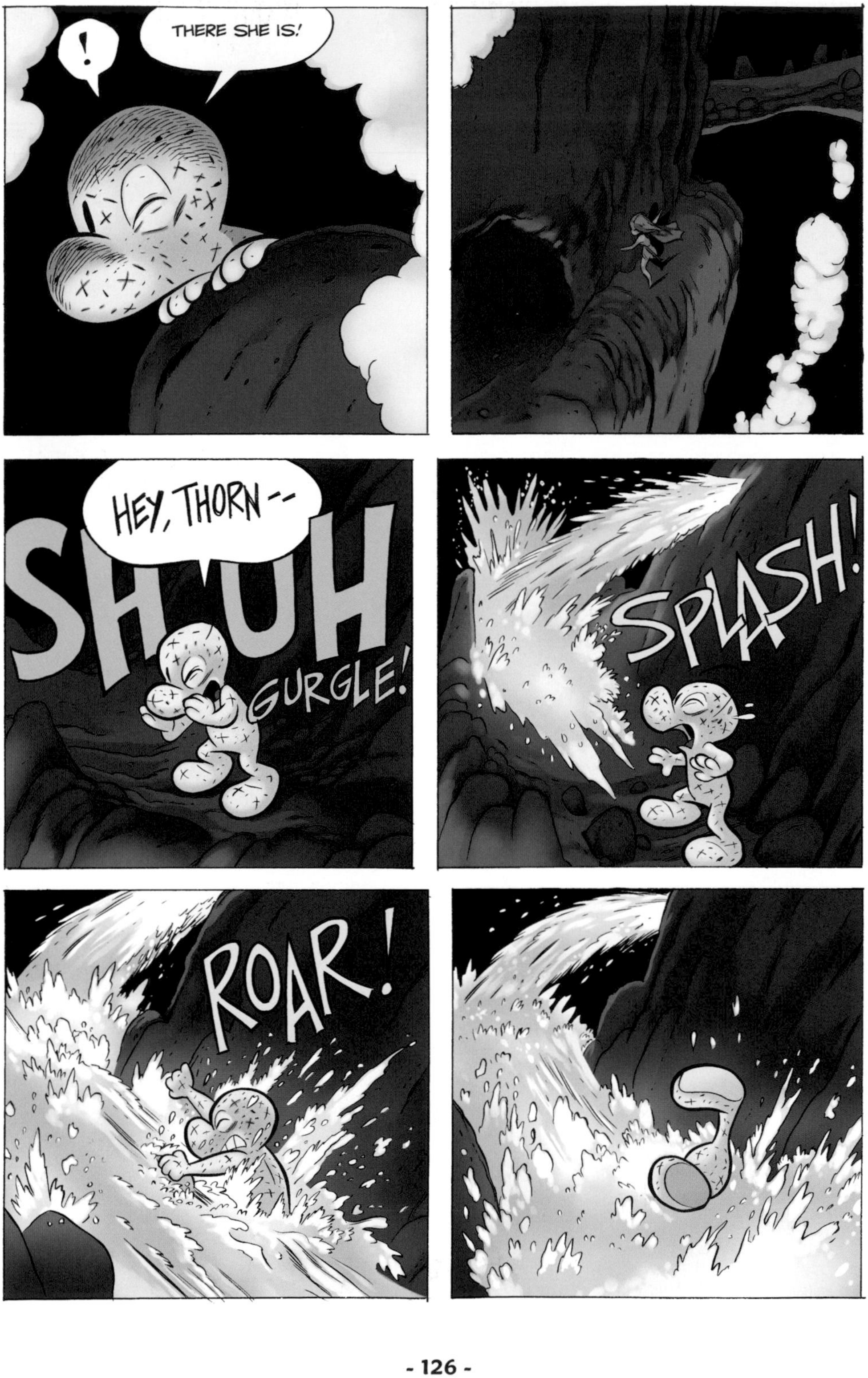
!
THERE SHE IS!
HEY, THORN --
SHUH
GURGLE!
SPLASH!
ROAR!

CROWN OF HORNS

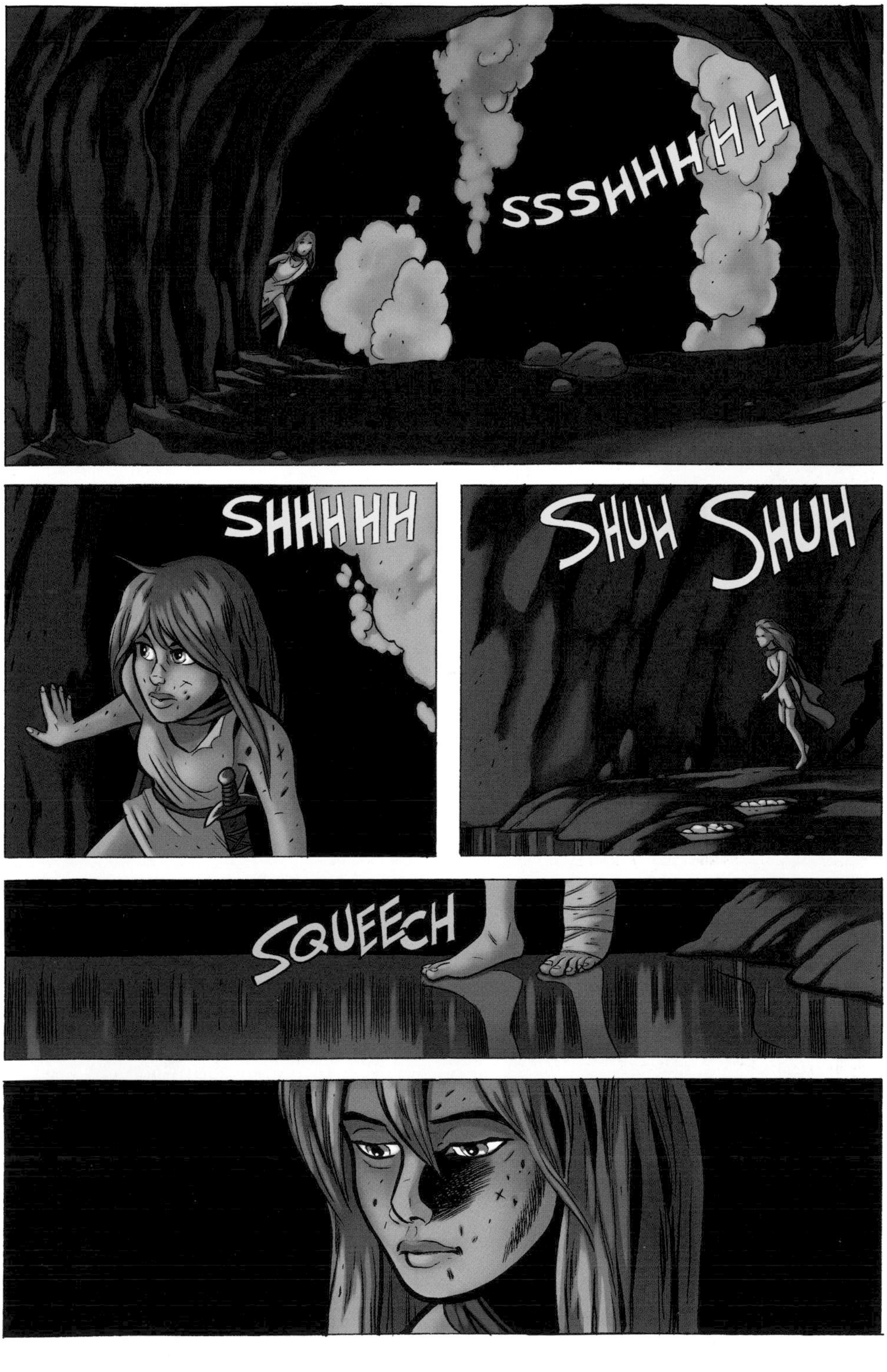
SSSHHHHHH
SHHHHH
SHUH SHUH
SQUEECH

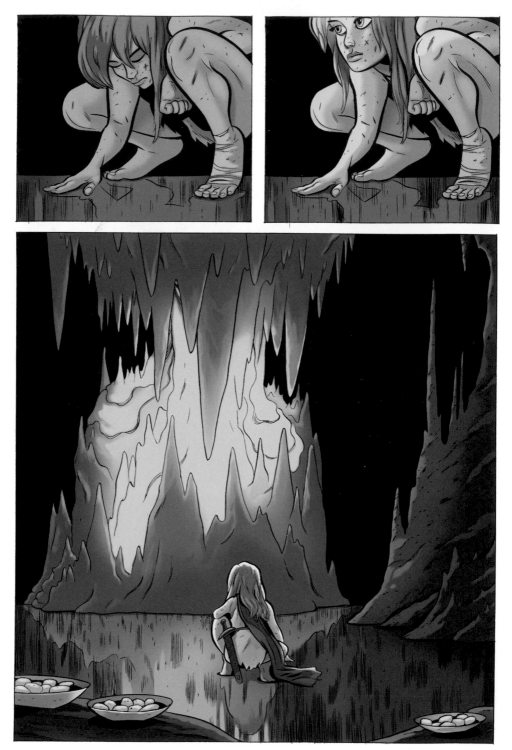

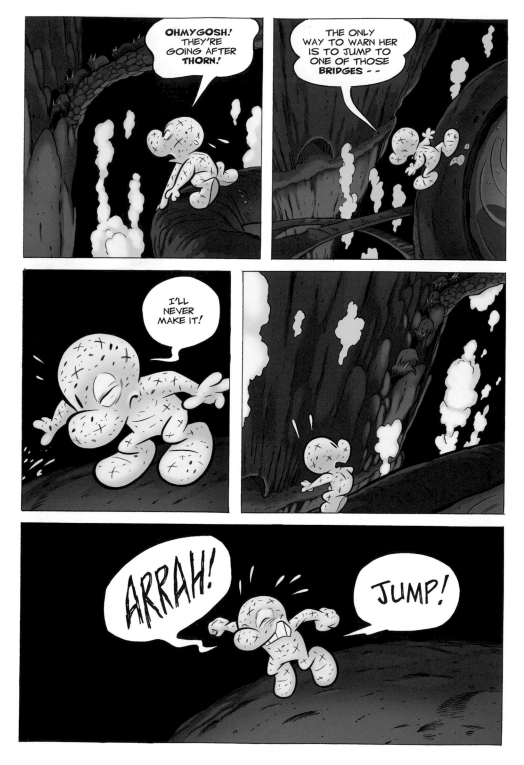

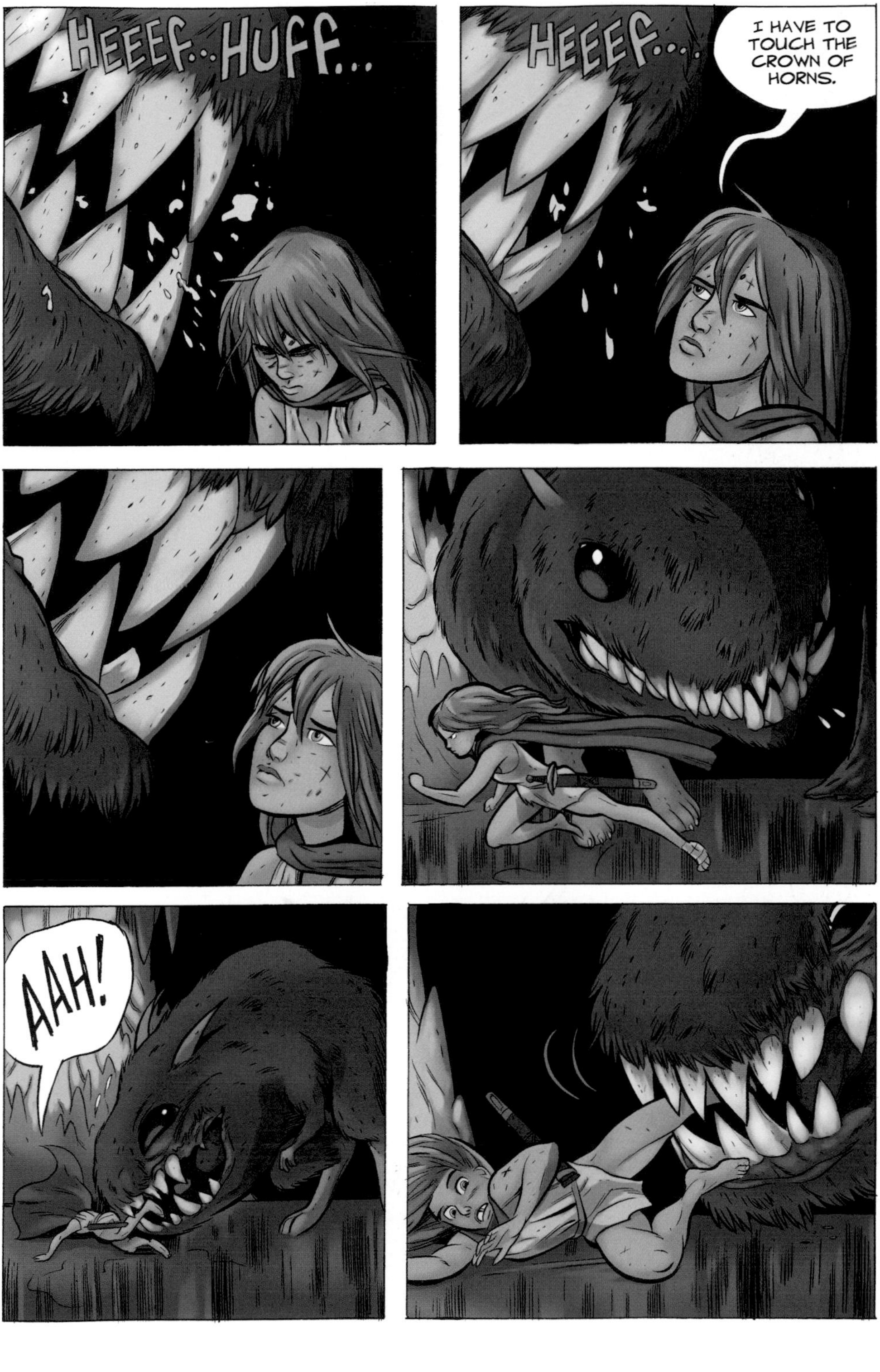
HEEEF...HUFF...
HEEEF...
I HAVE TO TOUCH THE CROWN OF HORNS.
AAH!

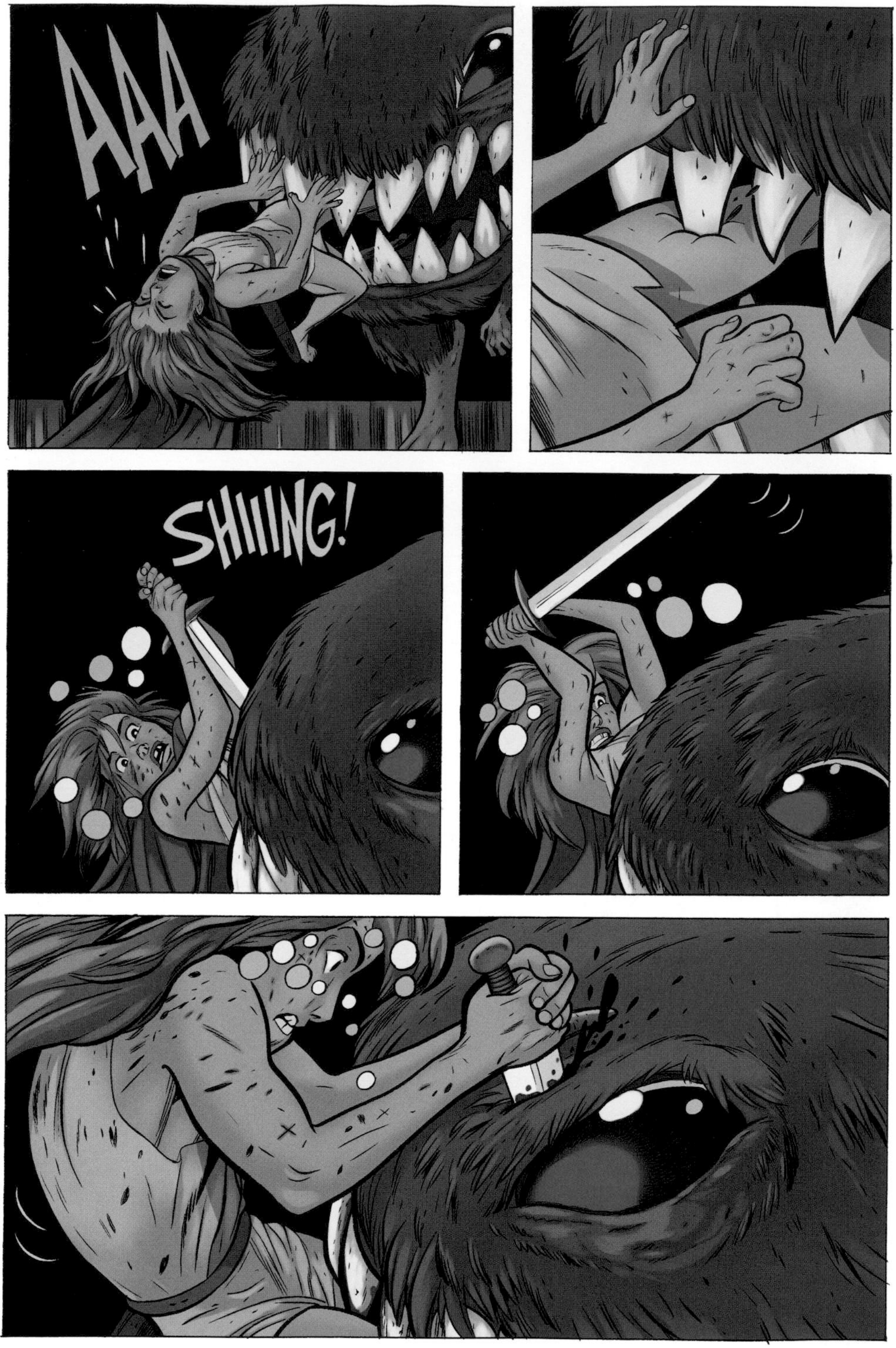
AAA
SHIIING!

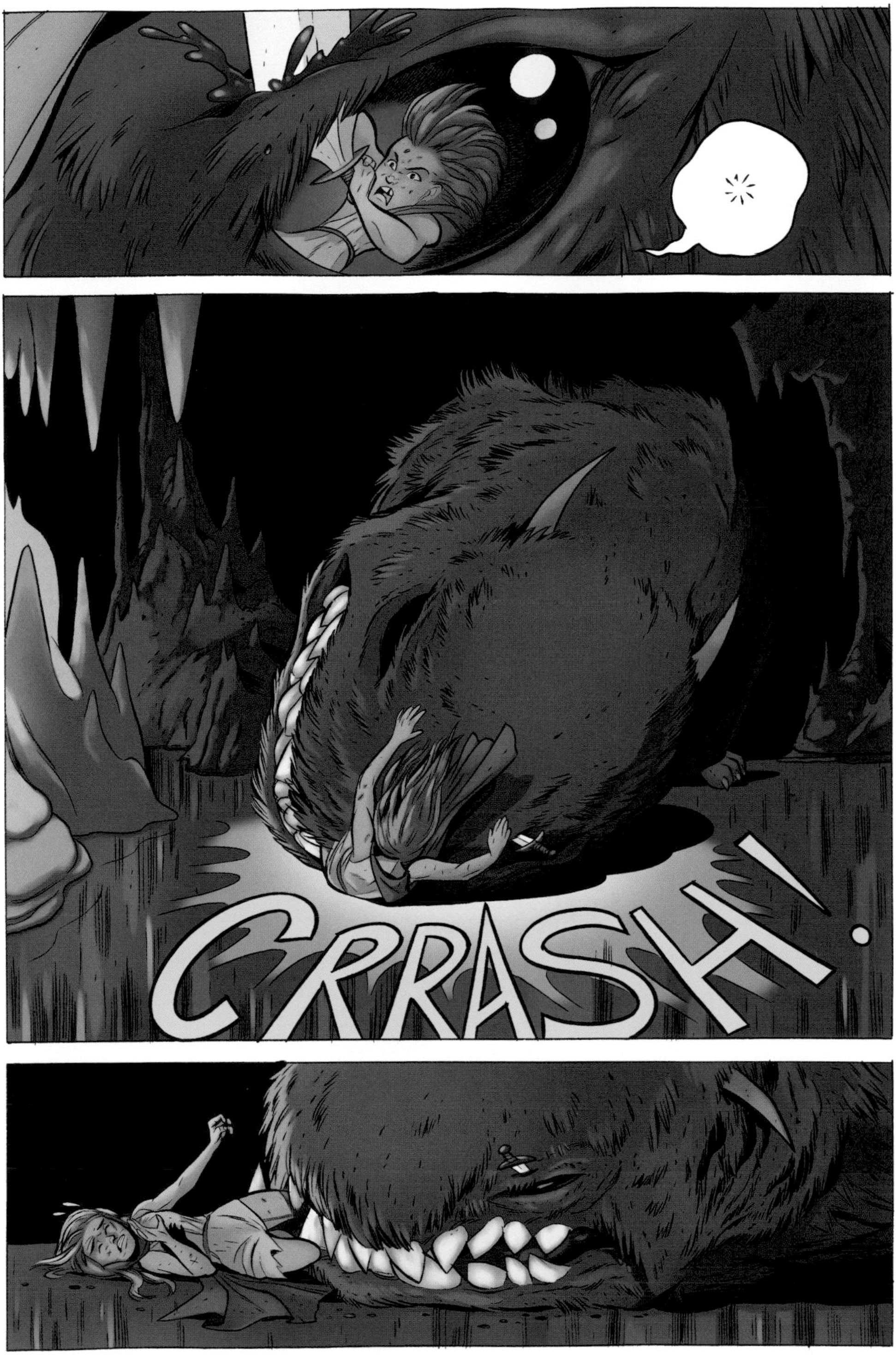
CRRASH!

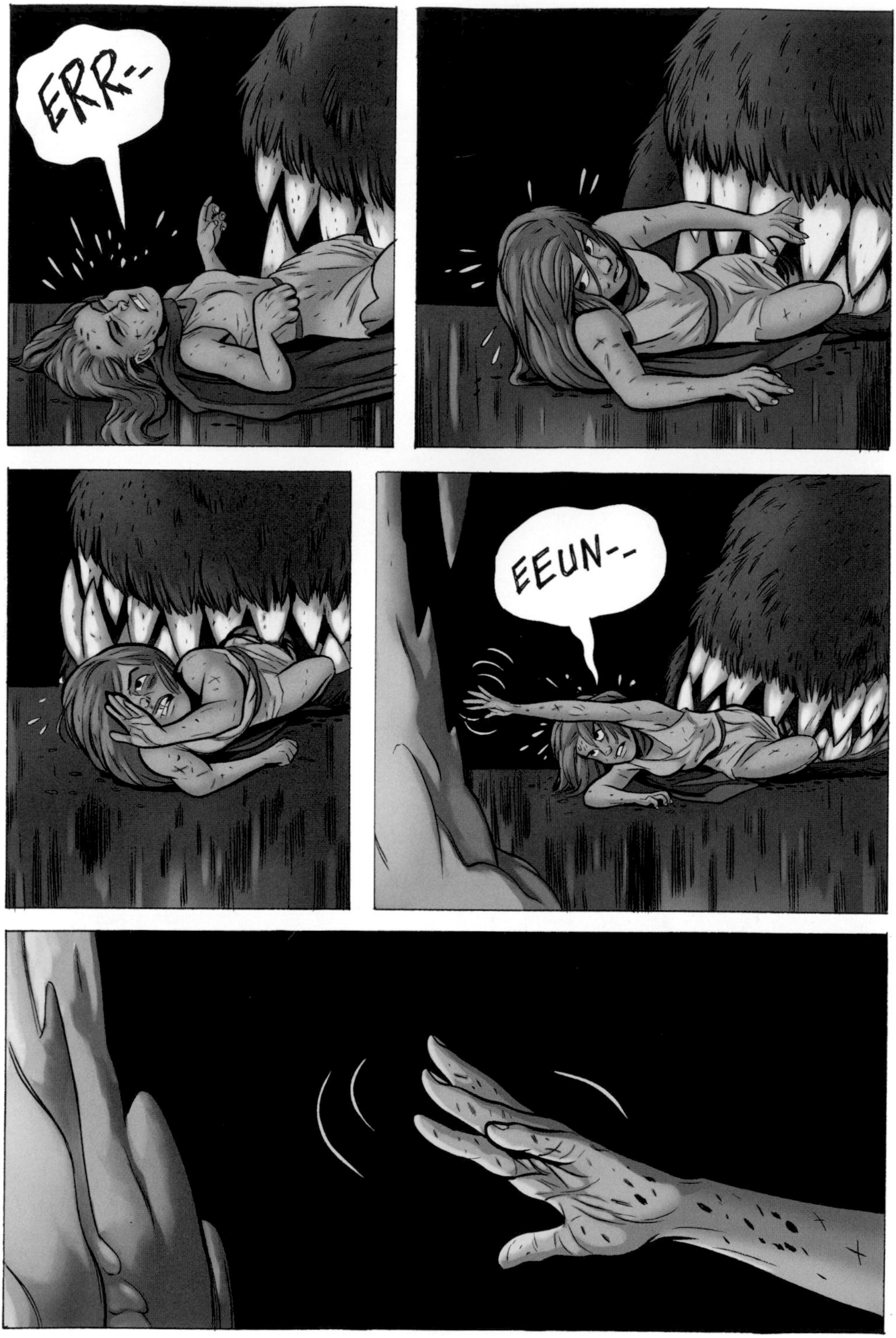
ERR-.
EEUN-.

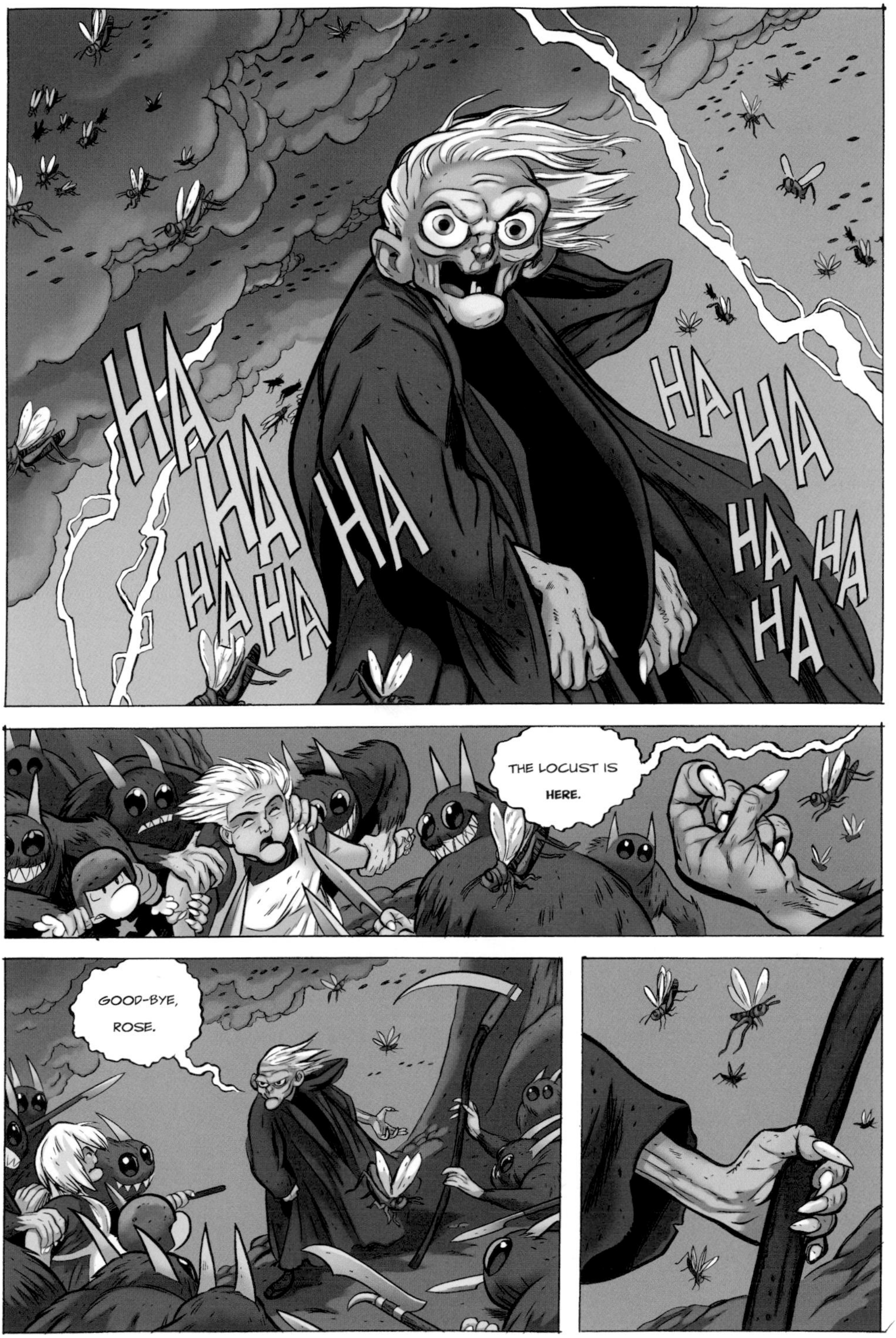
HA HA HA HA HA HA
HA HA HA HA HA HA HA HA
THE LOCUST IS HERE.
GOOD-BYE, ROSE.

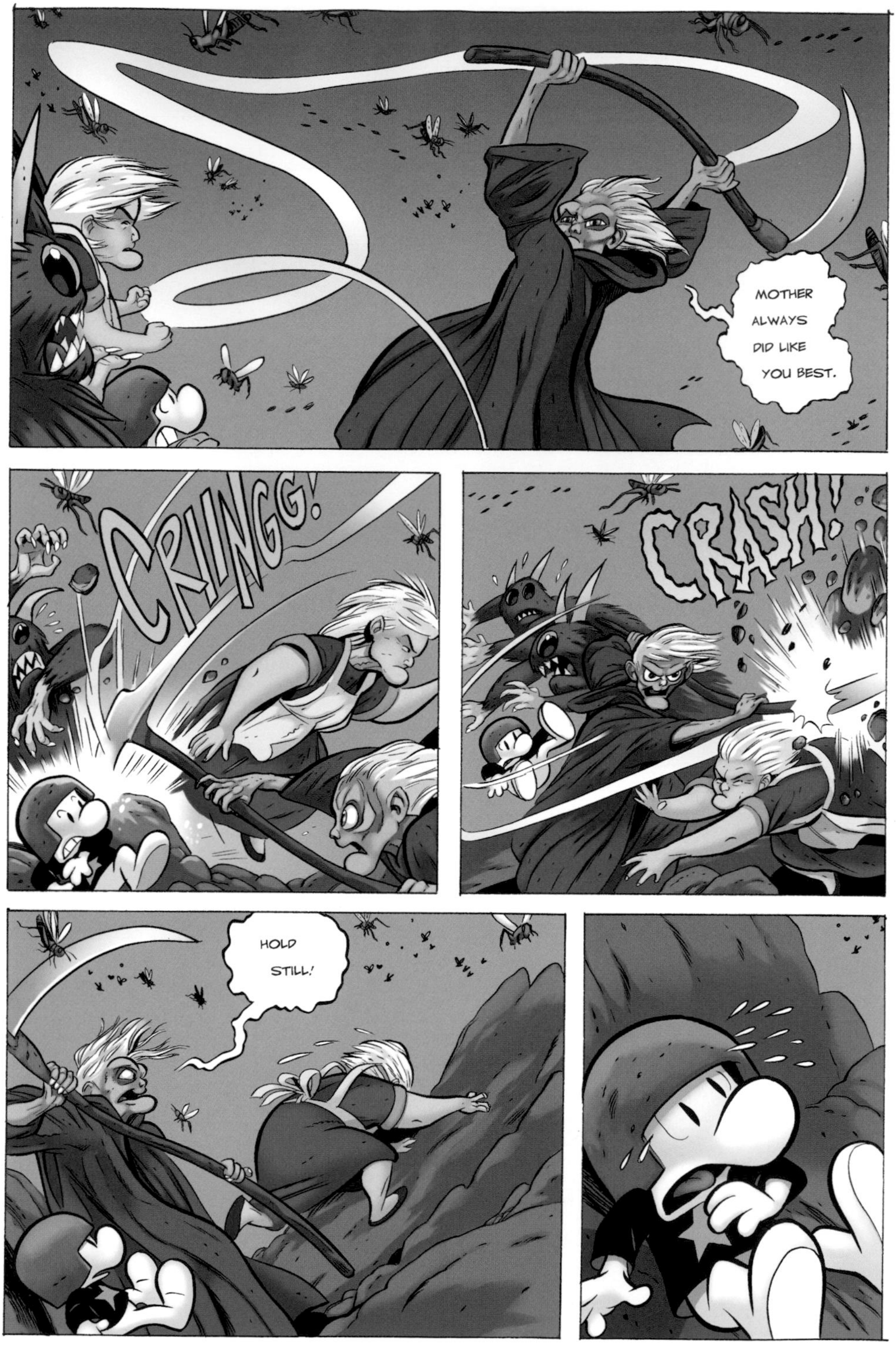
MOTHER ALWAYS DID LIKE YOU BEST.
CRIINGG!
CRASH!
HOLD STILL!

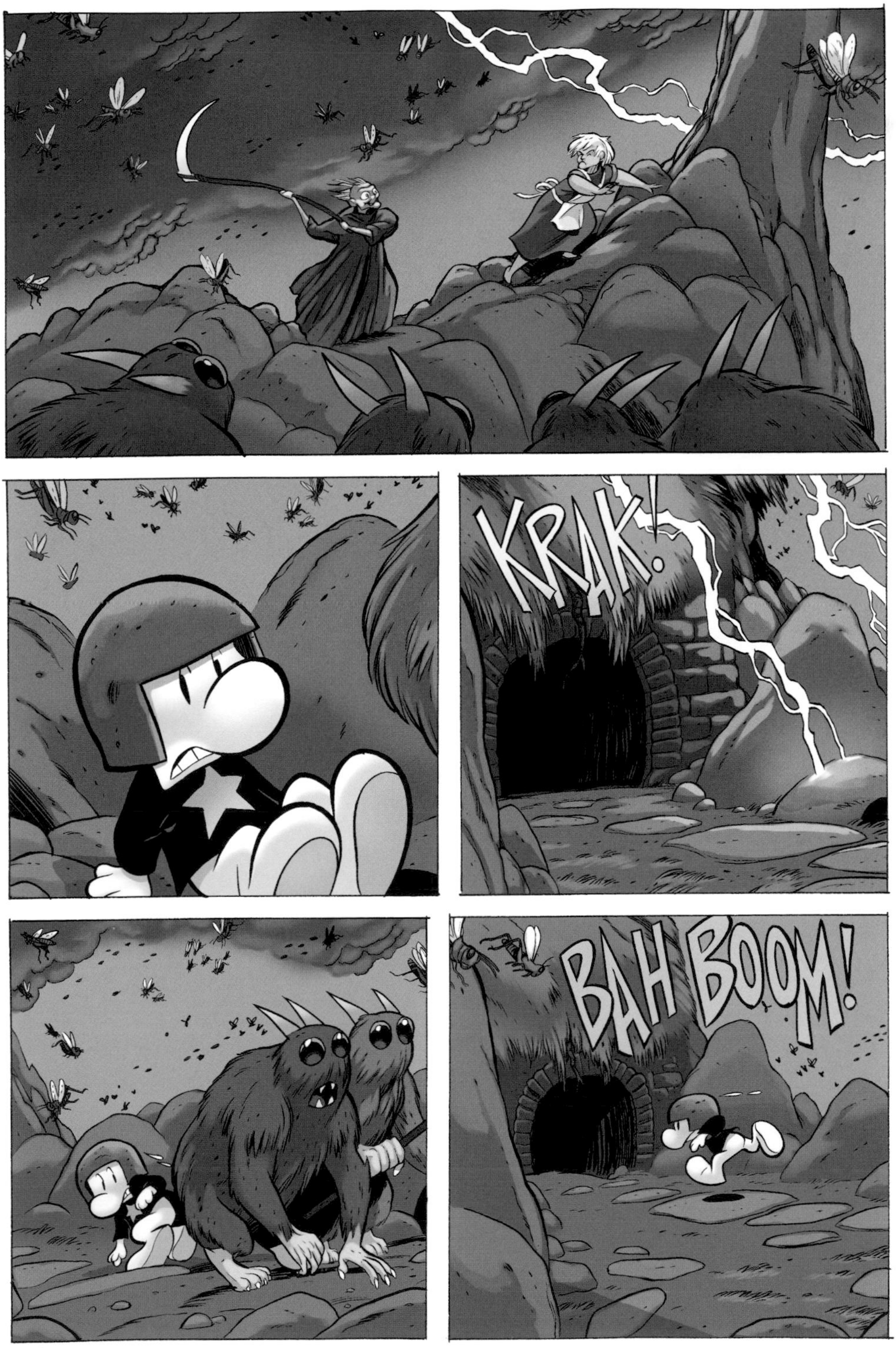
KRAK!
BAH BOOM!

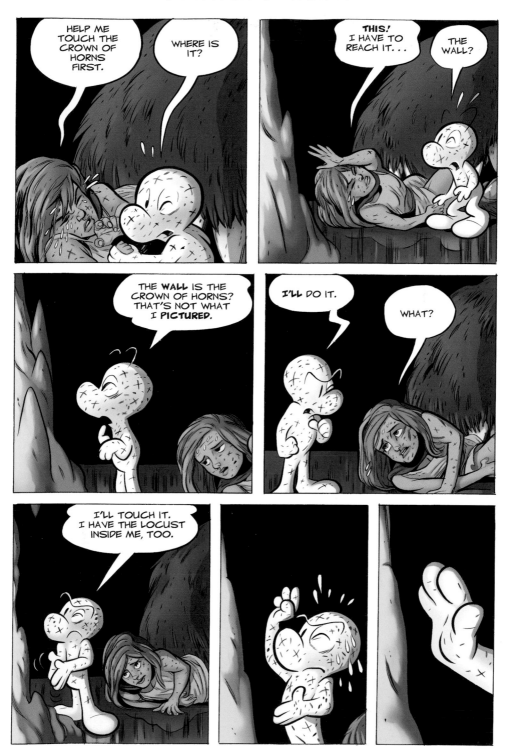

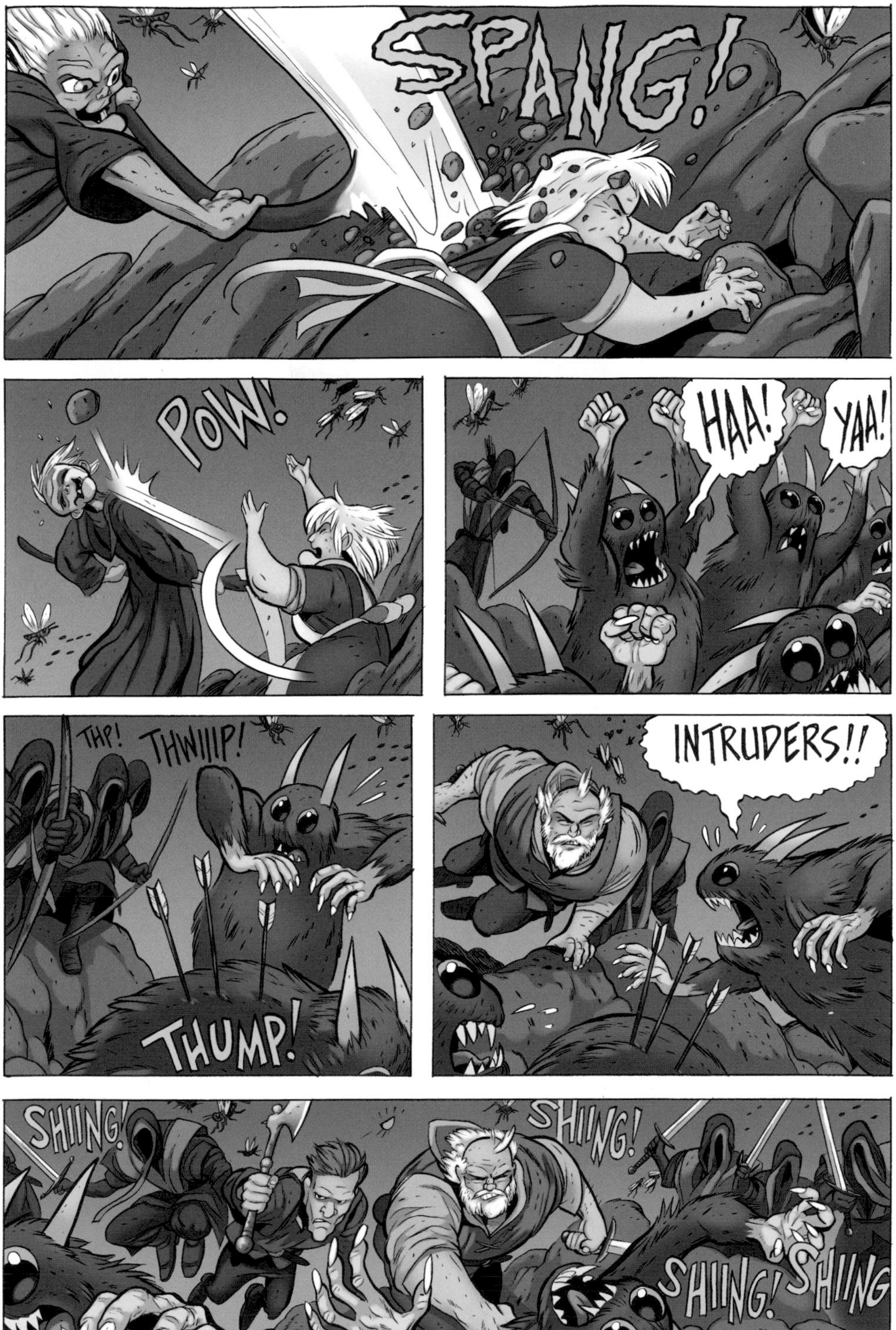
SPANG!
POW!
HAA!
YAA!
THP!
THWIIIP!
THUMP!
INTRUDERS!!
SHIING!
SHING!
SHIING!
SHIING

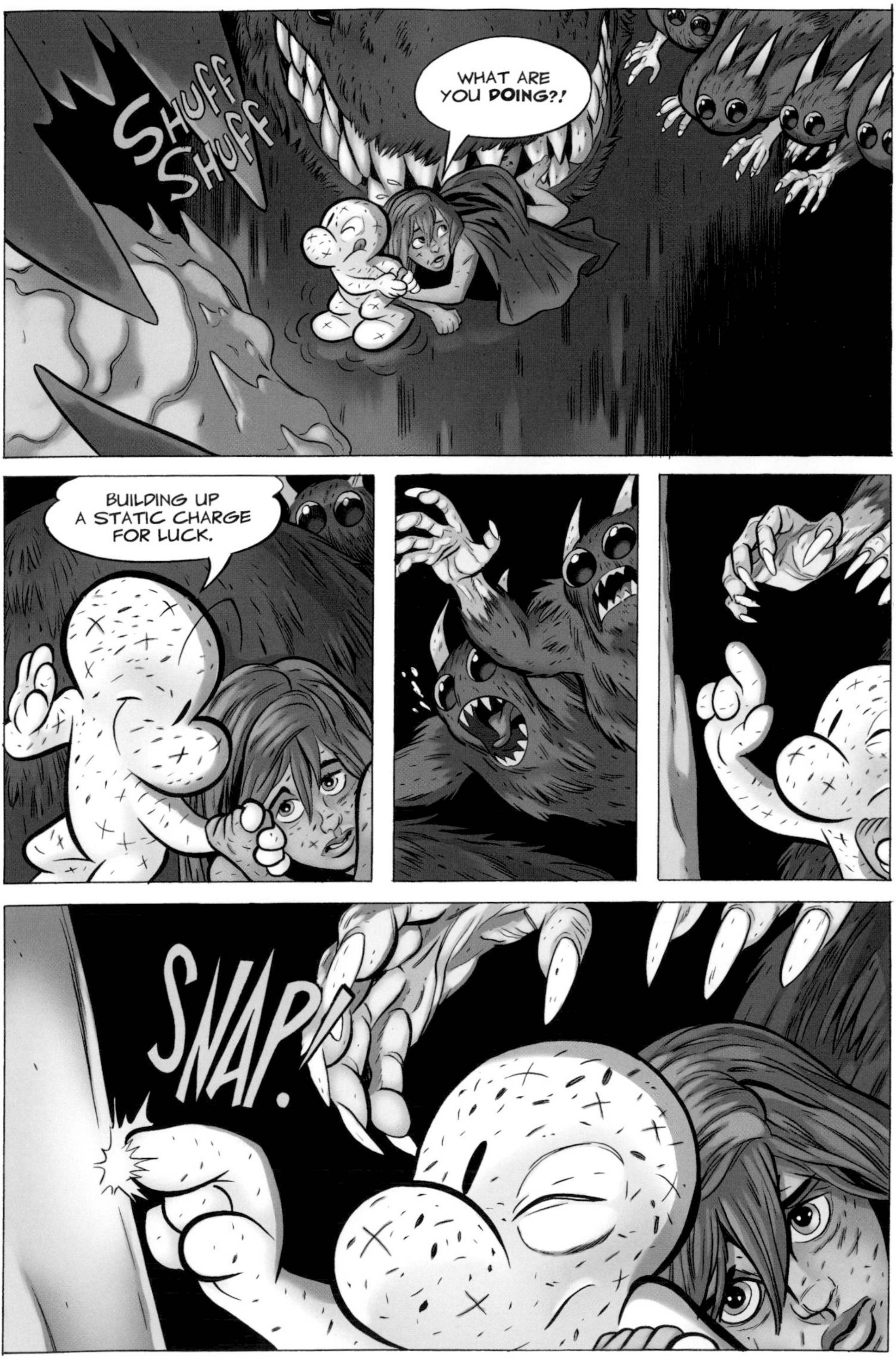
SHUFF SHUFF
WHAT ARE YOU DOING?!
BUILDING UP A STATIC CHARGE FOR LUCK.
SNAP!

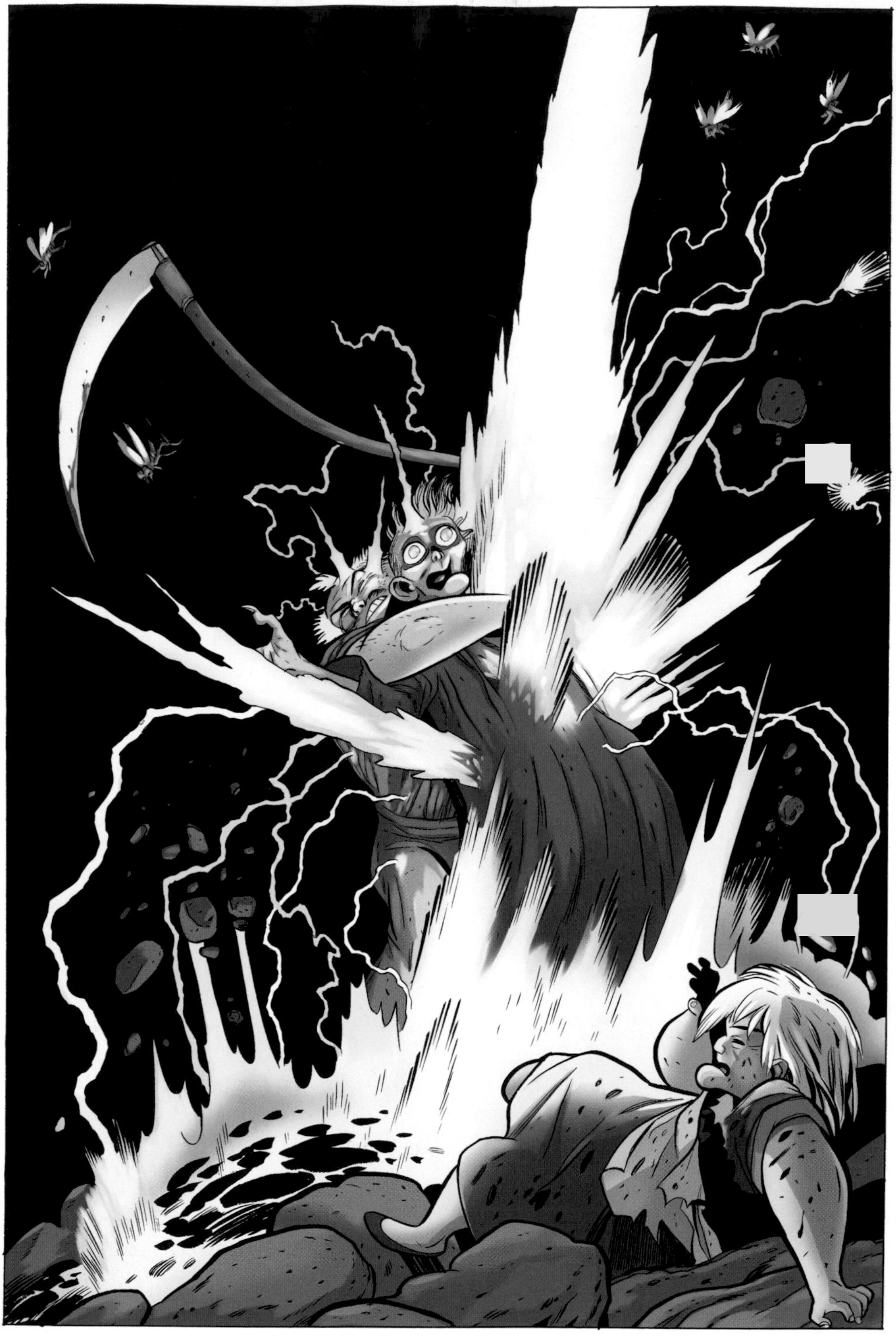

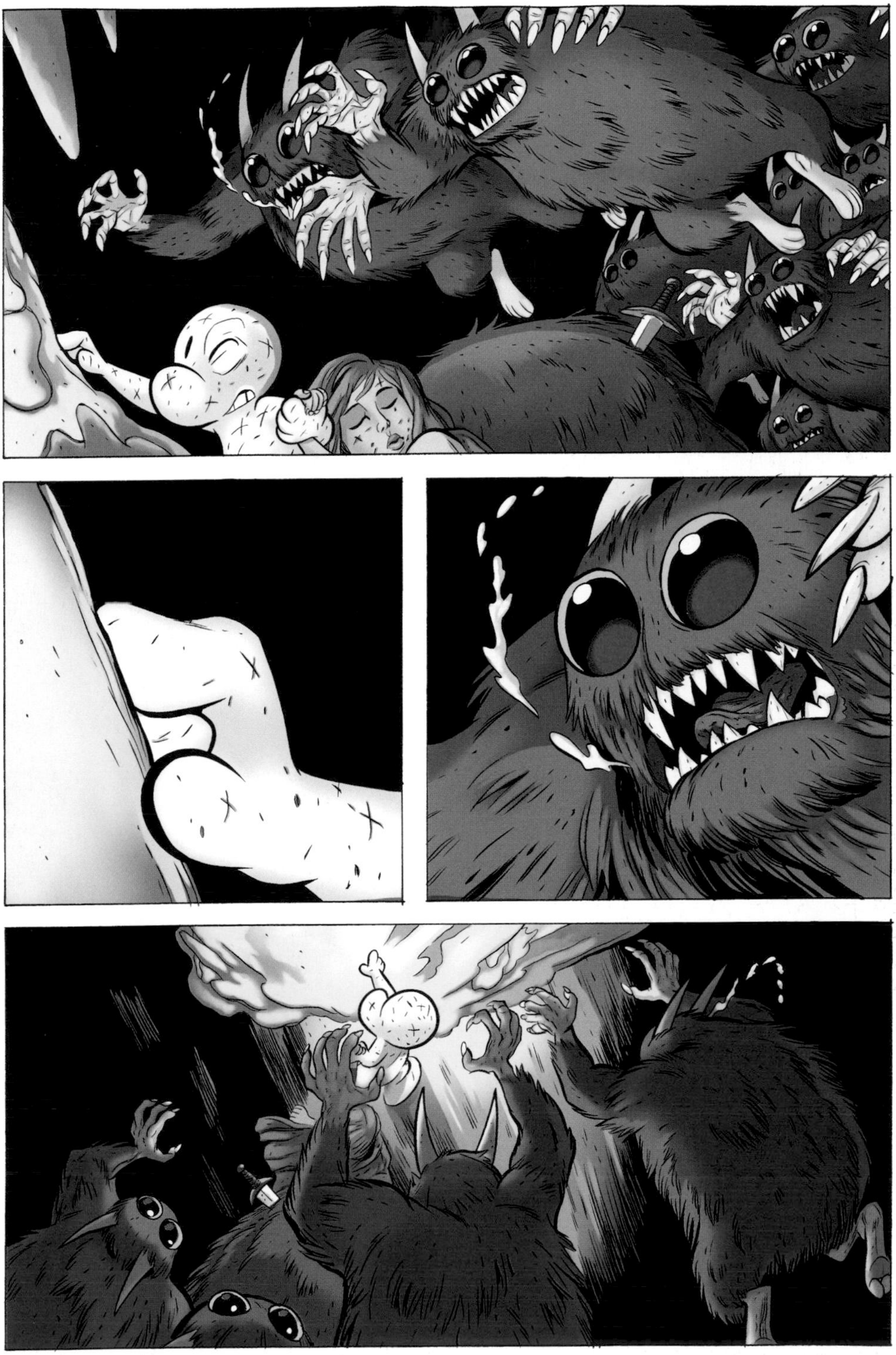

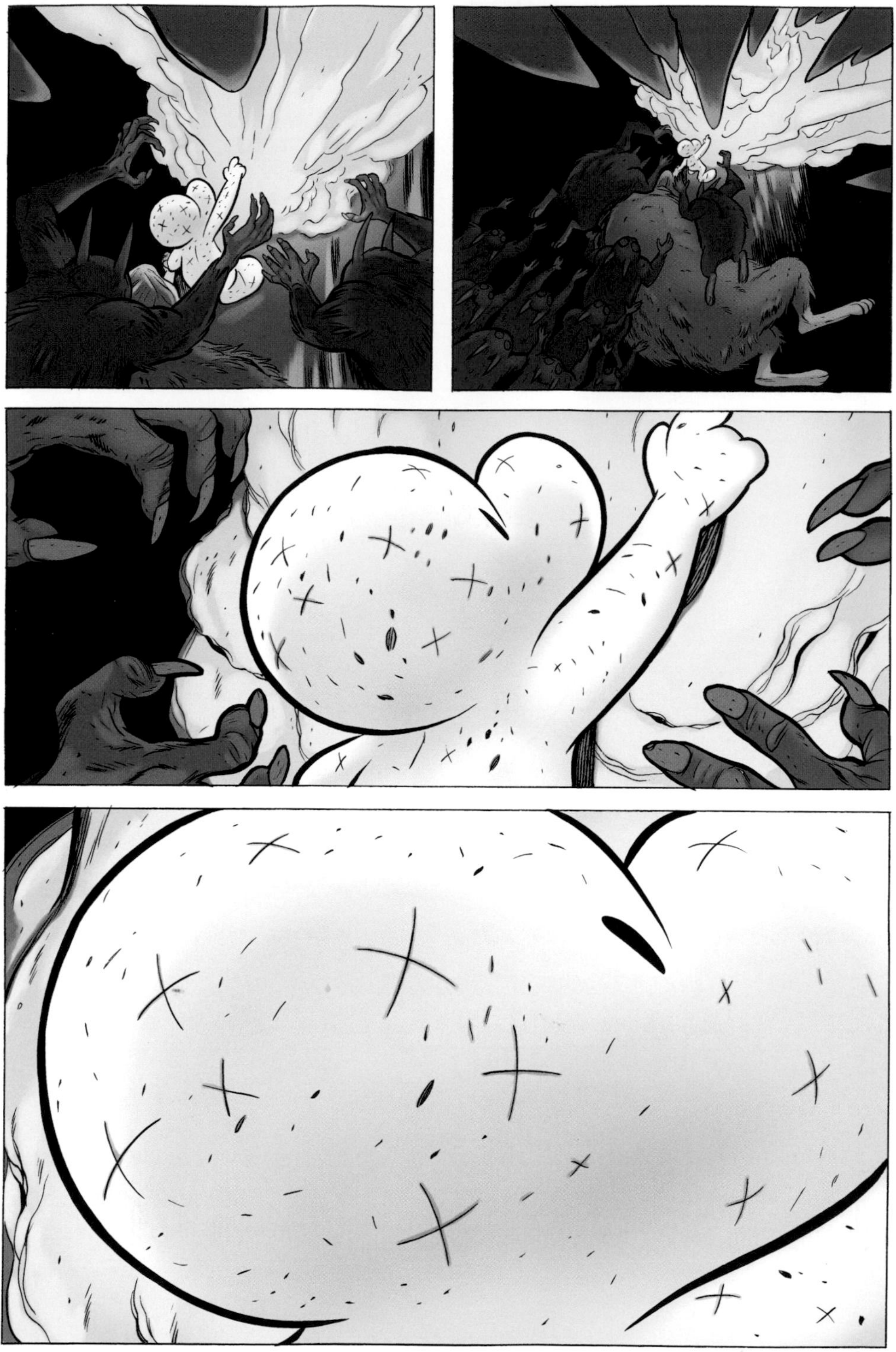

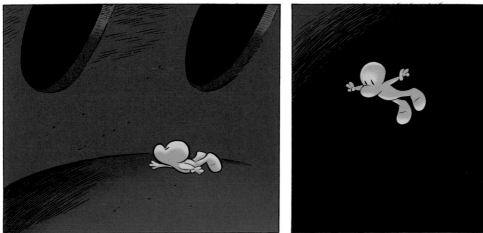

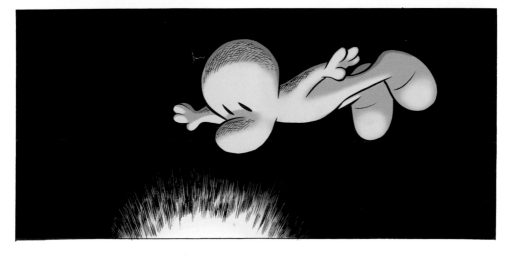

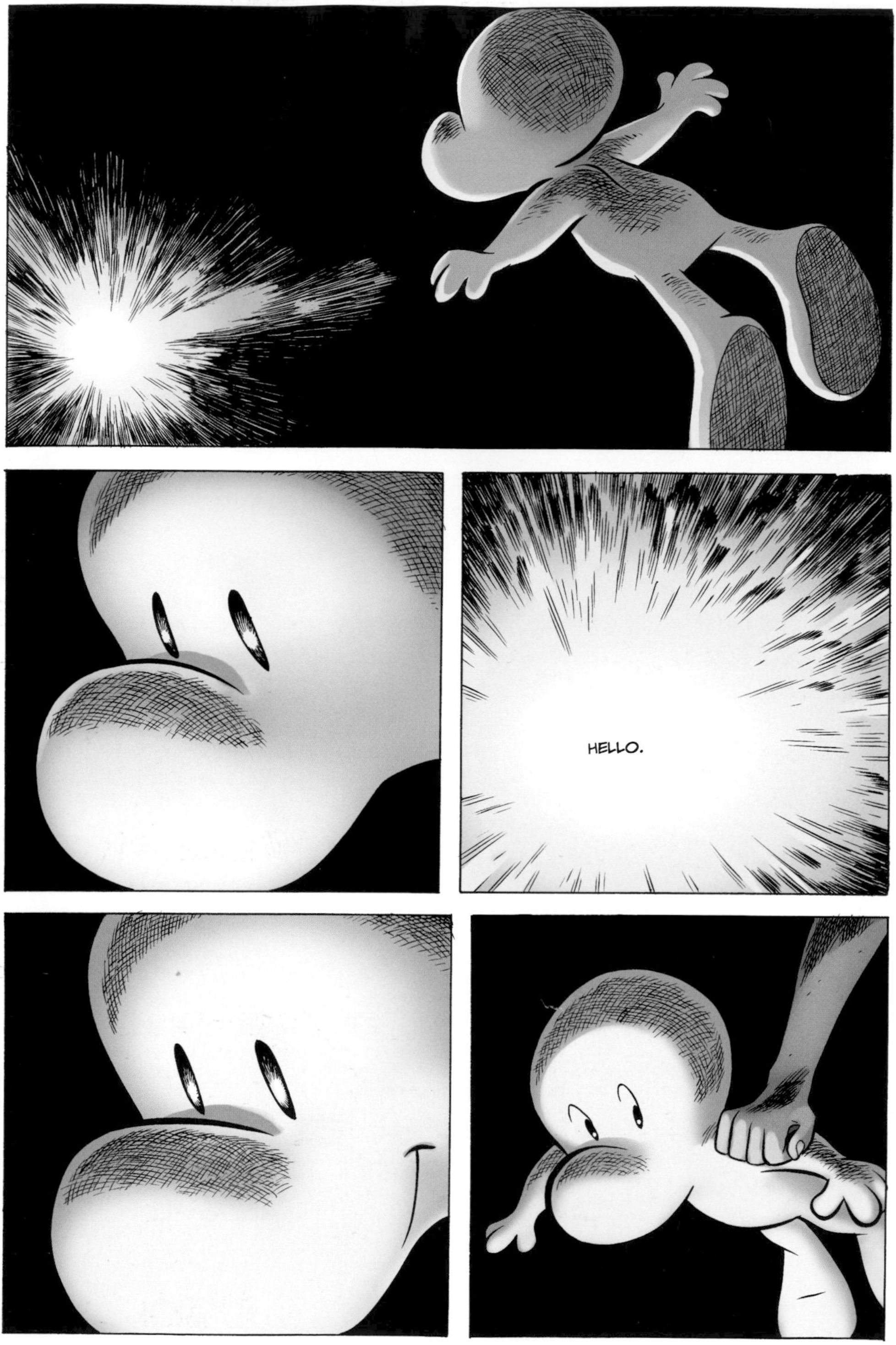
HELLO.

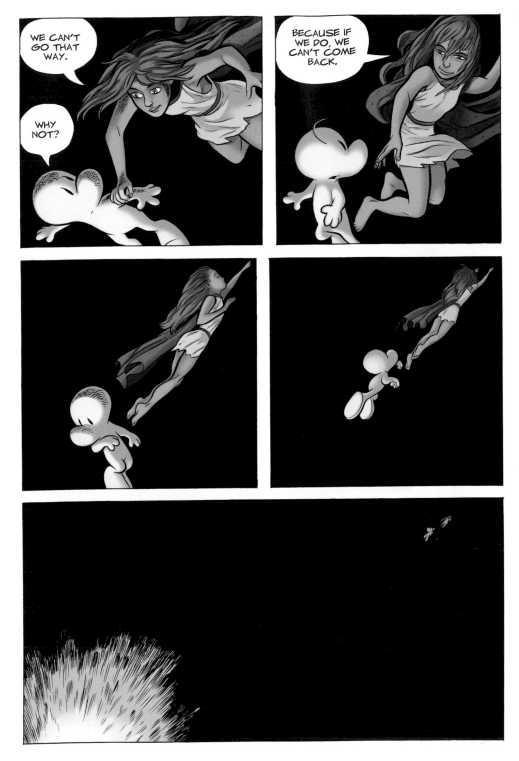

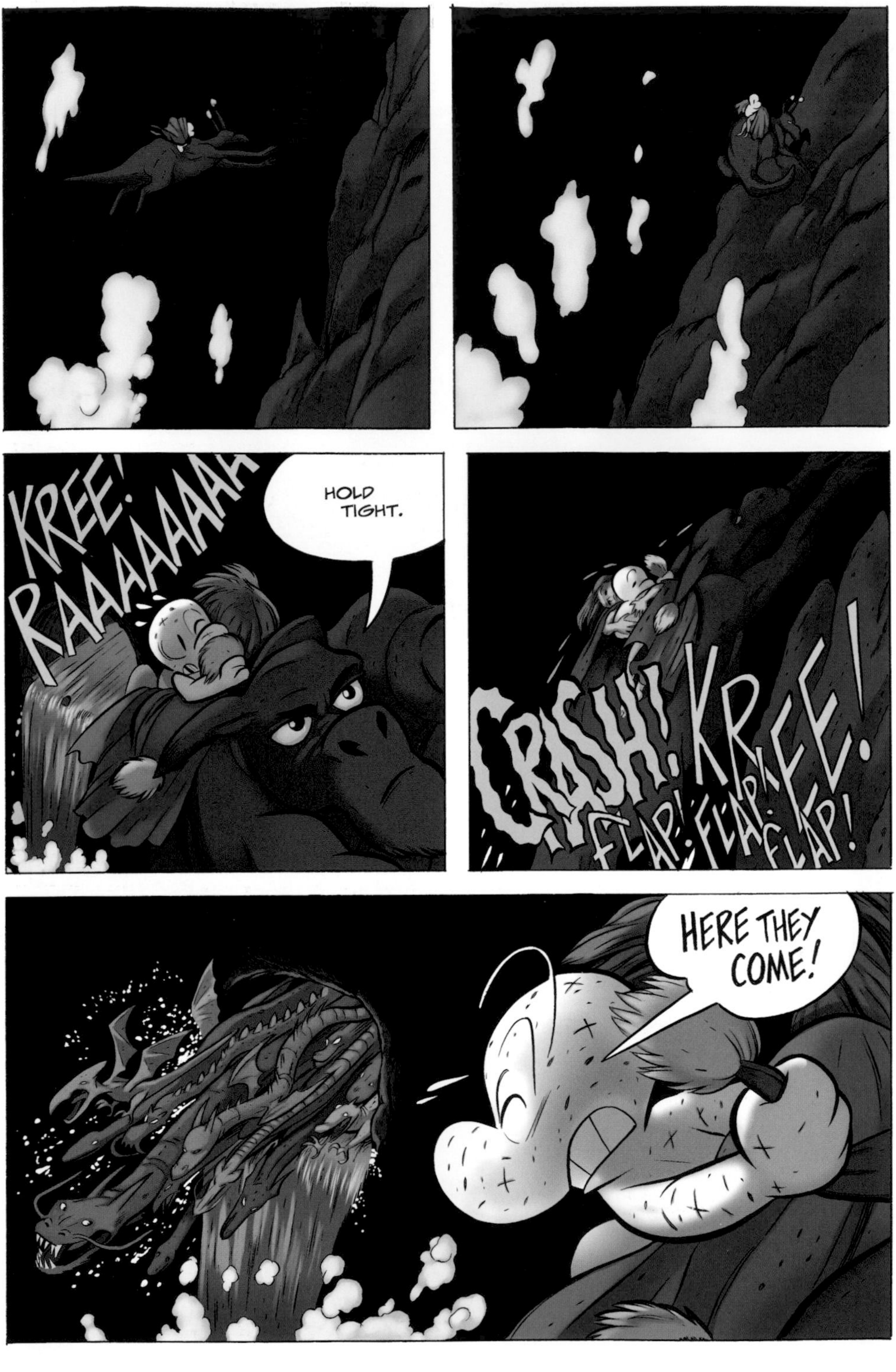
KREE! RAAAAAAAH
HOLD TIGHT.
CRASH! KR-EE!
FLAP! FLAP! FLAP!
HERE THEY COME!

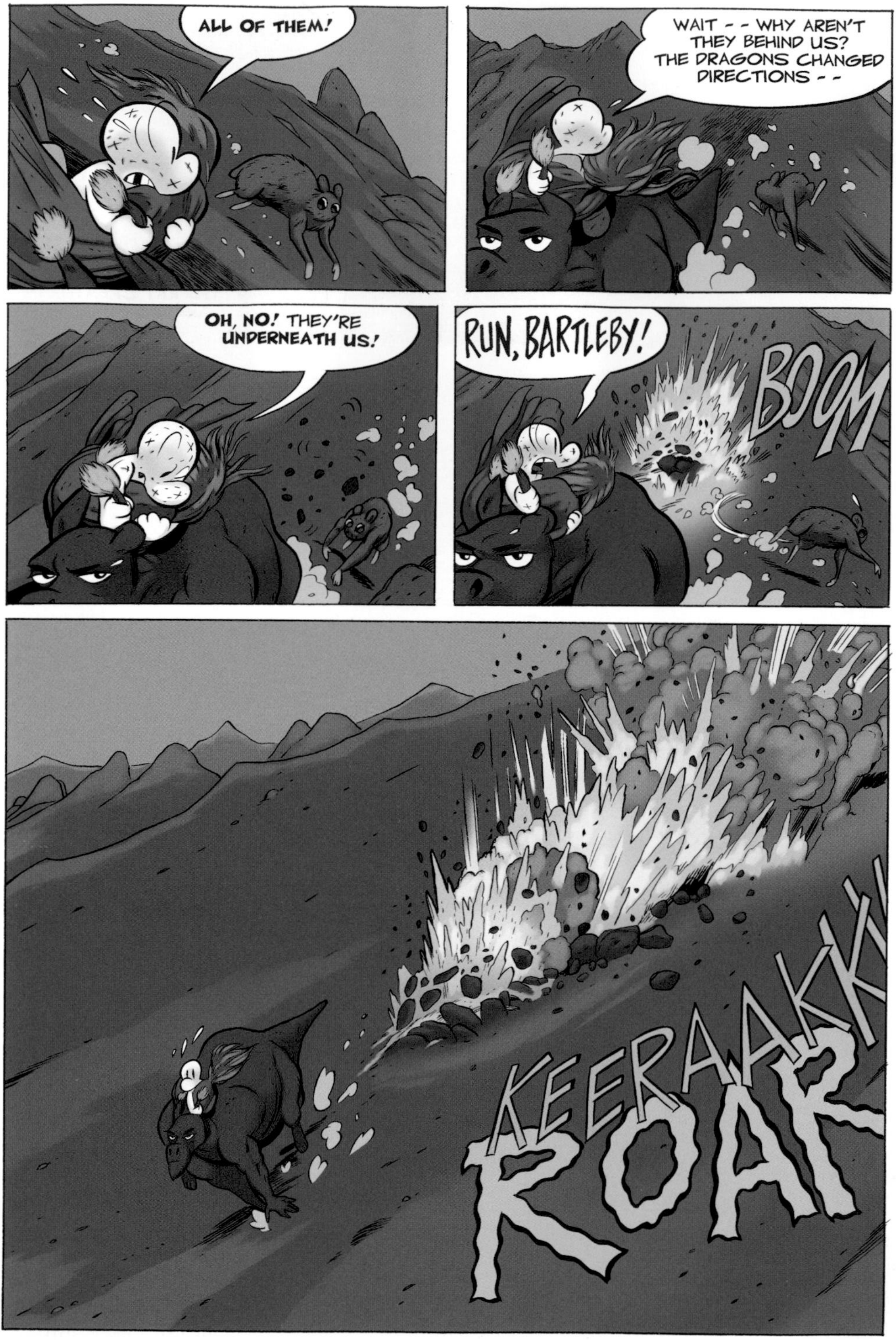
ALL OF THEM!
WAIT - - WHY AREN'T THEY BEHIND US? THE DRAGONS CHANGED DIRECTIONS - -
OH, NO! THEY'RE UNDERNEATH US!
RUN, BARTLEBY!
BOOM
KEERAAKK
ROAR

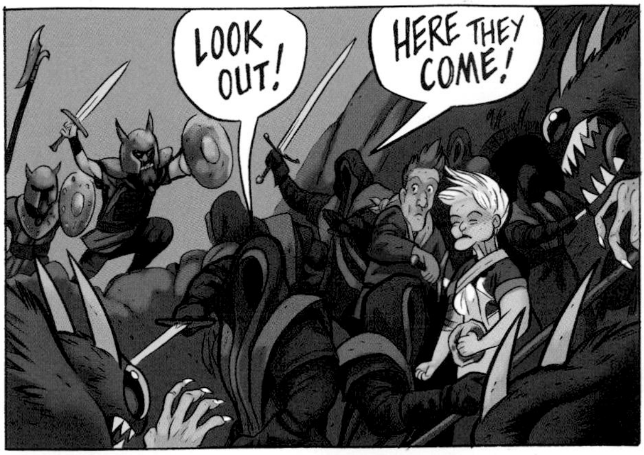
LOOK OUT!
HERE THEY COME!

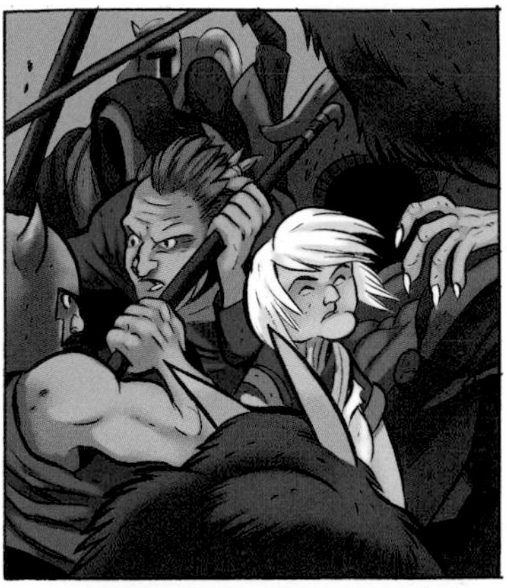

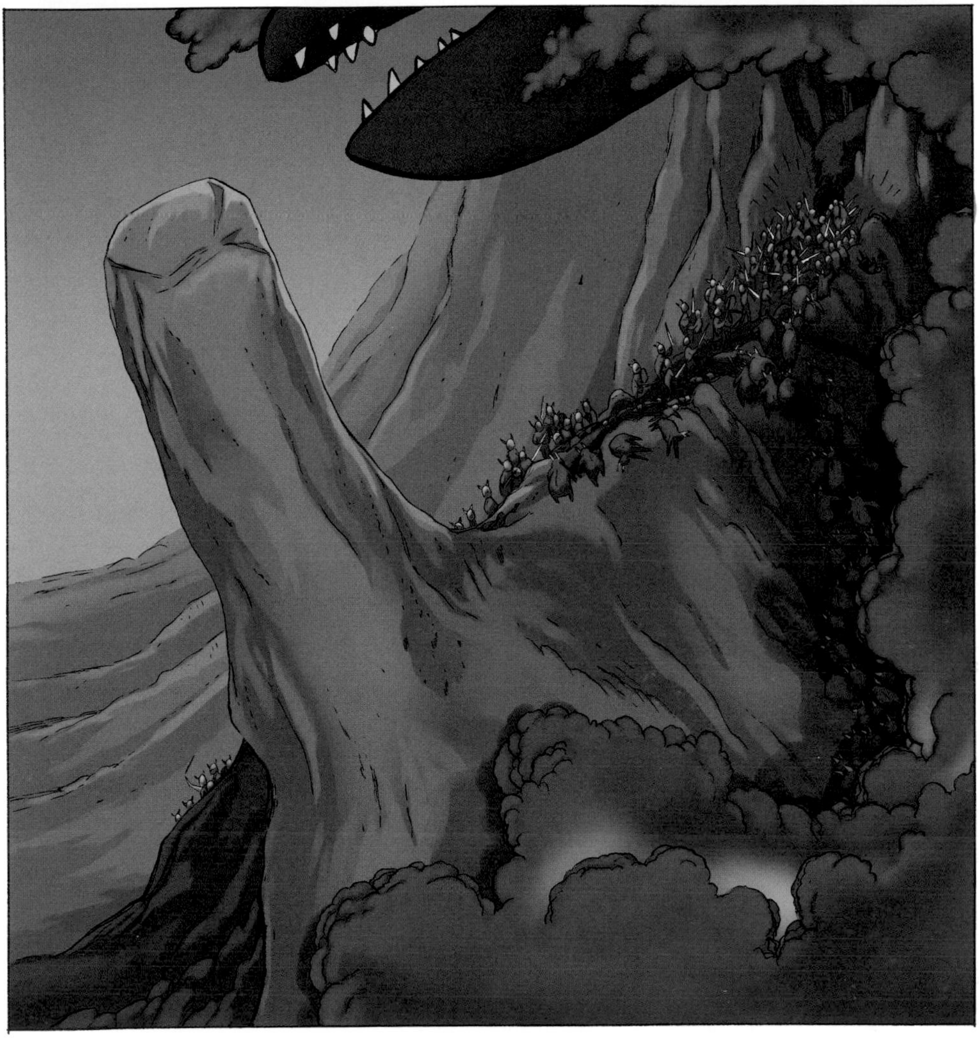

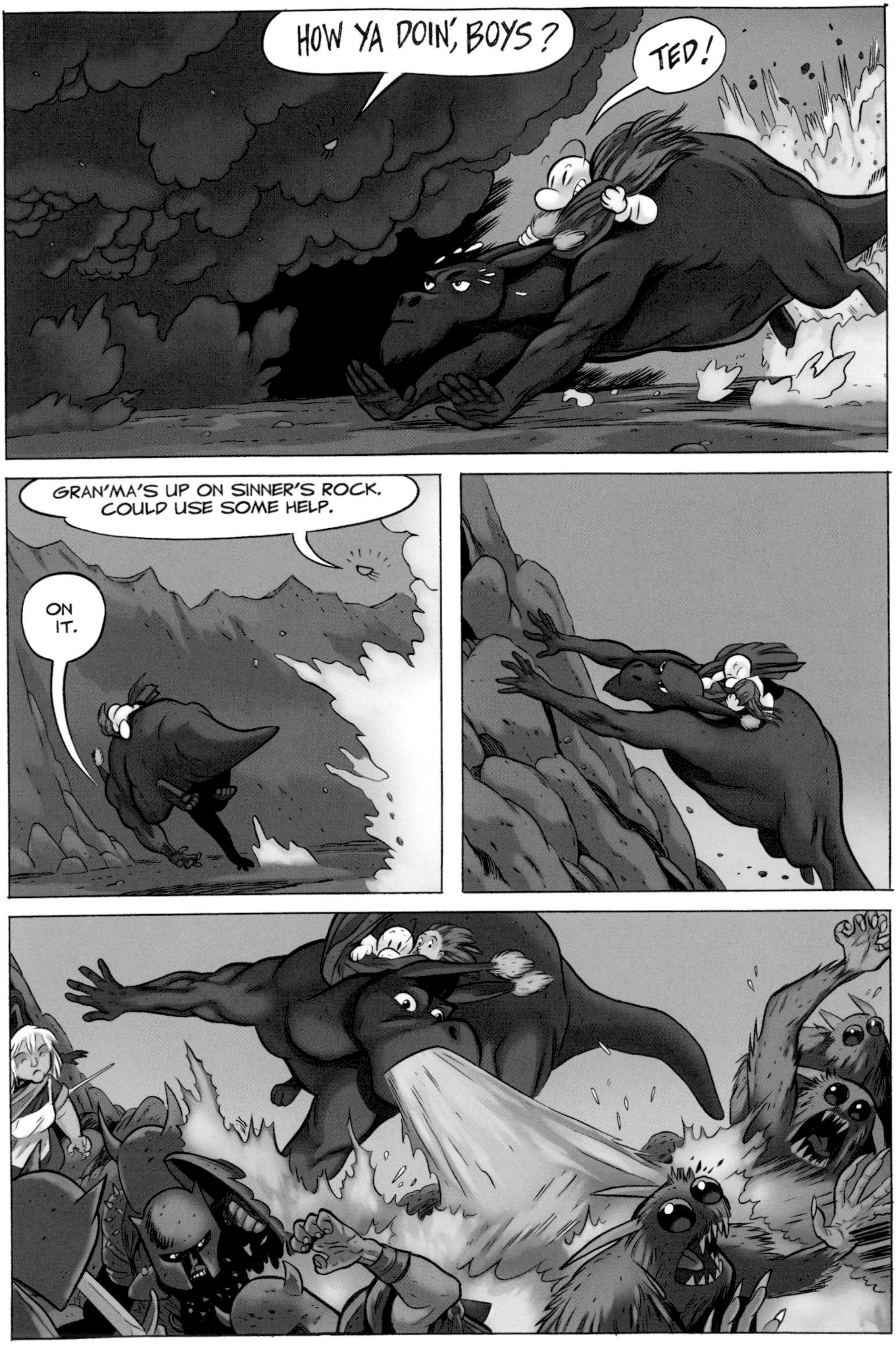
HOW YA DOIN', BOYS?
TED!
GRAN'MA'S UP ON SINNER'S ROCK. COULD USE SOME HELP.
ON IT.

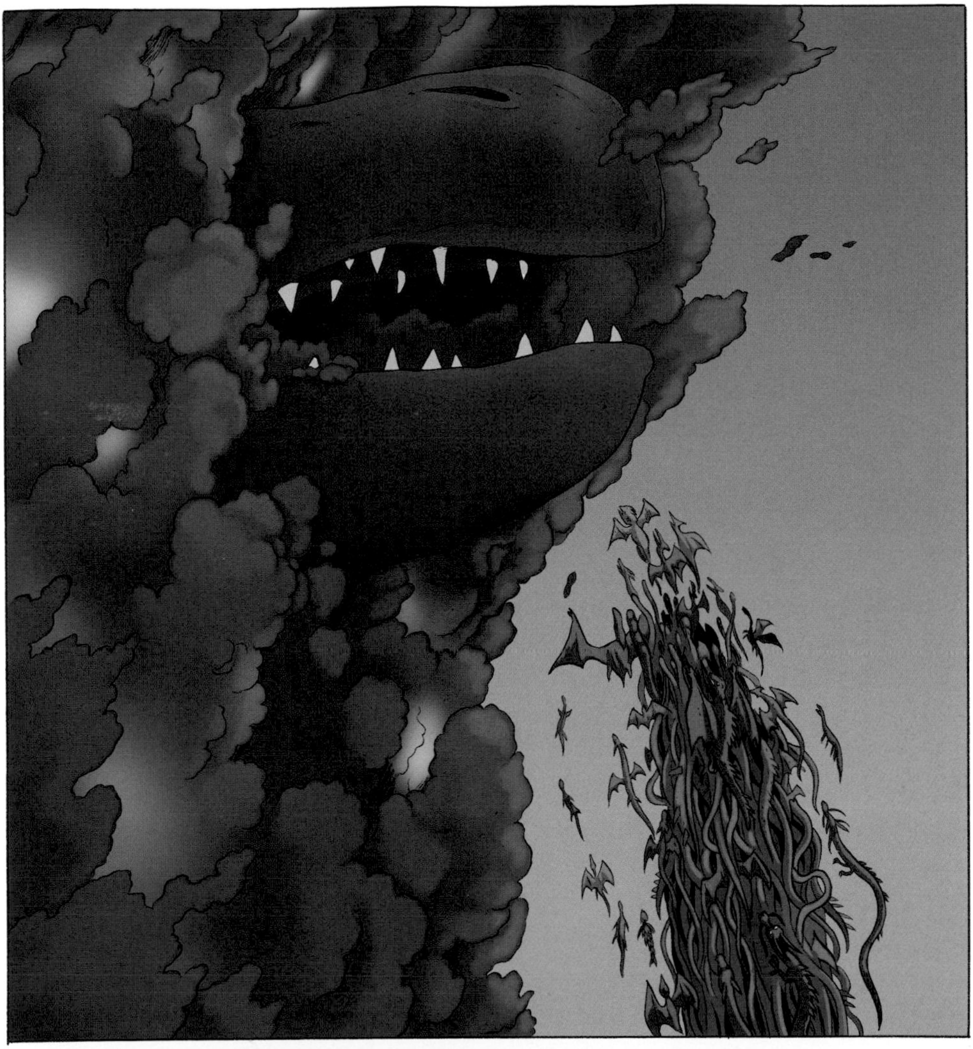

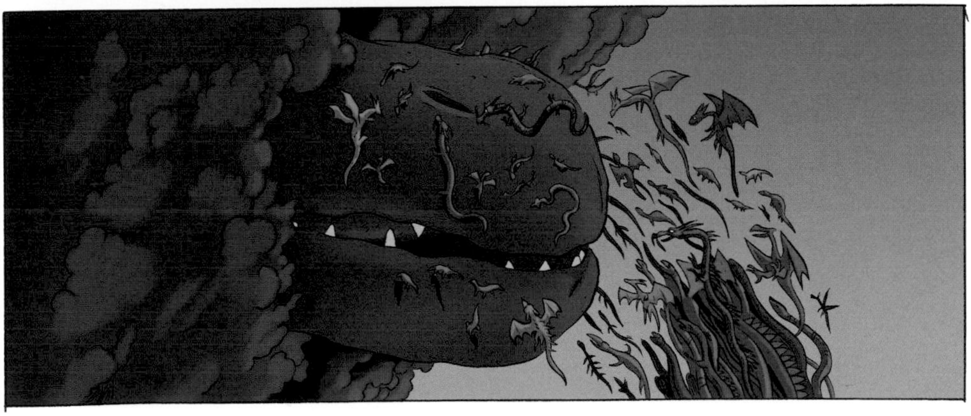

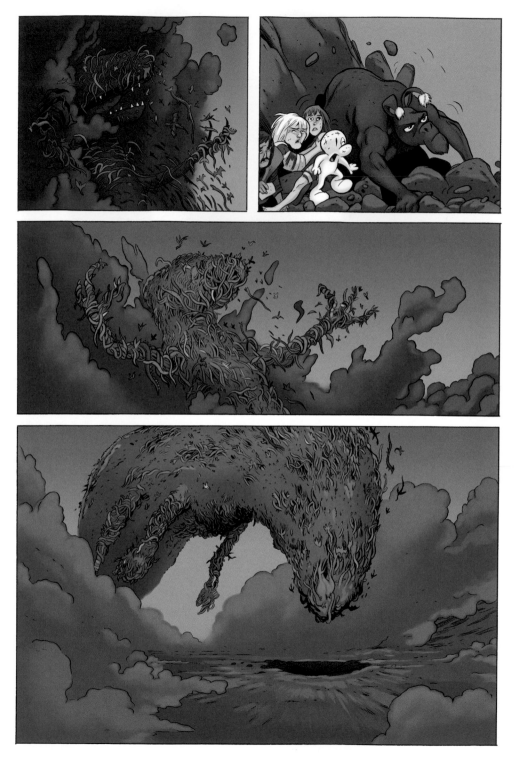

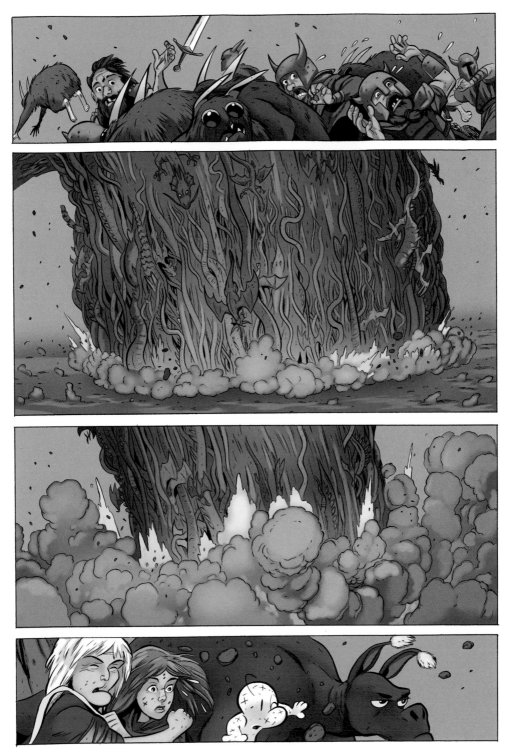

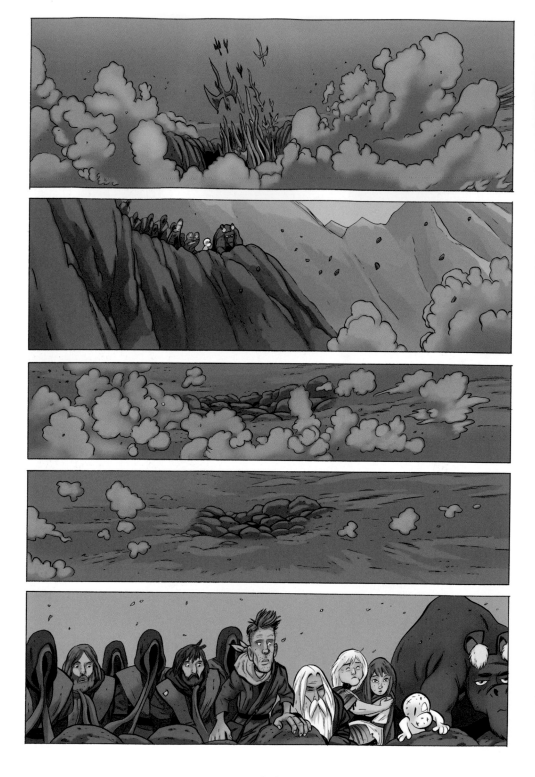

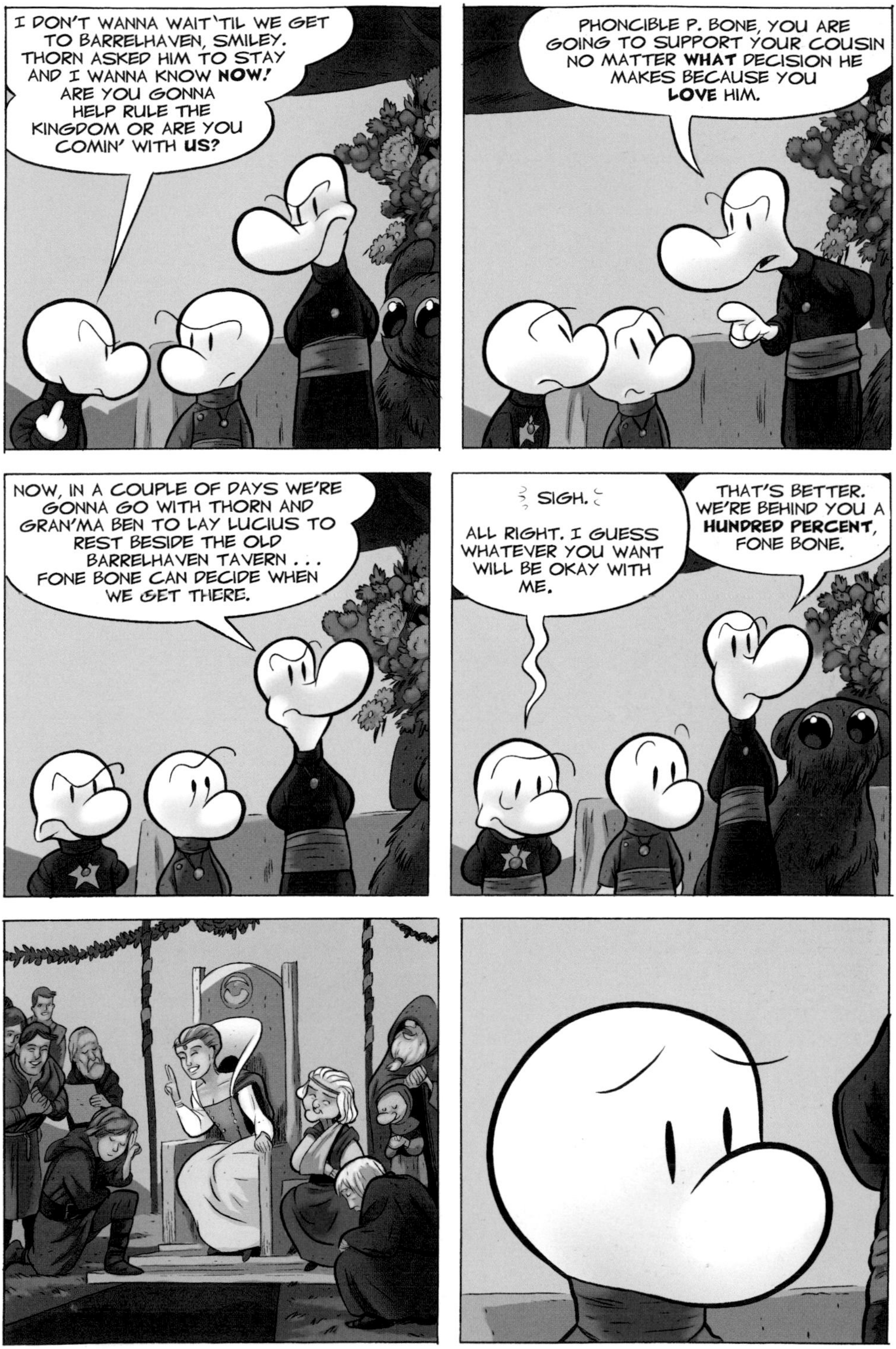
I DON'T WANNA WAIT 'TIL WE GET TO BARRELHAVEN, SMILEY. THORN ASKED HIM TO STAY AND I WANNA KNOW NOW! ARE YOU GONNA HELP RULE THE KINGDOM OR ARE YOU COMIN' WITH US?
PHONCIBLE P. BONE, YOU ARE GOING TO SUPPORT YOUR COUSIN NO MATTER WHAT DECISION HE MAKES BECAUSE YOU LOVE HIM.
NOW, IN A COUPLE OF DAYS WE'RE GONNA GO WITH THORN AND GRAN'MA BEN TO LAY LUCIUS TO REST BESIDE THE OLD BARRELHAVEN TAVERN . . . FONE BONE CAN DECIDE WHEN WE GET THERE.
SIGH.
ALL RIGHT. I GUESS WHATEVER YOU WANT WILL BE OKAY WITH ME.
THAT'S BETTER. WE'RE BEHIND YOU A HUNDRED PERCENT, FONE BONE.

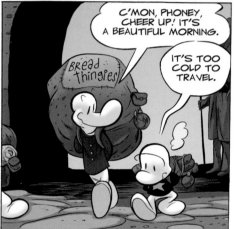

C'MON, PHONEY, CHEER UP! IT'S A BEAUTIFUL MORNING.

IT'S TOO COLD TO TRAVEL.

Bread Thingies

LUCIUS LOVED THE LATE FALL. I THINK HE'D BE HAPPY TRAVELING TO THE NORTH WOODS THIS TIME OF YEAR.

THANK YOU FOR DOING THIS, DEAR.

WAIT!

TANEAL!

I BROUGHT YOU A NEW PRAYER STONE! IT WILL BRING THE BLESSING OF THE DRAGONS UPON YOUR JOURNEY!

HOMECOMING

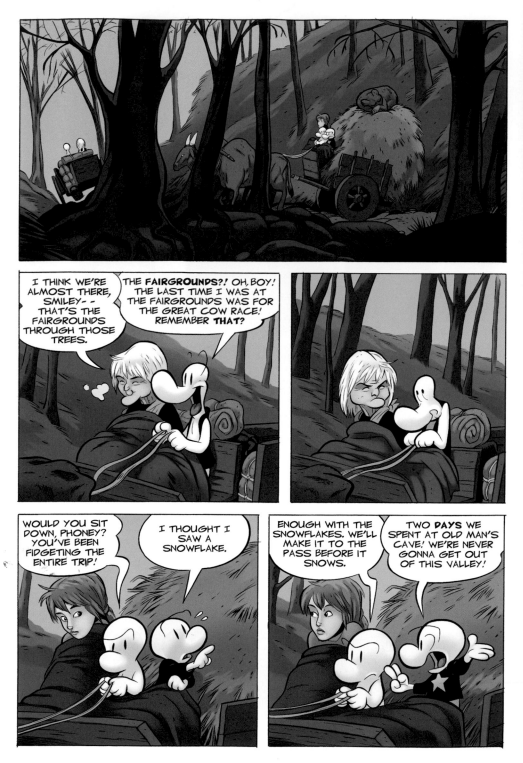

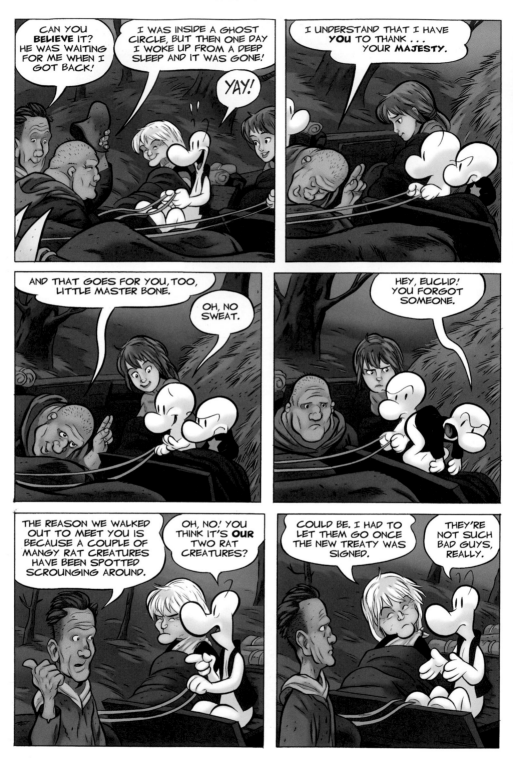

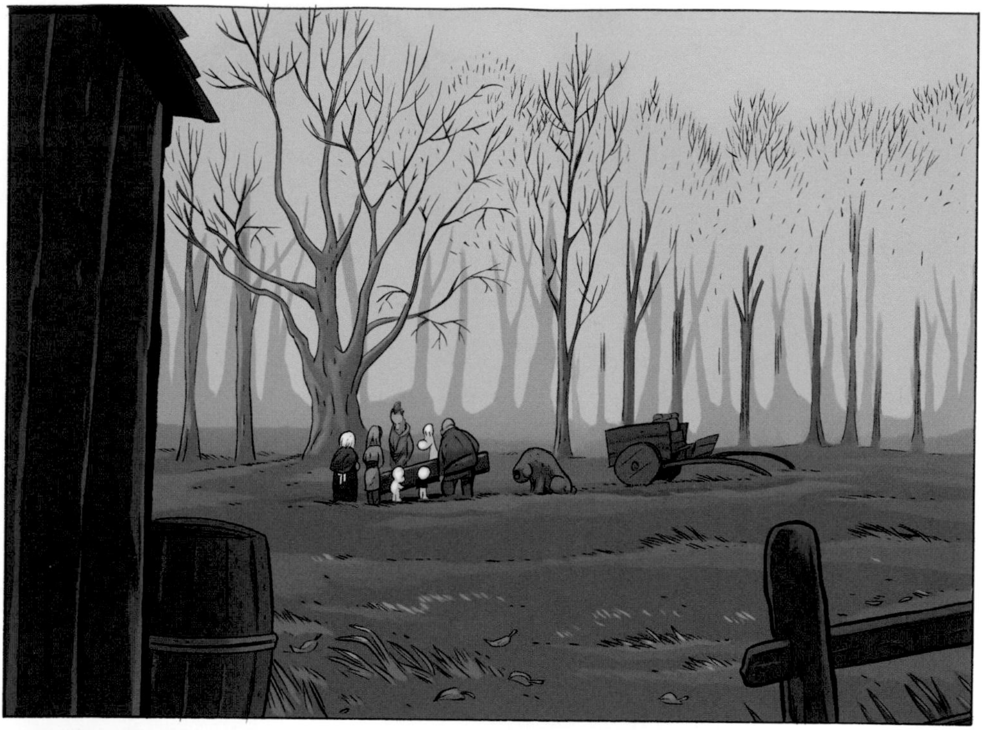

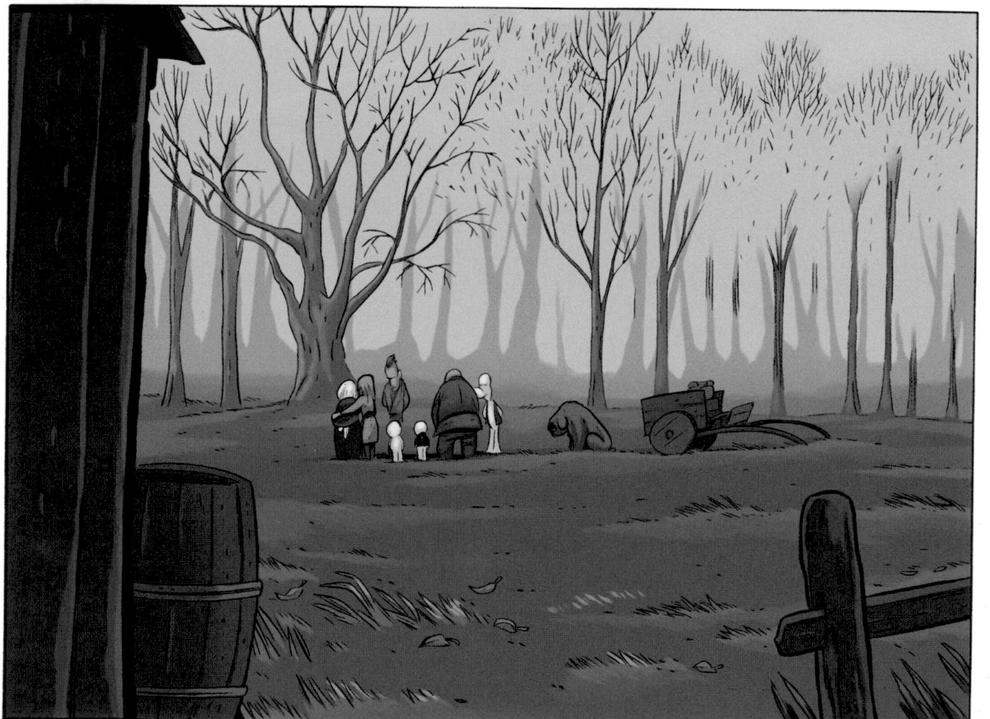

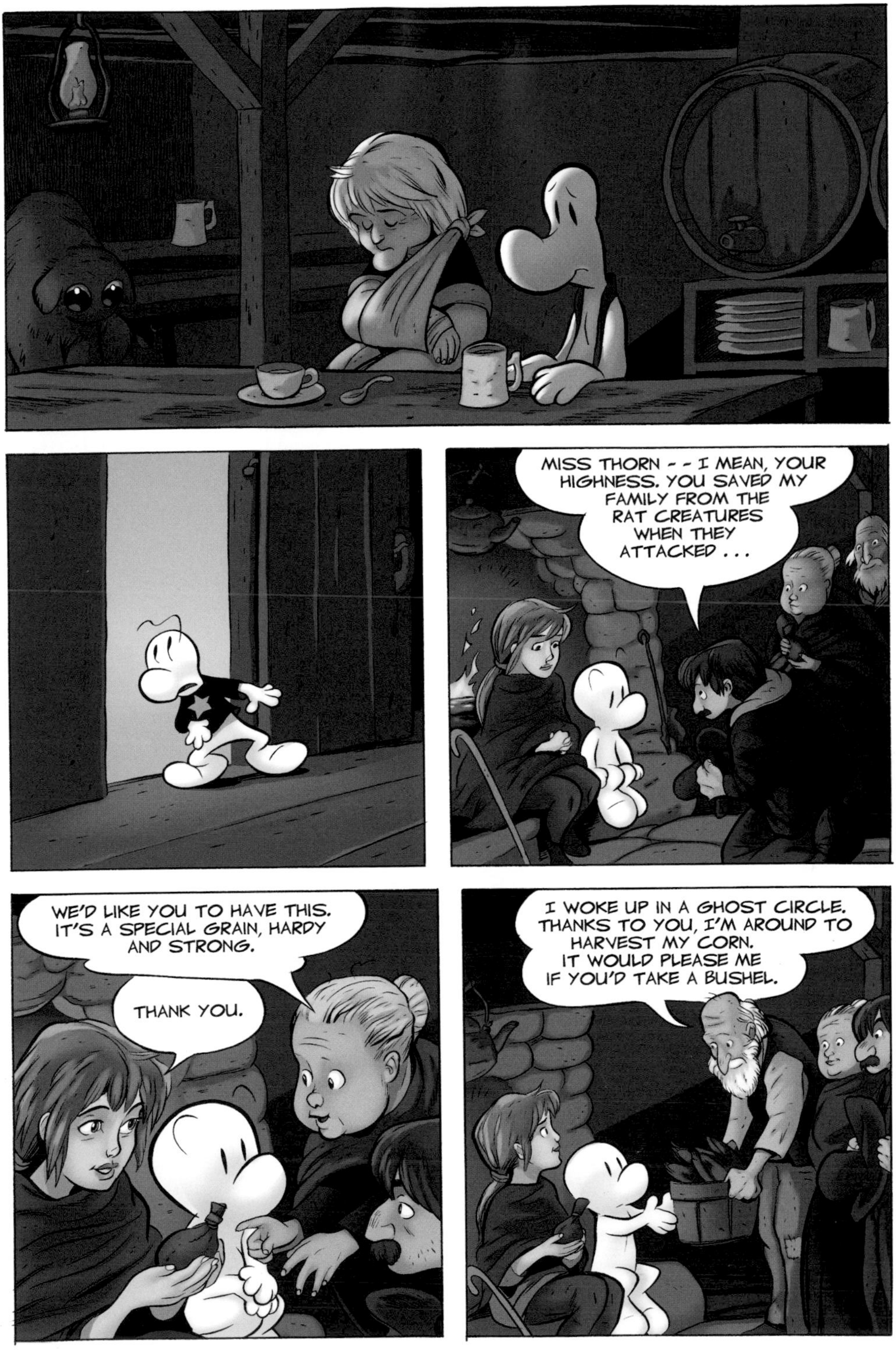
MISS THORN - - I MEAN, YOUR HIGHNESS. YOU SAVED MY FAMILY FROM THE RAT CREATURES WHEN THEY ATTACKED . . .
WE'D LIKE YOU TO HAVE THIS. IT'S A SPECIAL GRAIN, HARDY AND STRONG.
THANK YOU.
I WOKE UP IN A GHOST CIRCLE. THANKS TO YOU, I'M AROUND TO HARVEST MY CORN. IT WOULD PLEASE ME IF YOU'D TAKE A BUSHEL.

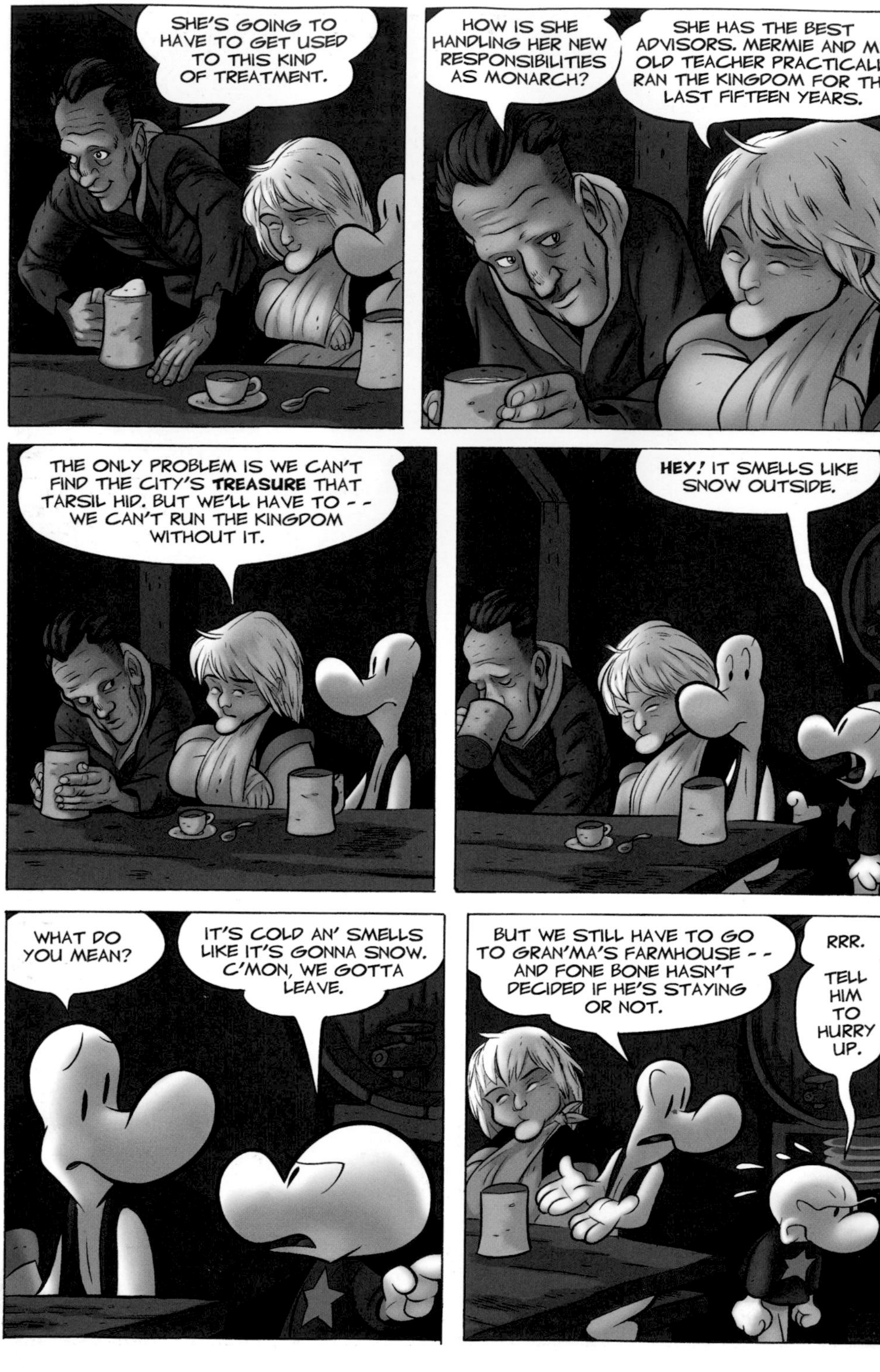
SHE'S GOING TO HAVE TO GET USED TO THIS KIND OF TREATMENT.
HOW IS SHE HANDLING HER NEW RESPONSIBILITIES AS MONARCH?
SHE HAS THE BEST ADVISORS. MERMIE AND MY OLD TEACHER PRACTICALLY RAN THE KINGDOM FOR THE LAST FIFTEEN YEARS.
THE ONLY PROBLEM IS WE CAN'T FIND THE CITY'S **TREASURE** THAT TARSIL HID. BUT WE'LL HAVE TO - - WE CAN'T RUN THE KINGDOM WITHOUT IT.
HEY! IT SMELLS LIKE SNOW OUTSIDE.
WHAT DO YOU MEAN?
IT'S COLD AN' SMELLS LIKE IT'S GONNA SNOW. C'MON, WE GOTTA LEAVE.
BUT WE STILL HAVE TO GO TO GRAN'MA'S FARMHOUSE - - AND FONE BONE HASN'T DECIDED IF HE'S STAYING OR NOT.
RRR.
TELL HIM TO HURRY UP.

HEY, BONE! WHERE YOU GOIN'?

I'LL BE RIGHT BACK, GRAN'MA!

HELLO?

HEY, GUYS! C'MON OUT! I KNOW YOU'RE AROUND HERE SOMEWHERE!

AH! **THERE** YOU ARE!

AAAARRRH!

PREPARE TO **TASTE INSTANT,** BLOODY **DEATH,** SMALL MAMMAL!

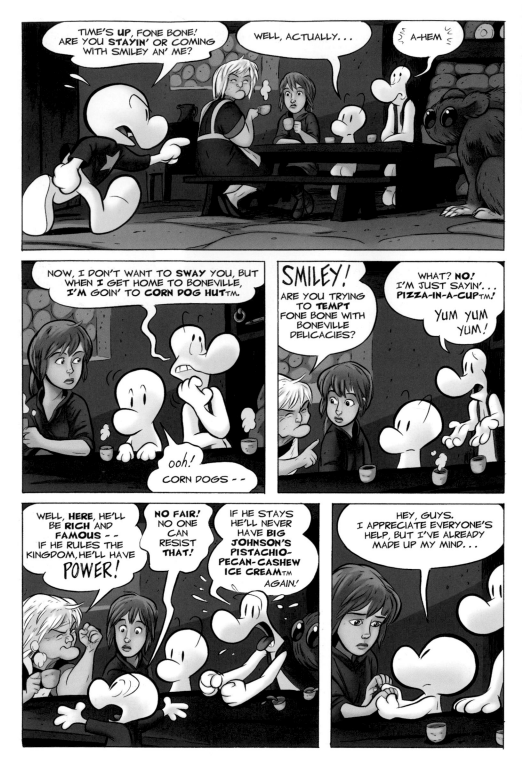

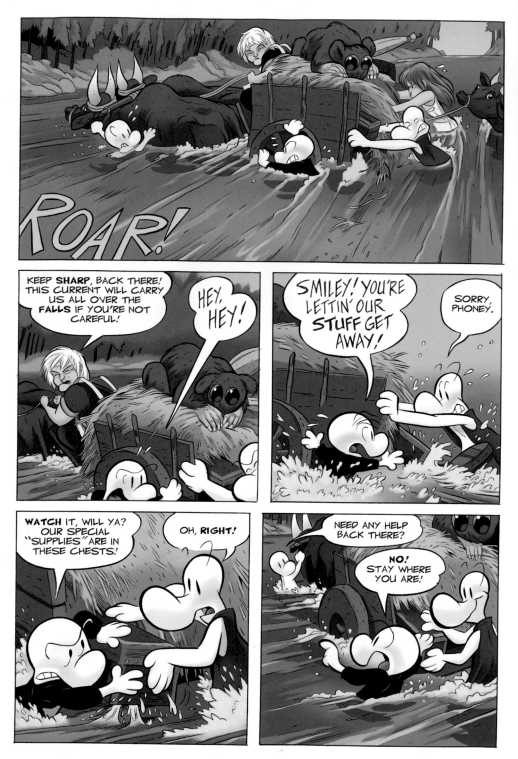

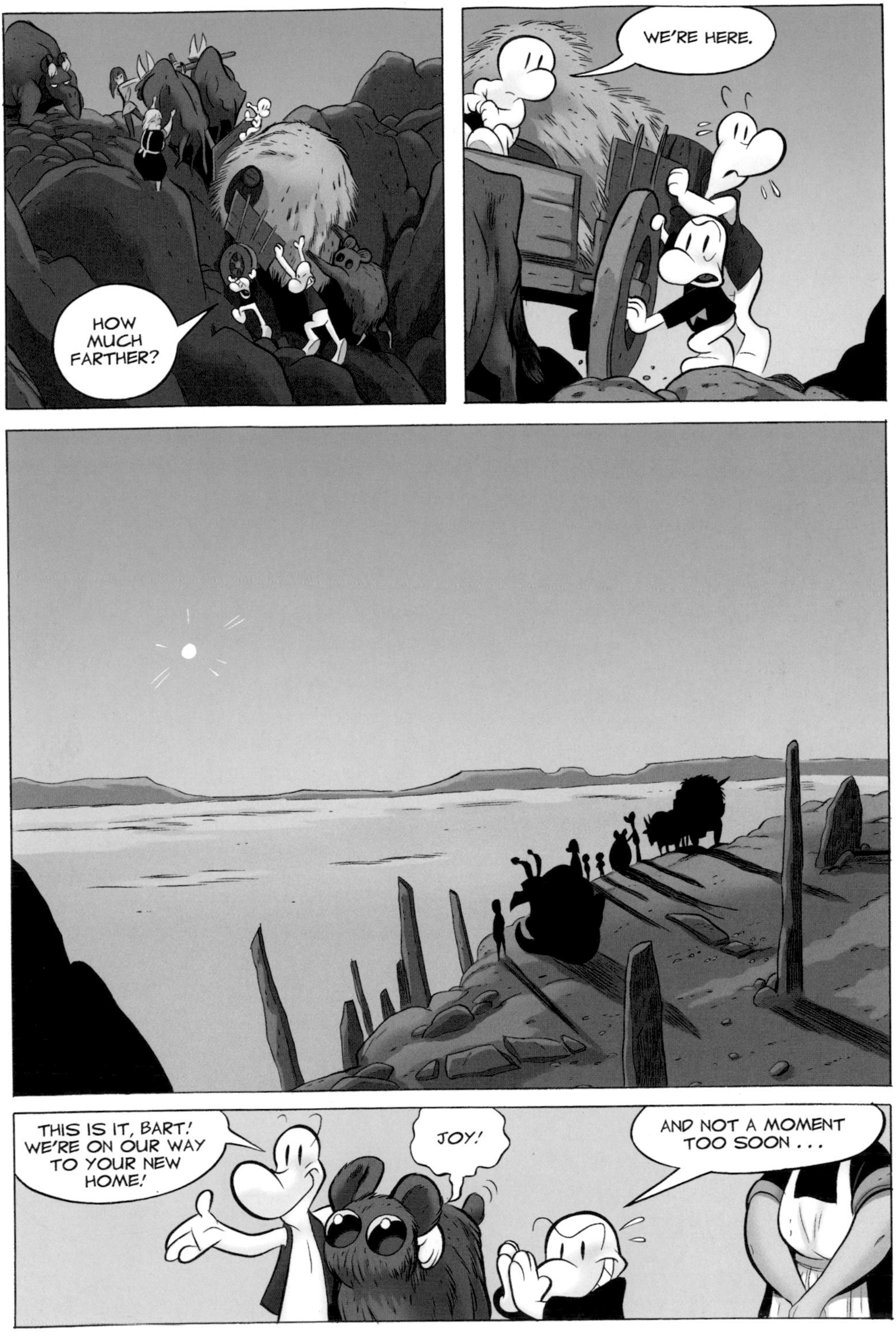
HOW MUCH FARTHER?
WE'RE HERE.
THIS IS IT, BART! WE'RE ON OUR WAY TO YOUR NEW HOME!
JOY!
AND NOT A MOMENT TOO SOON . . .

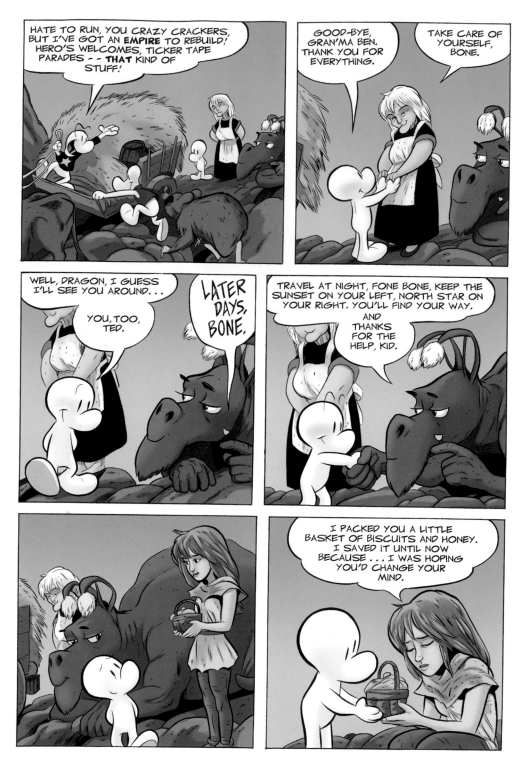

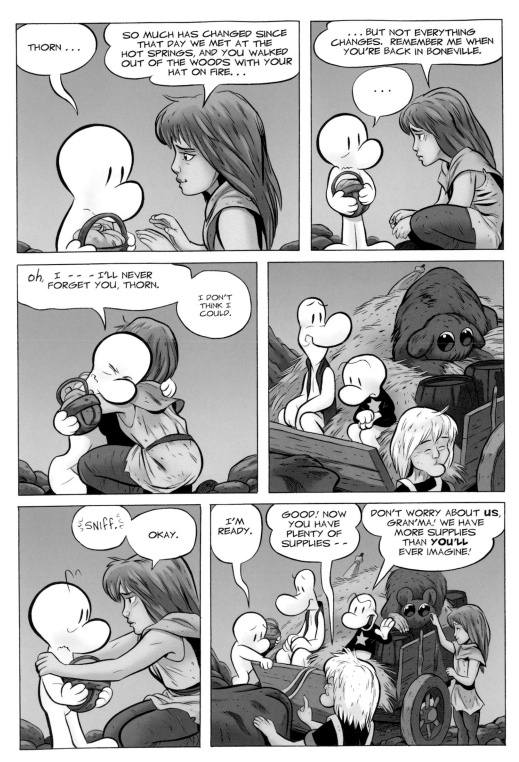

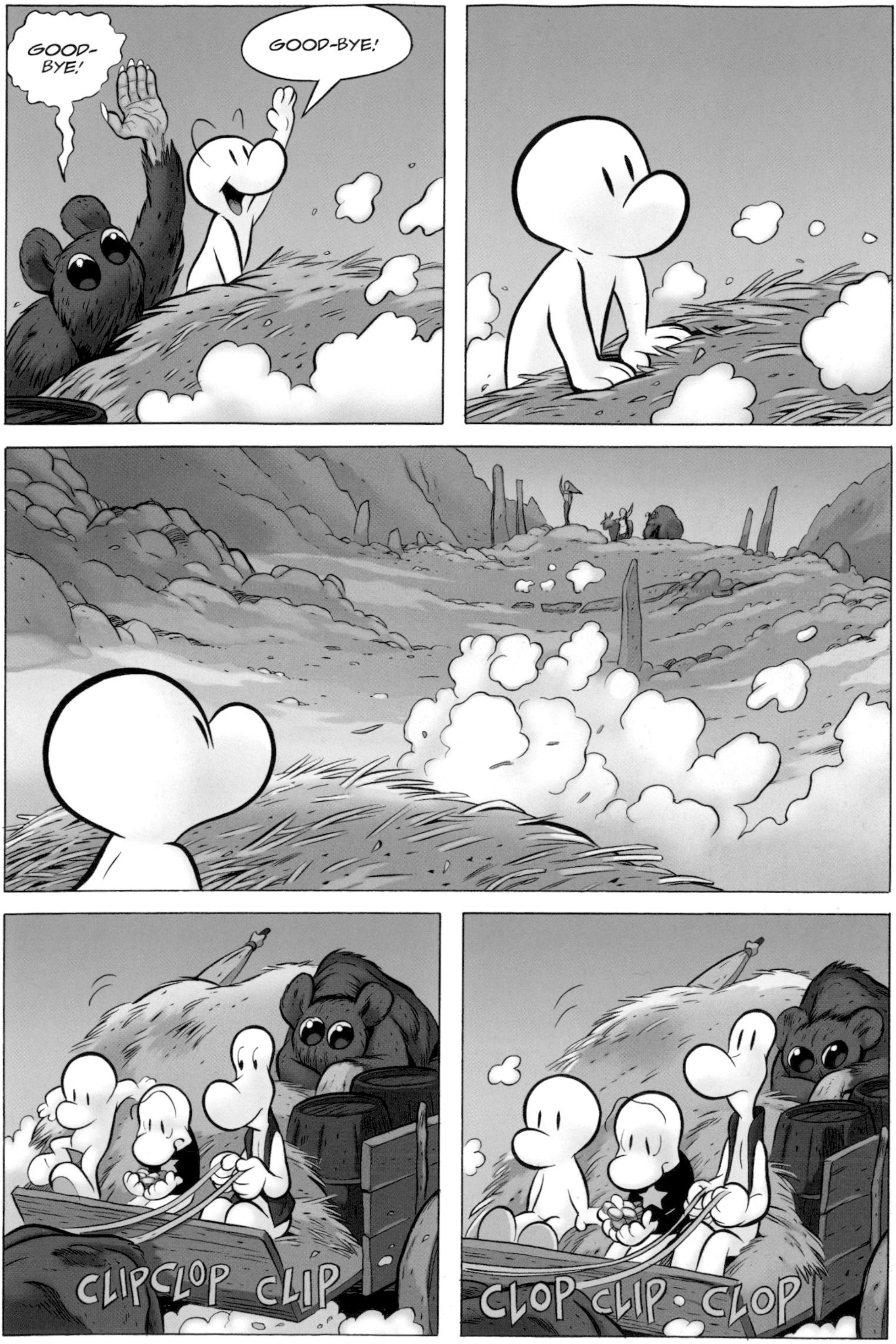
GOOD-BYE!
GOOD-BYE!
CLIPCLOP CLIP
CLOP CLIP · CLOP

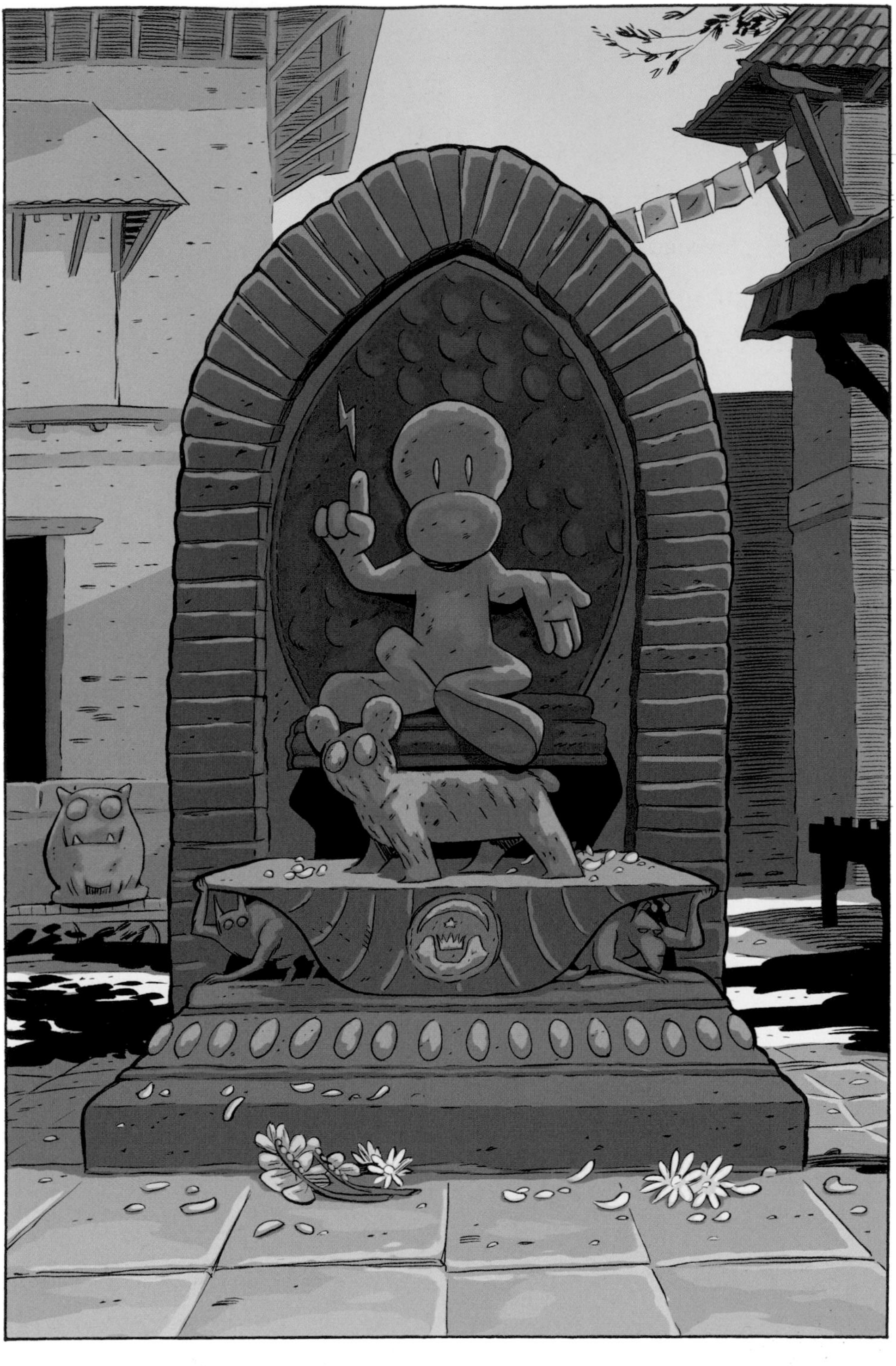

TANEAL'S SCULPTURE, QUEEN'S SQUARE, ATHEIA

About JEFF SMITH

JEFF SMITH was born and raised in the American Midwest and learned about cartooning from comic strips, comic books, and watching animated shorts on TV. After four years of drawing comic strips for The Ohio State University's student newspaper and co-founding Character Builders animation studio in 1986, Smith launched the comic book *BONE* in 1991. Between *BONE* and other comics projects, Smith spends much of his time on the international guest circuit promoting comics and the art of graphic novels.

More about *BONE*

An instant classic when it first appeared in the U.S. as an underground comic book in 1991, *BONE* has since garnered 38 international awards and sold millions of copies in 15 languages. Now, Scholastic's GRAPHIX imprint is publishing full-color graphic novel editions of the nine-book *BONE* series.

Look for the exciting prequel to the amazing *BONE* series, *ROSE*, written by Jeff Smith and illustrated by award-winning artist Charles Vess.

OTHER GRAPHIC NOVELS FROM SCHOLASTIC

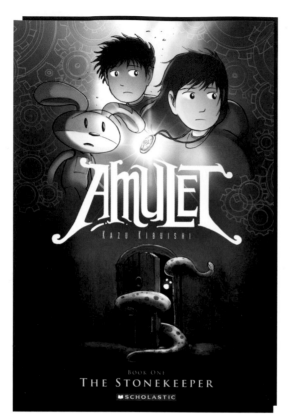

There's something strange behind the basement door. . . .

AMULET BOOK 1 - THE STONEKEEPER
BY KAZU KIBUISHI

After a family tragedy, Emily, Navin, and their mother move to an ancestral home to start a new life. On the family's very first night in the mysterious house, Em and Navin's mom is kidnapped by a tentacled creature. Now it's up to Em and Navin to figure out how to save their mother's life!

OTHER GRAPHIC NOVELS FROM SCHOLASTIC

One flying dill hero TO THE RESCUE!

MAGIC PICKLE
By Scott Morse

Meet the Magic Pickle, a flying kosher dill secret weapon created in a government lab under the floor of Jo Jo Wigman's bedroom. He's here to save the world from The Brotherhood of Evil Produce, who are threatening to take over the planet!

OTHER GRAPHIC NOVELS FROM SCHOLASTIC

FRANK CAMMUSO
KNIGHTS OF THE LUNCH TABLE
THE DODGEBALL CHRONICLES
SCHOLASTIC

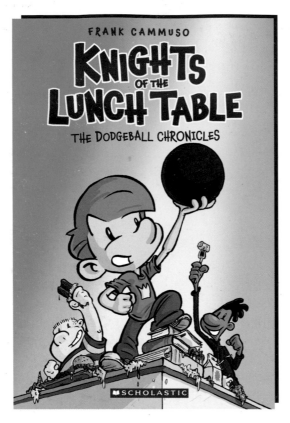

BEHOLD!
Artie King!
Ordinary hero!

KNIGHTS OF THE LUNCH TABLE
BY FRANK CAMMUSO

Artie King just wants to ease into life at Camelot Middle School. He's got new lunch buddies and a cool science teacher, but then there's the scary principal and Joe and the Horde, the brawny bullies who rule the school. The real trouble starts when Artie opens an old locker full of mysterious stuff, and Artie and his friends are challenged to a do-or-die dodgeball game. Losers get creamed!